Next Stop Hope
route 14

Editors
M Y Alam
Anthony Cropper
Ian Daley

route

First Published in 2003 by Route
School Lane, Glasshoughton, West Yorks, WF10 4QH
e-mail: books@route-online.com

ISBN: 1 901927 19 9

Cover Design: Jackie Parsons

Editors: M Y Alam, Anthony Cropper, Ian Daley

Thanks to
Isabel Daley, James Gilligan, Roger Green, Lorna Hey

Printed by Bookmarque Ltd, Croydon, Surrey

A catalogue for this book is available from the British Library

Events and characters in this book are imaginary.
Similarity to real persons and events is coincidental.

Full details of the Route programme of books
can be found on our website
www.route-online.com

Route is the fiction imprint of YAC, a registered charity No 1007443

YAC is supported by
Yorkshire Arts, Wakefield MDC, West Yorkshire Grants

This anthology of new writing is presented to you in three distinct collections:

Criminally Minded holds a dozen crime stories that contribute towards breaking the mould of formulaic crime fiction and explores the workings of the criminal mind.

Something Has Gone Wrong In The World has been drawn from the solicited submissions to this collection, the emerging theme questions if life was ever supposed to be like this.

Next Stop Hope is a series of commissioned pieces, and is a timely regathering of the writers who regularly graced the pages of route issues one through to thirteen.

Contents

Criminally Minded

Something Has Gone Wrong In The World

Next Stop Hope

Criminally Minded

Introduction
M Y Alam

For most of us, one crime story is going to be pretty much the same as the next – a perfect crime to be solved by any of the following: a demoralised but not beaten copper, a wise-cracking but decent private detective or in some cases an amateur sleuth with a thing for ornate dickie bow ties, classical music, opium or, on a quiet day, all three.

The collection before you has stories no doubt of that nature but this anthology has a much wider yet distinctive identity. The usual good cop/bad cop, tart with a heart or crook with a hook routines are all absent. Instead, you will find diverse, convincing and deeply developed characters with an equally surprising and diverse range of dilemmas and plots with which to engage: nicking a famous footballer's fish, having friends for dinner, avenging one big wrong with a series of smaller wrongs and a good old fashioned dose of TWOC-ing are just some of the crimes our writers and their criminals have fashioned. This collection symbolises the movement in direction that the crime fiction genre has been recently drifting towards: here you will find gangsters and guns, grit and guts, revenge and rage, lust and stupidity – narratives of the heart, stories of the soul, and, perhaps above all else, explorations of the minds that drive the crimes.

Finding and then putting these stories together has taken over two years. After sifting through over three hundred manuscripts, presented before you know are twelve stories of great stylistic and thematic diversity, each an imagining of a single author. The stories revolve around crime as both act and idea and therefore often deal with much wider issues including power, morality and that most human of conditions, desire. That doesn't mean the journeys our authors embark upon suffer or consequently become less dramatic and thrilling; far from it – they're loaded with distinct, fresh and the most engaging of voices which tell of events that occasionally disturb but never fail to excite. The majority being fast paced and complete pieces; no vague and incomplete three dot endings here, no excursions into personal neuroses that fail to become relevant or even remotely important to anyone other than the mind that pushes words onto paper. What is offered is contemporary, dramatic, thrilling, precision engineered and above all, readable literature.

The Rhapsodic Defence of Rudi Falsetto gets things rolling. Dai Parson's first person narrative is at times brutally delivered. That said, the story also manages to convey a sense of regret that may well become manifest after the desire to commit revenge is realised. In Dai's own words: 'A residual fear of having my head banged against the bar whilst the girls look on and shout "Leave him alone! Leave him alone, you bully!" is, basically, the impetus behind the story. Man meets horrible cunt. Horrible cunt humiliates man. Man gets him back big style. Man gets a bit lost on the way.'

Oliver Mallet's *Cause and Effect* is a story of violence involving two men, both looking for something. One is guided by a sense of responsibility whilst the other is guided by his penis. Which of them will get into trouble first?

Phil Hancock's (AKA Marvellous Phil) finest piece of criminal prose to date is one of those rare stories that leads us into believing one thing while we think we're reading another. *A Damn Good Finish* is a warning to all those who might think about talking down to and telling a time served tradesman how to do his job.

Fijian Rites, a story executed without fault. Denis Mattinson's minimalist but painfully meaningful narrative shocks but compels the pages to turn. What feels like a filmic, jump-cut structure is topped off with a somewhat disturbing but incessant undertone which, in all, manages to somehow fuse rhythm with plot propulsion. A story about eating.

At heart, James Bones' *Lifters* is an extremely simple boy meets girl romance store, the way that the characters choose to pursue their relationship is what makes this tale stand out a mile. Our heroes become so entangled in each other that their perspectives become warped. Their world is each other, and the loss of empathy with anyone external to their relationship has interesting – to put it mildly – consequences.

Murking back and forth in the dank water of (ex-international football star and local hero) Sunny Faisal's pond is beast of momentous propositions. Twenty-six inches of prime Chagoi Koi carp. Worth its weight in gold. It circles round, hour after hour, day and night. Thinking fishy thoughts. It's not the only one. Daniel Fox's *Getting Sunny Faisal's Fish* involves three local chancers with a van, a fish tank and a great big net. And they want that fish. An amusing, sharp and fast paced read: almost worth as much as the fish.

TWOC, by Jo Powell concerns teenage twocker Jason who grows up sharpish when he's caught in a dealer's – Big Danny – new Merc. We follow Jason from court to street and then back again. A cautionary tale in part but Jo's literary style and experience comes through in abundance.

One of those *Los Angeles Mornings*. Jason Parry's laid back and effortless style delves into the world before the day begins for the working and earning millions. It's hot in the city. Steve is early and has forty-five minutes to kill. Waiting for his job to start, Steve watches the early morning city life pass him by, conjuring up memories and fears and omens. The calm before the storm.

Andrew Oldham's *Spanking the Monkey* is one of the funniest and most intricately crafted short stories in the collection. Direct, to the point and a voice that just screams originality: an American detective, an American dream and a monkey with a gun.

Lee Harrison's *Stigby* occasionally slips into an almost documentary style that amuses while simultaneously propelling the pace and conclusion of the narrative to unexpected levels. Unlovable local lowlife Stigby undertakes his lowly round of Kingston-upon-Hull. But with rural animals being forced further and further into the City, could Stigby be about to meet his match?

Daithidh MacEochaidh's *The Player* is part noir tribute, part the end of the world: a captivating read. Here there is life, but hardly worth living and not lived for long. It's menace. It's unknowable and unexplained. You live. You're murdered. You play the game. That's all. Daithidh is fast becoming a successful writer with a gift of adapting his style and depth of analysis to several genres.

Bernie Hare's *This Happy Breed of Men* is not a simple story but here's a potted version: a woman plays a confidence trick on a man. The man, enraged, tracks her down, but then falls in love with her and eventually joins her in the con game. Years later, during a pub brawl, the man again becomes enraged with her, this time through jealousy. Bernie Hare's sharply observed comments on society become part of the whole seamlessly.

It's a fair bet that you'll see more work from these authors in the months and years to come. Each possesses the ability to imagine and then express characters, situations and resolutions. Not such a big deal; part of the job spec for most writers but what is rare is the ability to do so with such finesse and with a keen eye on the concerns of the reader: satisfaction, although never guaranteed, is highly likely. These writers are not really concerned with following rules or using textbook approaches. If anything, they're about breaking the mould and contributing towards the extension of the genre of crime fiction writing.

The Rhapsodic Defence of Rudi Falleto

Dai Parsons

'You have no fucking idea about me, do you? You have no fucking idea who you've messed with. Are you beginning to understand what could happen to you if you fuck with me?'

There was no reaction from the Pikey. He just stared at a point on Falletto's jumper. Both sides of his face had been clumsily scolded with an iron. He was sat trussed with rope to a chair. There were two dried clots of blood under each nostril. One side of his face was up like a beetroot - the side where Falletto had been hooking him with his best hand. It had got a bit embarrassing when he'd used his left. The Pikey had been afraid, but the blows hadn't inflicted much pain. The feeble left hands had, once again, brought home to Falletto that he was soft as shite.

The Pikey had more important things to worry about - tied to a chair, at the mercy of an angry weed. Still, he can't have helped registering the lack of power in Falletto's punches. Falletto didn't like that type of exposure. When he was on his own he didn't mind, he'd acknowledge his own weakness with a sense of relief, but not in front of the Pikey. The Pikey had already witnessed too much. He'd watched Falletto shit his muck big time.

Falletto had got hold of some cow tranquillizers at a friend's farm he used to work at.

'Look, that Pikey cunt, who drinks down the *Marshes*, put his hand up my girlfriend's skirt, and when she told him to fuck off he grabbed her round the throat and started shaking her. Well, I rushed over to the bar where they were, didn't I, and he sort of gave me a bit of kicking, like. Not just a bit, it went on for ages, in front of the girlfriend and everything. I just want to teach the cunt a lesson, you know. Put him to sleep for a bit. Give him a few bruises, maybe strip him off, then dump him in a field before he wakes up.'

The farmer got the tranquillizer gun out of the cabinet and handed it to Falletto.

'You'll need a smaller dose than for a cow,' he laughed.

Falletto waited outside the *Marshes*. The Pikey drunk there nearly every night and always took the back paths home. Falletto crouched in a hedge with the gun. He could hear the Pikey singing something as he stumbled down the path.

The Plan was to wait for the Pikey to walk past, then shoot him in the arse. But the Pikey didn't walk past; he hesitated right in front of Falletto and turned towards the hedge. He flopped his knob out and said, 'Piss. Kill the firkin wanker.' He then proceeded to piss all over the gun barrel. Falletto panicked, fired the dart and the Pikey sprang back, clutching his nuts. Falletto bolted out of the bush and stood in front of him. The dart had pierced the Pikey's ball bag and gone into his thigh. The Pikey tottered a bit, and then seemed to get his bearings. He pulled the dart out and started walking towards Falletto. 'Firkin Wanker. I'll firkin kill ya.' The fear hit Falletto crisp and clear like he was reading all about it in a tabloid headline - **Rudi Falletto Is Shitting His Pants Once Again**. Falletto started to panic and back off down the path. Before he knew it, he'd flung the rifle at the Pikey and began stumbling down the path, frantically looking behind, his legs moving sideways and refusing to straighten up, like some dizzy blonde in a B horror movie. 'Ya firkin shite ass, cum ye.' But the Pikey fell with a thud and the B movie came to an abrupt end. Falletto turned round and walked deliberately up to the Pikey. He took a slash all over his chops. But he grew bored with watching the piss splash off his face, so he finished the last half of his piss looking up at the stars. It was a beautiful night.

He dragged the Pikey down the path and got some of his piss back. He dumped him in the car boot.

'Right. You're Pikey fucking pie.'

He drove round for a while. He was hacked off he'd got so

frightened. It seemed like the Pikey had got one over on him again. The Pikey hadn't even been scared; he'd just carried on acting like poxy Jason out of *Halloween*. Falletto had to let out a laugh. But if the Pikey was such a winner then why was he stuck in the boot of Falletto's car with a mangled cock? Falletto gave himself a mental tap on the shoulder. However cowardly the plan at least he hadn't buckled. Okay he was a shit arse, but he hadn't taken the fact lying down. In a cowardly sort of way he was making a fight of it. He drove the Pikey back to the barn.

By the time Falletto had tied the Pikey to the chair he was shagged. He stared at the Pikey, still fast asleep, as he hesitated with the barn light switch. He was gonna get some kip and run the clock down on this one. He flicked the light off.

Falletto went into the barn early next morning. The Pikey was awake and looked right at him. Falletto stared back at the Pikey like a bad hangover. After that there was no going back. He couldn't go to the police. He couldn't let the Pikey loose - the crazy bastard would kill him. He didn't want to put his wife through the upheaval of skipping town, and he didn't really want to tell her that he'd shot someone with a cow tranquillizer.

There was nothing Falletto could do to erase the situation. He could stop now, go to the police before something crazier was done. But Falletto would still have to do bird. He was a pansy; they'd make mincemeat out of him and his arse. He touched his bum affectionately; he didn't want that. The world could no longer be reasoned with, the only thing to hope for was some diabolical luck. He walked over to the Pikey and cut one of his fingers off with a cigar cutter. That's how you speed the clock up a bit, which, in effect, is a quicker way of running it down. When he clocked the blood pissing out, he jogged up to the house, pulled the poker out of the coal fire, and cauterized the wound.

In the first few days each torture Falletto persisted in could still be recognized as another few months, or years, of bird on his sentence. Even, though he was well aware there was nothing to be done that could ensure he escaped the possibility of severe retribution, there was still much he could do, or refrain from doing, to prevent prolonging the misery of jail. But it is not every day that a man comes face to face with laws he cannot change and the sentences that are as good as passed. Hope looks like a gaunt and scruffy animal when the only thing you can do is make Hell a little shorter.

It took Falletto a while to get his head round this. And as he stared over at the already cut up Pikey, he began to see him as the catalyst for all this aporia. He walked over to the Pikey, sprayed hairspray over his head, flicked a match into it, and watched his bonce burn. After ten seconds he doubted the blaze with a bucket of water. He opened the barn doors to let the smoke out.

Falletto had already arrived at the end of something. Nothing much was going to happen - apart from torture, its cessation, thought, and the meagre entertainment received from more innovative forms of torture. But there were some colourful moments.

'You Pikey's don't have mothers, do you? I heard your father just digs a hole in the ground and fucks that instead. And then someone pulls you out by the hair just like vegetables. Vegetables you are, actually, like.'

The Pikey didn't like this. The Pikey wasn't going to give too much away for fear of being tortured more, but he couldn't hide it completely. And every time Falletto saw anything that resembled hatred or anger in the Pikey's eyes, he'd slap him across the face and say, 'Your mother's a potato.'

Falletto listened to his own words as a passer-by might. This must have been the first time in the history of torture that the torturer had claimed the torturee's mother was a potato. Falletto felt pretty bloody unique. He couldn't stop laughing. There wasn't anything so big you couldn't take the piss out of it. Or anything so disappointing - not even himself. He'd remember this – it was one of those moments that hung around, where he could rock on his heels, his hands in his pockets - smug as fuck. He knew what was coming - it didn't matter a shit - it would all be interrupted, and laughed at, same as everything else. A flash of brilliance.

But then he started thinking about how the Nazis must have taunted the Jews and gypsies about their background and come up with pretty much the same sort of shit as Falletto, funnier even. Falletto didn't feel his epiphanic jocundity or jocund epiphany was all it was cracked up to be, anymore, and he almost let the moment slip into the debris of experience. But then he thought, *Don't be so hard on yourself, mun, you still came up with it by yourself, you didn't have any help off the Nazis.* So, instead, it slipped into the debris of its own accord.

'Your mother's a potato,' Falletto said proudly.

The hate was still there. It was what made the torture worthwhile; but it was also proof that it wasn't working. The plan was to get so bad on the Pikey's arse that the only hope he would cling to would be being a million miles away from Falletto's barn, just living his life, nothing more – fuck revenge. He wanted the Pikey to believe that Falletto was so monstrous, so mean, so large, that if the Pikey even thought about revenge, Falletto was gonna rain on him. But, in some people, you just can't create those sorts of fictions. The Pikey was just too hard.

Besides, Falletto had gone too far - he'd done too much damage for the Pikey to walk away. If somebody had lopped off parts of Falletto's anatomy, he'd have run to the police. You see, really nasty bastards who aren't afraid of anything don't have to do nothing to you. They'd cut the Pikey's finger off and tell him to leave town or they'd lop his fucking head off. Or they'd just kill him straight off - end of story. What you need is the type of muscle and type of guts that is willing to put its neck on the line, and, if it comes to it, take on a caravan-site full of Pikeys. If he was gonna pull shit like this he had to be prepared to fight and risk losing. That's when people start to shit their muck - when they know you're prepared to lose. But Falletto wasn't even prepared to fight octogenarian holidayers in their caravans let alone Pikeys. This was the deal with Falletto: torture and kill a horrible bastard so long as nothing ever comes of it – end of story.

Domestics

Torturing somebody is a full-time job. Torturing is about striking a fine balance between inflicting pain and maintaining life.

Falletto had to get up an hour earlier. He had to feed the Pikey and

22

take him to the toilet. This would have been a laborious and extremely dangerous task, necessitating partially releasing the Pikey from bondage, had not Falletto come up with the ingenious plan of cutting a hole in the seat of the chair, replacing it with a sliding sheet of wood, and removing it only when the Pikey needed to shit or piss.

It was, however, a deeply unpleasant procedure. Falletto had to push the Pikey's prick down between his legs and hold it there until the Pikey emptied his bladder. He never stooped as far as wiping the Pikey's arse, but the increasing crud of shit on the sliding panel was beginning to grate on Falletto.

It goes without saying that the hours spent preserving the Pikey had a time-consuming effect upon family life. But, more disturbingly, it had a detrimental effect upon the torture itself. He became so involved with the upkeep of the prisoner that thoughts of torture tended to fall by the wayside. Falletto understood full well that the best torturers were able to preserve a minimum of life whilst still persevering in torture without any internecine consequence. But there were always a few of them there to muck in and take turns, whereas Falletto was on his own in this endeavour. The torture was intended to be about calculated anger, controlled slicing, elaborate methods of inducing pain, hours meditating upon how to crack the torturee's psyche, and all done in the flavour of tranquil revenge. Instead it took on the form of sporadic temper tantrums wherein Falletto was totally out of control, upset, angry and disheartened. The more pain he inflicted upon the Pikey the more he splintered the image he'd have of himself as a torturer. It was remarkable but he seemed to be taking on the characteristics of abusive, even neglectful, parent rather than a cold, committed and completely focused KGB-style torturer. It was all very unnerving. Toilet time was particularly volatile. The Pikey pissed so much once that the potty overflowed. Falletto got some piss on his hands and was sent into a filthy rage.

'You dirty little fucker. I should make you eat that up.' Following which, he beat at the Pikey's chest in the manner of a hurt and cheated-on wife. Then, in a gesture to some sort of procedure and manly composure, he paused, took a few steps back, and flung a flying kick into the cheekbone, sending chair and Pikey reeling.

The guilt was fucking horrendous. One minute he was guilty about not torturing the Pikey enough, the next minute he was feeling guilty about forgetting the Pikey's breakfast.

But it was the self-consciousness that really got to Falletto. After tea, he'd leave reluctantly for the barn to try his hand at inflicting some pain. But it had all got a bit staged; he couldn't even look the Pikey in the eye anymore, and would end up storming out of the barn in a blush. There was nothing left - he was all out of revenge.

The first couple of weeks had been different - he couldn't get enough of it. It had, admittedly, only been a day or two before he loathed even the sight of the Pikey and his suppurating wounds. But the more he sat at the kitchen table and meditated upon whether he should kill the Pikey or not, and about covering his tracks and what not, and the more he couldn't decide, the more he couldn't bear to be away from him a minute longer.

Some nights, he'd fall around the barn in a heap of broken promises - first turning to one and then the other, nagged by the fact that more or less torture was not now going to make a slight bit of difference to the amount of bird he served, muttering curses all night, til only exhaustion dragged him to bed.

It had made things really difficult at the house. He'd fidget round the place for about twenty minutes, eat a bit of toast frantically, switch the telly on and then off again, start preparing a meal, strike up a conversation with his wife, sharpen a pencil. Then he'd sprint down the garden shed just to give the Pikey a quick kick in the knackers, and then he'd run back up. And he had to end up telling his wife that he was making a surprise birthday present for their six-year-old daughter, and that they were to stay out of the barn. He kept the keys on him all the time.

The crap stained sheet of wood had become so inimical to Falletto he found himself picking up one of those antique shitting-chairs with a potty in a compartment underneath the seat. This, however, created further contortion in Falletto's original endeavour. Not only had he become preoccupied with the preservation of Monsieur Pikey but he'd actually begun to take pride in his good work.

'De de de de de de daaa! D'you like it? Only the best for you, my boy.'

The Pikey, in fact, did look genuinely chuffed. He was a bit groggy after being knocked out by the tranquillizer. But when he woke he was pleased to notice that he'd been washed (he smelt firkin lovely), shaved, was sitting in his lovely new chair, and was dressed in a very comfortable pinstriped suit. Falletto held up a mirror, and the Pikey clocked that his hair had been cut and neatly combed.

'Wakey, wakey. Hey, you look a bloody treat, wus. I've been putting it off and putting it off, till finally, I thought, bugger it, I'm going to bloody treat him.'

Falletto was grinning like a Cheshire cat and continued his sentimental recounting of the purchase.

'As soon as I seen it, I thought, that's the very thing for me laddo.'

It was a great moment - one of the best. Falletto promised himself that he would do the same for the Pikey every week.

Falletto spent the following week immersed in DIY manuals in a half-arsed attempt to build his girl a playhouse. The Pikey missed out on his bath nights. Some of his wounds were still festering, he was dishevelled, unshaven, and smelt of shit again. Falletto was no carpenter. He looked at the Pikey in despair. He would not tolerate it - he would not sit there again and watch the Pikey tumble into degradation.

He grabbed the Pikey round the throat.

'Listen to me, you lazy cunt. You're going to build that fucking playhouse. And you're going to do a fucking good job of it, understand? Now, I'm going to tie one leg to that stove. If you so much as look suspicious you're brown bread.

The Pikey was a good old carpenter. Falletto sat out of reach, eating buns, looking on with pleasure as the playhouse began to resemble a reality. Then, out of nowhere, Falletto felt something hit him square in the head. The Pikey had thrown the hammer. Falletto must only have been unconscious for a couple of seconds coz the Pikey was still cutting his rope frantically with the saw. Jason was definitely back. The Pikey, clocking that he wasn't going to cut through it in time, lunged at Falletto and tackled him round the shins. Falletto nearly screamed the barn down as he kicked his legs and made some unholy rodent sounding squeals from the pit of his stomach. He felt like he was being dragged into the deep by some sea monster as the Pikey pulled at his legs. Falletto would have gladly blown the whole thing and welcomed the sight of vanloads of pigs. But he got one leg free and managed to keep shunting the Pikey, who was holding on for dear life, in the head. Falletto finally managed to back-pedal out of reach. He squatted just out of arms length of the Pikey, who was breathing heavily and looking down at the floor despairingly. Falletto spotted the gun and was about to head for it, when he done one hell of a strange thing. The Pikey was on his feet by this time. 'Fuck it.' Falletto ran at the Pikey and dived into his stomach. The Pikey crashed into the oven and began fighting immediately. They rolled around on the floor in one of those untidy brawls with lots of short, inconsequential punches. After about three minutes, despite banging the Pikey's head against the floor a few times, Falletto realized that he was in danger of losing a scrap to a seriously starved and debilitated man, a mere shadow of his former self. The desire to live kicked in again and Falletto, once more, struggled to be free of the Pikey's grip. The Pikey was on top by this time, but Falletto managed to hold him close to his chest and bit deeply into the Pikey's neck. Unruffled, the gagged Pikey wrenched himself away and, once more, looked about for the hammer. Falletto managed to turn him over, roll away from him and scramble on his hands and knees just out of reach of the pursuing zombie. Falletto got to his feet and spat out some blood. He looked with relief at the Pikey flailing stupidly out of reach and was once again struck by the recurring but unfortunately ephemeral understanding that there were more important things than being a hard bastard. Falletto walked coolly towards the gun. He turned round, took aim, and fired the dart.

Falletto did not take hideous revenge on the Pikey. There was just too much logic to the attack. He smacked him in the face with the hammer a couple of times, but then left it at that.

After that, Falletto could barely be bothered to empty the shit out of the Pikey's arse and the poor bastard went without food for a day or two. This was more because of a complete exasperation on

Falletto's part rather than any malicious intent.

Falletto had just finished painting the playhouse, and was lying with his hands behind his head, staring contemptuously at the bedraggled wreck in the chair, when he noticed the Pikey beginning to convulse. A spume of vomit flew out of the Pikey's nose. Falletto ran across the room and ungagged the Pikey who proceeded to puke all down his front.

Falletto surveyed the view down the Pikey's shirt. That was the last straw for Falletto - he just didn't have the stomach to clean it up.

'You stinking little fucking pig.'

The Pikey started crying. He was feeling sorry for himself. Falletto turned his back on him and washed his hands in the sink.

'I know it's bad mate but you can't expect to go grabbing girls by the throat and then believe nothing's going to come of it.'

'It's too much, ye fucker.'

'I know that, wus. But, well, you grabbing my girlfriend round the throat like that, that was too fucking much wasn't it! If I go to prison for twenty years for a scumbag like you that'll be far too fucking much, but that's the way it is, innit? And if I get off scot-free that'll be too little. But it'll be just fucking right for me, mate. I just want you gone, pal.'

Falletto grabbed some masking-tape.

'Fuck! Nee more! Nee more.'

'It's all right, I'm taking you home.'

'Yous firkin lyin' bastard.'

'Shut your mouth, now, or I'll change my mind and blowtorch your balls.'

Falletto wrapped the masking-tape round the Pikey's mouth. He walked out of the barn and started the car up.

'I told you, we're going home,' he said, smiling, as he strolled back in.

He walked over to the wall and grabbed an axe off the hook. The Pikey couldn't see what was happening. Falletto genuinely wanted the Pikey to believe he was going home. But then, out of some banal but stubborn impulse to make something out of nothing he thought he'd leave the Pikey with a few choice words. He leant the axe at the back of the Pikey's chair and walked round to the front.

'I'm sorry mate. I don't get any pleasure out of this. I know you suffer an' that and I know you're not all bad. But lets be honest here, you are a bit of a cunt. You haven't said one charming thing since you've been here. Even if I let you go, what would you do, like? You'd just carry on being you most probably, wouldn't you? It's out of my hands, like. If I could let you go I would. But you were well out of order that night. Anyway, it looks like the cops might not find out. It's been six weeks now.'

Falletto shook his head. What a pointless fucking speech.

It didn't matter that he was gagged, the Pikey's eyes said everything. It was reminiscent of the two scenes in the Cohen brother's *Miller's Crossing* - the one where the protagonist doesn't shoot the pleading man and the one where he does. *'Open up your heart.'* Or was it - *'Look into your heart.'* It didn't matter, neither of them were gonna save the Pikey.

Falletto walked to the back of the chair and smashed the axe down on the Pikey's skull.

It was over. Not once had he ever considered giving himself up. But he had often imagined himself doing so. He was fascinated by the image of him bringing all that suffering down upon, not only himself, but upon his wife and child as well. He'd imagined himself understanding exactly why he was in prison and that he had some sort of philosophy - that the only way he could get what he deserved was to take on more than he deserved. But, fuck that, life was too short to learn from your mistakes the hard way. Never torture and murder a Pikey again.

Falletto chopped the Pikey to pieces and buried him in the hills. But he wasn't happy about it. And, by fuck, that felt like something. On another day it would have saved someone's life.

Falletto drove back to the barn. Still no cops. There was only one thing in the world that was out of his hands – whether he got caught. Everything else they could leave up to him - he could handle it. He hadn't felt that way since he wished his pregnant wife would give birth to a healthy child.

He looked up at the stars. It was straight out of an action film. He'd risked everything and to top it all off he might just get away with it. It was another beautiful night. One of those nights when even the ants feel like living.

Cause and Effect
Oliver Mallet

'What the hell are you ringing me for? ... What? ... No, just make sure you get here with the van by five.'

Danny hangs up.

* * *

It was nearly two in the morning. The club was packed but most people were now on the dance floor and the long stretch of bar was almost deserted. Periodically placed along the bar were thin, brightly lit fish tanks which rose to the ceiling. It was beside one of these columns that an attractive woman with a short, fashionably styled black dress sat alone.

A tall man approached, pushing the long hair back from his smiling face. The man made himself comfortable on the barstool beside the woman and said 'Nice fish. My name's Finn by the way, can I buy you a drink?'

The woman paused for a moment, looking Finn up and down before replying. 'Sure. A Tia Maria and Coke.'

Finn ordered the drink, glanced briefly down at the woman's expensive clothes and then embarked on small talk.

'Yeah, I'm alone,' she replied, gently laughing. She didn't look at Finn but instead watched the fish swimming lazily before her.

'No boyfriend?'

'Not tonight. My boyfriend isn't really one for clubs.' She paused before quietly adding, 'he isn't one for a lot of things.'

Finn downed the last of his beer and ordered another.

***

Trevor knocks at the solidly built black door. It opens quickly and Danny's head pops out and looks up and down the street.

'Hiya. Sorry I'm late,' Trevor says, stepping back to give his friend some room. 'Are you still up for this?'

'Is the van by the garage?'

'Yeah, just like you said.'

'Good, get inside.'

They enter the house and the door slams shut.

***

'So.. are you heading on anywhere when this place shuts?' Finn asked.

***

'... *and in the morning I discovered it was my brother!*'

***

'Heading on anywhere? I don't have any plans. You?'

***

'*Your brother? That's my husband you son of a bitch!...*'

'Turn that fucking TV off,' says Danny, beckoning Trevor from the sofa. 'C'mon, it's time to go.'

***

'Me? No, I never set anything in stone. I like to keep flexible, you know? I don't believe in planning,' Finn confidently replied.

'So what do you believe in?'

'Living in the now, to hell with the consequences, all that.'

'It's something you've given a lot of thought to, isn't it? I can tell,' the girl laughs.

'Well, it's just what feels right to me.'

***

Trevor stands, flicks off the television and turns to follow Danny from the room.

'I was enjoyin' that,' he grumbles. 'It was Jerry Springer and things were just about to kick off … Fuckin' hell!'

'What?'

'I didn't tell you about Mike, did I?'

'Gay-Mike? No, I don't think you did. Why? What's the mad fucker done now?'

'Don't call him that.'

'Don't call him what?'

'Gay-Mike.'

'Why? It's his name isn't it? He's gay and he's 'Mike'. Gay-Mike. What's wrong with that?'

'I don't know, but I do know he doesn't like it anymore. You don't wanna start upsetting Mike do you?'

'Okay, so what were you going to say? What's he done?'

'Well, I heard he's up for GBH. Smashed some guy's face in with a TV! Apparently he just kept pounding him with it, really fucking cut this guy up.'

'Jesus, what the hell is that about? Smashing some guy's face in with a TV? Why? Why don't people just kick the shit out of someone anymore? They're always tryin' to do something new and exciting to get in the papers. It pisses me off.'

'No-one seems to know why he did it. Larry reckons it was an 'ironic statement' but I think someone just said or did somethin' Mike didn't appreciate. Y'know what his temper's like.'

'That's what I mean. I can understand handing someone a beating; you know that. But you've got to have a fucking reason. Where do these wankers think they're living?'

'I guess. But it is kind of cool.'

Danny shakes his head in resignation. 'C'mon, we need to get going.'

* * *

'Nice place,' said Finn, genuinely impressed. He was standing in a high-ceilinged living room. Looking up he saw a large balcony that jutted out above the fitted kitchen. He was informed that this was the bedroom.

The girl sauntered into the kitchen and put the kettle on. 'Do you want milk and sugar?'

'Sure, thanks. I mean it, this is a really nice place. Like off 'Friends' or something. I didn't think there even were places like this round here. How the hell do you afford somewhere like this?'

'It's not as expensive as it looks,' the girl smiled as she poured boiling water into a coffee maker and replaced the lid.

'What do you do? You must earn a fair bit.'

'I'm in marketing.'

'Yeah? Interesting work is it?'

'I suppose. To be honest, I hate talking about my work. But, how about you, Finn? What do you do?'

'Not a lot really. I sure as hell don't earn enough to get a place like this. I'm pretty much between jobs at the minute.'

'You're a man who likes a bit of variety in his life then?' the girl asked as she handed Finn his coffee.

'Thanks. I guess I like a change, yeah. I get bored quickly.' Finn took the mug and strode over to an enormous window to admire the dimly-lit view.

'So you'll try your hand at anything, will you?'

'Er, yeah… I think so.'

'Good. What would you say if I told you there were some handcuffs and a sturdy whip waiting up in that bedroom?'

'Well, I… A little pain never hurt anyone, did it.' Finn paused. 'Only a little, mind you.'

* * *

Danny and Trevor walk down the back alley behind a row of terraced houses. It is beginning to get dark and the temperature is dropping. The water vapour that escapes their mouths forms a small mist around their faces.

'Oh, Jesus, not a list, man,' Danny curses as Trevor produces a crumpled piece of lined paper from his pocket. 'What the hell have you got that thing for?'

'What? What's wrong with a list? You told me to do so many things and I get forgetful. What's it matter to you?'

'I just hate lists, that's all.'

'You hate lists? Nobody hates lists.'

'Nobody but me. I've always hated them. They really piss me off.'

'How can lists piss you off?'

'Do you really want to know?'

'Yeah, of course. Tell me.'

'Okay. It was when I was like, eight or something, in primary school anyway. I was with my first girlfriend and it was pretty sweet as I remember. But, for some reason she made this list of the guys in school she fancied, right? One day I was having a root around in her bag, like you do, and I came across this list. Obviously I was curious and I looked for my name. I was fourth! Fourth, for fuck's sake. Second I could probably handle, I mean, you can kind of understand that, can't you? But fourth?'

'And?'

'Well, that put me off lists for life, my hatred's grown and grown since then. I lay awake at night thinking about them…'

'Are you serious?' Trevor asks as they stop beside a large white Bedford van.

Danny laughs as he tugs the side door open. 'Just get the fuck in there. Jesus, mate.'

* * *

Finn had woken early to find that his body ached all over. He never thought he'd feel so sore and yet so fresh and cheery. The previous night had been a hell of an experience, and she was an interesting girl.

He quietly got up, got dressed and hesitated before scribbling his phone number and address on a scrap of paper which he left on the bedside cabinet. He pecked the beautiful girl who had lain beside him on the cheek before stealing a can of Diet Coke from the fridge and making his way from the flat.

He eventually managed to navigate his way through the complex layout of the building's corridor system but once outside Finn realised he had no idea where he was. It was a rich area, that was obvious, probably on the other side of town to his own home. He lifted his collar up against the cold, rammed his hands into his pockets and began to walk.

* * *

Danny drives the van, frequently looking into his rear-view mirror and keeping his speed below the limit. Trevor fidgets, tapping aggressively at the dashboard.

'God, I wish Rob had a stereo in this heap of shit. You know? I hate drivin' without music.'

'Stop moaning, Trev. It's not like we're going miles is it?'

'I dunno, you've never told me where we're goin', have you?'

'Look, you can moan about Rob's van when you see him. For now just leave it.'

'Okay, okay.' Trevor looks out of the window for a few moments before reaching down into his bag and producing a small bundle of paper. He unwraps it and begins to eat the contents.

'What the fuck are you doin' now?'

'It's a kebab. Want some?'

'When did you get that?'

'This afternoon, why?'

'How can you eat that shit cold? It must be fucking disgusting.'

'Nah, it's nice. Are you sure you don't want to try some?'

'Yeah I'm sure. Just make sure you swallow a pack of breath mints after, I'm not putting up with your breath. I've got enough to deal with as it is.'

Trevor happily chomps into his sandwich as he watches the buildings outside his window gradually change shape and the distances between them grow bigger until they have driven out of the city and into the countryside.

'Where the hell are we going, Danny?'

'You'll see in a minute. We're nearly there.'

* * *

Finn slept like a baby. When he had eventually made it home he'd crawled straight into bed and fallen into a deep sleep. He was only

37

woken when a loud crash resounded from the hallway.

'Huh? W-what the fuck?' he grumbled as he tried to fully wake himself up.

This was hastened as two huge men suddenly appeared in his bedroom.

'Who the hell are you?' Finn cried as he jumped from the bed.

'I'm Mills, this is Smith. We're going to take you for a little ride in the country,' replied one of the men.

'Would you like that, kid?' Smith asked, chuckling to himself.

'Well, to be honest, fellas, I was out kind of late last night,' Finn told them, trying to hide the fear that fast overcame him.

'Yeah, we know,' said Smith.

'Get dressed,' ordered Mills, gruffly.

Finn did as he was told.

* * *

The van is carefully guided from the main road and onto a muddy track where it is dwarfed by dense woodland. Danny weaves his way along the track until it breaks from the trees and turns to gravel. As the van shudders to a halt, Trevor straightens his shirt and reaches for the door handle.

'Not yet, Trev. We're running a bit early and this all needs to be timed just right.' Danny reaches into his pocket and produces a crumpled pack of cigarettes. He pulls out two, handing one across to Trevor and lighting the other.

'Cheers,' says Trevor as Danny hands him the lighter. 'Do you know what you're doing here, Dan?'

'Yeah, I told you not to worry, I've got all the details worked out, it's gonna be fine.'

'That wasn't what I meant. Are you sure you want to do this? It's not too late.'

'You're wrong, Trevor. It was too late a long time ago. Heh.'

'What's funny?'

'Me. I'm starting to sound like some wanker off a film.' Danny takes a deep drag on his cigarette. 'Remember, Trev, this is nothing to do with you, feel free to stay with the van.'

'No chance mate. Besides, it's gonna be fun.'

Danny stubs out his cigarette and pulls on his sleek leather gloves. 'C'mon, let's get this over with.'

The two leave the van and begin to make their way across the gravel before Trevor suddenly halts in mid-stride.

'Shit.'

'What is it?'

'I've forgotten something, I know I have, I… fuck, this is why I needed my list. I told you… My bag! I've left my bag in the van!'

'Oh, for fuck's sake, Trev. Hurry up, we don't have time for all this fucking around.'

* * *

'Take him over to the workbench,' the old man instructed.

Mills and Smith dragged the squirming body of Finn towards a large wooden table covered with a wide array of tools.

They were in a huge depot, surrounded by trucks, but no people. They were in the middle of nowhere and Finn was scared shitless. 'No! Please, for fuck's sake, I'm sorry! I didn't know! PLEASE!!'

'Mills, you know what to do, if you wouldn't mind.'

The heavily muscled man known as Mills bent over and began to unbutton Finn's jeans. He then yanked them down, shortly followed by the Simpson's boxer shorts. Smith held Finn up from behind, halting all but the most insignificant of movement. Mills then lifted Finn's shrunken penis and testicles onto the cold metal of a vice.

'Please,' Finn whimpered as he began to shake, tears running down his cheeks.

'Now, Mister Finn isn't it? My name is Henry Stoaner and I am not a man to trifle with. Isn't that right, Mills?'

'Damn right, sir.'

'Before we continue I would like to tell you a few things about the haulage business if I may. The first thing to remember here is to always keep up to date on the maintenance of your trucks. That's very important. The second thing is NEVER have sexual intercourse with another man's woman. Is that clear? Well, I think that's all you need to know really. I mean, it's not as though you'll ever have the money to own a national haulage firm is it?'

The older man pulled out a large cigar from an intricately decorated metal case. He chopped off the end and lit up before turning his back and calmly saying, 'turn the vice.'

* * *

Danny and Trevor arrive at an imposing wire fence. Trevor produces an industrial pair of wire-cutters and passes them across. Danny makes short work of the fence and they quickly make their way through the hole he has produced.

Trevor pauses for a moment, looking across the greenery rolling away from them into the distance. 'Is this a golf course or something?' he asks.

'Yeah, why?'

'Well… it's a golf course, that's all.'

'Relax, it's not as if we're gonna be on the fifteenth hole or anything. C'mon, we need to keep moving.'

Danny leads the way towards a large, ostentatious building in the distance.

* * *

'How're you feeling Finn? Any better?'

'Pretty shit to be honest, mate. The pain killers are beginning to kick in, though. Never thought I'd be this happy to be in hospital. The only thing I don't like about it is the attractive nurses parading themselves around. That's torture.'

'Heh. You'll be alright.'

'Bruv, I…'

'Don't worry about it, mate. I've already spoken to some guys I used to know. I'm taking care of everything.'

* * *

'I'm gonna fuckin' kill you,' Danny bellows at the old man who is sat in a leather recliner in the centre of an otherwise unused smoking room. 'And may I ask what I have done to cause such offence?' the old man replies.

'How about sticking my fucking brother's bollocks in a vice?'

'Ah, you must be young Mister Finn's brother.'

'Yeah, I must.'

'I am afraid he is the only one to blame in this whole affair. If he had kept them to himself in the first place they would no doubt still be intact.'

'He's to blame? How about your whore of a girlfriend, huh?'

The old man visibly tenses up in his chair, his hands tightening their grip on the arm rests.

'Or, I know, how about you? What makes you think you're not to blame, you old duffer? Can't even keep your girlfriend happy!'

'Mills, if you please.'

A large, pot-bellied man suddenly appears out of nowhere and knocks Danny to the floor. The baseball bat falls from Danny's hands and is kicked into the corner of the room by Mills who then kicks Danny hard in the kidneys. A second man appears in the room, looming behind Trevor who remains silent and keeps a tight grip on his bat.

Danny regains his breath and continues, 'I bet you got this mother-fucker to do my brother for you as well didn't you? Can you even wipe your own arse?' He slowly picks himself off the ground. 'Your kind makes me sick.'

'And yours me. What an interesting dilemma, wouldn't you say?'

'No, I wouldn't.'

The hammer that had been concealed in his waistband suddenly swings outward. It lands heavily on Mills's face and knocks him to the ground with a high-pitched squeal.

While Danny kicks his former assailant into unconsciousness Trevor repeatedly hits the other heavily built man across the body and head with his baseball bat.

Once he's sure that Mills is a bloody pulp Danny stops kicking him and turns back to face the old man who sits frozen in his chair.

'W-what on earth do you think you're doing?' the old man stutters, trying to regain his composure. 'Leave now or I guarantee you spend the rest of your life buggered up against the bars of a prison cell.'

'Yeah, right, whatever. Your big hairy friends are gone, mate. I guess that leaves you to look after yourself.'

'Please, don't! I have money… my own haulage business. I'll give you anything you want.'

Danny looks at the blood-covered hammer he holds aloft with a forced smile. His gaze then slowly returns to the old man squirming in his leather recliner.

* * *

Finn stared up at the hospital ward's featureless ceiling. Despite the ward's size and his fellow patients, it was the first time in his life he had felt claustrophobic. He didn't like it much.

The growing sense of suffocation was temporarily relieved as a nurse approached his bed. 'Another visitor for you, Mister Finn. If you feel up to it?'

'Yeah, sure.' He carefully pulled himself up into a sitting position.

'Hi, Finn.'

'Hi… I wasn't expecting to see you here.'

'Well, I wanted to find out how you're doing, it's kind of my fault after all … I wasn't sure if you'd want to see me.'

'Of course I want to see you,' Finn tried to smile. 'Look, don't worry about … that. I'm trying to forget it all happened. I thought it was supposed to be easy to suppress painful memories but I don't seem to be doing too well so far.'

There was a moment of hesitation before they both laughed.

* * *

Danny stands above Finn's hospital bed, smiling down at his brother as he slowly wakes up.

'Feelin' any better, Finn?'

'Kind of. I've got so many fucking drugs in me it's kind of like New Year's. Plus I don't have any idea what the fuck they're gonna do with me. One doctor tells me one thing and then another comes and tells me something totally different. You'd think they'd at least get their stories straight. Speaking of which … the police ain't been round yet. I guess they will soon enough.'

'I don't know. It depends on who they speak to, really.'

'So did you…'

'Everything's sorted, don't worry about a thing.'

'Thanks. I…'

'It's okay, Finn. You're family, right?'

'Yeah… Oh, I forgot, the girl came to visit me!'

'THE girl?'

'Yeah, THE girl. She was really nice about the whole thing. She should be coming in again tomorrow.'

'Don't forget, she'll know by tomorrow. Just be careful, Finn.'

'I'm always careful, Bruv.'

Danny laughs before he warmly shakes his brother's hand and leaves the hospital. Outside Trevor waits with the van.

'How's he getting on?' Trevor asks as he clambers into the driver's seat.

'Not too bad, considering, but he's already started playing silly buggers again. Not that that's a fucking surprise.'

'And what about you? How are you doing?'

'Ask me again in a couple of weeks.' Danny looks back at the hospital before slamming the door shut. 'C'mon, let's get out of here, I hate hospitals.'

Trevor starts the engine and they drive away.

A Damn Good Finish

Philip J Hancock

I arrived at 'Bridgemont' on Monday just before eight o'clock. The morning hung still beneath a loaded sky. I was greeted at the front door by Pamela, David's wife. She appeared to be in one hell of a rush, her dripping wet hair forming dark spots upon the flimsy vest from which her fast nipples protruded. Her two young children squealed excitedly at the arrival of a visitor, stomping out a racket upon the wooden flooring.

'Mornin' Pam. You alright?'

'God! You'll have to excuse me. I'm in such a state. I'm taking the children to France for three weeks and we're so late,' she flustered. 'Please help yourself to everything. David will be around should you need anything, but you know what to do,' she smiled. 'Don't mind him too much. He can be a bit trying at times. I really must get going.'

'Don't you worry about it,' I winked. 'We'll be fine.'

The job in hand was far more complicated than usual. A complete change of style as well as feel was required by the lady of this house – a large Victorian villa that stood in two acres of grounds on the outskirts of town.

I'd arranged with Pamela to commence with the lounge. The high ceiling and prominently featured cornice were in good nick, and so required nothing more than two coats of 'off-white' emulsion. The walls were to be stripped of their existing Anaglypta paper, and judging by the way that the light from the bay window fell upon them needed to be extensively filled and redressed before finishing with emerald-green emulsion. The skirting boards, picture rail, panel door and architrave, fitted cupboards and shelving to the alcoves, were to be prepared and finished in matching eggshell.

David was a contemporary art dealer. He was due to fly out to San Francisco in ten days time to negotiate on behalf of one of the many art producing clients that he represented. The house was cram-full of extraordinary but dull works of art. Drab paintings and collages hung from the walls. Sculptures of expressive human heads and mystical African masks and wooden carvings were positioned in specific areas of the large rooms, already chock-a-block with cumbersome antique furniture. David passed by the open door as I was mauling a tallboy into the centre of the lounge.

'Morning David.'

The door to his study across the hallway pulled to. He didn't reply.

The Gods were with me. The brittle wallpaper fell from the walls. Buoyed by this good fortune I tore into the work and by lunchtime the walls were stripped clean.

'You're getting on quite quickly I see,' said David, who was standing in the lounge when I returned from lunch.

'Yeah. So far, so good. This prep is what no one ever sees. This is where all the hard work is.'

'Hmmm... Considering that the wallpaper has come off so well, do you think that a price reduction is in order?'

For a moment I was lost for words. People asking for discounts after agreeing a price always surprised me – even more so when wealthy people tried it on.

'Well. Err… As I said to Pamela when I last came over, the price is for what the job's worth. I can't really do it for much less,' I said, taken aback by his cheek.

'Hmmm… Well, we'll see,' he mumbled, and left the room.

'I suppose we will.'

David was still in bed when I arrived on Tuesday morning. I got straight to it, up and down the heavy wooden stepladders. I worked like a madman, scratching the walls with rough grade sandpaper. I sanded all the woodwork with a finer grade, and dusted everything down, bringing the job along nicely. After an hour or so there came a knock at the door.

'Good morning. Would you like a drink? Some coffee?' David called from the hallway.

'Yes please.' I replied, surprised by his pleasant tone.

I dusted myself down and went to the kitchen to find him milking the coffee. He was wearing plum coloured corduroy slippers and a grey silk dressing gown that matched his hair. He seemed cheerful enough.

'There you go. Sugar?'

'No thanks.'

'I see that's a neat kit of tools that you've got in your case,' he continued, eager for conversation. 'Why such a small case? I'd of thought people in your line of work would carry much more with them.'

'Nah mate. Much easier this way,' I said. If there's anything that I need and haven't got - stepladders for example – I can always borrow or hire them out. Pays to make a habit of packing the right tools for the job. Makes no sense carting too much stuff around with you. In a way, it's how I like to run my life as well. Travel light.'

'I don't agree,' he retorted. 'I think it is very important that one surrounds oneself with one's things.'

Oneself with one's things? Who did this idiot think he was? Royalty?

'Everything that I have here in my home, I absolutely must have!'

'Oh. I see.'

'So, you're a friend of Pamela's then?' he asked suddenly.

'Not exactly a friend. I, we, err…'

'Yes?' he smiled.

What was he thinking, I wondered. Did he suspect something between me and her?

'I'd better get back to it now.'

'Yes, you better had, hadn't you?' he replied curtly. Bewildered, I downed the lukewarm coffee and returned to the lounge.

I spent the rest of the day painting the ceiling and cornice. I was baffled by this David character. His manner was increasingly unpredictable and played on my mind. What the hell did this ponce know anyway? And he was a ponce: if taking fifty per cent off the sale of his clients' work didn't make him one, then nothing did.

The walls looked well considering what a mess they had been in. There was the odd mark here and there that needed a flick of filler, but I felt quite proud of the job so far. The ceiling had dried out nicely overnight, and the woodwork was ready for its first coat of eggshell.

It was during that third day that things became problematic. Looking for an empty tin, I found myself unfastening the security bolts at the back door when David appeared.

'Where are you going now?' he enquired.

'I need an empty can - something to split this new litre of paint into. Maybe I'll find something in the shed?'

'So that's where you're off to then is it? The shed?'

'Yeah. Why?'

'Why? You ask me why?'

'Yeah,' I shrugged. 'Why?'

'Why?' he repeated. 'I'll tell you *why,* shall I? Because this is my bloody house and I can ask whatever the bloody hell I like! When I like and to who I like!'

I tilted my head and fixed a stare. How easily I could just fang hold of his neck and throttle the living daylights out of him.

'I thought it was whom,' I said. 'Not who.'

'Don't you get clever with me, you…you bloody fucking oink!'

Pamela had warned me about this, but I honestly didn't think that he would be this bad. A spoilt, overgrown kid but with a wider range of vocabulary.

'Look, David, I don't know what your problem is, but…'

'Just shut up and get on with it!' he snapped, before scampering off to his study.

The shed was a converted air raid shelter built at the far end of the long winding back garden out of brick and corrugated iron sheeting. A single brick had been removed from the wall that faced the house, but the rest of the structure was concealed from view by a shambles of overgrown rhododendron and hydrangea bushes. I struggled to prise open the door - the hinges were crusted with generations of rust. Fumbling around in the darkness, I happened upon an ancient biscuit tin. I knocked it out clean and returned to the lounge, and that initial matter of first coating the woodwork.

I hoped to have most of the work finished on Thursday. The walls looked smooth and the Fancy-Dan paint that David had supplied produced a depth of colour that even I was surprised by. I was in the laundry room washing my emulsion tools when he barged in.

'I'm not satisfied with those skirting boards!'

'Oh? What's up with them?'

'Come here. I'll show you.'

'Just a sec mate,' I stuttered, fumbling the wet tools in the sink, 'Just let me…'

'I said NOW!'

His face was pressed an inch away from the skirting board when I entered the lounge.

'Do you see that edge?'

I saw a beautifully painted skirting board nothing else.

'Of course you can't see it, or you would have done something about it. I want that rectifying!'

'Rectifying? What's wrong with it?'

'What's wrong with it? That's bloody rough work! You've ruined my whole house you have! I want those skirting boards burnt off!'

I couldn't believe what I was hearing. There was nothing wrong with the job and he wouldn't know the difference between good and bad work so long as his arse-hole pointed downwards. If he wanted me to burn off the skirting boards then why wait until the job was almost finished before saying so?

'Well, I can burn them off if you want, but then the job'll take longer and I thought you said you're leaving on Saturday.'

'I don't care! Get it done!'

It took me all of Thursday afternoon to find a tool-hire shop that stocked a Propane blowtorch. The build of blistered skins fell like feathers from the blade of my scraper as I worked from the spot that David had picked me up on. When I was done, I called him to inspect once again.

'You're working this job as a foreigner aren't you?' he asked.

'How d'yer mean like?'

'*How do I mean like?* I mean the Inland Revenue would be very interested in hearing about you.'

'So?'

'So, I think a discount is in order,' he said smugly. 'After all the heartache you've put me through.'

Fine, I thought. Whatever would make him happy. And to think I'd actually felt sorry for this idiot when I took the job on. This would be my finest, most poetically justified piece of work I'd ever undertaken. This could even be my swansong.

'QUICK! QUICK! DAVID? DAVID?' I yelled. 'There's someone creeping around the back garden!'

He burst past me, his face full of thunder, out through the kitchen and into the yard.

'David. Sssh! Quietly.'

'Where the… I can't see anyone.'

'Up by the shed,' I whispered.

Half crouched, David crept along the lawn. At the turn of the rhododendron bush he paused to listen, like a cat about to strike its prey. He bolted up the side of the shed. The overhanging branches slashed at his body and whipped back at me as he made for the door. My pulse was racing, but my mind was set. He thrust into the shed like a wild thing. The door closed behind him. I dropped the steel brace across the frame.

'WHAT THE HELL IS GOING ON? Come on, stop pissing around! I'm very busy!'

His shouting became faint as I made for the house.

'NOW!'

No neighbours to speak of. No-one in earshot.

'I SAID NOW!'

It was weird seeing the reflection of David's spectacles from the hole in the shed wall.

'You can forget about getting paid now. When I get out of here you've had it!'

'That's alright. I don't really need the dosh, and seeing as I'm gonna be here for a couple more days, I may as well crash in your room. Is that okay?'

'What? he yelled. 'That's my bed! I'll see that you're locked up when I get out of here!'

51

'Locked up? Well, it'd be silly not to stay over. I mean, your bed's free - with Pamela being away and that.'

'That's my bed!'

'Oh, really?'

What a bed. Far too good for the likes of him, I thought. He didn't have a fuck in him. Pamela on the other hand, was the kind of woman who loved a good roasting. Not any more, though. Not on this bed. I managed to dismantle it in no time and carried it outside onto the lawn.

'Giz a shout if you need owt else. I've gotta get on.'

1961 was the year. My choice of 'Margaux' over many classics from David's vast stock of wine, washed smoothly over the excellent linguine and fresh mushrooms. The Marks and Spencer chocolate cake rounded off a well-earned dinner.

'I'm making some fresh coffee David, would you care for some?' I called from the edge of the dew glistening lawn.

'You sick bastard! I'll kill you with my own bare hands when I get out of here!'

'But David, then you would go to prison, and how do you think Pamela and the children would cope? She would have to find another man to take care of her, and what about the children? Please don't talk like that.'

'You have absolutely no idea of the trouble you are in. I know people. Serious people!'

'Look David, coffee or not? It's getting cold out here.'

I woke on Saturday morning and took the opportunity to have another look around. There really were some awful pieces of furniture and as for the artwork, well a three year old kid could do better. The extensive library and vast collection of CDs weren't up to much either. Nothing that David possessed, except for perhaps one thing, was to my liking. Throughout the time that I'd known him, David had constantly stressed his passion for his possessions. He had to own, have, control. His possessions were his life and his life was one of possessions. It was only right that they should be with him forever.

I shifted the tallboy, two-seater settee, and drop-leaf oak table from the centre of the lounge, and stacked them outside on the lawn. I washed the wooden floor over with a solution of oxalic acid before coating the skirting boards with quick drying acrylic. The way the job was going, I anticipated that it would be late Sunday afternoon before it would be all knocked off. There would be quite some time to kill in between coats, and where better to begin than in the clearing of the upstairs rooms?

'I beg you. Please let me out. I'm starving. It was freezing last night,' David whimpered.

'Well I did offer you coffee last night, and if you care to look, you can see that my hands are full.'

'That's my best furniture. What's it doing out here?'

'Remember what you said to me the other day. About wanting everything that you had around you?'

'LET ME OUT!'

A racket of banging against the corrugated iron sheeting followed his screaming.

'LET ME OUT! YOU BASTARD! I'M GOING TO FUCKING KILL YOU!'

'Language David! And I'd slow down if I were you. It's gonna be a scorcher today according to the forecast, so don't knacker yourself out shouting and banging like an idiot.'

Thank God I wasn't in the furniture removal business, and thank God that there wasn't a piano. I struggled against the sweltering sun that beat down on the back garden, and worked into the late afternoon. It was a real maul; shifting every single item of clothing, bedding, wardrobes, and cupboards, down the stairs, through the hallway, and stacking them outside on the lawn.

'I'm going to first coat them skirting boards now, then make something to eat,' I called to David.

'I need a drink. A glass of water. Please?' he pleaded.

'Okay. I think I can manage that.'

'Please will you let me out? I'll pay you double if you let me out. I'll forget everything that's been said. Just please let me out. Please?'

Saturday night. The food was once again delightful. I should have considered becoming a chef. Maybe there was still a chance? I mooched around the downstairs rooms making a note of what lay before me on the final day. The books, CDs, desk and chair, the oddments in the kitchen, and David's precious artwork that I had piled up against the walls in the hallway.

The lounge looked wonderful in the early light of Sunday morning. I decided to go out and check on David before attempting to rustle up some breakfast, out of what was now a threadbare refrigerator and pantry. Stepping outside, the piles of furniture looked eerie - all still and giant-like on the lawn. A cooling breeze shushed the rhododendron and hydrangea bushes as I approached the shed.

'David? David?' I called. 'Wakey-wakey! It's my last day today. It'll be all over soon. Can I get anything for you? David? David?'

I went back to the house and got straight to it. I shifted the fridge and cleared the kitchen. The desk in David's study was the only awkward item left, but on removing the drawers I managed to slide it around with considerable ease. I used the garden wheelbarrow to ferry out all the books, records and CDs, and wine from the racks, and tipped them in the few remaining spaces on the lawn.

'If it's my artwork that you're after, you can have it. Take it all. But please let me out! PLEASE!'

'David, chill baby. I couldn't live with myself if I stole from you. I'm not interested in your artwork. I don't need your money. My business is doing very well. I've got plenty on.'

'Take it all. It will make you very, very rich. But let me out. I'm not well.'

'You'll be cool. It's gonna piss down later.'

I stood the paintings upright against the chaos of clutter on the lawn. As the first spots of rain descended, I sheltered against the shed door expecting to hear David's last cries for freedom. The rain pelted down for some time, soaking everything through and making one hell of a din upon the corrugated iron. I listened to David sleep. I lifted the cross-brace and slowly opened the door. I watched him for a few moments before offering the gun to his temple… pays to pack the right tools for the job.

One last look around convinced me that Pamela would be delighted. I had completed everything that she had requested of me. The lounge was beautifully decorated, and everything was in its place.

Making a killing look like suicide isn't too difficult when you have a wife who will testify that her husband was going off his head. If the wife wasn't to be believed, then the contents of a household emptied onto the lawn should dismiss any further suspicion.

When the skirting boards were finally finished, I gathered my tools together and packed them neatly in to my suitcase, along with my business card that I recovered from one of Pamela's empty drawers.

BESPOKE FINISHER
Time-Served Tradesman
No Come-Backs Guaranteed

Fijian Rites
Denis Mattinson

Shuffling down into undergrowth not the most comfortable spot still needs must dictated to by the nature of the prey. Shit another briar hooked into leg penetrating camouflaged clothing. Nor the most Cheetah like of hunters therefore needing to ambush until demise of victim inevitable. Soon to be, skills honed to perfection after all succeeding in every prior attempt.

Pulse rate increasing dramatically on sighting prospective prey, young and tender moreover alone, easy meat. Heart pounding adrenaline flowing a few more steps required to point of no return. Rising onto toes like a sprinter in the blocks afore suddenly unleashing pent up power. Victim flung to the ground followed down to straddle like a lion. Smirking watching big blue eyes widen in shock, reacting just like the others. Steel blade flashing, priding himself on keeping tools of trade in pristine condition, honed razor sharp. Proven on deftly flicking off blouse buttons revealing bra. Likewise severed. Breasts flopping hardly the best ever seen but of little consequence serving their purpose, eventually. Mouthing large pink nipples mm tasting sweet, like nectar. Knife point circling each nipple ominously leaving red weal, yet so deft and accurate skin uncut. Watching face of terrified victim with disdain who like the rest to be slaughtered. Serial killer they called him, sick of mind, deranged, sadistic, barbaric, smirking, little did they know. Breasts heaving synchronised with pounding heart like eyes full of fear. Justifiably so for he her god having the power of life or death dimming eyes into eternal blackness cutting out this same heart if so desirous. Mouth opened. Finger wagged. 'Scream my pet and I will cut off your tits.' Grinning on orifice abruptly shut his dominance proved.

Unlike before when totally subjugated by mother that is until her timely death. Upon which assimilating her characteristics in the age old customs of the Fijians, well almost.

Knife point tracing twixt cleavage reddening but still no blood, wanting to conserve this precious juice for now, time in plenty for that to flow. Slicing through belt and skirt revealing red panties, an appropriate colour, silk cut revealing dark forest licking suddenly dry lips, eyes following dark central line. Ironically focused not on this den of iniquity but where leading, plump young thighs. Giggling, an adroit bird watcher and she a fine specimen indeed.

Needs to be said Tracy terrified no amount of training preparing for this scenario. Better not provoke. Eyes bulging burning gaze so intense almost searing flesh, nevertheless better this than cold steel. Oh god no, wincing on fleshy mound of Venus pulled when pubes grasped, short and curlies yanked straight. Had he done this to others plucking like a bird of prey, moreover while still alive. Part of his sadism. Slicing through, what when denude. Soon to know. Oh god now scraping bare, blade edge leaving sore. First sound involuntarily emitted emulating thoughts. 'Why?' Sickly smirk peered down.

'Simple my sweet innocent young thing, needing to be plucked and oven ready afore putting meat in.'

Realisation dawning wanting her to appear virginal before raping. Needs must having to act or too late. Faculties regained bringing knee up sharply between thighs. Target reached, object achieved denoted by sudden change in expression from smirk to pained wide eyed shock. Delivering a karate chop to side of neck in spite of bulk knocking sideways. Barely sitting before four detectives smothered him handcuffing.

John the sergeant in charge grinned pointedly. 'I knew you were too young for the job.' Eyes flashing angrily at this slight.

'You should talk, almost too late, he nearly had me.'

'Well wanting you to have a bit of a thrill afore moving in, all work and no play and all that. Like I said obviously too young not yet feathered.' Gaze fixed on where knife had worked. 'Looks a bit sore want me to rub some cream on it love or better still some hair restorer. Should stop playing with it or keep it covered, like a cat with its throat cut.'

Mouth dropping open glowing red on realisation dawning still nude for all to see situation quickly retrieved on wrapping skirt around covering embarrassment.

'That's better we can now concentrate on him without the distraction. By the way well done. Sorry for the delay must have dislodged or broke the wire you were wearing. We waiting like dummies deciding on instinct to come and find you. Never mind all well now having got your man.'

Avidly scanning through window the profuse growth of bushes and fruit trees. Smiling, at last after two years of absence the unmistakable outline of a waxwing feeding on the cotoneaster berries. This species held a special place in his heart leading to a lifelong passion of bird watching, an ardent twitcher. In turn leading to deep resentment for since new houses were built much to his chagrin creating a dearth of some species. Still unable to drive his pet away, safely caged.

Mother hated his Egyptian vulture there again perhaps why he loved it so much his one chance of defiance in otherwise dominated life. Constantly nagged if not bowing to every whim. An only child resentful always wanting a daughter perhaps why naming him Alma neither one nor the other. Still one day situation inevitably reversed. Likewise these newcomers, they too getting their just desserts. Giggling. Indeed phrase quite apt in more ways than one with what having in mind. Vowing a macabre revenge.

Whilst the influx of newcomers good for business destroying the atmosphere the ambience prevailing between the locals who having grown up together, these strangers not of their own. These middle class interlopers paying dearly for their intervention, curtailing his beloved hobby. Driven further into hatred of females by his one and only sexual experience. Under the influence of alcohol succumbing to temptation having sex with a prostitute. Not an unpleasant experience, initially, even contemplating an encore until finding having contracted a venereal disease. Too ashamed to have treatment suffering ever since mind like body painfully poisoned and tormented against females for treating him so therefore determined to wreak havoc against one and all.

Big, red faced the epitome of a jovial butcher, affable with customers outwardly yet inside like a seething dormant volcano, only awaiting the trigger to activate. Same supplied when Mother suffered a stroke paralysing down one side. Speech slurred but no less vehement far from subduing demands escalating more so on debilitating further by asthma. Driven to distraction the eruption nigh soon the bloody lava to flow.

The fateful day constantly harangued by mother who lay in bed banging on the floor demanding food, cups of tea, then a new inhaler to help with breathing. Patience finally snapping. Instead of supplying breath pillow conveniently held in place stopping forever, abuse abruptly halted free at last. However this not the total eclipse but the genesis of the nemesis. In spite of presuming to know each others business in such a close knit community presumptions incorrect. All assumed Alma to be the perfect doting son fawning on mother. After all staying at home solely to care for her having never bothered with girls. Naturally with death predictable due to afflictions the local doctor a family friend never bothered to examine. Death certificate signed automatically a foregone conclusion due to asphyxiation on sudden asthma attack. Diagnosis correct, cause not quite so.

Actions likewise predictable having coffin delivered to house wanting to lay out personally thereby spending as much time as possible with deceased before the final parting, what could be more natural.

However now released from bondage furthermore enhanced by inducing some of mother's strength and virtues into own being. Vengeance was his by enacting the age old customs of the Fijians.

At the police station on establishing name and address locked in a cell giving time to reflect. Laid on bunk a cynical smile touched corner of mouth. Getting caught inevitable, expected not that stupid in fact ironically welcomed. Objectives achieved how else would all be revealed especially to those victims who still alive. After all the deaths of the girls incidental, merely a means to an end.

Detectives together with forensic scientists visited his home to gather further evidence in so doing coming across more than bargained for. Using equipment designed to find human remains coming across skulls and pelvic bones buried in various locations yet curiously no other remains found. Dilemma solved by one detective offering a simple but plausible explanation. Nodding towards the Egyptian vulture in aviary. That quite capable of consuming broken bones, feeding on such in the wild. Skull and pelvis obviously too large or involving too much work to smash. However not knowing half of it, this but the tip of the iceberg.

John and Tracy the interrogating officers smugly revealed how having caught him by setting a trap. 'You developed a pattern, your last three victims ardent twitchers. Therefore simply releasing on the grapevine the location of a rare species to draw you. Tracy, here the bait.' Long hours of grilling expected trying to extract a confession by tripping up the last thing expected being a full and frank admittance.

Shrugging, resigned to fate candidly without regret or emotion stating 'Yes I am guilty the proof on the video you have seized.'

'We have seen it not amused. Finding the one depicting your mother in the coffin with leg bent under and you stood grinning brandishing a knife especially in bad taste. Surprised at you however that apart revealing little. We know what she died of, she wasn't stabbed.'

Giggling. 'Obviously not quite so astute as you like to think. Show it and I will talk you through.'

Initially of poor quality obviously learning. Hand raising dress to disclose empty space referring to missing leg. After which switching to dining table shown cutting off a piece from large steak raising to mouth 'Bon appetite mother.' Giggling. 'See I may have to make my own meals but make no bones about it she still feeding me in a sense.'

The inference still not grasped simply a macabre sense of humour not explaining the other killings. With enigmatic smile showing little regret proudly unbelievably volunteering the answers to their dilemma. 'You are unable to comprehend however having no bones

62

to pick with you I killed two birds with one stone, excuse the pun. Obtaining revenge on the opposite gender likewise those despising most. I am a student of nature therefore like in nature waste not want not, one complementing the other, where there is life there is death. To be fair tastefully done in the nicest way possible befitting their positions in life. Expecting and demanding the best so why not? Now watch my guests dine in Fijian style. All smiling affably at the camera willing posers one and all. Having a common denominator insofar new to the village, middle class, commuting to the city to work. Pointing out the new doctor, bank manager, police inspector and remarkably a bizarre exception in the vicar. All with respective spouses. 'Listen to the women commenting on my culinary skills requesting the recipe, none more than for the tender lean juicy steaks. Watch, watch me smile. Now suggesting attending my shop to be given preferential treatment insofar receiving mince from the same source.' Giggling. 'Now do you comprehend?'

Tracy shook head nonplussed. 'But these are the very people you despised so why the lavish dinner parties?'

Glaring back. 'Typical woman mouth opening before brain thinks why not keep it shut and appear intelligent? Think yourself lucky you not there, on the menu making a nice rump steak. Those tasty juicy steaks they are enjoying so much are from soft milky thighs. The mince consist of tender breasts and offal. In essence turning my auspicious guests into unwitting cannibals it is all human flesh. During ancient Fijian rites customary to eat enemies. By so doing not only showing own superiority but by partaking of their flesh preventing their entry into the afterlife. Having enough of females here and I certainly didn't want to meet mother again.' Licking lips suggestively before bursting into a fit of giggles.

Lifters
James Bones

Chloe brought me here.

I was kind of a blank slate when I met Chloe.

Twenty-five, single, worked in an office, rented accommodation, adult channel subscription, few qualifications, fewer prospects.

Chloe gave me definition.

Town centre, ten months ago: a light, pissy drizzle dances through the air. It's Saturday and the religious nuts are out. As I pass the Virgin Megastore some guy in an overcoat vents fire and brimstone at me, from my other side an in-store speaker informs me a new Radiohead album has been released; this second piece of news is of greater importance to me. I fish through my pockets looking for a few notes with which to purchase the album. The in-store speaker moves onto Dr Dre but the religious nut still tries selling me salvation.

My pockets are void of money. My footsteps slap wetly against the paving stones as I make my way toward the cash-point. I find a queue of shoppers. A young kid is screaming like it's being gutted, its mucus-covered face contorted in a grimace of non-existent agony, its mother too henpecked to really give a fuck.

I turn towards the street. I can still see the religious nut shouting at passers by. No one seems to be particularly interested in what he has to say. I feel a pang of pity for the guy.

A brief commotion somewhere at the other end of the street draws my attention. A blonde haired girl bolts past me, running like her life depends on it. For a second I get a clear view of the girl's face contorted in an expression of fear and excitement. I see that she's

66

dropped a silk scarf. The piece of fabric floats daintily towards the wet pavement.

I have an impulse to run after her. I decide to act on it. I quickly grab the now soggy and quite dirty scarf with a sense of urgency that has long been missing from my life, and begin to run as fast as I can after her.

She's quick and she's still going strong, but I'm fresh in on the chase. She's casting frightened glances back towards me as she runs now. I hold up the scarf and wave it around, 'Hey! You dropped this.' She turns as I repeat my appeal for her to stop. A look of ecstatic relief washes across her face as she realises I am her only pursuer. We both stagger to a halt in front of an electronics store, and for a few seconds we both lean breathlessly against the display window. The girl is beautiful. Shoulder length golden hair that contrasts vibrantly with the dull grey light of the English Spring. A little shorter than I am, with a slim build. Her eyes azure diamonds set in her face. It's a bit early to say really, I haven't even spoken to her, but I think I may well be in love.

I stand slack-jawed and panting holding out the scarf staring like an idiot, not quite sure what to say. She eyes me cautiously. I can tell she's trying to figure me out. Recovering my composure, I say, 'You dropped this just now.'

An amused smile cracks across her lips. 'You chased me all that way just to give me this?' She takes the scarf from my outstretched hand. For a second her hand touches mine.

I think I may be blushing. 'Well I saw you drop it as you ran past, and I, well…'

'It's just I thought you were…' she interrupts. 'Doesn't really matter.'

I laugh embarrassedly. 'You were going like a bat out of hell, you're lucky I caught you.'

'I was in a bit of a rush.' She smiles at me again, flirtatiously this time. 'Thanks. Here take this; it's probably too big for me anyway.'

She reaches into her long coat and pulls out a cellophane packaged shirt out from underneath. With a mischievous grin she hands it to me. Turning the packaged shirt over in my hands, struck dumb by the sheer oddness of this gift, I notice that the electronic security tag is still attached. Suddenly all the running and looks of abject terror make sense. 'Hold on,' I say. 'You stole this?'

'I lifted it, yeah,' she declares nonchalantly, beginning to walk away.

A moment passes as I take this in. 'Hey!' I shout after her, she's twenty yards away by now. 'What's your name?'

She turns around, flashing me yet another jellifying smile. 'Emily,' she says before rounding the corner and disappearing.

I stand with my mouth open for a moment, contemplating the chain of events that have just taken place. Saddened by the thought that I may never set eyes on this weird beauty again, I turn my attention to the electrical store display window. Several screens are showing the same thing: footage of starving children in some developing country, screaming at me silently from behind the glass.

This is how I first came to meet Chloe Russell. Of course at this point I still believed her name was Emily.

Initially Chloe was less than honest with me about a number of things. Her age, for instance; it wasn't until I'd been involved with her for a number of weeks that I discovered that she was seventeen years old, not twenty as she had originally claimed.

I'm still trying to coax the reasons for these minor deceptions out of her, but as of yet I have made no headway. She seems to clam up the second I raise the subject. I could put these embroideries of the truth down to some kind of urge to impress me, or perhaps they are merely another aspect of her warped sense of fun but whatever the case, I don't believe I'll ever be able to fathom it.

Love at first sight is rarely mutual. Our first meeting barely registered. During our second encounter we got to know each other a little better; this is when my own criminal behaviour began.

An unidentifiable greenish fluid smears my jacket, as I accidentally collide with the filthy exterior wall of the shop. Above me the gaudy Superdrug logo glares out into the street, the iconography of a corporate religion.

I take a step away from the shop's automatic door, allowing a woman with a pram to pass. I notice she has a lazy eye, and for a moment I wonder if the kid has a lazy eye too, but I can't tell. All that seems to be in the pram is a screaming bundle of rags and snot. My curiosity wanes and I enter the shop.

A pretty Asian girl sitting behind one of the checkouts gives me a vague look of disapproval as I pass. I can feel her eyes drill into the back of my head as I continue into the shop.

I make my way down the aisles, searching for the toothpaste. Artificial light cascades from strips lining the ceiling, giving the shop a synthetically oppressive quality. A girl in a long black coat stands with her back to me hugging the shelves as if pushed into them. I notice the brightly blonde hair pouring down her back, and I begin to wonder if this is Emily. Her image burning brightly in my mind, I begin to approach and realise I am correct. As I draw closer I notice that she is stealthily plucking bottles of peach shampoo from the shelves and consigning them to the recesses of her coat. Emily, now aware of my approach, turns her gaze to meet mine. The look on her face is one of stone cold rigidity, a poker face concealing her fear and apprehension of being caught in the act. Her face however melts into a look of relieved recognition and playfulness as a spark of memory flashes in her eyes.

'Hello, stranger.' Emily gives me the kind of smile that could make a dead man's cock twitch.

'Hi,' I reply. A little voice in my head chanting a mantra of 'play it cool, play it cool', but in a different area of my psyche I'm already down on one knee. 'Why is it every time I bump into you you're involved in some kind of criminal pursuit?'

Emily smiles ruthlessly. 'Well, the thing about pursuits is, the criminal ones are always the most fun.'

She casts a cautious glance over her shoulder and grabs me by my jacket lapels, pulling me closer to her and the shelves she's been busy pilfering. A wickedly mischievous look creeps across her face and she begins grabbing the shampoo bottles and stowing them in my jacket.

I struggle against her half-heartedly, cautious not to be too forceful. 'What the hell are you doing?'

'I think that's obvious,' she says, pausing for a moment. 'I'm implicating you in my criminal pursuits.'

'What if I don't want to be implicated?'

Emily leans closer to me, the smell of her perfume sending shivers of pleasure through me. 'It's pretty obvious that you'd love to be implicated in anything with me.'

I regain my composure somewhat. 'What the hell do I want with peach shampoo anyway?'

Emily ignores me and continues to expertly stash the bottles about both our persons. 'The trick is,' she says, 'not to make eye contact with them, but not to look like you're avoiding it either. The worst thing that can happen is if they make eye contact with you and you look away. If that happens, leg it.'

Emily links my arm and begins to drag me toward the checkout. A series of eventualities begin to run through my head: capture, court, disgrace then prison and all that comes with it including bad food and buggery. The events, however, have gained momentum and I don't think I could stop this even if I wanted to.

Arm-in-arm, we approach the checkout. I stare steadily ahead. Heart rate increases. Beads of sweat begin to prick my back. Time and space seem to sever as we make our way past the checkout; these moments seem to last much longer than they should. The gaze of the checkout girls surrounds us, a malevolent omnipresence. My heartbeat seems so loud I begin to wonder if anyone else can hear it. The shop door seems so far away. I don't think I can manage to suppress the urge to run much longer. Emily gives my arm a reassuring squeeze... My motivation is restored.

We emerge arm-in-arm onto the street. My heart still pounds furiously. The light seems blinding. I feel dazed and confused, like a newborn animal taking its first look at a dauntingly unfamiliar world.

I turn to Emily. An endless smile of ecstatic joy stretches her face to preternatural dimensions. I've done it. We did it. I begin to smile back at Emily. As my fear fades, a weird kind of contentment descends on me. A strange unspoken communion seems to join me, and the girl who links my arm.

'Better than sex,' she says as her knowing eyes penetrate mine.

About three minutes later the beginning of my first sexual experience with Chloe was heralded by the clatter of shampoo bottles cascading from our coats to the toilet floor.

Chloe and I were soon engaging in regular lifting trips. We became prolific. Experts at pilfering whatever came to hand. We very rarely stole anything of any actual use or value. It was the thrill that drove us, not the necessity.

I sometimes wonder where I would be now if I'd never met her. The answer's kind of obvious, I'd be sat in that fucking office, selling people I'll never even see stuff I'll never even touch, an indentured corporate slave, screaming impotently for freedom. I can now see that I was looking for a way out for some time before Chloe, and our unlikely, transgressive relationship.

About three weeks later, Chloe turned up at the door to my flat carrying a suitcase. From this moment on we lived together. I never asked about her past and she never asked about mine.

I worked through the week, so Chloe and I made our lifting trips on weekends, often hitting five shops in the same day. Afterwards, we'd have sex wherever we could. We rarely made it back to the flat before our urges got the better of us. The sex was always urgent and intense after a lifting trip. Our bodies would collide like a slow motion car crash, limbs buckling, muscles stretching, fluids leaking.

Pretty soon one or two trips a week weren't enough for me. I began to steal from the office. Small things at first, stationery and the like. Eventually I was caught on camera putting a piece of computer hardware in my car boot. I was sacked on the spot. This was when lifting became a way of life for us.

After a couple of months with no income bar the stuff we stole, the money that I had saved whilst I was working was beginning to run low. We needed an alternative source of cash. You can't survive on shoplifting alone. It was at this time that an opportunity arose.

An old acquaintance of mine named Taz came to visit us. I used to buy weed off him when I was younger, and we became the special kind of friends that only a man and his drug dealer are. Taz was primarily a purveyor of illicit pharmaceuticals, but had connections in anything that was remotely bent. It was Taz that gave us our first lessons in how to steal cars. He also later provided us with a contact, a guy who would give us three hundred pounds a pop for a car in decent nick. More if it was anything classy.

The secret to being a successful criminal is simple: do not look like one. For Chloe and I it was easy. Single men and women always look suspicious. Couples, on the other hand, are very rarely suspected of anything, especially well dressed, professional looking couples. For petty thieves, we took a great deal of care with our appearance.

We still went lifting, but only as a kind of sideline, the fire had gone out of it. Car theft was now our primary operation. Once again we were careful not to hit the same place too many times. We'd often get the bus or train out to another town and drive back in a stolen vehicle. Before we'd turn the cars in for payment, we'd park up in a lay-by and make love in the back. Chloe, seemed to enjoy this more than me. I think it was the defilement of someone else's personal space and property that did it.

Once or twice our benefactor would not accept the cars that we stole. In these instances we drove the cars out to remote areas of wasteland and torched them. I enjoyed watching the cars burn. Watching the metal buckle and fail with the heat, and the flames dancing, slowly consuming the shell of the vehicle. This is how Chloe got the idea for that surprise birthday present.

I look along to the other end of the counter at her, across the throng of faceless drones, and a smile breaks on my face as I think back to that night.

The car park. This is where Chloe told me to meet her. The air is heavy with the smell of piss and diesel, the black tarmac ground with indiscriminate spillages and splatters of unidentifiable filth. The change in my pockets is about the most interesting thing here.

After about five minutes a brand new black three series BMW drives on to the car park and pulls up right in front of me. I duck down to look through the window and see that Chloe's sitting at the wheel.

The window descends smoothly into the door. 'Jump in,' she says.

I enter the sleek black car through the passenger side.

We drive for a good twenty minutes out into the suburbs, and further out into the countryside. I gaze out of the window as we drive. In the fading light the crops dance to the mercurial melody of the wind.

Our journey seems to be coming to an end as we turn off along a side lane. The wooded road leads us up to a dilapidated old farmhouse. Chloe stops the car and steps out onto the grass-strewn gravel. The building has clearly been abandoned for some time, as a botanical garden seems to have taken root all over the stonework.

'What are we doing here?' I ask.

Chloe lights a cigarette and takes a moment to savour my agitation. 'Open the boot,' she tells me.

A little perplexed by the whole situation, I do as she requests and lift the lid of the BMW's sleek rear compartment. It contains three large jerry cans and a couple of rags.

'I've seen the way you look at the cars when we torch them.' Her hand strokes my spine in seductive downward motions. 'Happy birthday.'

Later as I watched the fire spread throughout the ground floor of the house from the car, Chloe's head sank into my lap. The flames are what really stand out in my memory, swirling ciphers of dissipating energy. I sat there transfixed, unable to spend myself into Chloe's mouth.

It was soon after this that our sex lives took a new twist. It was almost by accident that we discovered this new way of expressing our love.

Chloe's arm links mine as we make our way back from the Horse and Handmaiden. My thoughts are slightly clouded by alcohol consumption. I take unsure steps, as though the pavement is in a much worse state than it actually is. Chloe seems to be a tower of sobriety, supporting me when she thinks I may be about to stumble.

Gradually the cold night air takes effect and I start to regain mastery of my legs. Chloe notices this and loosens her grip on my arm. I snake my arm around her waist as we walk, and she lets her head rest affectionately against my shoulder.

This section of suburbia is like a labyrinth. We have walked back from the Horse and Handmaiden this way before, and in much worse states than this, but tonight for some reason we seem to be thoroughly lost. Each and every car and semi we pass seems to be cloned from the other. It's like being in a house of mirrors.

Chloe and I relinquish contact with each other while she lights a cigarette. 'Where the fuck are we?' I muse with a chuckle.

'Fuck should I know,' she exclaims wide-eyed, unlit cigarette hanging out the side of her mouth. 'You're the man, aren't you supposed to have some kind of inbuilt 'make-it-home-pissed radar'?'

'I think your oestrogen must have interfered with it.' I turn around in an unsteady arc to face her. She's not having any luck with her cigarette; the flint sparks repeatedly but the gas refuses to ignite.

Chloe throws the lighter and the cigarette into the road in exasperation. I wrap my arms around her waist and pull her to me. For a moment we share an intimate contact, but Chloe gently and tactfully pulls away with a kind of 'not right now' gesture. She seems distracted for a moment.

'That house,' she says, looking at one of the identical semis. 'It doesn't have a burglar alarm on it.'

I look briefly at the stupendously unspectacular house. 'I can't see one.'

'There's no car parked outside either.'

'So?'

'Lets try something different tonight.'

I don't think she means fluffy hand-cuffs and chocolate spread.

This became one of our regular forms of recreational crime. It was the fear that did it for me. Chloe's trip was more on an invasive level, a kind of female penetration. Whatever it was, she certainly reacted to it. These rank amongst the best times we spent together.

We never took anything valuable from any of the houses; like I said, this was one of our recreational activities: perhaps all crime has an element of recreation to it. We took only trinkets, souvenirs, and left only fluid secretions. From one house we removed all the light bulbs from the ground floor. In another we rearranged all the furniture in the living room and scratched 'getting the fear' into the underside of a coffee table.

From the way our relationship had been going I really should have foreseen the chain of events that would put me where I am now. You can never, however, account for the unpredictability of women.

I look at Chloe standing calm and statuesque facing the glass barrier of the counter surrounded by housewives, businessmen, screaming pram-bound infants and wonder: Would I change this in her if I could? The answer is, of course, no. Any change in Chloe would be a detraction from the love I have for her.

I stroll into the flat, allowing the door to slam behind me, to let Chloe know I'm back. She's in the shower. I can hear the sound of the water worrying the flimsy plastic shower guard. I discard my jacket onto a chair and seat myself on the sofa. I survey the room and an unfamiliar box on my coffee table grabs my attention. I reach across and pull it to the edge of the table so I can examine it more closely.

The box is the kind of plastic toolbox used by electricians. I pick it up to check its weight. It definitely contains something; too heavy to be empty. As I flick the catches open, a sense of childish joy seizes me, like a kid opening a birthday present. This leaves me the instant I set eyes on the box's contents. Two heavy looking automatic pistols accompanied by a package of what, I imagine, is ammunition.

I reach down, pick up one of the guns and lift it up to look at it more closely. Cold and heavy in my hand. A sense of empowerment emanates from it. I'm no expert but it doesn't look like a replica.

I hear Chloe enter the room behind me.

'Hiya,' she says.

I turn slowly to face her, the gun still in my hand. Chloe looks at me, then down to the gun, then back at me. Her face becomes stone cold. 'I was going to tell you…'

'Chloe, what is this?' I cut her off.

'A Glock Seventeen.' I stare at her coldly to let her know I'm not amused.

'Where did you get it?'

'Taz.'

'Is it real?'

'Of course it's sodding real.'

'Well what the fuck is it for?'

Chloe's eyes light up dangerously. 'I have a plan...'

And that's how I come to be standing in a branch of Barclays on a Friday morning with a fully loaded Glock Seventeen in my coat pocket.

Of course, I wasn't happy about this at first. I told Chloe her plan was ludicrous and that we'd never get away with it. But Chloe can be extremely persuasive, and over time I began to understand what this meant in terms of our relationship, both criminal and romantic. The bank robbery represents both a point of no return and an affirmation of our feelings for one another. Most couples get married; we're going to rob a bank. It makes more financial sense anyway.

I suppose at the moment we're getting ready to exchange vows. Although they'll probably be shouts of, 'nobody fucking move' or 'get the fuck down', and we'll be waving pistols about instead of swapping rings. Still it equates to the same thing, more or less.

I scan the anonymous faces that surround us. They're screaming for excitement, danger, change, any break from the tedium. These people must spend half their lives just waiting for something to happen, killing time til their personal apocalypse. I may be about to give it to them. I can just see all these fuckers at home glued to 'Stars In Their Eyes' or some such shit. Today Matthew I'm going to be robbing this bank.

I look to the clock on the wall: only ten seconds till decision time runs out. I look across to Chloe and she's looking back at me. There isn't a doubt in my mind. She begins to reach into her coat. Time to say 'I do'. This is when the screaming starts.

Getting Sunny Faisal's Fish

Daniel Fox

Pause. Freeze frame. Chris is at the front. Leaning on the counter, chinning at the receptionist or nurse or whatever she thinks she is. Telling her that Malc needs attention. And needs it now. I'm holding Malc up near the doorway while bruised pissheads and injured accident kids just gawp on. Malc's covered in mucky water and thick, thick blood. Gashes split his forearms and there's a nasty one deep in his belly. But he hasn't slashed anything major because the blood pours rather than spurts. He's lost loads, though.

The porters are rushing over and I'm slapping his face, trying to keep him awake. He keeps nodding away, he's whispering that he can see cherubs. That they're swooping down to kiss his head. Fucking hell. I'm slapping his cheeks asking myself how in the name of fuckery this happened.

Rewind. Spin back a few hours.

'I can't believe we're doing this. I can't believe it.'

'Will you shut up. Christ's sake.'

'Not to Sunny Faisal. I can't believe it. It's not right.'

We're sat in the Transit, down the lane from Sunny Faisal's house. Me and Chris are in the front. Malc in the rear, sat next to a shiny big fish tank. Where he belongs. He's jabbering on. 'It's fucking shit this. Not right'. He won't shut up. And he reckons he's got what it takes to be a pro'. A career criminal. Like me and Chris. My flabby arse.

'We're going to make twenty grand from this, you soft bastard, so fucking stop whinging,' I tell him through the rear-view mirror.

Chris turns round in the passenger seat as best as he can. He's got on this bulky Parka coat, so he can't turn proper.

'Look Malc. None of us likes doing it,' he says. 'Sunny's a big hero to all of us. Big star. An excellent sportsman and fantastic all round bloke. But… Twenty grand.' He tries a shrug in that hefty coat.

True. We all love Sunny. Every fucker does. Sunny Faisal. The Colombian wizard. Played for United, 1976-84. A star. Made the starting eleven every single match. Not one red card. Not even a yellow. A total legend. He was a hero to me and my mates. That ballet-like grace in the midfield. Self-deprecating manner and faltering English. And his diminished stature. Sunny Faisal. In so many ways a big man, only five foot five tall. Every inch legendary. The legend's legend. How could he fail to melt the hearts of an English kop? Even during those bleak times, mid-winter, midweek nil-nils we always loved him.

Even so…twenty grand. You have to shrug.

It's half-past ten. We've been sat here in Chris's Transit since half-nine. But it's a summer night so it's not proper dark. We thought the caper out over beers at Chris's house. When the missus was in the Yoga class. We planned it all out. Decided we should sit tight. Shouldn't make a move til gone midnight. And then only if we hadn't seen anyone lurking about in the last hour or so.

So. It's going to be a long night. We sit quiet.

'Do you remember when he came to our school for the sports day?' says Malc after a while. I shrug. 'Ah. You must remember. The same year we got to the League Cup final, it was. He handed out the certificates. After all the events. Signed them, too. Then he did autographs. He didn't have to do that. He was a big star.'

You can't help but crack a smile.

'Aye. I remember,' I say. 'He signed my away top. I asked him if it was true. About him going to Villa or going back abroad. That's what they were saying in the paper at the time.'

Sunny had come to United like a gift from above. From Benfica. We'd been drifting about at the bottom of the old first division for a few seasons. Always missing that special something. Perennial Also Rans. He was twenty-eight. At the peak of his game. He had a mane of dark brown hair and it wouldn't show flecks of grey till long after his retirement, when he would set himself up as a local celeb and amateur fish fanatic.

From 1980 onwards he was our team captain week in, week out. But that was more than twenty years ago. Christ.

'What did he say when you asked him about Villa?' asks Chris.

'He said; United, she my wife,' I try on my best South American accent. 'My lover. My diva. I wear the shirts of many more teams, many times in the past. Brief affairs. To wear another shirt. That would be adulterous. Wrong! I wear my United colours with pride. While I still have my fans to give me their love.'

'He never,' says Malc from behind.

'Nah,' I concede. 'He just said that the papers talk a load of bollocks. Any Bovril left in the Thermos, Chris?'

We're parked on Bunting's Nook, a narrow lane. High stone walls run along either side. There's a couple of trees overhanging from behind the walls, and they give off a bit of spooky vibe. We can see Sunny's house, dark, empty, looming alone a little further along the lane. In spite of the rural setting we're close to the city centre. Admittedly, there's a farm over one of the cobbled walls, but a little way back down the lane is a main road. Artery road, as the town planners and council bods would call it. It's attached to one of those Legoland housing developments. Barrett Homes or whatever they fucking are.

Bored. We eat the pack up, cheese and onion sandwiches. Lovely.

'Shall I put the wireless on?' says Chris. We watch a man, sixty-five plus, walk by with a dog on a lead. The dog's lurching and sniffing all over. We watch till they're out of sight. The Beatles sing *Eight Days A Week* on Classic Gold FM and I ask Malc to pass the evening paper forwards when he's finished with it.

Later. Man and dog walk back. I wonder what this looks like. Three men in a Transit beneath the cheesy moon on a Summer's night. But the old trooper hardly seems to notice us.

An hour shuffles past. We stare out the front windscreen. We do the crossword. *14+17 D, Local hero and former international sporting star (two words 5,6).*

We have a visitor. A sleek young coal-coloured cat with a coal nose.

It jumps up on the van. When Chris taps the windscreen it pricks its ears. It looks in and haughtily stares us down. So Chris gets out, expecting it to leg it. But the cat doesn't leg it. Chris strokes it and it arches its back. He lifts it off the front of the van and when he gets back inside it hops up onto his lap before he can close the door. Cheeky bastard. Chris looks at the collar.

'Fucking hell, it's Sunny's cat,' he says. 'Imagine having a cat with all those posh fish. Stupid get. It's a wonder he's got any fish left.'

'Maybe we should thieve the cat, as well,' says Malc from the back. We stroke the cat for a while. It sits purring on Chris's lap, its eyes slowly slipping shut. We chuck it out before it gets too comfy. We sit quiet again.

'I'll tell you one thing,' says Malc a few minutes after.

'What's that?' says Chris. Stretching back in his coat.

'I wouldn't mind a quick session. You know. With Sunny's missus.'

'Oh, not half,' I say. 'There's a real lady. You're not wrong Malc.' We talk about Mrs. Faisal's merits for a while. A proper lady. A local girl. Former model of women's underwear and nightclothes. Naturally beautiful. A classical beauty.

'You see the thing about a lot of these girls,' I say. 'They don't look bad in a certain light. But it's all down to that Max Factor shit they cake on themselves. Give me a natural looker any day over some bird with a bright yellow fuzzy-do and orange face.' Chris leans back, scratches at his belly, nods his agreement.

We all agree. Sunny's a top bloke. Top togger player. Shacked up with a top missus. Top house. Top life. Top cat. Can't fault him. Respect. Diamond geezer. All that Cockney bollocks. We sit, pondering our own thoughts.

'It's not on, this,' says Malc. 'It's not right. Is it?'

'I need to stretch myself,' says Chris, coming on all surly. I reckon he's getting pissed off with Malc's attitude. He climbs out of the Transit, wiping his nose on his sleeve. And me and Malc sit in silence.

'How's the water temperature in that fishtank?' I ask Malc.

This is mine and Chris's fourth job. Like I said, we're pros. It's Malc's second. Chris wanted to keep it between the two of us. But

Malc's a mate. And he's had the shittest time. Two years of fuck-up upon fuck-up. Things going wrong. It's left him with no missus and no job. He's in pretty bad shape (literally – he's turning into a right fat bastard, but then all three of us aren't as trim as we once were). And anyway. I reckon we need an extra pair of hands for these bigger jobs. So I twisted Chris's arm to let Malc in. It was me that did that. And now I'm beginning to regret it. Because Malc's showing no gratitude.

At a half past eleven we go for it. After Malc starts complaining again. Saying that it's not right. That we're doing something bad or something.

'Look, it's a fish Malcom. A fucking big fish. If some Colombian cunt can come to this country and spend twenty grand on a fucking fish then I am morally obliged, morally obliged, to relieve the fucker of it. Okay? It's not like he can't afford the fucker, is it? Think about it. Think about what we're doing. We're stealing a twenty thousand pound fish *off of a man who can afford to buy a fucking twenty thousand pound fish*. So don't think I'm going to feel guilty. No matter how many times I've seen the fucker turning out in my team's strip. Between the three of us we've virtually paid for the fucker's fish.' I point at the massive stone building up the road. 'Have you seen the size of that house?'

Chris just sits looking out the window, mouth muscles all taut. Malcolm just shakes is head. He looks like he's about to roar, his brittle face reflecting in the glass tank.

'Come on. Let's have it now,' I say climbing out the van. 'Get the net.'

'*Have you got it?*'

'It keeps ducking out the way… You should see the size of the thing.'

'*Have you got it?*'

'Nearly. It's fucking massive. It knows I'm after it.'

'*It's a fucking fish… Have you got it?*'

I keep seeing it swerving about in the murk. But this is a pretty huge pond. And there are other fish, too, obstructing the view. There's no mistaking which one we're after though.

Massive. Twenty-six inches. Chagoi Koi carp. One of a handful of its kind in the whole country. Bred in Japan. It's beautiful. For a fish. But it doesn't look delicate. It looks like a hardy fucker and I reckon it'll be fine in the huge tank in Chris's van.

Once it's in the Transit we've got to get it round to Chris's house. Get it into his little plastic-mould pond for a few days. Until we ship the beast. We've already managed to flog it to some fish freak in Belgium. Cash on delivery. Easy money.

But I'm getting ahead of myself. First we've got to nail the bastard.

'*Have you got it?*' Chris is stood back in the lane, over the wall and the miniature conifer trees that line the end of Sunny's garden. He's keeping watch. Ready to relay the fish back to the van while me and Malc scramble through the shrubbery and climb back over the wall. Chris's got the least risky job. If anything goes wrong he can scarper, and leave me and Malc to take the shit. Not that anything will fucking go wrong. We've planned this right. Like pros. We know Sunny and his missus and the kiddies are away on holiday. This fish is ours.

But anyway. Chris deserves the least risky job, just in case. After all, we're using his Transit van for transport and we're going to be using his pond to store the fish in.

We know Sunny's away for another fortnight. So by the time he comes back his prize specimen will be all chilled out in its new home courtesy of some Belgium fish fancier with too much money. It's important we shift the fish, quick as can do. Because as soon as Sunny discovers his pond's been plundered he's bound to get the local press involved. Just hope that whoever comes to feed the pond and the cat while Sunny's away doesn't notice one of the critters is missing. The last thing we need is some div raising the alarm, premature.

'*I said, have you got it?*'

'I don't think this net's big enough.' I shout back to Chris, turning to look down the garden. I turn back to catch Malcolm gawping up at Sunny's monster-monster size house. He definitely had a good agent, did Sunny. Must've secured him the best signing-on deals. Malcolm is stood peering at the custom-made conservatory. Like he's not a care in the world. 'Malcolm! The fish! Keep following it with the torch Malcolm, for Christ's sake. Don't lose it now.' He carries on gawping.

'Are you sure this house is empty?' he says.

'Yes. Positive. Sunny's away. And besides we've been sat watching the bastard for two hours or more.' Malc shrugs.

'Must be me mind. Playing tricks.' He points the torch into the water, uses it to mark out this beautiful, beautiful creature, scales glistening, reflecting.

And after so much anticipation I can hardly believe it, as she sails, almost cruises into the net. I watch the fish. I'm holding the net in my hands and then I'm gently raising it up from the water. And she hardly twitches. It's like it was meant to be. Almost like she is compliant. A more than willing protagonist.

'Come on,' says Malc and then we're legging it down the garden, towards the van, wriggling net in hand.

This is how it happens. The van's shafting us up the backside. Chris is at the wheel now. I'm in the passenger seat. Malc's still in the back next to the fish. It's pretty much stationary, glubbing away in a tank that's hardly big enough for its meaty proportions.

But the van. It doesn't start first time. With each turn of the ignition key I'm shitting it more. Getting more anxious. Chris is too. But then, thank Christ, he manages to coax the engine into life and it lets out a growl. So he speeds a little way down the lane, up to third gear, and we're all a bit more relaxed, bit giddy. The vibe's good. We are *the* fucking pros. Anyway. We want to be back on the main road. Back in the opposite direction. So when we come to a little driveway Chris uses it to spin the van round. He does a tidy little U-turn. We're all dead keen to get back.

But it's all over in seconds. That good feeling that we'd hoped would stay a while. When something moves in a bush. Sprints across the road. Shiny black and shiny eyes. I see Chris, or I imagine I see Chris, swerving the wheel and I see his right thigh tense as he shifts his foot down on the brake. I want to tell him to fuck it. Keep driving straight. Squash it, Chris, just don't stop. But he's clamped his foot down through instinct or shock and we all jolt forwards.

Malc goes flying. The fish tank goes flying and the two connect in the space in the rear of the van with a sickening crash.

Then the van's still. It's dark. We can hear the fish thrashing about but Malc's quiet. Chris and I, we jump out and go round the back. Swing open the doors to get a look under the light of the moon. Water gushes onto the road.

There's broken glass all over. The fish is heaving, frantic, cutting itself on the fragments, its electric blue body stripping on the slivers to pulpy ribbons before our eyes. Mouth pop-popping open, an eye trickles out the socket like a blob of jelly on a dirty knot of string, the other is staring blankly. We can't see Malc properly because he's facing forwards.

'Put it out of its misery,' Chris tells me without actually looking at me. 'I'll have a look at Malcolm. Malcolm?' There's a groan.

I feel ill. I grab at the fish by its tail. Its wriggling turns up a notch then quickly subsides. When I hoist it up half its tangled innards pour out of it. It wreaks something awful. Chris wretches. I'm relieved a little to hear Malc is coughing, too.

I drag the fish onto the side of the road. I look around for inspiration. I take a loose stone from the top of the wall by the lane, intending to bash its head in, quick. But just as I raise my arm to strike I hear something pewling, scratching. Something on the road. It's trying to crawl. The fish is still flapping, feeble at my feet.

I go and look. It's Sunny's cat. I just gawp. It's almost flat from the pelvis down. Its back legs are crushed. They're matted to the extent that you can't really tell what they used to be. Just bone and red mash and black fur. It can hardly muster the strength to cry. And I thought it had made it across the lane. So I gawp. From fish to cat, cat to fish. I'm thinking, fuck me, this is bad. Then I shake myself. Do the business with the stone, crack, then go and finish off the fish, too. Crack.

TWOC
Jo Powell

Tuesday morning, Number One Youth Court – windows blinded by tired grey nets, uninspired graffiti on wooden desks. Jason in ripped jeans and washed out Kickers sweatshirt standing next to his brief who has dog breath and can't keep his eyes off the prosecutor's hemline. Court clerk reading the charge against him – twocking a car again. Kira, his social worker, in nose-ring and Doc Marts, acting as appropriate adult in the absence of his Mum. Kira's been blahing on about a place on a course on addressing aggression in Spain. The wankers don't care if he's only going for the suntan. The Youth Justice Team – it makes him want to crack up.

Charlie, his brief, shuffles a few papers as the bench file back into court.

Jason still standing, shifting his weight from foot to foot. Bored. Waiting for the beaks' decision – needing a fag.

Beaks staring down at him from their wooden perch like those vultures in his kid brother's *Jungle Book* video. Two old grey men in faded suits sitting at the wings. The middle one – ugly old bird with thin ciggy smoke hair and puke-coloured suit - eyeballing him over the top of her specs.

'We want you to know we are taking this matter very seriously.' Old bird pulling her mouth in a thin red gash, lipstick bleeding into the powdered wrinkles around her mouth.

Then: 'Have you anything to say before we announce our decision?'

Jason rounding his shoulders and concentrating on his trainers, laces fraying, designer jobs - a tenner from Honest John. Wanting to say 'Fuck you'. Instead saying 'Sorry.'

Head still bent, trying his best not to laugh. Thinking, sorry he's been caught. At sixteen Jason knows he's one of the best twockers in the North West. He's two cautions and seven previous convictions but he's done twice as many jobs than he's been pulled for. He should know the score by now - after all he's been taking without consent since his twelfth birthday. He's just crazy about motors. Mad for it!

Usually he nicks cars for cash but often he does it just for the buzz. Like the one he is up for this morning - old Jag, classic job, leather upholstery, walnut dash…the lot. Reminded Jason of that Inspector Morse on telly.

Chairwoman saying to Jason 'We are imposing a twelve month conditional discharge.' Watching him for a reaction. Jason giving none. Wouldn't give them the heat off his shit.

Then: 'Our clerk will explain what it means.'

Jason saying cheerfully. 'No sweat - I know what it means, I've had CD's before.' Ignoring the warning look from his brief as a Mexican wave of muffled snorts ripples along the back of the courtroom.

Beaks retiring, everybody standing. Respect. What's all that about?

They all bow.

Except Jason. Bowing, what's that all about? Leaving court. Charlie Henderson following on his long legs like a pinstriped crane fly after his client. Charlie saying 'Giving lip to the chairman of the bench isn't the best move you could make.'

'Silly old bag asked for it.' Jason sniggering as he shoves a B and H between his lips. Asking, 'Got a light?'

Charlie taking a deep breath, probably remembering.

Mortgage.

Three kids.

Ex-wife.

Current girlfriend.

Fishing in his pocket before obliging with the matches he always carries round for his legal aiders. Warning, 'Don't forget Jason, you're nearly seventeen – that makes you a candidate for the adult court.' Then: 'That puts you in the running for grown-up chokey.'

Jason grinning, saying 'Yeah, but I'm still a baby yet.' Adding,

'Can't do much to me. The law's great innit?'

Charlie saying 'Not when it's sending you down for six months.'

Jason knowing Charlie thinks he's a little git. He knows he wants to kick his under age ass. But he can't. Jason is his client and ass kicking isn't in the code of conduct for dealing with young offenders. Jase knows all about the code. Jase can quote from it.

'Well you know what they say man,' Jason adds, his lip curling in his best *don't fuck with me* face. Followed by: 'If you can't do the time don't do the crime.'

Charlie, Solicitor of the Supreme Court, watching as Jason swaggers out of the building with his mates.

No education.

No jobs.

No dosh.

A cul-de-sac in this toxic city.

Charlie still studying his client. Jacki, Jason's Mum, has been around a bit. Charlie wondering whose capricious chromosomes have given Jason an above average IQ.

He has the brains to make something of himself, but not the sense. Charlie wondering if Jason realises. Deciding not.

Jason swaggering out of the courthouse, knowing he is different from the rest. He has style. Class. He prides himself on never nicking a car priced at under twenty grand in *Parker's Guide*.

They leave through the Youth Court exit. The law says it's bad for juveniles to mix with adult offenders. But then, as Jason knows, the law's an ass. An asshole. The entrance to the adult court is just a few feet away and Jason nearly walks smack into six foot three of navy blue Gucci. It's Big Danny, the biggest dealer in town up at court for a spot of Class C possession. Nothing heavy, just a bit of resin. Big D's too clever for anything else. Respect. Jason moves aside to let him pass. Outside it's brass-monkey weather. On the court steps a few groups of defendants huddle smoking their fags till the dog ends burn their fingers. Others are just chewing like cattle at the cud, waiting for their cases to be called. Jason shouldering his way through them, sculled by his boys, Sumo and Numpty George. Numpty gobbing on the pavement.

Jason frowning. Hungry. Asking: 'Got any dosh Numpty?' Remembering that he's left his own cash at home in case the bench fined him.

Numpty answering: 'Amb skint,' struggling as usual with his enlarged adenoids.

Sumo adding: 'Me too.' Then: 'Want me to go and lean on one of them for a few quid?' Gesturing with a meaty finger towards the hollow cheeked gaggle of defendants nearest to them.

Jason shaking his head, play punching Sumo on the bicep. Blonde girl in a short leather skirt watching him. Too much slap on, but not bad looking. Good legs. Jason making eye contact, checking her out. Thinking, maybe she fancies him. Maybe not. Wondering if it will make a difference.

Probably not.

All he has to do is take her – with or without consent. Take what you want – that's what his Dad says. His old man's inside now – three years, dwelling house burglary. Mum's moved Uncle Geoff in. To help with the rent. What a joke – the fat bastard hasn't worked in years.

Jason saying, 'I think we can arrange our own transport, boys.'

Sumo looking at Jason vacuously for a moment.

Penny dropping. Then: 'Oh, right Jase, you mean nick another motor?'

Numpty rolling his eyes but grinning. Joining Sumo in undisguised admiration. 'Better watch you don't get pulled mate. You heard what the beaks said.'

Jason grinning, exposing a row of tombstone teeth. Saying 'They have to catch me first.' Then: 'Anyway if they do catch me what are they doing to do to me?'

Sumo and Numpty shaking their heads, waiting in the vacuum before he answers. Lights on but nobody home.

Jason saying, 'I might get a fine, or another CD.' Eyes widening in mock fright, 'I might even get probation.' He does a parody of a trembling hand. 'See lads, I'm that scared.'

Weather turning for the worse now. The three of them slouching across the nearby car park, backs hunched against the driving rain, eyes peeled for a suitable motor.

'How about that?' Numpty George pointing to a blue hatchback, new reg, parked in a corner, away from the security cameras that haven't been trashed. 'Get in it no sweat – goes like shit off a stick as well.'

'Nah,' Jason shaking his head. 'I think we can do better than that,' nodding over to a shiny Merc. The car's paintwork is polished as a Rottweiller's arse, tinted windows, leather upholstery. Class. Just the job.

Numpty George looking worried. Saying, 'Alarmbed.'

Sumo laughing and reaching into his puffa jacket like Michelin man.

'No sweat.'

Two minutes, forty-three seconds and they're in.

Sumo silences the alarm and wires the ignition.

Two minutes forty-eight seconds and they're off. Jason driving, knuckles white against the black leather steering wheel.

Saying, 'How's this boys?'

Thinking, might as well do a good one before he goes to big school. Adult court – remands in custody. Beaks and briefs, they're all a bunch of knob-heads. Bail Act. What a laugh!

Inside the Merc, smell of new leather, dashboard lit up like the machines at the local arcade. Nice. Full on turbo-charged motor. Numpty bending his ear about the speed as he takes the narrow side road. Soft sod. High revs to Manchester Road.

Jason slamming his foot down. Swerving to miss a woman with a pram.

Silly cow.

Short cut across Sainsbury's car park, the Merc skewing between abandoned trolleys. Heading for the motorway.

Then, Sumo yelling 'I smell bacon,' as he cranes his neck to see out of the rear window. Laughing as his bulk is thrown about in the back. No seat belt.

Marked car behind, siren going, 'stop' sign up. Jason looking in the rear view mirror, grinning. Screaming 'Fuck you!'.

Anchors on. Foot down.

Handbrake turn.

Jason laughing out loud – loving it.

Better than E's.

Sumo shouting 'Next left.'

Numpty shouting but nothing coming out – his face white, eyes just staring at the windscreen.

Bottle gone.

Jason flying......

Soaring and swooping, over the bridge to the by-pass.

Opening it up. Faster, faster, faster......

Flying on to motorway slip road.

Straight onto carriageway, no signals, weaving in between artics. Jason slamming his foot to the floor. Burning the fucking rubber. Doing a ton, outside lane, radio blaring. Traffic thinning out rapido – leaving him to it.

King of the road.

Master of the Universe.

More sirens. Motorway patrol cars, flashing lights. Jason remembering his Dad's old videos – *Dukes of Hazard*. Way to go!

More cars.....

Police Land Rover now.

Sandwiched in.

Lights blinding.

STOP, STOP, STOP.......

Jason yelling, 'When I'm ready pal.'

Finally, smiling, pulling over to hard shoulder. Pulse still racing. Saying, 'Ride's over boys.'

Then getting out slowly, staying cool. Jason holding out his hands, palms together. Saying 'Treat me gently lads, I'm only a baby.'

Cuffs snapping on, head pushed down. Into the meat wagon. Radio crackling – police computer check. Somebody swearing. Then, Sergeant smirking.

'Guess who the car's registered to?'

What's the silly cunt on about?

Then he tells him.

Big Danny. The main man. Nobody messes with his wheels. How was Jason to know he'd got a new motor?

Jason is dead.

The radio crackling again. Another officer opening the boot of Big Danny's motor. Saying, 'Better get someone from CID down here.' Then: 'Looks like our Jason's working for the big boys now.'

In the boot, Big Danny's stash.

Jason is not dead. Scratch 'dead'. He is very dead.

Motorway patrol guy saying 'Out of his depth here.'

Then another voice asking, 'Do you think little Jase has done it this time?'

A third voice saying. 'Nothing's going to happen to him. He's still a youth – custody sergeant will probably bail him.'

Sumo and Numpty in the car behind, watching Jason.

Jason saying nothing for once. Thinking about the size of Big Danny's fists and the scorched earth policy he has for the tossers thick enough to cross him. Then picturing the Big D's minders. A cell would be welcome right now. But Jase is just a youth. Just a baby. If you can't do the time don't do the crime. Jason sweating, heart racing, wishing he was somewhere else. Most of all, wishing it was his birthday.

One of Those
Los Angeles Mornings
Jason Parry

It's one of those L.A. mornings. The colour and mood of waking sleep, a distended blue sky domes high above the closest stars and the sun smashes light across 6am. Smog and haze the colour of burnt orange sit heavy on the city; smother it; already promise a heat that makes Steve want to be by the pool come midday. But right now he drives a car. On his way to work.

The superheated air inside the car swells against him, so he pushes the button to wind the window right down; cool wind roars past his right ear; deafens him. The traffic is light, as it's early yet and as school is out for the summer. Steve parks the stolen Honda up at the side of the road and looks out over the buildings of Leeds that carpet this low and wide river valley. The University tower up on the far hill; multicoloured flats over to the right; a scattering of tall office blocks in the one-sided bowl of the city centre. In the field directly below him piebald ponies have grazed perfect circles into the grass – to the end of their tethered radius.

He knows he can't stay at this place; it's too public, with the early commuter stream already beginning to flow strong. He can't draw attention to himself, this morning; him standing here too long, too many people might remember the car and him. He knows where he has to go. He gets back into the car and continues his drive into town.

He parks at the pre-selected disused factory site, tucked away by the canal in an underdeveloped corner of what had been the industrial heartland of this city. He hefts his kit bag from the back seat. After taking a quick check around for problem on-lookers, he torches the car. Leaves the petrol cap on, so there might be an explosion. He once saw a TV programme about the Second World War, and his mind rolls over these heard-once ideas about scorched-earth policies. His own is marked by quick orange flames rearing upwards, biting after never catching the billowing black smoke. He turns his back and sets off to walk the last three miles, past the call centres and out-of-town offices, into the new beating heart of the city. All shopping malls and boutiques. The sun, hot breath, licks at the back of his neck.

Steve is early. He has forty-five minutes to kill.

Steve chooses a quiet landscaped square, he knows is just a few short steps from where his job will start. Conifers grow tall enough to shield him from earlybirds. He likes the sharp-edged fleshly desert plants that cut up against the conifer trunks. Studies these plants that would never meet in nature but are neighbours in the city panorama. In the shade he feels a chill. The T-shirt he chose to wear this morning is not enough in this shady spot. He leans against a low wall and takes his time to light a cigarette; killing time; savours the first puff; takes time to imprint in his mind the rasping heat and burn suffered and borne by his lungs.

Looking through his shady green curtain, Steve watches an old man who basks in a sharp-edged patch of early morning sunshine across the other side of this sheltering square. The old man enjoys the moment. A walking stick leans against his legs. He carries a paper, but makes no effort to read it here – this is something he will do, later, once he reaches home.

As Steve takes a fresh cigarette from his packet, the man decides he has had enough sun this morning. He picks up his stick and shuffles forward. The man gets closer, and Steve sees he looks old, but is probably only around thirty-five. Lesions associated with AIDS scratch across the man's face. The man returns Steve's stare and Steve can do nothing but smile.

Morning.

Good morning.

The sight of the young dying man provokes Steve's memories. His mind closes his eyes; jumps him to the last time he saw his grandfather. His father's father. Steve had been to see the old man, who was dying of cancer. They hadn't talked about much: how the old man was feeling; the horses; Steve's first proper job. Nothing profound. Nothing with a meaning that would last beyond the car park. At the end of the visit, Steve walked away. Something made him look round before turning out of sight down the next corridor. The old dying man had come to the door of his room. He looked as Steve turned. The old man raised a hand. He just raised his hand. Goodbye. At that moment, Steve knew he wouldn't see his grandfather again. That had made him overwhelmingly sad, but he didn't go back. No truths. No peace-making. Nothing.

This is a bad omen for this day of days, thinks Steve. I don't want an omen of death. See something good. Happy. Alive. He opens his eyes and sees...

Derelicts have been ejected from a nearby hostel. Two men and a woman. All unkempt. All wearing filthy clothes. Another trails behind. Already weaving drunk. Sports bottoms with poppers up the dirty flourescent yellow stripe to the knee. Non-committal anorak, flapping half-on half-off his shoulders. Already drunk, or is he all there? He clutches a can of beer to his chest and rails against the world in general. He berates passers-by, but his language has a cadence all of its own. Scottish. The words indistinct, but the rise and fall suggest an inner poetry bursting with energy. An inner story. He rises into a song. Only he knows the words and tune. He stops in front of Steve and stares.

The man stinks. Of booze. Of being unwashed. Steve pulls himself upright and turns to face up to the mad derelict. Steve blows smoke at his round ruddy cross-eyed dog-happy face. The drunk recoils in fear. He bleats and beats a hasty retreat. Stumbles down a step in the square and sprawls in the gravel. He scrambles up. Bumbles away. The knee to his jogging pants newly ripped, the only new thing about him.

Steve drops the cigarette to the ground, stamps it out and roots another from an inner pocket.

You got a light?

He didn't see the girl come up. And starts.

She begins over. What did you say to him?

Steve lights her cigarette.

The down-and-out. What did you say to him? He ran from you.

I didn't say anything. He just ran.

I work up there. I was watching you from the window.

Yeah?

Yeah. You looked deep in thought.

Yeah?

The girl looks at him; feels slighted; only wanted to talk to the nice-looking boy in the T-shirt; the boy who stood at peace with himself; who looked as if he was going somewhere simply by standing still.

You're hard work.

Yeah?

Yeah. I just came over to say hi.

She is pretty. She had come over to speak with him. Her eyes promise plenty. He can smell the light flowery perfume she misted onto her skin that morning. Some creature within him shivered and sparked when she tucked that loose soft strand of hair back behind her ear. He has always had a passion for girls with dark hair. Like Cat. She reminds him of Cat. The gaudy fake jewels Cat loved to wear; plastic beads, primary-coloured like a child's toy, tight against her tanned neck; tickled by the chopped short ends of her dark hair. The baby. The reason he left Cardiff. Chased by brother Cagney, who promised to fuck him up. The baby; the reason he's on the run. This girl in front of him now. Offering him something. Normality. A laugh. Fun. But he can't. Not today. Not now.

He fails to recognise his omen. Instead, speaks words he knows will send her away. His focus on. His focus on the job.

Well, hi.

The girl turns her head, so as not to blow smoke in his face – polite, in spite of this boy's wall-faced emotional silence. Blankness. She considers him for a moment. Then turns and walks back across the road into her office block, sorry she bothered to try to force a change on this bright summer's day of warmth that had made her feel so open to change.

Another day, Steve would have taken her home. Perhaps she would have saved him; married him; lived happily ever after. Not today, on this day of days.

Steve looks at his watch. Five minutes. His adrenaline levels are way up; his neck arteries feel solid; metal rods forcing him to stand straight and only face the front. He doesn't feel the cold of the shadow that is risen over him.

Time.

He drops his cigarette. Crushes it beneath his boot. And hefts his bag up onto his shoulder. He steps to an alleyway just across the way – next to the door the girl used to enter her building. In the alley, Steve checks both ways before taking a jacket from the bag. He puts it on. Brown with badges to the shoulders. Not a security guard; a traffic warden. He takes a cap and puts that on. Slings the bag crossways on his chest. Bandolier.

Emerges from the tunnel; walks into the next road. A dead end road. Like he was told. Begins to slowly check car windows for parking tickets. He sees a man sitting in a car with the engine running. A forest green Mondeo ST200. Steve walks over. Taps on the driver's window. The man inside turns his head and winds down the window.

Ready?

Steve pushes wax plugs deep into his ears. A passer-by would ignore this conversation between traffic warden and driver; would not see the stranger aspects: the traffic warden's cross-slung bag; the earplugs....

Ready.

Steve keeps his head down, as if they are still talking. At the top end of the street a second traffic warden raises his arm in a standard hello. Steve waves back. He pulls his bag round to his front. A security van turns into the dead-end street beside the second traffic warden; this man walks down the road behind it. The van passes Steve and the man in the Mondeo. It stops at the end of the road at the back door of a bank and a guard gets out. The guard approaches the back door and speaks into the intercom. The man in the Mondeo pulls sharply away from the kerb, speeds to the dead end of the road and blocks the van. Steve pulls a sawn-off shotgun from his bag. The second traffic warden is running now and already holds his shotgun en garde. He runs past Steve and covers the security guard who has seen the attack coming and already holds his empty hands out to either side of him.

Steve runs up to them; past them; bangs on the van door; open up he screams or your mate gets it. The second traffic warden discharges his shotgun into the van's windscreen and cranks another round into the chamber. Steve doesn't hear the report; just sees the screen crack into glass crazy paving. A slow picture of the dry cracked floor of a desert dustbowl leaps into his mind's eye. Dry. Parched. The second hand on his watch drags round. The sun throws down its life on him. Enriches him. As from above, and sliding down sideways, he sees himself standing crouched, alert, waiting to live or die. He needs water; throat suddenly dry enough to split. The exposed guard pisses himself. Steve forces his gaze from the growing flood and screams again. COME ON. Discharges his sawn-off into the city sky. Stone chips shatter from a nearby building. A car alarm blares. The second gunman knocks the legs from under the shivering guard. Lifts his shotgun. The guard looks over at Steve. Right into Steve's eyes. The guard raises his right hand. Not two in surrender; one in goodbye. Steve can't look away.

Come on, screams Steve. Do the right thing.

Spanking the Monkey
Andrew Oldham

Now girls, I don't profess to be a nice guy but Friday afternoon means one thing and one thing only to me, it's jazz day, porn intake. Bet you thought I was going to tell you that I love the licks of Theolonius Monk, that Charlie Parker rocks my boat. Bullshit. I love licks but I pay for them and the only thing that rocks my boat is a cheap motel room or the back seat of a Dodge. Here's the trick, I find, and I mean this, I find the most crowded shop in the city, normally in a train station, Waterloo, Euston, you know the places, some magazine vendor that stocks the shit. A little aside thought for you all, why can you find porn in any terminus in this country but get nothing on any high street shelf? Zip, nada, nothing, but hey, go to your local, friendly choo-choo stop and there it is, top row, opium glistening, legs parting, lips pouting, softcore shit, what the fuck are the railways trying to tell us? Are they endorsing spanking the monkey on trains? Choking the chicken on the underground? Come on, we've all seen that one. Is this why there's this spate of train drivers missing the red light?

So, get the packed shop, the more people the better, the more indignant, the sweller. Why? Well, you have to learn that it's time to cut the embarrassment factor from your week and your life. If you spend most of your day up to your neck in human sewage, going through people's garbage, clearing the embarrassments out of their lives you're not going to come up smelling of roses. And it's time you got over the fact, that when you tell people you're a private dick, you shouldn't tell them in that apologetic voice. Get over it, you're not a lawyer. Say it proud, *I smell of shit but I make more money on a good day than you make in month, a year, a fucking lifetime*. I don't get invited to many parties; do you have to ask why? So, cut the embarrassing shit from your back, hit the store, get a copy of Razzle in one hand and a flapjack in the other, get in the queue and pay. Pay for the sniggers from the women, and there always is, pay with your cash and fuck with their heads. Because what the fuck does a raspberry flapjack have to do with a Razzle mag? Is this porn and eat? Is this wank to oats? If you can surf this, you can do anything, you can crawl, eat and swim in shit, you can even ask some dumb fuck who owes you money to cough up because you have an insurance policy on them. Bribery or blackmail? Take your pick. Come on, do you know how many people hire me each year to catch their cheating partners when they're doing the hustle on them as well?

One time, I shit you not, I tailed this woman for four blocks, she was meeting her husband at some fancy restaurant in the West End, that place where that fat little twat from TV cooks in his smalls, and surprise-surprise who pulls up after her husband? Another dick hired by the wife. Some shit smells sweeter than others.

So catch the choo-choo with the rest of us, dump the porn in the toilet, come on do you think I actually read the stuff? Who needs it? That's for embarrassed parents to explain about to their kids. Why did Little Johnny come back from the john with a brand new copy of Razzle? Because. Yes, I'm the guy who loves to make you feel awkward. Ain't that a sonofabitch? No, but I know a guy who is.

If you can do that, you'd think getting paid was a breeze. Wrong. Friday afternoon, hit the train and go client calling, you know the ones, the kind you invoice and will hear dip shit from until the end of eternity, the people with ansaphones. Sure, on the Monday, you're all sweet, even apologetic for asking them. Asking them? Do you get this shit? Asking them for the money they owe you. By Wednesday you're tepid, not quite brutal but getting there, Thursday spins around and you're worried, pay day coming, rent needs paying, bills need brushing under the carpet. Come Friday and you're one brutal fucker, you're Mary Poppins on crack, you're Charlie Brown with a studded baseball bat. You're pissed.

There's this one fat guy I've been calling on for the last two years, my shrink says that it's become an obsession for me, that the tub of lard is 'necessary' to my Friday routine. I told my shrink that if the guy paid up, and that's looking less and less likely, the fat fuck would be off my 'necessary' routine and I'd be off her fucking cosy forty quid in chair, and she'd be waving goodbye to her cash.

So, this Friday, under the advice from my shrink, I'm hanging out at the zoo, casing the joint, remaining calm and breaking the so-called routine. Watching Ma and Pa Yappy cover the eyes of Junior Yappy because the monkeys are doing what monkeys do best. Whilst fat tourists with fat wallets, and melting 99s, snap off happy porn pictures, that they can turn into slides and force feed friends and family over fucking cocktail wieners, fries and beer, and scream at them that this was the highlight of their fucking holiday, so watch the monkeys fuck. This is what normal people in a normal world do and it makes me feel pretty damned good about myself because I know that psychiatry has a fucking lot to answer for.

I'm pretty centred in all this because I'm wearing sunglasses. Never leave your brain without them. They help me get over the hangover that is Ma and Pa and their constant yapping and camera flashing, and their need to expose tropical shirts to hapless single dads and traumatised kids. Whilst catching an infomercial from them about their hatred of other tourists, especially Jappy ones with grey clothes and even greyer cameras. Like I said, I feel fucking great, I feel normal as hell compared to these freaks. Ma and Pa really fucking hate those Jappy guys because they always, they always fucking get to the penguins first and that isn't right, is it? Ma is letting me in…do you get this? I've just met her and she's letting me in on her theory that all these grey Jappy tourists are little aliens and big cocksuckers, her theory, not mine. I have a whole dictionary of words that would describe Ma but I choose to dump them in favour of shoving her ice cream cone in her face, because (A) she's an asshole, and; (B) she's a bigger asshole than me. (C) I hate competition, and; (D) I've seen something short, fat, extremely sweaty, pushing through a group of Jappy grey tourists who are bitching about yappy fat Yanks who always want to see the monkeys fuck.

The sweaty fat guy is Leon, that's his name. Why isn't fat and the name Leon not a surprise to me? It's like there's two types of Claire and Clare in the world, and one of them is always going to wind up fat. That's Leon's as well, fat, sweaty, dull, shit heads that fuck up parties just before I get there, skip town with my money and fuck up my brand new Friday routine. I have no desire to see the penguins anymore. This is bad. I should pray to my shrink or at least phone her, even beer might help but it all costs money and frankly Leon owes me a bundle. I wouldn't be so pissed off if it was couple of quid, let's get that straight and on the record, so you can play it back to me later and throw a party. The fuck owes me a whole bank vault of money for such jobs as getting him the country.

You see, Leon isn't from England, but then again neither am I, you know I will never get royalty and what all the fuss was about when one of them died, what is it with you lot? I live here, I've been here fifteen years, I've seen rapes, killings, child abusers and the whole merry go round of shit you call news and not one tear, not one outcry, unless it's furry or banging an Arab. But Leon, bless him, loves this country, loves furry animals as well, even the authorities got wind of that one. He hired me to get him off the leash that time.

Leon is an animal trainer, pure and simple, judging by the zoo overall and the smug getting-laid grin on his face, he works here, probably still training wild bears to crap in living rooms, dance on balls and get poked with sticks. Which is a step up from the trick of making them live in cages with budgies and walk on their back legs for Bonio. In fact, before Leon came to this country he was famous, sure it was the circus kind of fame but people loved his bears and so did Leon. Do I have to draw you a picture? Do you want that image to last longer? So, Leon hits your shores in the early eighties, sometime after I crash land here with a party of Americans on a hoot to see the Mary Rose get dragged up, can you believe that some of them thought that the fucking thing was still intact? Do I have to tell you why I came here? Does the word retard spring to mind? There I am, in limey world, division of Disney USA, no bucks, no place to stay, and in need of a job and who comes along but Leon and his bears. Still trying to make them dance on tight ropes and shit, and running from every animal activist in the country. He tells me that he needs someone to get him off the hook, somewhere to hide the bears until the country comes to its senses and realises that getting a twenty stone bear to dance on a beach ball is entertainment and not cruelty. Cruelty is, as Leon says, *getting some dumb idiot to dance on the ball with it.* You can guess that Leon's entertainment break never came.

That was the first job I did for Leon. I got him off the hook, shipped the bears out to Afghanistan, where the furry fucks surrendered to the Red Army for fish sticks, pork pie hats, tiny tricycles and cigars, that kind of stuck in my craw, ticked me off. Leon was going to follow them a couple of days later but he ended up in Pentonville. So it was goodbye to bears crapping in the wood, Leon playing the lumberjack and my fee. Ever since then I've been cleaning up other people's mess and on occasions, Leon's.

Leon in nineteen eighty-six owed me about eight hundred pounds, today he owes me, roughly speaking, about five hundred and sixty-eight thousand pounds and thirty-six pence, sorry, forty-eight pence, and my shrink wants me to let it go. Would you? You probably think I'm a schmuck for working for Leon but what the hell do you know? Most of the goddamn money is compound interest and the courts in this country just think it's a hoot that a Slav has torn a new ass for a Yank. Ha-ha and you wonder why we're not a colony anymore? You gave us independence; we gave you our Presidents. Hurts don't it?

So there's Leon and I think this could be divine intervention, that or the coke I'm drinking isn't sugar free. This is fate. I should kiss my shrink for suggesting a visit to the zoo, but that'll only buy me more therapy and a one way ticket to a padded room at the Hilton.

Anyway, I knew the fuck was here.

Leon's given me the slip quite a few times over the years. In the last eighteen months he's changed his name, his address and the way he looks, five times. One time he changed his name to Elvis Presley, I shit you not, that was the hardest; he wasn't easy to find, do you know how many crappy Kings of rock n roll you have in this country? Play the *Wonder of You* in any bar and one of the little freaks will crawl out of the woodwork and into your booze, try it and find out. Leon even changes his looks. When he moved over to Tooting, he started wearing a bright orange wig and an even brighter beard, claimed he was a Scottish Buddha. Ever seen a Slav master a Scot accent whilst in transcendental meditation? It's like William Shatner from Star Trek reading for the role of Macbeth. Bizarre but compelling. That was the easiest time to find him. Not many guys slip through Tooting Broadway with an entourage of crazed hippie fans tracking them. Of course, each time Leon slips away, I find him, and each time I add the cost to his bill and send it to him, still polite, still cool. Sometimes he skips town when he gets the bill, other times he hangs tough and tries to blank me, tell me it's not him but you see, Leon is Leon, dumb, and wherever he goes he always ends up working for a zoo. Dumb but easy.

The Yappy and Jappy tourists are calling it a day and are striking out for bars, strippers and guided tours on the Thames. Doesn't that sound strange? How completely fucked up is a guided tour on the Thames? Hi, I'm your guide and this, the Thames, stinks like shit, moves through London like shit and probably consists nine-tenths of shit and on your left is Parliament, which is full of…and so on and so on. Which leaves little old me and sweaty old Leon alone in a big, empty zoo with the bears.

But this time round he's training monkeys, different animal, same love, some might say it's commitment, I just say that he should be committed. Which is why I'm here, I want to get my money before they do and before Leon can train any more animals not to jump fences and chew faces off yappy tourists…that is one of the other ways I tracked Leon to this zoo, the so-called accidents. I should have seen it, each time an animal went nuts, I should have known that Leon was behind it, literally. You see, the animals only attacked certain people, one time it was a night guard, another a zoo keeper, at one place some fat kid who got its nose bit off, a pregnant lady, some dumb zoologist that got too close, all random. All the newspapers tell you about are the injuries or how this or that animal got a bullet for its troubles. They go into great detail about how a bull elephant smeared the zookeeper like shit across its pen or how the pregnant lady got so scared she dropped the kid and the monkey tore it to shreds before her face. Real sick stuff like that. Real vomit in throat stuff that empties your stomach but never the real fact that linked them all. America. A-M-E-R-I-C-A-N. Y-A-N-K-S. Do I have to spell it out for you? They were all Americans, all with their screwy but cute accent, all identifiable as foreign, all targets, all trained by Leon.

Let's run over some figures again, five hundred and sixty-eight thousand pounds and forty-eight pence. Now if Leon decided to pay me, on his wage, he would take approximately, I don't carry a calculator but he would take roughly eighty-four years, twenty-eight days, four hours and twelve minutes to pay me back. That's before interest. In other words I'm never going to see the money, he's never going to pay me back and by the time I retire I would be a fictional millionaire. The money is out there, Jim, we just don't know how to get it.

Well, screw that shit, this is money, real money. I'm taking the opportunity to reacquaint myself with Leon, using the universal language of the fist. My shrink would deem this to be aggression therapy. Very bad. I've decided to take the sting out of it by calling it a clambake and inviting the fucking Waltons. Billy Bob, John Boy, Missy Sue and whatever the rest of the twisted in-breds are called are invited to a bake-up in the monkey house, so I can show them how to stuff party crackers up a Slav's ass. It should be very educational. So, it comes as no surprise to find that Leon has invited Mr Chuckles, a three hundred pound chimp, and that the Waltons have split.

I've seen it all in this, the big bad city, it's big, it's bad, and it's a city that sometimes gets the better of me. Like today. But what I want to know, and stop me if you want to duck out and get a tape recorder or book yourself a room next to me in the Hilton. What I want to know is how the hell does a monkey get access to the personal contents of Charlton Heston's gun rack?

Leon has somehow figured out that I won't quit on him, ever, period, I don't know who told him, probably my shrink phoned him and told him that I suffered from a compulsive barrier, or obsessive behaviour, all very bad, all very ill, all very screwy and bad for the wallet. Mine or hers? She probably even advised him to try and kill me, as this is a very positive way of expressing negative feelings.

So, here I am, back against the wall fumbling for an exit that isn't there, praying for that sick fuck from Candid Camera to let me in on the gag. Any chance of yelling for help is zero because the yappy-jappy tourists have fucked off on pleasure cruises and all I can think is how are the papers going to write this one up? *Robber in monkey house maul? Banana or bullet?* I also don't know whether there are any decent photos of me in existence for them to plaster all over the front page. This is worrying.

The sick thing is that Leon will back the monkey up, call me a stalker, the shrink will back them up by telling them that I'm a compulsive fuck and the monkey will be the hero for shooting me dead. That's real twisted but this is how my life will hit the streets, strike out across the tabloids.

This is it. I'm not going to wake up on the train home with porn stuffed in my pockets. This isn't a show on HBO, I'm not that lucky to get a crappy dream sequence with a chubby kid asking his mommy what big and bouncy is, whilst some guy with a G2 and chubby fetishist rottweiler in tow, smiles at me from his seat with *oh aren't kids that age cute?* look, just before I get the chance to lean over and punch him. It isn't going to happen, shame. No kid with a stereo and packed lunch is going to get my back up with his modern, hip, cutting edge crap, cats fucking in alleyways music. I'm never going to crunch his Monster Munch under my feet, smear banana peel and orange rind over his face, and scream Doors lyrics at him. I'm never going to be fined fifty for smoking on the train and I'm not going to be there when all the shit flies off those bumpy rails taking them into someone's front living room. Which is my normal Friday routine, except the bit about the train and the living room. That and the fact that I'll never get the chance to leer and stalk the cute brunette in snake skin boots who lives across the way, making out with her galaxy of boyfriends. That has slipped away, along with the fantasy that one day it might be me. None of it is ever going to happen because there's this monkey with a gun, trained by a Slav who's figured out that I'm never going to give up.

Stigby
Lee Harrison

In the dead quiet of night, or at least, under the distant factory echo that passes for quiet in the city, Stigby notices the *things* on the estate. He's seen them flitting through the after-hours shadows. Their subtlety is not flawless: they sometimes empty bin bags out onto the street; but even so, they're slinky and discreet enough that he notices them. Stigby notices them for all their slink and discretion. And like all sticking out nails, Stigby knows they have to be hammered home.

Stigby's mate Deano from round the block has been in trouble and is clearing out. He has a cheap air rifle that Stigby wants. He lets on that he wants to kill the thing because it had his little sister's rabbits out of the hutch; but Stigby doesn't care about the rabbits any more than his snot-nosed and ungrateful sister ever did. He'd have shot them himself if he'd had the rifle then. Stigby wants to hunt and he wants to kill something, anything.

Stigbys typically form small social groups, and our Stigby is no exception. His typical day involves a working co-operative between himself and an older male, named Doddy. They have formed a partnership of a kind, with a concern for their mutual prosperity in territory regulation and rights. Stigby and Doddy know that together they can make quite a stink: and in fact, they literally do. Smelling of multiple ashtrays, a pungent waft surrounds them at all times, one so strong that if you were unfortunate to get close enough you might actually *taste* the nicotine. Appearance and presentation is an important part of identity to the Stigby. The peaked cap, for example, is likewise a statement of potency. You can see this in the positioning; the cap will

114

be balanced as far back over the scalps as can be managed, perched precariously like a type of pious skullcap. Stigby and Doddy though, are far from pious.

The sporting looks are finished off with a tracksuit which is buttoned and zipped down the legs, then stylishly stuffed into grubby white sports socks. The sport theme here is misleading; you will never see Stigby and Doddy at the gym, nor indeed at any form of recreational physical activity.

Though distinctive, they are not without resource; their distinctive plumage can double to secret advantage. Stigby in particular has learned to adapt. *His* plumage doubles to ply his trade as he sports a nice new MINT SMART white smock with lots of pocket space for cigarettes, chocolate bars, packs of sports socks, whatever he takes a fancy to. The extra space in his pouch-like pockets give plenty of room for removing those pesky security tags out of sight of the security guards who know them so well.

On a typical day our two will be out doing the rounds in town, an everyday activity known as *Jobseeking* - where they go on the daily trawl for various opportunities. Their bustling walk can be very distinctive. They move swiftly, with heads hanging low from slumping shoulders, and tab-ends cupped in secretive paws. Though boisterous looking, their beady eyes are very watchful; Stigby and Doddy are as opportunistic as hyenas. Typical opportunities range from the collection of discarded tab-ends to cash machine loitering (NOW TAKE THEIR CASH), anything to keep them going until something else pops up.

At the end of the Jobseeking day, the two retreat to an embankment near the local KWIK SAVE to count up the opportune findings of the day - a tot's football shirt, CDs and nappies; not bad. Since Stigby is conscious that it's chucking out time at the school fairly soon, he makes his way off in search of under-aged ladies, leaving Doddy to inhale aerosols and finish off their crumpled bottle of White Lightning.

Sometime later, as the orange car park lamps stretch out over the road and the sound of passing cars wind down to an occasional hiss, Doddy staggers through a hole in the fence onto the KWIK SAVE car park. Drunk and slovenly, he collides with a loose trolley and gives it a sloppy, frustrated kick. This attracts the attention of the trolley attendant, a WORKING LAD, and this attention in turn causes Doddy in turn his eye on the red-coated lad who is just DOING HIS JOB. Doddy begins to wonder and indeed, it is in on the tip of his tongue to ask, what the WORKING LAD might be looking at...

Stigby is on call for bother at all times, so when Doddy calls him with bother on offer, Stigby slaps his phone away, turns and sets off at a sprint to join in, despite being halfway home. With spite on tap, he's already cursing under his breath, and already threatening his unknown opponent.

He eventually comes skidding around the corner to the yard at the back of the KWIK SAVE, near the staff entrance where Doddy struggles with two lads in red coats. Arriving on call like this, the logistics mean little to Stigby; it's another fight, it's us and them, it's game on. He doesn't resort to his older companion's tactics - Doddy will typically intimidate and distract opponents with a stream of curses, threats and fabricated accusations as he strikes - whereas Stigby just throws himself straight in, at a second WORKING LAD, who had only just come out to try and pull Doddy away. Stigby pulls his hair back, punching repeatedly into the unfamiliar upside down face as if his desperate life depends on it. Doddy takes this cue to continue striking the first working lad, who now lies curled up on the floor. And here, in both instances, a startling innovation comes into play, another doubling up of the plumage. Like Doddy, Stigby has ten NICE sovereigns, one for each grubby finger, and these are much vaunted amongst their kind not so much for their sovereignty as for their astonishing resemblance to a legalised knuckle-duster.

Within seconds it's done, only Stigby and Doddy are standing, but Stigby isn't finished. He helps himself to a cracked bottle jutting out of a skip and goes to emphasise his feeling of victory by jabbing it into the floored victim's head.

As the first WORKING LAD watches his would-be aide have his hair matted with blood and scattered with glass shards, he can only scramble backwards in horror. He slams against the corrugated wall of the warehouse, pleading with them to LEAVE IT, banging against the panels in the hope that someone comes out. He is bewildered and can only think that he was just DOING HIS JOB.

In one sudden efficient moment Stigby snaps out of his bloodlust, demands his victim's mobile phone, and turns to run, almost clear of the yard even before his discarded and bloodied bottle smashes on the floor. Doddy is left standing over the two with his glazed and empty eyes when the shift supervisor leans around the staff door. He ignores her, threatens the two WORKING LADS once again, then lurches along after Stigby, wanting to get away before the rozzers come, but not wanting to look like he does.

Doddy explains along the way that this WORKING LAD called him a DAFT CUNT and was looking at him cockily; he had been STARTING. They walk a little further in a satisfied kind of quiet. Doddy though, is DECIDING as he puffs and pants with his stitched side on the fast walk back to the estate. Doddy explains that he is older than Stigby and has a brood to consider. He's DECIDED to lie low for a little bit, starting abruptly there and then, before either of them have even got their breaths back. As Doddy walks off, Stigby DECIDES privately that Doddy is a FANNY.

Stigby can't sleep. Late in the night he finds himself staring at the ceiling and breaking out in a sweat, still tensely thinking about maiming and bottling, recalling his fight with gritted teeth, savouring the feeling of his punch-numbed knuckles. Then, in uncanny harmony with the broken glass in his imagination, he hears a tinkle outside, and lurches over to the window.

Stigby sees it there, the *thing* in his own garden, daring to be subtle and graceful, as if it was ACTING CLEVER. Seeing that the thing has upset a carrier bag full of rubbish, Stigby opens his window, grabbing for something to pelt.

He expects it to run, but to his surprise it stops and looks directly up at him. For a moment, unguarded metallic eyes catch the light and gleam back at Stigby. FUCKING BASTARD. Then he does but blink, and the Fox has vanished, leaving a loose tin rolling all night on the path, leaving Stigby evermore unsettled, sweaty and anxious.

The neighbourhood needs to be watched. So it's lucky that Stigby has a small band of lookalikes already trained in this - all made in his image with caps, trackies, filthy trainers, premature frown lines and translucent, pre-pubescent taches. They gather in the park, on a hill overlooking the savaged playground which has long since been stripped of rope and chain, painted, battered and bent till it matches the estate. Stigby and his contemporaries are very conscientious nestbuilders. Having been made so homely, the estate park is then host to all kind of meetings and social events.

Well after closing-time they do the rounds of the local streets, keeping their eyes peeled for those open windows, houses that have shown no lights for a few nights running. This patrol can be very detailed; they may even get used to the timetables of others to find out their comings and goings, all in the name of course, of neighbourhood watch. Mr. Curtis has been arguing with his wife, one of the Stigbys had heard him - he's had to put his fishing gear in the shed. It's a rickety shed. Mrs Cross is cooking a stew, you can smell it from the alley because she leaves her back door open, but Eastenders is always on in the other room and she can't miss her Eastenders. Ashley at number 56 has just got a job working nights. That stupid couple on the corner were throwing bags and cases in their car on Friday...all is taken into account. Yet more and more, Stigby himself is watching for the slinky shadows...

Some of the trainee Stigbys are very young indeed, and can easily be put in through small windows. Stigby makes a bit of an old Fagin of himself on nights like this, watching and waiting from the outside for a safe entry, once the doors have been opened from inside, coming to lend a bit of muscle where appropriate. Putty is scraped, windows are cracked and forced, smudged fingerprints left on sills and kitchen counters. All for a good cause - the next morning's mobile carrier bag jumble sale - a nice new Lego set, some nice nappies, a nice new stereo, still in the box. Bargains galore.

But it's not all graft. When not working so hard seeking opportunities, Stigby and his young tutees/trainees enjoy discount bottles of white cider from the local shop. This is the same corner shop whose windows they've put through time and time again until it needs to be boarded over. The same corner shop that sells them alcohol and loose cigarettes and turns the occasional blind eye precisely because of the cost of windows.

Once sorted for liquor, the Stigbys can roam the street at leisure, sometimes preferring a venue. Finding pubs and clubs to be somewhat passé, and a little uncouth, they opt for the more sophisticated haunts, all the admit-only places; on the Park, outside the corner shop; behind the supermarket car park; or perhaps the railway embankment.

Stigby and usually Doddy hang around growing steadily more intoxicated, as they drink and talk of their exploits, of FUCKS and CUNTS. At some point the female element will arrive, usually in intrepid pairs who wander up within viewing distance, pretending privacy like foul-mouthed coquettes, just as full of FUCKS and CUNTS as Stigby or Doddy. In appearance there is not much to distinguish them from the male - Millennium fashion being so unisex - they also are sporting the tracksuit. A ladylike hue can be impressed into the shell of their suit, a pastel blue or lilac, or pink maybe, in a subtle contrast to the male navy, white, and ecru. Tonight at the embankment are Shelli and Leanne. Leanne is the leader of the two. She is loaded down with heavy, Mr. T style jewellery, and thickly plastered make-up (which is sometimes known to run with tears due to the painfully tight ritual back comb of her hairline). She has her usual sour-faced expression, hard and unimpressed, one she learned from older sister Chantelle.

Stigby is proud of his post-pubescence, knowing that it, along with drunken white lightning maturity and ashtray fumes (scent?) will attract only the choicest young girls from the estate. Masterfully, he demonstrates his ability to curse, do press-ups and fight; and his beloved thatch of pubic hairs are never far from display. The younger Stigbys can't wait for theirs. Soon the two, Stigby and Leanne, edge their way together with an exchange of insults, until the sun has sunk low and the smaller Stigbys have to go away. So they make themselves scarce, sniggering to one another, sensing that *show me yours show you mine* is about to occur. Mating is generally brief, usually restricted to a damp ten minutes up the slope of the embankment. Insults are sometimes exchanged before the pair part.

It's not long before Leanne has become sweethearts with him, and she can be seen rushing eagerly at a quarter past three to meet her Stigby at the school gates so that they might indulge in a bit of *standing about smoking fags dispassionately*. Then, before they move off to the Park, the Embankment, or wherever, Leanne would fall into step a few paces behind her moody and humourless Stigby. He might take her to the amusement arcade, where he'll stand outside with her. Each person to pass is Stigby's MATE; he gives everyone the benefit of the doubt at first; but those who haven't got ten pee spare to LEND instantly become DAFT CUNTS. Soon he'll go inside, leaving Leanne because she's too young to go on the bandits. Sometimes Shelli will come and stand with her on this evening out to share fags and White Lightning, but as soon as Stigby comes out it's off to mate in the graveyard.

This goes on until the stork smiles on them, and little Miss Stigby is blessed with the pitter-patter of tiny white trainers. It is she who is blessed for sure, because the whole thing is NOWT TO DO with Stigby; he NEVER TOUCHED HER. The Stigby parent is known to be somewhat stand-offish with regard to its offspring. In any case, Stigby has something else more pressing in mind; with the recent carrier bag sales having been given a further boost by the phone he's snatched at the KWIK SAVE, Stigby's gun fund has reached target.

The chosen night soon arrives and Stigby places himself, huddled and rooted in his smock on the lichen-coated roof of the garage, just in sight of the bulging bin bags propped up outside his broken garden gate. It's a cool evening, and he entertains himself with a smoke. The hunter is thus marked with a dot of orange floating about his face. He keeps his firearm steady.

The first few hours of this vigil are spoiled by one of Stigby's little sisters who should be in bed unconscious but keeps running about the house, dangling out of the windows to practice her ARSEHOLES and BASTARDS. In the end, Stigby has to jump off the garage to run in and slap her, and by half twelve, maybe one, the crying stops, and the night draws on in full.

Stigby comes to and from the house during the night, and then, after a pot noodle, several pieces of toast and more smokes, the grey of the early hours arrives. It will be here soon. He'll stay up right through and go sign on afterwards.

'What have you been doing this week?' the lady behind the desk at the head of queue A will ask. He sees himself throwing the dead fox across the desk. Something unfamiliar like a smirk nearly forms on his face at this, but is choked as always by Stigby's cynical lack of humour.

The almost-smirk is barely gone from his dry lips when he hears the faint rattle of a tin on the street, just two doors along. He sprawls out, lying flat into the corrugated roof, and levels his gun. A few more rustlings sound out, and then a grey shape drifts silently out into the street looking scarcely real beneath the orange lamppost. The sleek and feral figure is alertness itself, constantly testing the atmosphere.

Stigby has never concentrated so much in his life. The fox pulls back out of view, the hunter holds his breath. A soundless flickering between the gaps in his fence are all that give it away. Stigby swallows, and his eyes narrow in promise of cruelty. A moment later, the nervous creature steps away from the line of the fence to test the air, as if it's caught some of Stigby there. Its raised nose bobs ever higher, until it must be looking right at him. Stigby's looking directly into its shiny black eyes when his trigger finger tightens. The sharp crack is accompanied, first by Stigby's gloating obscenity, and then by a quiet, painfully confused sounding yelp. The creature spins in shock and agony, then tears away along the line of the fence. With a look of vicious triumph on his face, Stigby drops heavily from the garage roof, falling into a roll across the tarmac, crunching on the ever present sprinkling of broken glass. He sees a shape curl around into an alley, rather more slowly now, as if the shock is already wearing off. He scours the scene as he runs, his smock rustling in the cold air, reloading quickly.

As Stigby bursts around the corner, expecting more chase, he is shocked out of his skin when met by savagely bared teeth and a grinding growl. The fox is in a rabid spin just around the corner, and its wildness frightens Stigby, causing him to stagger back, dropping his gun as he falls over an overstuffed bin-liner. His falling hands slam down into shards of broken glass that have been carelessly put in a spilling black bag. As he hits the floor, Stigby happens to notice a line of smaller shadows slinking away at the end of the alley.

His Fox stands determinedly holding their retreat, bleeding from the ear and still baring teeth. Stigby rolls to get up without driving the glass further in, but the Fox moves forward looking to bite him again. As the Fox nips at his tracky, Stigby scrambles away through the rubbish in a careless panic that grinds the glass into him.

By the time he's scrambled to his feet, the mad Fox is between him and the gun. For a moment all the hunter can do is stand wincing and clutching his bloody hand; the Fox calms down after a moment of Stigby's wide-eyed, heavy breathing, and the intelligent shine returns to its eyes, as if it thinks Stigby might have learnt his lesson. A meek cry comes from the alley, and the Fox turns with almost thoughtless care to follow the noise, leaving Stigby scared and bleeding in the street.

He wraps his glass-jabbed hand in the pouch of his NICE smock, quickly colouring it red. It is only when he bends over to retrieve his gun, swearing contemptuously all along, that he feels a tweak in his tracksuit bottoms, and his good hand reaches back to find a used syringe sticking into the back of his thigh. Cursing yet more, he flicks it out warily, takes up his gun, summoning all his seasoned rage and spite, and tears off after the Fox, down the old gap between two garages. After he's killed it, he'll string the pups up on the washing line.

Stigby knows how to go around to a wall that winds around between the two buildings. Once he's climbed onto it, he'll be able to take shots at the cornered Fox before kicking it to death. He's soon up on top looking to find his vantage point over the gap between his wall and Curtis's. The wall of Mr. Curtis is a jagged great glass lined battlement of a thing, forged in vengeance itself after years of intolerable trespassing and break-ins. Stigby edges along, winding his torn hand in the smock and scouring the dark gap with wet eye and warm gun.

As Stigby moves, he's not looking, but pointing his gun down into the dark gap, looking for the slightest gleam or whimper to betray the presence of the Fox or one of its cubs.

Stigby really ought to pay more attention to his footing; but the years of using the shortcut have given it an over-familiarity he can't shake off. So he overestimates his balance, and when the Fox calls out unexpectedly from the opposite corner of the gap, Stigby whirls on it faster than his feet can manage, and loses balance. He drops the gun, and with his hand already entangled, he falls chin first onto the glass lined wall of Mr. Curtis. After the uppercut effect of the wall hitting his jaw, several shards of glass, in a variety of colours rend Stigby's throat. His skin tears as he continues to fall down into the dirty gap. He flails in a moment's panic, making a rough gargling sound and spraying blood openly across his beloved smock. The panic makes this worse so he tries a choked stillness. The nearby Fox is still on guard in the cluttered gap where Stigby lands, still growling to warn him off. There's no need. Stigby dare not move.

Without Stigby the father-to-be, Leanne will have no partner to claim joint benefits with, and the twins - poor little Diadora and Ellesse - will be without a father. If they survive, the Fox-pups will be young adults by the time the girls are born, and if *they* survive, then Foxes and little Stigbys alike will all have to find their way in the estate somehow. In this moment, neither Stigby nor the Fox are thinking about that; the hunter soon begins to sag; the Fox settles and watches him start to die with impassive black eyes.

The Player
Daithidh MacEochaidh

The sky was charcoal quiet, blistered with dull city-red from street-lamps, taillights or cheap neons selling lonely time. Wind tugged clouts and rags of rubbish, made them dance and jig on the wind as if possessed with some sudden vitality. A freight train clanked overhead, working its way into the distance. He hunched a little more inside, pushed firmly on his crow-black Fedora. Tightening his ripped raincoat, he shuffled down-street. Even here there were blanched, white frogs hopping from the grates, some dying in front of him, others though getting there fast: all dying. They stank, even the ones still twitching, they stank and the feral alley cats didn't bother to torment them.

He glanced behind, Klora was still following, taking it all in, wide sweeping hand-held shots and steady close-ups on the sweating frogs. There was a scurry, a scamper, from a side alley. Klora turned round to take that in too. She got it all and she wasn't bothered. The rats were getting bolder. Why not? They were winning. They'd made it across the river; any day would come the swarm. A helicopter up above sprayed in wide arcs intersecting, slowly covering the grid, but it was too late. The sector was lost.

He'd come to the right place.

His grey eyes scanned the toothed skyline of offices, apartments and old, decrepit apartment stores that thrived on bargain basements and imported fake merchandising. It was starting to look familiar, but he couldn't be sure as yet. Mistakes had been made, they'd been glossed over, passed over and under-reported, but it was a fact, his job carried errors; it was something that almost made it worth the risk.

Klora panned it all. He signed for her to come near, to come close. He couldn't afford to lose her now. At first it had annoyed him that his camera-operator was mute. Then it amused him. He still laughed over the fact that Klora had her tongue ripped out during a game of forfeits. She'd won. She never complained. She was that good. She was in close-up again, some feral dog with blistered eyes and red-worm chewing through its sides. He knew already how good it would look after the shots were polished up on the cutting-room floor.

He checked the address again, walked further down the street to where these concrete steps folded down to the sidewalk. The building was still good for another fifteen years, maybe more, but he couldn't be sure. It wasn't his job, but he always liked to speculate, just before a move was made, something about cheating years made him want to guess, even though he could never be quite sure. He felt the evening drizzle squeeze down his collar. He couldn't stand out there all night. Time was ticking away for someone else. Once more, he checked the address. He was certain now, certain for the time being. He whistled for Klora.

The lobby was quietly lit by filtered streetlights and this dim amber lighting that failed to hide the squalor of rabid graffiti, growing urban ivy-like up the walls. The desk clerk, a solid bald man, behind the counter didn't look up from his late evening paper and a certain kind of glossy extra trapped between the sheets of newsprint - somehow they never do. It would have been all the same even if that silent, squat man had looked, had ventured his opinion, maybe even tried to call somebody. It couldn't alter a result: the result was fixed. Klora wanted a shot, wanted him in close-up as he fumbled the pages of his porn mag. Klora was signing excitedly. He looked. It was all pretty average: amputee porn and animals. Klora filmed but it wasn't worth wasting film to him. The low-life stuff had all been done before. Still, Klora was a professional and the result was in.

The result was fixed but you couldn't squeeze out all the errors. He tilted back his Fedora to see which way the lift was shifting: up or down. Sometimes just for the exercise he'd take the stairs. Sometimes just for the tension he'd take the long route. Today, the lift would suffice as it whined to a halt and the doors gutted open.

The lift was a sealed tin that stank of piss, and the mechanism groaned as if already tired, as if it had done, seen or heard enough, fighting gravity up and then down, day in and night out. There were these felt-tip scrawls by the buttons, 'Shulia takes it in the head'; there were racist slogans in cheap hot red, sprayed on all the walls and the ceiling too. The small box of welded steel told him nothing that he didn't already know, save someone had had the wit to give out the local Samaritans number in fat, happy Day-Glo italics. It was the humorous touch that he appreciated most - you had to make a game of it or it was no fun at the end.

Klora filmed.

The lift stopped to a grating nicety. He stepped off, working at his composure, giving the right corporate image and quietening those small irritating doubts that would at times plague him.

The corridor seemed thin and straight and cold as a stiletto. This was a lie. It wasn't quite that straight and plumb, truth was it snaked a little, but no one noticed this at first. Klora panned, shewed all the angles and had it down on tape 'fore he made his next move.

A gang of anaemic skins sniffing glue massed around a dimly-lit fire escape. One youth, oblivious, was pissing in the door-crack. There were distant hints of sniggers, stray one-liners and sharp intakes of something illicit. Shit-house rats the lot of them, they looked and glared in his direction, but that's all. They weren't nobody's heroes, not even their own. They just whispered, shuffled and took deeper, sharper intakes of breath.

Klora went in close. The urinating skin turned round and displayed his small tattooed prick.

Some doors were boarded up, others kicked in, and then there were the odd one or two doors where people were known to be still living behind, keeping the door locked, the letterbox sealed and a baseball bat handy. The bat made him smile. He hadn't come across one yet that had stopped cynical determination. And nothing stops a result.

Harling his lamed leg he hirpled past door-numbers, counting, making sure he was on the right floor. There was his door, bust plastic lettering like splintered bones that spelt out, just enough, the winning number. He could be wrong. He rang the bell, briefly waited, then rang again, impatient as always at the end. He whistled, then shouted for Klora.

'Mr Sam Hubbert?'

'Who?'

'Mr Sam Hubbert is down in our books as a player. May I come in?'

He was of medium height, sported a blue-black beard and had several chins that gave him this sad dog look, especially when he shook his head.

'He don't live here no more.'

'Can I come in?' he said and passed on through as normal.

'Mr Hubbert has moved on, he don't live here no more - I tell you.' The fat man with a beard waddled after them, panting slightly, his jowls shaking, doing his best to keep up. A lie, of course, the television was going and the game was up and running. There only remained the result.

Klora slammed the door shut. The skins fell silent, waited, tense and sick at heart, but too concerned not to show it. They hadn't liked the guy, didn't really know him, but they knew he didn't deserve this. The long, thin corridor ingested this awkward, strained silence; for a while, nothing further was heard.

The television was going. The game was on and the smug host in this dazzling, purple-starred jacket minced and camped it up, sometimes stopping to give a knowing wink or an exasperated roll of the eyes. The game was on, and flopped in an armchair the man who claimed not to be Mr Hubbert sweated, his winning numbers already held tightly in his hands.

He signed to Klora to follow as he took in the room. There was nothing unusual in any of it save this six-foot tank of tropical water holding diverse varieties of fish, flitting ignorantly and perhaps content amongst the twisted ribbon weed. This was vaguely attractive and he stopped to examine this item most carefully. Pristine bubbles burst at the surface, pieces of brightly-coloured coral glowed iridescently from hidden lit strips and not so much as a piece of gravel seemed out of place.

He tried to think back to his training, back to the old days when he had just been a SOCO: a scene of crime officer. He wondered if he saw this room differently from those eyes. He wondered too what Klora saw as she took it all in, thought about angles and the best way to hang a frame on this.

He looked round.

The room was a pit: balls of rubbish and take-away pizza boxes littered the floor. There were hairs from a longhaired Persian cat striping the dark stained sofa. This cat seemed to have the run of the place, but it was safely ignored now, as it licked its arse, crouched over in a far corner oblivious to the game. By his whiskey glass the contestant was holding a ticket and praying earnestly. Beads of sweat gathered in his puckered brow, he could be hyperventilating but that wouldn't matter.

Any second the TV host was going to make the draw. The man's blue eyes flitted, stole a glance at him. 'What you want?'

'You know. You've got the ticket. It's there just by your glass, go on take a drink, a long dig and enjoy it.'

'It ain't drawn yet.'

He took out his 9mm Beretta laid it on his lap, folded it within his fingers as delicately as a napkin and again he watched the screen flicker.

'I don't want to die…give me a reason, one damn reason why?'

The game was still running, but it was a foregone conclusion. This fact was sinking in fast and the man who wouldn't be Mr Hubbert was sweating hard. He could see those huge fat pearls of perspiration through Klora's lens and he shivered.

'You need a reason? What makes you so precious? There're plenty getting dead with no good excuse for the result. You want a reason, give me a pen.'

The sarcasm backfired, Hubbert was taking him on and there was nothing funny in this: it made a joke out of the joker. Hubbert was up, moving towards this fake walnut-veneer dresser. He wasn't taking any chances. 'Sit back down, keep your hands on your ticket or your glass.'

'Looking for a pen.'

'I do the looking.'

Hubbert was sat down roughly. He noticed how Hubbert's hands trembled like a drunk's, like an Alzheimer sufferer – and he was suffering now. Hubbert dug deep from the glass, topped right up and hit again. In a drawer in the dresser, there was nothing more offensive than an old pair of nutcrackers, a pile of betting slips and the cheap plastic pens that they give out at such places. It would do. He tore off a slip, picked up a pen and hurriedly he scribbled down six numbers, holding it up to the camera then placing the slip by Hubbert's glass.

The punter wouldn't look. He knew what was on that paper already. He just drank and sobbed a little, almost mewing like a kitten. It was time for the draw: a tense, media moment that had the Hubbert man mouthing silent prayers, despite the facts, he still had hope or perhaps no hope at all.

As for himself, he had no such emotion; hope wasn't important, certainty mattered more to him. Klora filmed and he just wondered how they'd handle the sound back at the labs. Fixing a sound on this was the most creative part, framing correct and expected emotions to every shot, every sweep of the camera, making sure things were felt right. It was a science.

Music from the TV blared and there was no longer any time left for speculation.

It was getting round to countdown time, the captive studio audience knew it; their rehearsed mad-clap clapping, screeching cheers and whistles whooping between wolf and bird-calls announced it audibly enough for any to hear. The dyed blond presenter in his purple-starred jacket almost danced in his pants, unable to contain his professionalism. He was an entertainer, he was earning his money: sycophantic as a dockside whore, happy as a laboratory puppy. He was loved by all. His ratings proved it.

There was a celebrity to push the button. She looked glamorous. She looked like something the cat dragged through the flap in spring. It took real money to look that bad, but she could push a button and smile. It didn't look a hard thing to do, putting a finger on that button. It took more strength than it looked. He knew that and stole a glance at Hubbert, rocking back and forth in his seat, deranged as a dancing bear.

Any second now. Some things only take a second, or, less. A whirr of numbers, random or not so random finding of a certain chosen ordering, and the audience loved it. You only had to look at the ratings.

The second was up. There were cheers. There was a synthetic re-mastered fanfare and firework ending. It was all over for another week. Klora's camera never left Hubbert once.

'How do you want it?'

Hubbert was still staring fixedly at a screen, swaying slightly, bewitched, enchanted and damned.

He stole quietly behind him, squeezed a bullet into the back of Hubbert's head. There was a dull thwack, soft thud as this body edged down the seat, like a supplicant, like a slave or a devotee, to gravity.

He left the television going. The results would be broadcast later; everything fixed.

***

Outside it had been raining, raining hard, some of the ghost frogs, these blanched, fallen angels with limbs spread in rigour mortis, had been washed to the gutter. In the blend of night and streetlights, they almost looked beautiful; their swollen stomachs glistening like mother of pearl. Briefly fascinated like a child, he bent down, hunkered down to the sidewalk and watched. He flipped the dead frog over with his ancient, beloved Beretta, still vaguely warm in his hand. He tossed the amphibian back into an open grate. He'd made no mistake and the camera rolled.

This Happy Breed Of Men

Bernard Thomas Hare

It was a quarter to eight on a cold, crisp February morning. I sat outside the main gate of the Wetherby Young Offenders' Institution in a red Vauxhall Corsa GSi. I felt a vague sense of unease and oppression. Probably something to do with the thirty-foot-high wire-mesh fence topped with swirling razor wire that ran off into the distance.

A red sun low in the sky tried to poke its nose through the dull, grey clouds. A light coating of frost covered the car park. Handel's Water Music droned out from the radio. I thought it might rain.

Frankly, I'm not a big fan of classical music, but the radio had defeated me. The car was a ringer and I wasn't yet familiar with all the controls. There were two rows of buttons on the radio. The top row were okay. I had no problems with them. They were clearly labelled, 1, 2, 3, 4 and 5, respectively. Concise, succinct and to the point. No one could ask for more. The bottom row were labelled, UML, EPS, AB, BB and D. These had me foxed. I'd been pressing them at random in a futile attempt to discover their function by means of trial and error. Nothing doing at all. None of them seemed to do anything. Dismayed, I'd surrendered myself to the Water Music. What else could I do?

I was waiting for our Len, my stepson. I accidentally married his mum a few years back and he'd been like a son to me ever since. To tell you the truth, his mum wasn't quite with us half the time. She had, what you might call, a few little peccadilloes. She couldn't control the drink and drugs like I could. Don't get me wrong, she was a fine looking woman. That's probably what attracted me to her in the first place. And she was fun to be with. A laugh a minute, all day long. I can't deny that. Unfortunately, on the negative side, she was as mad as a dustbin and she didn't give two hoots about anything. All she cared about was getting smashed out of her face from the minute she got up until the minute she went back to bed again. Brandy and charlie were her favourite tipples, but she'd settle for cider and weed if there wasn't much money about. Or brown, or E's, or phet, or anything that was going, really. You wouldn't call her fussy.

At first, I tried to keep her in the manner to which she was accustomed. I did a bit of this and a bit of that to try and make ends meet. You know how it is. We were doing alright, as it goes, until some bastard grassed me. I got collared half way through changing the VIN plates on a long wheelbase Transit. There you go. Such is life. I served twenty-two months of a three-year sentence.

Len was twelve when I went in, fourteen when I got out, and our lass was worse than ever. She'd gone right smack downhill. Literally. Needle-marks on her arms and the lot. After that, it was a case of making the most of a bad job. I didn't want to leave her, because of Len. He wrote to me every week when I was inside and I know he thought the world of me. I thought the world of him too.

I was almost content there for a moment, listening to Handel and mulling over my happy family circumstances. I was disturbed from my reverie by the sound of a big Group 4 meat wagon pulling up to the main gate of the prison. I was surprised the driver didn't beep his horn. Any normal person would have beeped their horn without even thinking about it. Not this bloke. He revved his engine instead. That's how dumb they are in the prison service. Vroom, vroom, vroom, as if that were the magic password to get into the place. A screw came out and swung the gate open. It squealed like an ancient oak door in some deep, dark hole of a dungeon. The screw had a red face and malicious eyes.

I noticed that the system for letting vehicles in and out of the prison worked like the lock gates on a canal. First, the outer gates were opened and the wagon drove into a large compound. Then, the outer gates were firmly closed before the inner ones were opened. At no point were both gates open at precisely the same moment. I surmised that this was a precautionary measure against prospective escape attempts.

Five minutes later, a Farm Fresh Frozen Foods van pulled up to the gate. This time, much to my satisfaction, the driver beeped his horn. He must have been one of the unruly, undisciplined rabble, like me. I beeped my own horn a couple of times in support. He was, after all, one of us. I can tell. We're like the Freemasons. We have our own secret signs and hidden means of communication.

This time, when the fat, ugly freak opened the gate, I wound the electric window down and called over to him. 'Hey up, Boss! What time do you let people out?'

'Eight-ish,' he called back. 'Who you waiting for?'

'Our Len,' I called.

'Len? Len who?' he called, as the van drove past him into the compound.

Just to wind him up, I called back, 'Len DG4975. Why? What's it to you?'

He gave me a right dirty look and - with a resounding clang - slammed the gate shut in my face without further ado.

'Silly bastard,' I mumbled under my breath.

I couldn't wait to see Len. He was sixteen by this time and had a kid of his own. His bird had therefore taken most of the Visiting Orders. Fair enough. He wanted to see his kid. We may be criminal types, but we do take our parental responsibilities seriously, don't you know? I wrote to him regularly and sent him a P.O. every week. Prison isn't all bad, if you've got plenty of burn. I can guess why he wanted his bird visiting every time. I think she was taking him a bit more than burn in. I dropped her off one time and she was fiddling with her minge a lot. You know the score. None of my business, so I keep my nose out.

He got worse after I'd been inside, did Len. He was running wild by the time I got out. He'd got in with all the twockers and was out nicking cars most nights of the week. I used to see him doing displays in the street on my way to the pub. Him and his mates doing wheel-spins, burn-outs, doughnuts, handbrake-turns, people coming out of their houses to watch them and egg them on, a cheap, entertaining and enjoyable alternative to staring at the one-eyed lodger all night like a poor brain-dead cabbage. I know you're all blaming me, but I couldn't say much to him. He was too big for me to control anymore. Besides, when he'd finished with them, I was buying some of the cars off of him and stripping them down for parts. What else could I do? I'm a mechanic for God's sake. It's the only way I know how to make a living. You try getting a straight job when you've just come out of nick.

I couldn't care less in any case. What do I care? I'd rather be a criminal than a mindless zombie ant, slaving away in some stinking factory sweatshop for peanuts. Fuck that! What am I? A muppet, or something? They think we're all dumb, just because we're in between jobs at the moment. They think we can be controlled by economics, now that religion is dead. My analysis of the situation is that we, the white urban underclass, are treated like shit. From the minute we're born to the minute we die, we lead lives of pure, unadulterated shit. Kids are killing each other in the streets. Everywhere you look, society is rotten and corrupt. Nobody cares about us, so why should we care about anyone else? That's not how we want it. That's just how it is. Anyone who doesn't see it is a fool.

I must have passed some of my spiritual and philosophical beliefs onto Len. He didn't read or write too good, so he wanted to be an orator. He wanted to change the world by means of reasoned and rational argument and debate. I told him he was wasting his time, but he wouldn't listen to me. His mum reckoned he'd have made a good actor, or a stand-up comedian. He always had something to say and a uniquely curious way of putting it over.

About ten past eight, he finally emerged from a small side gate carrying a model plywood yacht. Jumping out of the car, I ran towards him, arms akimbo. I expected him to sling the dumb plywood yacht into the air, run towards me and try to punch me in the stomach like he used to do in the old days. When he was little, I always used to let him punch me in the stomach. It was one of our things. He couldn't hurt me in those days, so it was no big deal. As he got bigger and it started to hurt, I asked him to stop doing it.

Nevertheless, he still gave me the odd one for old time's sake.

But no, he just stood there looking listless and confused. I tried to give him a great, big hug, but he didn't respond at all. He was about as much use as a lemon. I punched him gently on the shoulder, 'Hey! That's it. You've done your time. You're out. As free as a bird. It's all over.'

Still he stood there, looking down at the ground, hopeless and forlorn, almost dejected. I stood before him and looked into his eyes. They were dull, lifeless. 'My God,' I said. 'What have they done to you?'

'I've been bad,' he droned. 'I must be good in future.' I couldn't believe my ears. He was talking like a robot, like one of the mindless zombie ants.

They must have done some *Clockwork Orange* shit on him. That wasn't Len. Len was bubbly and jaunty. He didn't knuckle under and be good. That wasn't his style at all. He saw himself as a big hero, a knight in shining armour fighting the forces of darkness and oppression. And how he loved to recount his adventures. He was always the hero and the police were always the villains. He could make you believe that he was Robin Hood. I remember once, he stumbled into the house, his coat-sleeve torn to ribbons, his arm dripping blood all over the carpet. His mum started panicking, but Len brushed her aside. He refused to have his injuries tended until he'd told his tale. He planted himself in the middle of the room and took up the *orating* stance of the bold knight-errant.

'We led them a merry dance,' he began. 'Up hill and down vale.' I can almost remember his speech, word for word. 'Me and Johnny McMahon twocked an Astra GTE. We were just doing a show on the Drive, when the T5 came flying round the corner. We took the chase. They had the power, but our mount was nimbler and lighter. We headed for the park and led them across the playground. A snazzy little hundred and eighty-degree handbrake-turn and we were heading back towards them. They veered off, crashing through a hedge and desecrating the bowling green. 'Dispatched!' cried Johnny.

'As we bounced off the park onto Osmondthorpe Lane, a Rover 200 was upon us. I swerved to avoid them and headed for York Road at speed. The bog-standard Rover couldn't live with us. I had to slow off to let them keep up. Another patrol car was waiting for us at the intersection, but I whizzed the wrong way round the roundabout and headed for the Ring Road. We shot off towards Barwick-in-Elmet, hitting the ton on the little country roads. You can't beat a nice drive in the country.

'Soon, the helicopter was above us and we knew that whatever happened now, we were the better men. I spurred my mount to greater effort, a hundred, a hundred and ten, a hundred and twenty. A record! But no matter how fast we went, there was no escaping the copper-chopper. I knew that our only hope of freedom lay in the Zoo.'

He meant Halton Moor, a well-known centre of misery and deprivation, also known as a council estate. The American writer Michael Harrington, once said, 'In almost any slum there is a vast conspiracy against the forces of law and order.' Halton Moor was a perfect example.

'There was a dead-end street with bollards at its head,' he continued. 'We'd already demolished one of the bollards so you could get into the woods. It would be tight, but I felt we could squeeze through. The law seemed to guess our intentions. A jam-sandwich tried to block us as we entered the culdy. Unceremoniously, I rammed them out of the way and sped up the street. Johnny was crapping himself. 'It won't go through! It won't go through!' But I had my plan and I went for it. Okay, I took three or four inches from either side of our mount, but we made it. The pig cars screeched to a halt behind us.

'Into Temple Newsam woods, I raced along the dusty track like a maddened jockey, the copter still above us. Here, our trusty chestnut failed us. More accustomed to the flat than the hurdles, our steed hit a carelessly discarded tree-trunk and we careered into a ditch. Undaunted, we ran into the woods to avoid the hawk-like endeavours of the eye-in-the-sky. Ah, but we hadn't bargained for the fact that the evil tyrants aren't as dumb as they look. They learn, they respond, they improve, they counter our every manoeuvre. They've got a new trick, effective if dishonourable. They've taken to carrying police dogs about with them in the passenger-seat. When you bail out and run for it, they loose these hounds of hell upon you

'We thought we were in the clear, but I was soon dismayed as a vicious set of flashing gnashers hurtled towards me and enthralled themselves with my arm. We debated the issue. No quarter was asked nor given. The matter wasn't resolved until Johnny hit the brute over the head with a scaffy-bar he found lying about in the woods.

With the beast now unconscious or dead, we hid down the old mineshaft till they got fed up of looking for us.

'And here I am,' he concluded. 'Gloriously victorious!'

He wasn't, of course. The scuffers had videoed his every move and they were round to get him within the hour. But that was the real Len, bold and defiant. Now he just stood there like a drugged up automaton. I brushed the fringe away from his forehead and looked into his eyes. I saw not the slightest flicker of rebellion.

'They've broken your spirit,' I sighed. 'They've taken you away from me.'

I'd made a serious mistake. Standing before Len in such an exposed and vulnerable position was not the best of moves. He'd been pumping iron – hard – for four months. His muscles were solid, like steel.

Suddenly, I saw a glint in his eye, a sign of life, a massive, contemptuous amusement. He dropped the stupid plywood yacht in the middle of the car park, pulled his right fist back and whacked me in the guts like I've never been whacked before. I let out a pained '*oof*' and slumped to the ground like a brick.

Len, in turn, doubled up with laughter. 'Got you, you muppet!' he goes. 'I never thought you'd fall for that one. You must be getting past it, you old fart.'

'He's probably right,' I thought, as I struggled to get up. Maybe I was getting past it. I used to be able to take his punches all day long. Apparently, prison hadn't broken his spirit after all. But judging by the pain I was in, he might well have broken one of my ribs, the little swine. Not only had his spirit survived, but he'd obviously learned a few new tricks while he was in there. Prison's a bit like finishing school to the likes of us. It makes you, or it breaks you. You can handle it, or you can't. He'd handled it. He'd passed his final exams with flying colours. 'A's, all round. I was so proud of him. He'd come of age, finished his apprenticeship, gained his *City and Guilds*. He was now fully qualified and should be ready to start working with us on some of the bigger blags. There and then, I decided that he was no longer a kid. He'd come through the white tribe's gruelling initiation rite and he was now - officially - a man.

'Happy Barmitzvah,' I said, tossing him the car keys. 'You're driving.'

His little eyes lit up. He couldn't believe his ears. He launched into the driver's seat, twisted the ignition key, and revved up the engine. I barely managed to get into the passenger-seat before he wheel-spinned off with an ear-piercing screech. I gripped my seat as he performed a wild, swirling doughnut round the stupid plywood yacht, then drove over it, crushing it to matchwood.

Boldly, he accelerated down the car park like a maniac. Defiantly, he executed a sensationally accurate, ninety-degree handbrake-turn at the exit. Bravely, he careered out onto the main road without bothering to look whether anything was coming. Cheerily, he beeped his horn a couple of times for luck and we headed back towards Leeds at speed.

Something Has Gone Wrong In The World

Introduction
Anthony Cropper

There was something about each of the stories contained here, something, initially, I couldn't quite work out. But then maybe that's what I found attractive about them. Each of the pieces deals with everyday situations, they deal, as Peter Bromley writes in *Skylight*, with the 'small collisions' in people's lives. These collisions could be the search for a lost orchard, sex with an older man, unexpected happenings in a bus station, a chance meeting over a lunch break or the simple loss of a few pieces of a jigsaw. What is good about them is their ability to make the everyday appear not so plain and not so simple. They make the everyday appear extraordinary. They explode the world, and that, for me, is what writing is about.

This extraordinariness could be the loss of a partner, it could be a story revolving around a battle with alcohol, a battle with work colleagues, and, ultimately, it is about a battle with ourselves.

What brings these stories together is the idea that something has gone wrong in the world, that something has ended, that something has changed.

These stories offer a glimpse of life, and in that glimpse you're left with the impression that the person at the end is different in some way from the person at the beginning. The small collisions that have brought about these changes may not be so clear, may be barely perceptible, but, in each of these stories, they are there.

Something has gone wrong in the world, things haven't worked out as they should, life wasn't supposed to be like this. That's the impression you get from reading these stories.

Was it really meant to work out this way?

Who knows?

Why People Dance
Roddy Hamilton

I'm on that college course now. And I've moved flats. First floor now - smaller, but I don't care - it's got my books. I never really thought about books before. It's on the other side of the city, that's all that matters. I'm a kitchen porter at the Neptune, part-time, because the government don't give a grant for mature students and I need the money. Not much chance of seeing Lisa there either. Or Samuel. Or Mr Richardson. Not that it matters.

Being on the first floor I've got people underneath and above me. And being that I don't do the same hours anymore, I can hear them. The couple upstairs argue. Down below there's that bump-bump music they used to play at the Hacienda. I can hear folk coming in and out. I wonder what they're up to.

If I miss anything it's the quiet times I used to have after work when everyone else was sleeping. And I miss Lisa coming round. My fridge is a mess.

The old flat was a top floor. I'd finish about three-thirty, be home by four. I'd open the window right up and sit at the table - with the wind coming in, and listen to hear the seagulls' cries echoing against the tenements. Hours I'd sit there. I suppose if I'd got to sleep straight after finishing I could've got into some kind of pattern but I don't suppose I wanted to. Just me and the seagulls, the odd car, the odd siren down below. I liked it that way. Three cups of coffee. I didn't want to go to my bed. Eventually I'd go, around seven-thirty or eight. Be up at two or three, next day - out for a paper or chocolate, come home and watch the box. I'd probably fall asleep until mid-evening. Unless Lisa came round, that is.

She'd come in with her boyfriend sometimes, a real rag-tag lad, hair down to his nose-ring, not much meat on him. I'd seen them at the club a couple of times but they weren't in too often. Then the boyfriend stopped coming and it was just Lisa. I wondered if it was over with the boyfriend. Whenever she came round to mine, she sat on the old couch, dejected. I didn't ask, though, about the boyfriend. Not my place.

In fact, it was always tricky trying to find out where my place was.

'Won't your dad think it a bit strange you come here?' I asked, once.

She had bare arms, a tattoo - you know, one of those celtic rings, around her arm. The other arm had bangles round the wrist. She shrugged. 'He doesn't know I'm here,' she said.

I got the feeling Mr Richardson never knew where she was. It seemed like she didn't live anywhere. Certainly not with him. Maybe she did the rounds of friends, staying a bit here, a bit there. Once, when I came home she was on the top landing outside the door. It was January, freezing, the snow outside was up to your knees.

When I saw her first I thought it was some tramp - just a pile of old clothes, looked like. Then I saw it was her, cut above the eye. She was so pissed she could hardly stand. I thought, 'Oh, no.' Who could I phone? I couldn't phone Mr Richardson. It was quarter to four in the morning. The club had just shut. Mr R wouldn't want to be disturbed.

So what did I do? Took her in. I locked up behind her, I put the kettle on, cleaned her eye up a bit and stuck a band-aid on the cut. I pulled the gas heater over to the couch where she lay, and turned it up. I took off her parka, which was soaking wet. I left her jeans although they were wet too. I took off her shoes and got a blanket to wrap her in. By the time I'd made coffee she was out - gone - zonked on the sofa. Big z's. I thought, 'This isn't a good idea, Edward.' I opened the window.

'You're a bit of a dark horse,' she said in the morning. She'd made a good recovery. There was no sign of a hangover. I was still awake. I couldn't have got to sleep anyway. 'There's nothing dark about me, Lisa,' I assured her. She said, 'Well… you don't talk much about yourself, do you?' To which I said, 'That's because there isn't much to talk about.'

She felt her head. For the first time she realised there was a plaster on it. Then she went to take a piss. I could hear it from the kitchen. The sound of her groaning with relief. I wonder if she'd left the door open.

Anyway, she was there for a while. Kept asking things like could she borrow some toothpaste. She dried her socks on the gas heater because they were still damp. Then she made coffee, then soup and a sandwich, all drawn out, all over a period of time. I kept making hints, but she wouldn't go. Somehow I couldn't spell it out. Eventually I said I was working that night and I had to get some sleep, but instead of leaving she said, 'That's all right. Go to sleep and I'll tidy.'

'I don't think that's a good idea,' I said. 'Go on,' she said. She more or less pushed me back into the bedroom.

I couldn't get to sleep. I heard the noises of her moving about in the kitchen, in the hall, in the living room. When I got up a few hours later she was gone and the floor, the cupboards, the fridge were all cleaned. I thought, 'This isn't a good thing to be happening.' It was all right for her to clean my fridge on a Sunday when all I was doing was reading the papers, but not when I was lying half-clothed in the bed next door. Mr Richardson wouldn't have liked that. He wouldn't have liked that at all.

Course, I never let on to Samuel. Samuel is Mr Richardson's son. Appearance-wise he's very much his father's son. In every-other-way-wise he isn't. He'd done his official training same as I had to, except he didn't listen. Samuel was above all that Proper Restraint Technique stuff.

Obviously I was working with him the night it happened. Although Samuel was only there every now and then. Pocket money he would've called it. Helping dad out of a tight spot. There were always staff shortages at the Hacienda. Anyway, I'd worked with Samuel enough times to know what he was like, and he didn't like me. He used to wind me up - 'You not getting a bit old for this, Edward?' he'd say, laughing. 'Only saying for your own good, pops.'

Then he'd say, 'Stand against the wall behind me if you want. In case there's a rush.'

Once or twice I told him it wasn't a joke being a doorman. It was a lot of standing around in the cold, being bored so it was, saying, 'Evening Gentlemen. How you doing, Ladies?' and all that stuff, keeping a smile on, acting as if you were loving it, so it looked like a really welcoming kind of place, but paying attention to the fact that out of it could come at any moment some nutter mistaking you for Joe Bloggs at the club down the road, or some nyaff you threw out so long ago you couldn't remember him, harbouring a grudge - maybe even harbouring a knife - fancying himself a bit of a face-carver. But it always went over his head. Samuel always knew best.

One exception was the time after he'd been up seeing his dad in the office. He came back and I reckon he'd had a dressing down about something or other. He was as quiet as a mouse the rest of the night. He left all the hello's to the punters to me and skulked into the side lobby biting at his thumbnail. Not quite classic doorman but it suited me better than his big flapping mouth. Afterwards I remember him saying to me, 'What you were saying about some guy with a knife, Edward. Is that how ye got that?' I left him to wonder. Lots of things aren't my business. Lots of things aren't his.

Anyway, that was a while ago - and maybe he talked to his dad about me and his dad put him right. Mr Richardson and myself used to be on terms, you see. I had a bit of respect there, a bit of dignity, and that's what it's all about. It's all about dignity.

But what's important is what happened the night I'm talking about, and all that talking to Samuel just hadn't made any difference. He was up the whole night, looking down on people, running his beady eyes over them, trying to exercise prejudices in a world where prejudices don't count for anything. Like I'd told him - you can have a guy in a sackcloth, jeans and spiky hair and so many earrings you could hang curtains on him and he's Sylvester the Pussy. And you can have Mr Business, straight from the financial sector with a wife and two kids in the country, out for the weekend with a split personality and a Stanley knife. It's dark, it's drinking time, Samuel, and prejudices don't work.

Intuition does. Which is where being an old fuck like me comes in handy sometimes. But it all depends who you're working with. It's all about teamwork.

I had Samuel in my team.

About twelve it gets busy. Most of the pubs are closing and people are moving on to the clubs. The Hacienda was no different, except that there were less people in it than there had been a month ago. That didn't bother me, particularly. Fashions change. Clubs dress themselves up just like the underage girls who go out on a Saturday night, and the word from Mr Richardson was that they'd be refurbishing soon.

So anyway, shortly after this we get a buzz from the bar. Someone had seen something, some dealing or something, so we had to go inside and take a look. Samuel went, I stayed behind on the door - that's how it worked. For security. If he wasn't back in a few minutes, or if the buzzer buzzed again I'd go in too. No need to worry. In the meantime, I stopped people coming in. Nothing strange there - we kept a queue most nights, especially week-nights, whenever it was slow - it makes the passing punter think something good is happening inside. Give people a queue and they'll queue. Don't ask me why, I don't know.

So after a while, when he didn't come back, I told the punters to wait at the door. I shut it, saying I'd be back shortly, and went inside. What I saw was Samuel with his hand round this scrawny guy's throat. Hardly in the Stewardship Manual. I grabbed Samuel by the collar at the back of his neck. 'Get him outside, Samuel,' I shouted above the music. 'Head down.' So Samuel took the punter through, past a dozen or so people at the bar. I walked behind him, checking he did it right. I was also smiling to the punters. 'Carry on, folks! Nothing happening! Drink up your drinks, enjoy yourselves!' I was just trying to calm the clients, you know?

I'm following up behind Samuel until we get to the door. Into the lobby, and Samuel's got the guy one-handed round the back of his neck. His other hand is pulling his arm. Suddenly he shouts at the guy, 'Not in here!' and to punctuate it he smacks the guy's arm off the door. He whirls him around, says, 'Come on. What ye got?' The guy mumbles something and holds his shoulder, which must already be bruised. 'What ye got?' repeats Samuel, face beetroot. He pushes the scrawny guy up the 'Staff-Only' stairs and the guy falls over, can't find his feet - Samuel looks back at me, bawls, 'Shut the door!'

Course, I look back at the door, just for a second, and when I look back again, Samuel has taken his fist off the guy's mouth. He pulls him up and delves into his pocket - the scrawny guy's pocket. He pulls out a bag, saying, 'Is that it? Is this all you've got?' and he starts pushing him. He gives him another big punch to the stomach. The guy gags. He looks over at me for help - but it's bad form for one doorman to compromise another - so I pretend not to see what's happening.

But I need to help the guy out. Samuel pulls him up by the lapels and I take over, pushing the guy into the street, past the queue of punters - handing him a hanky to make it look good, saying, 'Don't bother coming back. You're barred!'

'Bastard!' the guy says. 'What about my friends?' He points at the door. I feel something press on my shoulder. Samuel, behind me, shouts right past my ear, 'Friends? Shite like you doesnae have friends!' I see him sticking the bag in his own jacket pocket.

To give the impression of normality we let another four punters in. They were looking shaken but a few drinks inside and they would forget about it. Samuel grinned and rubbed his knuckles. 'A bit of light exercise,' his expression said. 'What the fuck's that?' I said, nodding my head at the pocket the bag was in. 'Mine,' said Samuel, 'Here. Let some in, it's dead as fuck in there.'

I let it go. Afterwards, when all the punters were gone I usually stay around to check the place out, nobody sleeping or comatose in the toilets, everything secure, that sort of thing - I had to pass Samuel in the bar.

He was usually long gone by this time, but he was sitting at a table with a long drink. His legs were splayed, sticking out under the table and I stood between them. His pupils were wide. You notice these things when you work on a door. I said, 'Your dad wouldn't be too happy about that.' I was meaning the hiatus earlier. He laughed and sneered, leaning over the table at me. His head was cocked. 'It's only whizz, Edward. No need to get moral. Dad's got his coca. Do you really think he cares about me?'

I was about to go home. I hoped the sunrise would be slow and colourful. I also hoped Lisa would come by the next day.

Anyway, a bottle had been dropped on the floor and I kicked it. Accidentally. Things in a club seem really quiet when the music's switched off and nobody's there. Or maybe it's just your ears adjusting, I don't know, but it sounded loud. Loud enough to get the other staff looking. Samuel laughed. 'Hey, Edward!' he said. 'You're hitting the bottle again!'

I turned. Samuel waited while the bottle spun to a stop on the floor. His eyes were wide. He said, 'Oh, sorry. I forgot. Lisa says you're dried out. Well, she'd know, eh? Getting pretty close to you, my sister, eh?'

I said, 'I don't know what you're talking about, Samuel.' He pushed his arms flat on the table and eased them slowly to the edges, daring me. I moved forward, leaning on the table with my arms. One of my hands covered one of his. 'You're not like your dad, are you?' I said. I put pressure on the hand. His expression changed. I could feel him squirming away underneath my hand, trying to get away like a cat with its tail stuck. 'Do you want to talk about what you did tonight?' I said, 'I don't care what your dad thinks. It's me who's got to work with you. My neck. So, do you want to talk about it?' '

You could see him working out if he could punch me with his free hand, working out that even if he could, would it stop me leaning - because I'm a big man, getting on maybe, true, there's grey hairs and rheumatism in my hand - but I do my press-ups and I eat steaks when I can and christ almighty I was laying some weight down on his knuckles. Not only was I pushing on the hand, I had my fingers wrapped round the edge of the table and was using them to squeeze. No way was he getting away. I didn't care if his fingers got crushed. I'd tell Mr R. he fell.

He looked at me. His free hand grabbed my sleeve. I flipped my hand round and put my thumb knuckle onto his tendons and pushed even more. The man dropped out of him. He breathed in. He started talking to me as if I was his dad. 'Okay, okay, I'm sorry.'

156

I said, 'You sure you don't want to talk about it further?' He nodded, sweat like mercury on his neck. When I was half way out, he collected the bottle. I looked back to see what he'd do but if he'd thought about something, he'd changed his mind. He rubbed his hand. 'You better talk to somebody, Edward!' he shouted. 'You better talk to somebody about getting another job!'

The sunrise that early morning was nothing spectacular. For the first time I could remember I was tired, but the open window and the cold air kept me awake. I read old newspapers to keep me from thinking.

The next few nights Samuel wasn't working. I didn't see much of Mr Richardson either. Mostly he wasn't there because of the meetings he had during the day. I knew something was happening but I didn't know what. I thought maybe it was the refurbishment we'd been waiting for. And it wasn't until a few nights later that Lisa appeared - but when she did, it was for two nights in succession. She'd never appeared after work before. It was always the day after, except for the time she was drunk and had cut her head.

'Why do you like watching the rooftops?' she said. 'Nothing happens.' 'Maybe that's why,' I said, 'Because it's peaceful.' It was far from peaceful with those gulls screeching but the noise was far away, almost like music, and I think she knew what I meant. She didn't say anything for a while. We just watched the gulls wheeling and shrieking round each other, bickering on the chimneys of the tenements, landing on the roof of the electric company building and the spotlights of the rail yard. Lisa had a parka on, with the fur-lined hood up. I had the gas heater on but close to the window it didn't make a difference. She got up and shifted from one leg to the other. Then she put her arms in the air. I thought she was tired, stretching. Out of the blue she said, 'Edward? Why do people dance?' I didn't answer her. I didn't even look at her. There was a gull, a big herring gull on one of the chimneys below. It was bending its head back and shrieking up to the pink sky, shifting from foot to foot. I said, 'I don't know.' She rested her hands on the table, sitting so I couldn't see her face behind the hood.

'You know anything about interior design?' she asked after a while.

'No,' I said.

She said, 'I think I'm going to do a course on interior design.'

She left about seven, saying she had something to do. Next night she'd changed. She was more animated, lively. She said, 'Can't you clean up after yourself? You don't do anything round here but read the papers and eat breakfast.' I said, 'What do you mean, 'I don't do anything'? What do you mean? I clean up when I have to. Nobody makes you clean up.'

'Of course not,' she said. 'I never thought they did. But you don't do anything. Why don't you do something. You just sit there.' She tried to pretend she wasn't angry, that she was just joking, but I could tell she was serious. 'Maybe you should go,' I said. I'd thought about the situation. I'd turned it over in my head for the last few days and the whole thing was a bad idea.

The Hacienda shut down.

Mr Richardson, who'd said nothing about Lisa's visits, bunged me a couple of hundred, which was nice of him - but I was out of a job. He moved to that fancy restaurant in the centre. Before I went, he said, 'I'm moving to the Portico. We're selling up here, it's not worth overhauling. Buy yourself a drink.' He looked at me in apology, 'I'm sorry. Don't buy yourself a drink, then. I forgot.'

I took the envelope. For the first time in a year, my hand was shaking. 'Let me settle at the Portico,' he said, 'There are some other faces there. But once I know what's what I'll give you a shout. I might have a job for you.'

I shook his hand. Why not? Mr R had been good to me. He gave me a suit and a tie when I needed it. And with it came dignity. Respect is something you earn. Mine was earned in that suit and tie and it was in that brown envelope.

The call came one Wednesday when it was raining. I'd tried every club and pub up and down town trying to find work, and although a few places had promised to phone back there was nothing solid.

The Portico is on a plaza underneath a tower block of offices. It's plush. A new building right in the centre of the West End. Blue lights light up its fifteen storeys. 'The Portico Restaurant' is in red neon script above the door and the windows are tinted so you can't see in.

'Nice place,' I said, when I met Mr R. He showed me into his office, which had red and blue prints of fish on the wall. 'Glad you think so. Maybe you'll eat here sometime.' 'It's a bit exclusive for me,' I said. He said, 'Lisa did some of the interiors. Well I say "did", she gave us some ideas.' I nodded. 'You haven't seen her lately, have you?' he asked, 'She's gone off somewhere.'

I told him I hadn't.

And I hadn't. I had got used to the idea, too. Mr R. looked out the window at the sandwich place across the road as if he expected her to come out of it.

The job was for the following Monday evening. It turned out not to be a doorman's job. It was a one-off - moving some stuff from the shell of the Hacienda, some fittings that the new owners wanted taken away and wouldn't pay for, and Samuel was picking me up in a dropside van. Mr Richardson provided the gloves and I provided the back for fifty quid the evening. I didn't want to see Samuel but I had no choice, my landlady wanted to see the fifty quid.

So that's how we ended up with a van full of stuff, headed for the dump - Samuel making good use of the old man jokes as I struggled with sink-units and bar frames. He didn't use much muscle himself, only for his mouth, as usual, until I said, 'Hey, are ye doing this?' and he took a token piece of copper piping out of the back of the van and threw it into the pit.

I was doing all the work. He just sat and watched me. 'It's amazing the things people throw away,' he said. 'Look. Good copper piping. Hey, did you not use to work for the council, Edward? Someone told me you used to work the rubbish.'

I ignored him. Down in the pit there were washing machines, cardboard boxes, bent metal bedframes, wardrobes, squares of turf. All of these things were familiar to me. Part of the past, still familiar. There were seagulls above a mound up on the hill. I threw one of the broken metal barstools in. 'But you got binned because you were always pissed. Is that it?'

'Why don't you help?' I said.

He lit a cigarette from the packet in his shirt pocket. 'You ever seen

Lisa, bin man?' he said.

I focused on a rat I saw squirming under someone's old mattress. 'Your dad asked me that,' I said. 'No, I havenae.'

'Must miss her,' he said. He was goading me. I should have seen it coming. In retrospect it's a surprise it took that long. Fifty quid or no fifty quid I wished I'd turned down the job. 'She got down about something and disappeared.'

I said, 'I havenae seen her.'

'Dad says you're lying.'

I was getting tired. 'Let's get this finished and go,' I said. 'I havenae got all night.' I turned to see the orange flick of the cigarette, then one of the bar-stools was coming down on me. I managed to pad it away and caught my wrist on its metal leg. 'Hey!'

I was right at the edge of the tip, with a drop of fifteen feet beside me. The stool sprang off my hand and then went in. It was a stupid game to play at. Then I realised it wasn't Samuel's usual horseplay, I could see by his eyes. He picked up and threw another stool. 'We'll go back to yours and wait for her after this, will we? You old fuck. She's twenty-five!' Another stool.

Twenty-five? What did he mean twenty-five? Of course I knew she was twenty-five.

'Maybe we could have a drink while we wait,' he said. 'See if there's any meths down there.'

I got my balance, finally.

The third stool missed but I nearly went in, watching him pick up another. This last one I caught by a leg and swung back at him. By a stroke of luck it caught him in the chest. The reason it hit so hard was he was coming down off the van. It lifted him right up. But I'd swung it wide. Just like those council bins when I'd to lift them into the lorry.

It's all about dignity. I remembered the feeling as soon as I got it back. One hit could have knocked sense into him, probably. It might even have shut his mouth. I did it twice.

But Samuel's mouth belonged on that tip. I like to think of him waking up there later, smelling like his words. I took a quick look around to see no-one was watching, then I lifted him up. The seagulls on the mound exploded into the air. I watched them crowd the sky for a moment, lifted him back into the van, then put the dropside up. After that I disengaged the handbrake and let the whole lot roll in.

Autistic Angel
A S Hopkins Hart

Autistic Angel had had enough. Truth was, this clumsy, nearly middle-aged lady, half-deaf, and blind to the ways of the world, couldn't understand anything anymore. The world just wasn't making sense.

She'd wanted a boyfriend, once upon a time, years ago, even longed for a boyfriend, yearned to be considered 'normal'. But these days? No way! She'd never 'fitted in', so why try now? It was too late. Enough was enough.

She cast her mind back to the happy times, if living life as 'a waif' could be called 'a happy time', that was. But at least then she'd had some contact with 'the outside world'.

TC had understood her. Probably the only person who ever did. He'd watched her from a distance, made friends with her like you would with a half-starved stray dog, made her cups of freshly-ground coffee, she liked that, even let her lay down on his bed to while away the day-time hours till it was time to find 'shelter' again. 'Shelter' from what, she wondered. 'Shelter' from whoM? 'The world, of course,' her body and mind screamed in unison. The doctor had told her to 'think in opposites' - if she thought a glum, gloomy thought, then she must try and think of a cheerful one, at the same time.

It was allright, this 'thinking opposites' till she got round to trying to find her way round Hyde Park. TC lived at the end of Hyde Park Road, through the tennis courts and at the bottom of the park. She walked up and down the road seven times, thinking in 'oppostites'- opposite directions, that was, till she got so tired she mentally told the doctor to 'get lost' and finally arrived at TC's house. She rang the intercom.

'Hello.' A man's voice crackled, still distinguishable through the tinniness.

'It's Angel,' she muttered; ashamedly, ashamed of being herself, ashamed of her creased clothes and unkempt hair, ashamed of 'being thirsty' and calling round in need of a drink, though truth was, she was fond of TC, genuinely fond; she would have called to see him anyway, but the cups of hot, steamy coffee were most welcome.

Three flights of thinly-carpeted stairs later (the lift was too claustrophobic, even with its mirrors which read 'Welcome to Hawthorne Court') she arrived at a passageway that looked a bit like those films you used to see on the telly, of the inside of a ship.

She banged on the door with her fist, hoping he'd let her in. He didn't always. She knew, sometimes, he peered at her through the spy-hole in the blue painted door and went away again. Today she was lucky.

'Hi, Angel,' he smiled, a warm, gentle smile that would have greeted a princess.

'Well, I'm glad you came round,' he said, frantically trying to empty the overflowing ashtrays, as he struggled with dirty coffee-cups and kicked shoes under the bed, shoving the laundry into the wardrobe. 'It's the only time I clean up,' he confessed, 'when anyone comes round.'

One time he tried it on. Oh, not for sex, particularly, TC wasn't like all the others. He'd said to her, casual-like 'Clean up for me, will you, Angel? The place is in a right state. It needs a woman's touch.'

She'd refused outright, surprising herself. 'No way, TC, I'm not allowed.'

'Who won't allow you?' He took his eyes away from the ever-increasing layer of dust on the sunshine-filled windowsill.

'Joan of Arc.' Her words came out like a dream come true. Any other man and she wouldn't have dared refuse, in fact, some she did clean for, and washed, and cooked, and scrubbed for, like the scrubber they took her to be, but TC was different. She didn't want things to be like that, she didn't want to be 'his scrubber'. It was nice things being different, romantic-like even. She smiled at him from over the top of the coffee-cup.

'I knew you'd say that' he smiled back, 'and stop nicking my tea-bags, Angel, stop taking them with you when you leave.' He tried to look stern.

'How do you know I've been taking your tea-bags?'

'I've counted them. You're not allowed in the kitchen anymore.'

Her heart sank. Not that the kitchen was anything to write home about, inches of grease and grime, why it would have taken ten cleaning-ladies the best part of a week to get it anything like, but sometimes, just sometimes, there was a crust of pizza or a few pieces of rice and peas left on a plate. Once there'd been a whole onion bhaji, she'd enjoyed that.

'Well, how do I get tea-bags, then, TC? I won't be able to make cups of tea anymore.' Tears welled inside her.

'Buy some.' His gentle voice had patience in it. She liked that.

'Buy some? Where from?'

'The shop.'

'Which shop?'

'That shop you pass on the way here. You've got money, haven't you? The Asian shop on the corner.'

So he sent her to the shop, and she waited anxiously in the queue, but came out triumphantly with her first packet of tea-bags. Her first lesson in 'life-skills'.

* * *

Visits to TC's were enjoyable. She started calling most days. He gave her his phone number.

'Can I lie down, TC? I'm tired.'

'As long as you take your shoes off.'

He sat in the chair. He only had the one room. Two comfy seats, one single bed, one table with a chair and computer on it, and a wardrobe next to the bed. It was really a bedsit.

Brown-leaved yukka plants stained the windowsill where the sun was invariably streaming through the open window. The central-heating was always on full, winter or summer.

'Can't you turn the heating off, TC?'

166

'It comes from a boiler in the basement. It's the same in all the flats. You can't turn it off.'

He kept his hair short and neat. She admired the way the grey strands blended with brown from the single bed in the far corner of the room, the sun irradiating her outstretched legs, highlighting the blond hairs on her arms. They talked. He'd got a son in Edinburgh who he'd never seen. He must be nearly eighteen now.

'Don't you miss him?'

'No, I've never seen him, never been part of his life.'

'Why don't you get in touch with him?'

'I wouldn't know what to say to him, and anyway, I don't know where he's living. He could be in America, anywhere.'

He put some music on the second-hand stereo, asked her if she liked it, she nodded, too sleepy to speak and fell pleasantly asleep, waking up in a bath of sunshine and duvets.

'Where's my shoes, TC? I've got to go.'

'Where you put them.'

'See you later. Thanks for the coffee.'

* * *

Some visits to TC's were 'special'. She used to get on the bed, wrapped in duvets and sunshine. Never before had she felt so much at ease, at peace with the world, herself and her body, drinking in the atmosphere of smokey sunshine and warm duvets, in love with the world, the peace, the moment. She kissed away the hurt, the pain of her life, caressing herself with love.

TC watched her from the chair, following her fingers dancing under the duvets, listening to the sound of cotton sheets on fingertips, watched her face quiver with pleasure and desire, and then, that final sigh.

The second or third time, he came over and sat on the floor next to the bed.

'Want me to do that for you?'

'O.K.'

She smiled at him and he drew closer, as if to kiss her, but she

167

turned her head towards the wall. He moved away and she looked at him in grateful relief. She hated kissing! How do you explain to people, life, and especially men that you hate kissing? Everybody kissed, she knew that, and most of the time she obliged, covering up the deep disgust she felt inside.

He slipped his hand under the duvet and found hers, traced a shape round her index finger pressed closely against her 'love-bump'. His hand against hers, her passion, hunger, desire returned. Wet fingers slipped slowly against her body, tracing the lettuce-leaf shape of her inner lips, finding, feeling that bump grow and swell until it finally burst.

'Oh, TC, that was lovely.'

He smiled.

'Can I get a bath?'

'O.K. But clean the bath out after you.'

She never did clean the bath out after herself. Sometimes she used his toothbrush and toothpaste, too, but if he noticed, he never said.

* * *

Bliss-filled days kissed against nights of torment, nights with men pressing themselves hard into her body as she reeled in painful disgust, their selfish, slobbering lips oblivious to her silent screams of protest.

Days were oh so, very, different. One time TC asked her 'Do you want me to go inside you? Use a condom?'

'No, thanks, it's allright.'

'O.K.'

He was the only person in her life who had never used or abused her, had always done just what she wanted to do, nothing more, nothing less, and those stupid Social Services people had said he'd 'taken advantage of her'. If only they knew.

One time she asked him 'What do you do, TC?..I mean, what do you do for a living, you know, money and that.'

'Oh, I'm a property developer,' he replied.

'What does that mean?'

'Oh, you know, buying and selling land and that. Mainly by phone.'
She could understand that, he had a kind, lovely voice, a friendly speaking manner.

'So that's what the computer's for.'

* * *

One day as they were sitting on the comfy seats sipping coffee he said to her 'Oh, don't come round at weekends 'cos I've got a girlfriend.' She looked at him. 'But you can still visit during the week, she's at work then.'

Still, once or twice she did visit at weekends. A couple of times she met his girlfriend, on one occasion they went for a walk in the park, just her and his girlfriend. Gabrielle was her name. Long, blond hair, waving round her shoulders. They got talking. Eventually they talked about TC.

'He's a lovely man,' Gabrielle smiled. 'I'm glad I met him. He's been wonderful to me, takes care of things, you know, the car, and money matters and everything.'

'Yes,' Autistic Angel piped up. 'And he's good in bed.'

His girlfriend, Gabrielle, looked at her strangely, giving her a sort of sideways glance that upset her somehow. The conversation continued.

'How long have you known TC?'

Eventually they parted at the picnic area - taking separate paths.

'See you later, then.'

She never saw her again. Never saw TC either.

She tried telephoning. The last thing TC said to her before he replaced the receiver was 'It's not your fault, Angel.' She'd cried. No, she didn't want another boyfriend, not even another TC, if there was such a thing that was, not these days, nearly middle-aged now, and anyway, she couldn't do with all the things men wanted to do, all the kissing and that. No way. It was too late. Enough was enough.

American Policeman

James Dean Garside

They're watching me in black and white. Not the pregnant teen looking for a place to sit, or the young boy hunched over in front of the second hand bookshop. That place is known for trouble. Of all the people they could watch, the camera has singled me out. I'm not supposed to smoke here.

I was stoned when the coach pulled in. She wasn't on it this time either. A woman in a red dress stepped barefoot from the coach. She wasn't my girlfriend but I stared at her anyway. She leaned over, stretched her long legs and slipped on her sandals.

'Have you got the time?' I said.

She looked at me disgusted; so disgusted that I didn't ask anyone else. Maybe she was meeting someone? I've seen them do that. They kiss and hug and quote each other, taking turns to finish sentences.

The driver waddled round, white shirt untucked; stretching his legs, but that is not the same thing. He lifted up the side panel on the coach and helped people get out their luggage. The coach was like a dead horse, opened up, with everyone gathered around it. My girlfriend wasn't in the crowd. I looked at them all in turn as though they might be her. The man in the blue suit didn't qualify. She would never wear blue, only black. It matches her pupils.

The passengers took up too much room now they weren't on the coach. I wondered what would happen if I got up and walked away. The surveillance camera pointed right at me. Would I be made to sit back down and wait for her?

I crossed over to the shopping precinct. There is a café and some toilets that you pay to enter. Where you take a shit is now a restricted area, guarded by a turnstile with a slot in the side for your coins. Low enough to step over, but high enough to draw too much attention to yourself when doing it. Someone got paid to measure these things.

Painted arrows pointed down concrete steps into the male toilets. Fluorescent strip lights flickered on and off, buzzing louder than the flies they attracted. My stomach lurched at the brown detergent smell of a hospital. That's when I saw the body on the wet floor.

A man was curled up in front of the urinals. I looked around for an empty cubicle to use instead. The nearest one had no door and was cordoned off with black and yellow hazard tape like a crime scene. The middle one was empty, but I heard two men's hushed voices in the other cubicle. The door said occupied and banged at regular intervals. I didn't want to know what they were doing, so I approached the man instead.

'Can I have a piss?' I said. He had a lumberjack shirt rolled up under his head like a pillow. I stepped over him. He groaned, but got up as soon as I unzipped.

'I couldn't sleep anyway. Got any change?'

'You don't have to pay to get out' I said.

'No, but I have to make sure I can get back in.'

'Even tramps pay to get in here?' I thought, then stopped mid-flow, unsure of whether I'd said it out loud. He moved over to the sink and turned on the taps.

'Men throw me out. They have their own staircase.'

'I can't help you' I said. In my head I saw him glare at me through the mirror and struggled to finish.

'Now wash your hands' he said. He wasn't there when I turned round. He'd left the lumberjack shirt in a puddle by the sink. The cubicle door banged faster and louder; one man whined like a kicked dog. I sniffed my hands and walked out.

As I flicked through the crumpled notes in my wallet I realised that I'd told the truth; I couldn't help. Since I'd paid for the toilets, I didn't have any change. There was a newsagent stand just round the corner. The small fat woman eyed me with contempt as I handed her my money.

'We don't give change' she said.

'But I need to use the phone.'

'You'll have to buy something.'

I picked up a newspaper without looking at the headline.

'I'm not changing a tenner just for that.'

'Alright, a pack of cigarettes.'

'Which one?'

'I don't care which one. The cheapest.'

'What kind of man doesn't care what brand he smokes?'

She gave me my change but didn't say how much it came to.

The phone box was worse than the toilets. You could tell someone had pissed there. My girlfriend would kill me for not putting her before the toilet. City traffic blared outside, so loud and constant that you only noticed when it was cut off by the booth door. My coins dropped into the metal box with exaggerated clunks. I tried to get through to her mobile.

'This service is not available. Please replace the handset and try again.'

The metal box decided to keep my money anyway. My head just hung up on the idea. What is the point of having a phone if you can't talk to someone on the other side? What if I'd been waiting in the wrong place? And what if she'd gone to another station to meet someone else instead of me?

That's when the bad things started. Myself and the sky are no longer on speaking terms. It began to chuck it down as soon as I stepped out of the phone box. All around me the buildings ran in weighed down colours. Rain made them dirty, the bus station drained through a coffee filter. I ran across to the stand where I'd been waiting. The coach was no longer there. Oil patterns slid on the wet road in its place. I've seen oil slicks in a grey sea, and a rainbow in a black sky, but this one ran straight into the gutter.

The newspaper was too wet to read, stories blurred together, hands smudged black from the cheap print. It's not like I was in the mood anyway, slumped cold and wet on the same plastic seat as before. The newspaper went straight in the bin along with the shrink-wrap from my cigarettes.

I tried to do something with my eyes other than just looking at the floor. As I smoked, the warmth in my lungs made me want the words I do read: Nazi propaganda, Mayan codices, and every manner of bus timetable that I can lay my hands on.

A man came and stood in front of me.

'All I need is an American Policeman' he said.

'What?' I said, talking to muddy hobnail boots.

'All I need is an American Policeman.'

He had an alcoholic's red nose and a pock scar dug into his left cheek like a question mark. I couldn't tell if he was the man from the toilets. He wore a Benny hat, but rolled up wrong, half mast on his head.

'The last thing you need is to talk to a cop, mate.'

He grinned. 'Normally I'd agree with you, if it was just your average beat bobby. But this is different.'

'Why American?'

'Well it's the way they move, isn't it?'

'Are you for real?' I said.

He shook his head at me. I didn't know if he was laughing or choking as the words spilled out of his mouth.

'I need one now or else I'm gonna lose it, go crazy like. No-one cares, so I'm all *why me* inside, you know?'

'And a cop would care?'

'No, but they'd know what to do.'

He sat down too close to me on the green plastic seat and leaned in even closer. His bad breath stung like raw onions. Mismatched brown and blue eyes watched me; each had nothing to do with the other.

'I'm like a bomb, see? An American Policeman will stop me from going off.'

The blue eye blinked and the brown eye stared at my mouth.

'Smoking is bad for you. This is a no smoking area.'

I could taste him on my cigarette so I handed it over.

'Here' I said. 'Keep it.'

He snatched the cigarette then just held it for a moment, like he didn't know what to do with it.

'What are you doing?' he said.

'Waiting.'

'But, you could go places.'

'I'm waiting for my girlfriend.'

'A man should wait for his woman to come, the TV told me that. Does she have a name?'

'Yes, but it doesn't suit her.'

He seemed to have calmed down a bit, and took a long drag on the cigarette. I'd smoke the rest of them when he'd gone.

'I say that I'm waiting, but that means I'm getting somewhere, if you see what I mean?'

'Coaches go places. They have horses.'

'They have Horse Power' I said. 'Do you know, the only time I saw a horse outside of a book or movie was on the road at night? There was an accident. The horse had bolted. Bolt is the word they lock the horse with, I could never understand that. It galloped down the busy motorway, ran itself to death in all the headlights.'

The man's brown and blue eyes blinked together.

'Your girlfriend's dead, isn't she?'

I took back my cigarette and ground it out on the green seat, melting the plastic.

'I told you, I'm waiting for my girlfriend.'

'All I need is an American Policeman' he said.

'Well, I hope you find one.'

'It's not your fault' he said, and walked right out into the rain.

The surveillance camera stayed on me. A new coach rounded the corner, so I stood up on show for the security guards. My wallet was missing; the bastard must have stolen it. I was patting down my pockets when the coach pulled in. I had to choose between chasing after him and waiting for my girlfriend.

I looked for her through the tinted windows.

It Is All Right
Helena Hoar

It is all right, I am telling myself, to meet someone the age of your father for dinner. Not someone who could be your father; he is not your father, your father is different, unpresumptuous, would not go on holiday by himself and ask someone the age of his daughter to join him for dinner. I know I am uneasy but am not able to admit why. There may be some interesting people there; I will be polite and well mannered and only tell them tiny parts of myself and I will never have to see them again. I have, after all, torn out the pages in my book.

It takes me some time to decide what to wear, how to wear it.

I bring the postcard of St Ola with me. I will have time to write it to my nanna. I sit outside the tourist office where there is a post-box so I can pop it straight in with no excuses for forgetting. I write large and clear and can only fit four lines on. I tell her where I am, for how long, that I hope to see her soon. I write that on all the postcards I send her when I take a few days away, and on the cards I send her at festive times throughout year, just to stay in contact, but I never see her soon. I will send cards to the rest of my family tomorrow, when I have done something real.

I walk down the street and look for the restaurant. I am a little puzzled when I cannot find it; I make myself pause and look out to greying, ruffling sea for a long minute before I walk back again, more slowly, looking carefully at each shop front this time. Here I am, neat-dressed, hair brushed, mascara and eyeliner and lipstick and hungry too now and I cannot find the meeting place in this tiny town. I consider the bread and cheese. Even though it had only been planned a couple of hours ago, even though I am not sure I would normally look forwards to an early dinner with a man who is the age of my father, I am feeling disappointed. I face the plate glass of an optician and make myself choose a pair of frames as if that was the reason I came out tonight. I become engrossed.

'Do you need new glasses?'

Robin startles me and I am surprised that nervousness grabs at my sternum. 'No,' I lie, and then say more truthfully, 'I don't wear glasses.' I should wear glasses and have already decided to have an eye test in Kirkwall tomorrow. 'I couldn't find the restaurant.' I tilt my face up to him. He has, just by being here, curtailed my movements, made my voice level and soft. He has dressed in different clothes, slicked his hair; I can smell a twitch of soap, or perhaps shaving cream.

'It's changed its name,' he tells me. 'Shall we try it anyway?'

He does not mention any other people and I realize that the evening will be just him and me. I am concerned I will have nothing to talk about with him. What would I want to disclose of myself to a man the age of my father? We descend the steps and are seated in the dim and mostly empty restaurant, a table for unromantic two, and he waits till I have sat before he pulls out his own chair. I feel as if I am strangely back on the ferry, a sway, a yaw at an unanticipated moment.

Robin orders an old fashioned single gin and tonic but barely drinks it. He is keen to set himself out, a la carte, a portion of each part of himself discreet on the plate and he works through the courses of himself in an intelligent but unemotive way. He tells me he is a magistrate, a scout leader, a flight engineer, has been to bed with an air hostess in need of comfort in a hot and tropical country, he tells at length of the success of his eldest son. I listen carefully and make supportive comments but I can find no way to wriggle under this tablecloth surface.

I eat my meal so, so slowly and neatly with cutlery precise, hold my wine glass by the stem, tuck my elbows in and cross my legs at the ankle. 'And do you have just the one child?' I ask as I sit inside myself and see what the few other diners might surmise, he with a younger woman, me with an older man.

Robin sets down his steak knife. 'We have another boy,' he says.

'Oh?' I say, and am surprised; there seems no gap for him.

'He has...' and Robin pauses, a dish not available on the menu, 'well, he has mental problems.'

'Does he?' And at last I find something I can relate to; words teem but I do not want to mention myself, and then our plates are cleared and the moment with them. Robin has said all he will. Once more there is no one near me; I hide the sad times of anger and tears in the paper napkin screwed up in the palm of my hand and I smile practicedly at him. 'I'm just going to the toilet.'

I spread on more lipstick and I put my forehead against the mirror. I talk aloud in a low rumble because just thinking is too flighty and am appalled and pleased with the tragedy of my voice. I look into eyes that, after wine, seem dark and beautiful to me.

'You do not want a man like Robin. What the fuck are you doing here? The food was adequate, the company poor, he is a bore. Even if you yourself had nothing to tell him. Say goodbye now, go to bed with a cup of tea and be ready to begin tomorrow.' But I am feeling the pull of the inevitable.

'I've asked for the bill,' he tells me.

I acknowledge it and wonder if he will pay my part, and when he does not I smile to myself and wish it was a sign of independence. Now I owe him nothing but I have not been flattered by him either. 'Well,' I say as we enter the wine-enhanced still day-lit street, 'thank you for a pleasant evening.' I turn to go, I have my itinerary to plan, tomorrow to prepare for.

'It's early yet,' he says, 'would you like to come for a drive with me, see a bit of the island?'

He is dull and safe, and I tell myself there should be no threat or imposition. 'Oh,' I say, 'that would be nice,' although I do not think it would be nice, but I need to see the island.

His small red car chugs on diesel, it has a compass stuck to the top of the dashboard and a tape of organ music in the player. 'I play the organ,' he tells me, 'in our church.' And then he explains all about it, at length, just him talking; I let him tell me some things I already know. We climb steeply out of the town and through this foreign land of grey-green grass and hay meadows and single stunted trees blown bare of branch by the wind. I open the window, lap the air with my tongue, wanting it to taste specific; it does not but something from out there leaps into me, joys me and I wish I was outside the car and alone.

'I'm heading west,' Robin tells me, jolts me out of myself, 'perhaps we can see the sun set.'

'You old romantic,' I say, for something to say, inside saying, just shut up and leave me alone.

'I am romantic,' he replies seriously, 'I buy my wife chocolates and flowers.'

'That's nice,' I cringe but that is not what I'm thinking. He is the sort of man with a list on lined paper that I'd despise in Sainsburys, that I'd dismiss in the park with grandchildren on Sundays. Part of me wants to smack his smug face and shake his steady shoulders, to uncover what's underneath; but I am not really that interested. The sun, so far north, is still a while away from setting; there is a hedge of clouds between it and the horizon. Robin consults the compass, plays the organ music on the steering wheel. We drive through a grey modern village and I suddenly feel depressed, a sudden crashing fall through breaking branches into my centre.

Robin pulls the car into a gateway. A knobbly herd of young calves are licking the gate, lowing, stretching for the tall dry grass on the far side. 'Shall we get out? I think the sun will go behind those clouds before it sets.'

We watch the sliding sun and I pretend to be interested. He moves too close to me and I move away from that too-closeness, from the prickle of his polyester trousers and the fabric-conditioned soft top each time he comes too close to my gently browned skin. There is no sunset; the light lingers greyly. We get back in the car.

He leans forward to turn the key in the ignition and asks, 'How do you fancy a kiss and a cuddle?'

A huge and silent wail lodges itself in my throat; every time, every bloody time. I close my eyes but I know he is looking at me. I feel lonely. I can say no, I can say no, and I am not afraid of him, I do not believe he would make me this man who is a father of two sons, a magistrate, a scout leader, who flies and dives, who plays the organ in his church. I want to ask why he thinks he can ask that of me, of me, when I have not flirted or alluded but behaved perfectly. Too many answers bang in my ears and I say nothing.

'Do you fancy it?' he repeats.

I look out of the window at the cows behind their wire fences. 'Not really,' I slump, heavily. It is getting darker, he switches on the headlights.

'Why not?' he persists.

'I don't know,' and I feel like a sullen teenager.

'How do you know you won't like it until you try it?' His voice is steady, assured but there is a hint in there of bright hope.

My head tells me to be safe, to join him in this confidence, to improve my position, to be level with him and this compounds strangely with not wanting to hurt his feelings. So I say, 'All right then,' but it is only grudgingly that I acquiesce. Robin doesn't seem to notice. I am back at my old feeling; if that's what they want, they can have it, but it doesn't mean they have me. I had foolishly thought I could leave it behind.

He stops the car again after several more miles; I have not looked at him at all but have been bracing myself. There are no hedges, no trees for shelter, but the air is turning grainy with the dark and the car is off the road down a dim and peaty track marked by the wire fence that ties the land to the rock beneath on all this windswept island.

'Come on then,' he says to me.

I lean towards him over the handbrake and I touch him. I have never touched a man who is old enough to be my father in this way before; I am appalled by the thinness of his iron-grey hair slicked to his scalp, by the flab of his fresh-shaved jowl. I think about how I will have to write him in my book.

'Kiss me,' he says, his lips on my cheek. I smell the soap, the shampoo, the oil on his hair, a hint of juniper on his breath.

I try, I tear a small tight kiss from his mouth and I try again but it is choking me. 'I'm sorry,' I say, drawing back, 'I don't like kissing very much.' I wonder if we can go now, this dry encounter done with.

'Let's climb into the back,' he suggests.

He pulls his driver's seat forward.

I pause for a moment outside the car. There are crickets and birds and moths in the grass that sounds like the sea. There is a farmhouse with one light bright up on the slope of the hill. The gloaming sky is huge above me, stretching from one fingertip to the other of my outstretched arms. I swallow it all down, hard, and get into the back of this small car.

With no pretence at anything else Robin puts one arm around my shoulder and rests his hand on my breast through my dress. He does not look at my face while I stare at his and note each dark follicle on his cheek, each speck of dandruff on his scalp, each spring of hair in his left ear. He moves his hand gently, talking all the while in a soft and lulling voice. 'Is it all right if I feel you here? Do you like that? Does that feel good?' And they are real questions even though I am quiet, I say nothing, and I am almost ready to humour him. 'Can I touch you here?' and he slips his hand down my neck, down my sternum, under my dress.

I watch him at work, I am surprised by him and by my own involuntary pleasure. He takes off his glasses and folds the arms neatly and places them in the rear window. His eyes are bright, clear, in his wrinkled face. Then as he lifts one breast from my dress, plump in his hand, he sighs with deep pleasure, 'Oh, such firm breasts,' and I feel in his palm the shadow of how my flesh will become. 'Can I lick you here?' and he gorges himself and I had not meant to, do not mean to, but I find myself breathing hard, rising to meet him.

'And here?' he carries on, pulling my legs by the crook of my knees onto the seat, 'Can I touch you here?' and he reaches through my dress between my thigh, and I cannot help it, I am pushing towards him. 'Can I do this?' he asks and slowly stirs as if waiting to be stopped with his fingertips from my knee to my thigh and further.

Now it doesn't matter who he is, it doesn't matter that if I look down I can see his hair jagged on his sweaty nape. He pulls off my knickers and begins to lick me, parting my lips so he can lap over my clitoris and I should be ashamed to be so aroused but the blood is plumping my skin and I don't desire him, I only desire what he is doing. And he is good, he knows how to play me and I am moaning now and he slides a finger into me and I know I am burning hot and with the other hand he rubs at my fiery clitoris and I am coming noisily, terribly.

He keeps me going, working me with more fingers until there is no sound in me and I can barely breath and I am still coming. My hand is sourcing rivers down the condensated windows. I float with the stars in that wide wide sky and then I curl away from him, curl up small and he just holds me.

'Did you enjoy that?' he asks but I cannot speak, I just regard him with eyes as wide as that sky.

The windows in the car have steamed up; I am still for a long, long time. He smiles and begins to touch me again, his palm between my legs, cupping, and I am so fully flooded I am coming at once but have not enough energy to come. I push him away and find my voice is hoarse and incoherent.

'No?' he asks, then leaves me alone. And then, much later, 'We ought to go.'

My legs are unsteady, ungainly, stiff as the calves by the gate, and with my dress a bundle around my stomach I am cold. It is almost dark proper; the clock in his car inexplicably says midnight. He plays the steering wheel to the tape again and says to me in a flirtatious way that makes me feel sick, 'You liked a bit of this, and this, and this,' his fingers rolling and tapping and pushing. I have laid myself open to this man and once more I cannot understand why or how; his eyes and skin and body breathes satisfaction. I feel sorry for him that I have made him proud. I put my hand on his knee and caress it and the skin on my hand feels so fresh on the polyester cloth. I move it up to his thigh and rest it, my little finger in the crease of his groin. He drives on. With no encouragement from him, no twist of pleasure, no quick, deep exhalation, I give up.

Before we park on the pavement outside his place he encloses me in a tight fatherly hug against his chest, his spreading belly. 'I'll get some stick off that lot,' he says, nodding to the house behind, 'I told them I was taking a young lady out to dinner.' He hesitates. 'Would you like to do it again? I'm busy tomorrow. How about Tuesday?'

'I'm not sure what my plans are really.' I don't want this to be what my being here is about but I know that I am not in control, that I may be enticed.

Robin takes charge. 'Well, meet me here at seven if you do.'

'Thank you for a pleasant evening,' I say, polite, and we peck each other lightly on the cheek before turning away.

Jigsaw
Rachel Feldberg

One hundred pieces. Maybe. Or maybe not. Maybe that's just what it says on the box. Maybe there's more, creating their own maverick picture with no relation to the main event. Neil is charged with counting them out. In another place they'd do it automatically, they'd have a gadget. Here the machinery along the belt is old, because Dan Johnson can see no reason to replace it. Now or ever. That's what he says. When it breaks down he gets a set of spanners out of his bag and crouches under the casing, trails of oily sweat running down the side of his face. The machinery went in his father's day and hasn't been updated since. The shed - everyone calls it the shed, although no one remembers for certain where it got its name- is boiling hot in summer. There are no windows, only opaque patches of something that isn't quite glass, and in winter the chill creeps up from the ground and in through the cracks until your hands are too cold to hold the pieces of 'Britain's Best Buses' and 'Summer on the Inland Waterways'.

Neil's place is at the end of the line by the supervisor's office - a shack inside a shed. More like a ticket collector's booth if you look closely, the planks stained dark as an old fence. He's been counting all day every day since 1954. He never seems to tire. His voice doesn't waver.

'Ninety-six, ninety-seven, ninety-eight -'

Such a familiar undercurrent that no-one hears him anymore. Cherry used to listen, when she first came. It had a comforting rhythm. His voice, rather high with just a trace of a Scottish accent, lulled her through days when she still had to concentrate on scooping the pieces into the boxes which ran along the belt. The pace of the belt is never right. Some days it's unendurably slow. Others, so fast the boxes twirl away before she can fill them.

'The pace never alters,' the supervisor tells her. 'It's impossible to alter the speed. It's preset. Been the same for fifty years.'

Cherry says nothing, but she's unconvinced. There are days when the boxes fly past like ducks on a fast flowing river, and others when they meander so she has to pause and wait for them to come up level, her hands brimming with freshly stamped pieces. It's uncomfortable to hold them in one hand, they don't look sharp, individually. In fact individually they're perfectly painless. But when you hold a great bunch of them, crushed together in your fist, the points dig into your palms - her hand is pitted with angular red marks. The corners are worst. Maybe there are only four of them, but her hand feels full of thistles. When she washes in the shabby lean-to washroom at dinner time (the only light coming in through a half frosted window, Mr Johnson had never been keen on light) she sees her fingers are swollen.

She's used to both - lack of light and swollen fingers. Mother doesn't like to sit directly in the sun, and avoids the bright light of midday, draping a sheet askew from the curtain rail.

When the belt changes speed it interrupts Cherry's flow. Her fingers repeat the same task thirty times a minute, seventy-two thousand times between Monday morning and Friday five o'clock. Taking into consideration two weeks in Tenby (by coach, Mother doesn't like the train) two weeks at Christmas and a week at Easter she calculates that in each of the seventeen years she's worked at Johnson's there's been three million three hundred and eighty-four thousand of those repetitions. It's scarcely a wonder that her mind's been wandering off to other things. Eight hours a day dreaming of something, somewhere other than where you are, It's a disturbing indulgence. Like spending every afternoon watching black and white films with a full box of Milk Tray. She always feels a little sordid when she comes blinking into the light at the end of the day.

The others talk. It doesn't seem as if they talk about anything of substance. Just a familiar dance without excitement. Much more inviting to slip inside her head and pick up the threads of yesterday's story. Some weeks her ability to travel anywhere, to evoke any place overwhelms her. Today she's in Italy. A pavement cafe. Near the Ponte Vecchio. But there's still the question of her clothes. She had thought of a white linen dress, but somehow it doesn't seem right. Too glaring and obvious. Probably too young. Now she's rerunning the whole scene - from the moment she stepped through the door, down into the dark interior - in a dress that isn't so much white, as a gentle beige.

'Ninety-six, ninety-seven, ninety-eight -' Neil pauses in the counting. It throws his rhythm out he says, if you have to stop.

'We're short. Two short over here.'

Neil holds the box close to his eyes as if he were reading the label. Cherry knows he's looking at the picture. Neil doesn't read.

'Bridges of the World.' He says at last, still squinting.

'Different bridges. All kinds.'

Brenda is passing the word back -

'Tell whichever fat cow's on number eight she messed up.'

Cherry glances at the floor. Sometimes the pieces slip out of her hands as she sweeps them into the box. She lifts her feet carefully, setting them down just wide of where she's been. There's nothing under her heels.

Neil empties the pieces onto the table beside the belt , they come out of the box with a rush.

'Do you want me to give you a hand?'

Neil nods. He seldom speaks except when he's counting. It's never worried Cherry, some of the others find it strange. She begins to lay the pieces face up.

'Do you like to start with the edges or the middle?'

Neil shrugs.

'Not bothered.'

Mother begins with the edges. Cherry picks out the pieces with one flat edge and lays them together, aware of Neil waiting beside her. Then she pulls the inner pieces towards her.

'You can do the edge if you want,' she says at last. 'It's all there'.

'Not bothered.'

Cherry props the box lid up in front of them, so they can see the illustration. It shows an unlikely maze of bridges. She recognises a few, less than half. Mother would know them all: their names, the rivers they pass over. Tower Bridge in the centre, open to let a majestic looking liner pass through, Golden Gate Bridge, dwindling away to infinity on the left, down at the bottom the Pont Du Neuf. Well definitely something French. There are blobby flower sellers along the embankment and a row of paintings hanging from the railings. The rest are unfamiliar.

Neil is hanging over the pieces.

'Might be a lot got in the wrong box,' he says gloomily.

In her experience of puzzles it's unusual. There's no shared sky at the top. Each bridge has its own patch of blue, and its own flowing river. They cross over and above one another like Spaghetti Junction with no regard for the reality of the water flow. 'No regard at all.' She says to herself and begins putting the pieces into little heaps, each one a different colour.

'Twenty-two along the top. You'll be needing the same along the bottom.' Neil's sounds more confident. The first pieces slide together as if by enchantment. Sometimes she can visualise what should go where. Or it may be a glimpse of colour. A tiny scrap of detail. Mother holds the pieces she's trying to place just above the puzzle with her finger and thumb.

'Now whereabouts do you think I'll find that shape? Come on Cherry, I'm looking for the outline.'

Otherwise when they do jigsaws it's mostly in silence. Mother doesn't like anyone to talk. Not while she's doing jigsaws, or playing Scrabble, or eating poached egg. In Summer she recites the names of the Wimbledon tennis players in alphabetical order - right back to nineteen-fifty, although she can't always be bothered with the men. Long after Mother has turned out the landing lights Cherry can hear the determined mutter from next door:

'Goolagong, Henman, Ivanisovic, Billie Jean King; Rod Laver..Martina...'

She looks down and sees that her fingers are piecing the fragments together of their own accord. Neil's working on a scrap of crowd at the end of the Sydney Harbour Bridge. Now they have the piers finished it's quite clear what it is, you can see the rounded cones of the opera house beyond, but the two halves of the picture don't quite fit. Neil's forced the pieces into place and now they're misshapen and bulging upwards. She smooths them out , stroking them into place.

The red bus on Tower Bridge is easy. It goes together so quickly her fingers can't keep up. Every time she slots a piece into place there's another waiting. And then another. And another. Her hands don't move fast enough, her breath is coming more quickly, until she's almost panting.

'There.' She says at last. All across the table are little islands of colour. Miniature icons with bright jewelled images. The flower sellers on the Pont du Neuf. Runners crossing Sydney Harbour Bridge, the lights of the cars above San Francisco Bay. Neil is worrying at the edges. He's made a ragged frame, a biscuit with the middle eaten out.

'Move it closer,' she says, 'then we can join them.' He looks blank.

'See. Like this.' She stretches across him and the backs of her hands brush his shirt. She eases the frame down until she can join it to the pictures, it's like doing up the poppers on the mother's old slip.

'It all goes in together like this.'

She patches and fiddles, fingers skipping between the remaining pieces until it's done and they can see the gaping hole in the centre of the Ponte Vecchio, showing the scratched table underneath.

'There's two bits gone.' Neil says, passing the word down the line. 'From the Italian bridge. People in a cafe. Talking.'

Cherry slides the pieces out of her pocket, still warm from the heat of her body. She eases them carefully into place. Neil is looking at her. She doesn't say, 'I found them on the floor.' Mother often says it would be better if she spoke out. 'Give people more of a chance to get to know you'.

The pieces fit so tightly you can hardly see the join. Cherry steps away to ease her back, and sees the woman in the beige linen dress is raising a glass to her pasteboard companion.

'One hundred' she says to Neil. And smiles.

Taking Stock
Lolita Chakrabarti

Tiffany Butler was on her lunch break. She was late and hurrying back to Furniture Land where she had worked for only two weeks. She didn't want to give the wrong impression. She was only sixteen and she needed this job. As she approached the large display window of the shop where the new black leather suite was displayed, she saw that a man, of West Indian origin, old, was sitting on the window display. She thought he may have been trying out the top of the range black leather suite with white leather trim and though he looked a little odd in the window, she rushed into the staff room to put her coat away and don her shop blazer.

A couple of minutes later Tiffany was back on the shop floor and no one seemed to have noticed her absence. She ambled around the floor, asking customers if everything was alright. They would jump, then smile and say they were just looking. She walked on, enjoying her authority and glad to be doing her job well. Always keep the customer's needs in sight, Mr McLaine, department manager, said.

It must have been almost twenty minutes later when she happened to stroll past the window display again. And there, sat on the deep-seated, plush leather three-seater, was the old West Indian man. Tiffany was disconcerted to see him still there. Had he fallen asleep? It didn't make the shop look very classy. She looked around for a senior member of staff but saw that they were all at the opposite end of the floor dealing with customers. Use your initiative, she thought to herself. You are a member of staff here, deal with the problem intelligently.

She looked at the man. He must have been in his fifties she thought. He was wearing a suit and tie, well used, so he wasn't a tramp or a drunk. And he wore a brown trilby which was not something you saw very often. She noticed his fingernails were very clean and she flexed her own acrylic fake glue on nails in appreciation of his good standard of hand hygiene. "Scuse me?' she almost whispered, afraid that she might cause offence. The man did not move. "Scuse me!' she said louder, trying to be more confident. He stirred a little. 'I wondered if you'd fallen asleep or something. Perhaps you're interested in buying our black leather plush suite with stylish white leather trim? It's extremely comfortable as I'm sure you've noticed. Sort of holds you like a big hand and moulds to your contours. I'd be happy to help you with the sale or to answer any questions you might have.' She waited.

The man was stirring, rocking himself into consciousness it looked like. He turned very slowly to look at her. The trilby obscured his eyes but she knew he was taking her in. She lost confidence. 'It's just you've been sat in the display window for almost half an hour now and I wondered if you might have fallen asleep or something. Or if you don't feel well?'

The man removed the hat from his head in a polite way and held it in his hands. He did not move from the sofa as he spoke. 'I am not ill thank you very much for asking,' he said, 'but no, I do not feel well at all.'

Tiffany couldn't make out the meaning of this conundrum. 'I'm sorry,' she offered, 'but I don't think I follow your meaning exactly.'

'Where are you from?' he asked.

'Peckham,' she said.

'I'm from Jamaica, long time past.'

'Right,' she said, unsure of what to say really.

'Jamaica's a land of great beauty did you know that?' he asked.

'I always thought that was where they film the Bounty advert, but I didn't know for sure,' she offered.

'I think it might be,' he said nodding sadly. 'How old are you?' he asked, 'if that is not too impertinent a question to ask a young lady?'

He was so old fashioned, gallant she thought. 'Sixteen', she answered without hesitation.

'Sweeeeet sixteen, ' he crooned, ' when I was sixteen I ran along the beaches of Negril and swam like a fish in the sea. Seven miles of white sand beach and water as warm as your heart,' he said. He chuckled to himself lightly and she longed to ask what he was remembering but did not want to intrude on his private thoughts.

'Peckham's got a bit of green but it can be warm in a different way, if you know it,' she said.

'A philosopher!' he said. 'Are you a philosopher?'

'I don't think so', she answered, 'but I think for myself.'

'Good, good. That's all we have in the end,' he said tapping the side of his head, 'make your choices wisely young woman and you will regret nothing.'

He said nothing for a few minutes and Tiffany was starting to feel conspicuous standing by the door, at the window display, talking to this strange man. 'Would you like to buy that suite? There's a discount this month and no interest credit for three years, if you'd like it,' she said. He stroked the plump leather beside him in a lost sort of way. 'Why are you so sad?' she asked without thinking. He looked sharply at her and she realised she'd overstepped the mark. 'Sorry,' she said, 'being nosy.'

'It is very pleasing to be asked to share one's state of mind. To be given an observation on one's emotional state by a stranger confirms that we can all speak to each other if we really want to. I would like to answer your question, if you have the time?' Tiffany was intrigued. She looked back at the floor and saw that her colleagues were still busy, so she stepped up into the window display and sat opposite the old man on the matching leather chair. It squeaked as she eased herself down.

'I came here from the beautiful island of Jamaica in 1965. Of course I didn't think it beautiful then or I would never have left it. That is an old man's romanticism for what could have been. I met a glorious woman called Yvonne while working on the buses in central London. She was from Barbados and carried the strength of the sun in her arms. We had two sons. We were not well off at all and we would dream of our fantasy home with a real fire place and a broad, expensive, deep leather sofa. All the luxuries of life. But disappointments lead a man to make choices that are not always good for his family.' He regarded this young woman before him and years of his life flashed through his mind like a video fast-forwarding to the correct point. He saw his endless job applications as a master carpenter rejected within days. He was never to build wardrobes, design sideboards, shape tables, carve dining chairs ever again. A passionate talent wasted by lack of opportunity. It became an all-consuming frustration because of his second class citizenship in this foreign land. He'd been called Blackie on the buses and after the first couple of fights and the possibility of redundancy, he'd allowed it, acknowledged it. Given in. He said none of this to Tiffany. This was history he thought, why spread it's shadow across today.

'I drank,' he said. 'I drank a lot. All the extra money we had I would drink because it made me feel better about myself. The more I drank the less sober I was and I could hide away from disappointing myself. I never once struck my boys or my wife but I didn't need to. I betrayed them in every other way. She threw me out after trying to cope with my immaturity after fifteen long years. She put her time in. She tried hard, I see that now. I sobered up. I drank again. It's been a lonely road. Now I am almost sixty but I'm sober. And today my eldest son got married to the most lovely Welsh woman with a lilting voice and a sunshine smile. And I saw my wife after, oh I don't know, three years, and she broke my heart with how beautiful and strong she is. We were able to talk and be dignified. It was a milestone. We talked of our foolish dreams of a house with a real fire and a broad, expensive, deep leather sofa. Then she went home with all her friends and I was going home when I saw this in your window. It is a beautiful thing.'

'Will you buy it for her?' asked Tiffany hopefully. 'It's very good value'.

He sighed a heavy sigh. 'No, I don't have the money any more and she wouldn't accept it after all this time. Bad choices. But I wanted to sit here and imagine what it could have been. If I had chosen differently.' He eased himself off the chair and stepped down out of the window display. Tiffany followed behind him. He put his hat on his head and tipped it slightly to her as he walked out of the door. 'Thank you for listening to an old man's regrets, young lady. I wish you great joy and good choices and a broad, expensive, deep leather sofa of your own.'

He was gone. Tiffany turned back to the display. She stepped up into the window and sat for a few moments where the man had sat, contemplating her philosophies.

Sky Light
Peter Bromley

We sang hymns and drank beer straight from the bottle the day the harmonium arrived. Its dead weight had made us sweat and graze our knuckles on the wall of the stairwell as we carried it up the four flights of stairs to her tenement flat. But Sheila had rewarded us with the beer.

'Why a harmonium?'

'I love them,' she says.

'...but why?'

'I love the sound. It's beautiful'

..and later she picks out some hymns. *Rock of Ages* and *The day Thou gavest Lord is ended*. Then she tells us that the devil has all the best tunes and plays a mazurka but ends with *Abide with Me* to lead us in our singing. Our noise fills the room, sharp-edged against the reedy softness of the harmonium notes. The singing and the tune float out of the skylight of her flat roof into the night. For the rest of the evening we drink her beer until we fall asleep where we are. When we awake, Sheila has gone to work, so we spend the morning hanging around in her flat. We play her albums, make breakfast and do a bit of tidying up. She lives on her own, has kids to bring up and works hard. We all like to help.

Before we leave, I open the skylight to let in some air. I stand with my head out of the window and look out across the rooves, open spaces then the tree tops to where the distant hills are blue and green in the clear sky. I turn around from the opening and look back around Sheila's small living room. From the kitchen comes the noise of my friends fooling around. There is a potted plant on the ledge above her fireplace, with a bright crimson flower floating like a sun in the horizons of her flat.

Sheila has pinned a note to the inside of the door to remind us to lock the door as we leave. She has been burgled before and she is very wary. We tell her she should move, but she asks 'Where to?'

My friend at school who was in my class, Gregor, told me that there was an orchard at the end of town, just beyond the last houses, where the farms began to spread out, which we could get into. He told me of the fruit trees, particularly the apple trees, with fruit as big as he's ever seen.

'Where ?'

'I've been there,' he says

'When?'

'Lots of times.'

'On your own?'

'Mostly.'

He tells me we should go there and I say yes, but hope he will forget about it. And I say no more for several days. But he does not forget and he pulls me into his plans to go back to the orchard when the apples are ripe. He says that we will need to bunk off school because if we go at the weekend there will be too many people around. So we have to think of an excuse to get off school. Already, I am worried about it. So I convince him we could do it after school, and we settle for that.

Next time we meet, he takes me to an empty house on our estate. It has been boarded up by the Council but he says he knows a way in. We climb over the rubbish at the side of the house to get to the back door, but it is nailed shut.

'You used to be able to get in,' he says.

'There's no way in.' I turn to go.

'There usually is.' But he too turns away.

So we go to his house, which is a flat in a new high-rise block. He shares a bedroom with his brother, but he is not there. So we sit and stare out of his window at the houses and streets below, and think of when we can go to get the apples. He tells me there is also a barn that you can get into and you can sleep there in the straw and the farmer will not find you. And there are rabbits you can shoot with your air-gun, but his is broken. And why was the house boarded up again? His brother had told him you could get in through the back door dead easy. It's where his brother and his mates go to drink and smoke. Through the window I watch the people cross the open spaces below us. Some boys from our school are kicking a football around against the lock-up garage doors. I know that there is a sign saying ' No ball games' on the side of the garage. Someone has crossed out the word 'No' so it now says 'Ball games'. Through the window, from down below, I hear the boys singing football songs as they play. Then they chant 'You're going to get your fucking head kicked in'.

When I arrive, Sheila is playing her harmonium. I hear it from the flight of stairs below her front door. It is a soft, breathless sound. As I reach her front door I can hear the sound of her feet moving the pedals to operate the bellows. A gentle rhythmic rocking which cuts through the tempo of the tune. I wait until she has finished before I ring the bell.

'Don't stop.' I say as I go into her room.

'I've been at it for ages.'

'You're good.'

'I'm crap.'

I make us coffee and we talk about our friends. One of them, Fiona, has two teenage children, but she doesn't hear from any of them anymore. She gets to hear about them from people around the city, including Sheila. They turn up in a squat or in a friend's house somewhere. They get into relationships and leave them. Of course she worries. 'They're her kids.' says Sheila. 'I hear about them from time to time.' Then she shows me a few chords on the harmonium and we sit next to each other as she plays the right hand melody and I play the bass left hand. She moves the stops in and out to change the volume and the tone.

'You're a natural,' she says.

'Yeah. Sure.'

'We'll get you onto the right hand soon.'

'I can't do two things at once.'

She tells me that she worries that Fiona's children are on hard drugs, or she wouldn't be surprised if they were. She just wants to know where they are. Fiona has got to stay sane herself, though, and she cannot worry about them all the time, but that's what it feels like. 'That's why I do some of the worrying for her,' says Sheila. As I leave her, she begins to play another tune, and its melody follows me down the flights of stairs, but I imagine it drifting upwards through the skylight. I look up at her window before I walk off down the street.

Gregor has to stay in. His mum has told him he cannot go out. He went to the house again to try to get in, but it was still boarded up. The police caught him trying to kick open the door along with his brother, and took them to the station to be cautioned. His mum opens the door when I knock. She looks at me as if she wants to hit me. I am scared of her. Gregor says she's OK though.

'He's in his room.'

'Thanks.'

'He can't go out.'

'No.'

'He's a little shit,' she says.

My mum is a Catholic. She has family in Ireland, so she says. She goes to Mass every week, but the rest of us don't. Sometimes, though, she makes us go. Me and Sarah have to walk with her to the big ugly church. She says that the Protestants took all of the pretty churches off us years ago and left us with nothing, so we had to build the new ones. I don't believe in God, I don't see the point. The church is big and ugly like nothing I have ever seen. It is worse than Gregor's tower block, and it is always empty except for a few of my Mum's friends.

There are words that I do not understand, too. Like Emmanuel, and Hosannah. Words that I might understand if I went more, but that just stop me understanding. Words I cannot get past. Words like immaculate and words in Latin. At Christmas there are even more, like magi and epiphany. The words sound nice, but mean nothing. The service is so long, but mum glares at us if we start to talk or muck around, so I turn the words around in my head. I repeat them over and over. 'Hosannah, Hosannah, Hosannah in the highest. Hosannah, Hosannah Emmanuel.' They do not make sense. I cannot understand them, so I repeat them like a chant in my head. Epiphany, epiphany, epiphany.

In Gregor's room he tells me about the boarded-up house and the things he has done in there. I hope he has forgotten about the trip to the orchard, so I do not remind him. He tells me instead of smoking and of drinking bottles of cider. His friend sniffs glue and he thinks that his brother's friend might take drugs. I ask if Gregor has ever taken drugs, but he says he has not. I do not know whether he is telling the truth. The boys are playing football again on the concrete square and I ask Gregor if he wants to go and play.

'I can't, can I?'

'Oh no. I forgot'

I do not stay long. I am bored and realise that if I am not doing things with Gregor, we don't say much to each other. He just ends up telling me what he does and more usually what he wants to do and as he talks now, I end up looking out of the window. I shout goodbye to his mother but she does not reply. She is watching the television. Out on the concrete square I look back up at his window. He is still sitting there and I wave. He waves back. I feel sorry for Gregor, but I cannot really understand why. He is so distant, framed in the window high up in the tower block. He looks down at the square below his window, where I am standing and where the boys are playing football.

There are a few of us meeting up after work to get a drink and something to eat, and I tell Sheila to come along. She says that she might. When I arrive in the restaurant after work she is there with many of our friends and my work mates. The two groups kind of blend into each other. Most of us are in social work and most of us know each other in some way or other.

Sheila is sitting and laughing with a couple of her female friends so I sit with my colleagues. I am at the end of the table because I am late, but she looks up and gives a little wave. She also imitates playing the harmonium with her hands and laughs some more. Her friend nudges her and I watch Sheila turn to her and, I imagine, explain what she is doing. We are the biggest group in the place, and our noise drowns out the rest of the music and conversation in the room. It is fairly dark and claustrophobic. We are in a basement with a low barrel vault ceiling. It is just brick that has been painted over. My colleagues talk about office politics and I join in as best I can. Two of the people in 'Personnel' are having an affair, it seems. I cannot picture either of them, but I go along with it until, eventually, it feels as if I do know them.

'They should know better,' says Malcolm.

'Especially being in Personnel'

'Sex knows no boundaries.'

They then ask me, because I am single, who I fancy in the office. The people around us have joined in the conversation so they are egging me on to answer.

'I've never really thought about it' I say.

'Sure you have'

'What about Becky here' says Malcolm, pointing to one of the women.

'She's good for a shag' and they all laugh. They laugh so loud that the rest of the table turns round to look at us. Even the woman laughs, after she has let out a short scream at Malcolm.

'He says he wants to shag Becky,' says Malcolm to the rest of the table, pointing at me. I just smile as they all look on. Sheila raises her eyebrows in mock surprise, and then pours herself and her friends another glass of wine. I too reach for a bottle and pour a large glassful.

Outside Gregor's block of flats, the boys playing football are shouting and swearing at each other. Some are wearing proper football kit. My mother cannot afford it, so I just do without. I'm not really bothered. As the boys play, one of them kicks the ball so hard it bounces against the garage doors and rebounds towards where I am walking. I was hoping that they would not notice me, but the ball rolls straight towards me. I stop it with my foot, and it bobbles slightly. Then it keeps rolling slowly down the hill. I want to kick it back, but cannot get properly behind it because it has not stopped moving, so I keep shuffling to try to get in a better position. Eventually one of the boys shouts out.

'Kick it you wanker.'

So I kick it as best I can, and it rolls pathetically towards them.

'You big fucking Jessie,' shouts out the boy and they all laugh. I walk on, and just before I turn off towards my house, I look back. The boys have carried on playing football, and Gregor is still at the window. I wave again, but he must be watching the game, as he does not wave back.

'So, you want to shag Becky,' says Sheila.

'That's not what I said.'

'Sure' and she opens the door fully with a smile.

I go in.

She tells me that she has had some news about Fiona's children and she is just on her way to try to get in touch with them. She has an address on one of the large council-built estates at the edge of town. She has work's car to get her there. I offer to go with her.

'It might not be pretty,' she says.

'I'll cope.'

'Where are your kids?'

'They're at their dad's.'

The car is a small Ford, with the words 'Social Services' written on it, and is bright yellow.

'Not much chance of sneaking up in this, then.' I say

We are just going to look at the flat at the address we have, she tells me, and that officially we cannot do anything as they are both over sixteen, but Fiona wants to make sure they are alright. She has even considered registering them as missing persons but then they might just leave the city.

'She doesn't know what to do.'

'I'm not sure I would, either,' I say.

The journey to the housing estate is slow. It is the after-work rush-hour and the roads are crowded, firstly with cars then, as we get out into the housing schemes, more and more buses. Here the streets are emptier. It has taken nearly an hour to travel the relatively short distance and the difference between here and the city centre is vast. I had forgotten just how these estates felt. Not since I used to visit Gregor have I really been back to places like this. We look at the long lists of street names at the entrance to each part of the estate. Some road leading to another street leading to 'Something Way'. They are named after people, after other towns, after long gone features. 'Croft Road' or 'Orchard Place'. Blocks of flats named after foreign politicians. We turn round in a bus turning-circle, which is full of broken glass, and on our way back, we see the name of the street we are looking for.

'Into the valley of death,' says Sheila.

'What?'

'It's a poem,' she says.

There are two other cars in the parking area, and the rest is just empty. In one corner are the remains of a litter bin that has been burned. We get out and head towards the block of flats. The lift does not work so we walk the seven floors to the floor we want. I am genuinely worried, but Sheila seems relaxed as she knocks on the door.

'Who is it?' The voice is faint. The woman sounds drunk.

'It's Sheila McVeigh.'

'Who the fuck are you?'

'I've come to see Fiona Gibson's daughters.'

'Well they're not fucking here.'

We wait and Sheila speaks again. This time, after a short while, the person comes to the door, and opens it slowly and only partly. The woman inside is only about sixteen. She is small and slight, skinny almost. It is one of Fiona's daughters. She is high on something. She and Sheila talk on the doorstep for a short while and I look over the balcony onto the ground below. I can see the car, and some lock-up garages. There is a sign, saying no ball games. Beyond the houses and the tower blocks, the city centre is visible. The big Victorian and Georgian buildings massed together, crowding in towards the main square. Beyond those are the streets of tenements and houses where Sheila and I live. And Sheila's skylight that lets the harmonium notes out into the night.

Sheila calls me. We are going into the flat. It smells of piss and is a complete mess. The mattresses are on the floor and the sheets are filthy. There is no furniture. A small CD player is in the corner, with a few CDs scattered around the room. Fiona's daughter sits on the mattress with her knees drawn up to her chest and her back to the wall as Sheila gently asks her how she is and does she want anything.

Gregor's mother opens the door.

'He still can't come out, you know.'

'Yes, I know.'

Her front room is clean and tidy. She has a model lighthouse on the fireplace, and a picture of Gregor in his school uniform. The walls are bare, except for a picture of Christ on the wall between the windows and a blue plate on the wall next to Gregor's bedroom door. In Gregor's room he is sitting on his bed. We talk about the boarded up house and his brother. His brother was caught doing drugs and has to go to court. Gregor's mum is really mad, but he also tells me she cries a lot. Then I suddenly say to Gregor, for no reason that I can think of,

'I am going to go to that orchard.'

'When?' he says.

'Tomorrow. Before we go back to school.'

'Wait for me. Until my mum lets me out.'

'No. I can't.'

And I sit on his bed and half look out of the window and half listen to him. He talks of how he will come with me to the orchard when he can and how we can break into the boarded-up house and drink some lager. In the Christmas holidays we will bunk off the school concerts and go into the city centre. We shouldn't be wasting our time singing carols, he says. It is as if my mentioning the orchard has opened his eyes again to things outside his room. His mum gets worse at Christmas, he says. She goes all religious and she makes him go to church nearly everyday for a week. And all those carols and songs.

'Hosannah, Hosannah, Hosannah,' I say

'Yeah, and Emmanuel.'

'..and Magi, and In excelsis Deo.'

'…and epiphany.'

'Yeah. Epiphany.'

The silence rushes in after our shouting of the strange words and the laughter. Soon after this I leave, but before I do I ask Gregor which bus to catch to get to the orchard.

'They're the biggest apples ever.' he says as I go. Down on the concrete square, I look up again at his window, and he is not there. The boys are not playing football.

Back near Sheila's car, I look up at the windows of the block of flats. I am not sure which one we have just been in. Sheila tells me that it is no use looking, as Fiona's daughter will be inside the flat on her mobile phone, the one she gets given to do the deals on, arranging to move to another flat. She will be telling her older sister that they have been found. That is not what they wanted. But she had also promised to get in touch with Fiona, just to speak to her.

'Even if she doesn't, at least I can tell Fiona they are alive!'

'You were brilliant up there,' I say

'Just doing my job, sir,' she says in a mock American accent.

I see a group of youngsters standing near to the car as we leave the building. The ground floor flats are boarded up, with thick graffiti on the wooden panels.

On our way out of the estate we take a wrong turning and end up heading away from the city, out up towards the hills that ring that edge of the built-up area. The pylons begin to spread out, marching ankle deep in mud across the ploughed fields towards the horizon. The houses and blocks of flats stop abruptly as we cross the bridge over the ring road.

'I'm lost,' says Sheila.

'Long-term or short-term'

She continues up the road to look for a turning place. Behind us, the tower blocks are as pale as dead elms against the evening sky. We eventually find a tuning place, in a lane about a mile or so up the hill. The landscape around me looks vaguely familiar, but then perhaps I have just seen so many places on the urban fringe, they all blend into one. There is a lane, with a couple of houses at each corner. A woman is at the kitchen window in one of the houses, standing at the sink looking out onto the side road. A man is walking his dog away from us along the lane. A sprinkler is going on someone's lawn. These small collisions in our lives make me think even more that I know the place, that I even know these people, but it is probably because it is just familiar from the many situations like it that I have seen. But I still ask Sheila to drive further up the lane. Just in case.

'There's a farm at the end of this lane,' I say

'There always is.'

'No. I've been here before.'

'Long-term or short-term'

We pass the man with the dog. He watches us go past as he stands in the verge out of our way. Sheila waves a 'thank you ' to him as we pass. He does not respond. We drive along the lane, running parallel to the edge of the city and the ring road, until eventually we arrive at a farm which has buildings on both sides of the road. In a yard, a worker is moving large cylindrical straw bales with a tractor and fork lift attachment. He too watches us pass. I had forgotten about the colour and wording on the van. We go through the farm buildings and again the lane is lined with scrappy hedges.

'Stop here,' I shout as we pass a gate.

I get out and Sheila stands next to me looking over the gate, up the hill away from the city.

'It might be the place,' I say.

'What place?'

'Somewhere I came when I was young.'

We look at the hill and follow its slope up towards the horizon.

From the bus, I walk up the road away from the city and then turn down a lane, as Gregor had told me. He had wanted to come with me and promised to take me to the boarded-up house with him if I did wait. I came on my own, though. The lane worries me. It is like nowhere that I am used to walking. What if someone sees me? What if they ask what I am doing? I do see a farm, and beyond it the fields and hedges. But I do not see an orchard.

I walk past the farm house and the out-buildings and on the other side of the farm a high wall runs along the road-side. There is still no orchard. I begin to believe that there is not one, or I have got the wrong place altogether. I walk on a bit further, but then after I have passed the farm and turned a corner out of view, I stop.

'There is no bloody orchard.' I think.

So I climb over a gate and follow a track away from the road, down the hill towards the city's edge. And I see a tree in the corner of the field that has low branches and a good flat top. I will climb it. It is easy climbing, with strong branches and firm footholds. For a short while I disappear into the greenery and leaves. I cannot see anything, but I can see ahead of me the light coming through the crown and so keep climbing. Gradually the leaves begin to thin out and then my head emerges from the top of the tree and I can see all around me. I find a good point to sit and I gaze out over the fields. I can see the farm, I can see the road I came along and, in the other direction, I can see the city. I can see Gregor's tower block and just beyond that the area that I live in. I can see it all clearly from here.

'Let's go,' I say to Sheila.

'I didn't want to stop.'

'I just thought...' I say.

Back in the car we head back towards the city. In the evening sunlight it glows deep red.

'It's a really beautiful city,' I say.

'I love it.'

'Do you fancy a drink...something to eat?'

'Why, who is going out?'

'No-one...just us I mean.'

She is silent for a short moment. Then she says,

'Yes...I do. That would be great. That would be really, really great.'

211

February Nights
Jane Scargill

You wake again and there's this weight pressing on your gut telling you you are dying for a pee, but you cannot move yourself to get out of bed for one.

Ray hasn't called yet. He won't call this week after what he's found out, perhaps he'll never call, but you know he's not up to receiving calls without shouting at you just now.

These things always happen in February. So much for summer heat and riots. In your books, it's this time when people really lose it: their tempers, relationships or lives. It's now they decide they've really had enough, worn out like frost-strangled flowers. How many times have you lost a job in February or split up, or what about Dave, cancer finally finishing him off at that time of year, and all the elderly people who've finally had it then?

So you lie back, hoping to drift back to sleep when there's a knock at the door. You try to pretend it hasn't happened, like the strong desire to pee, but the knocking comes again, harder that before.

You switch on the lamp and see it is half past two in the morning. You get up and put on your big jumper and go out into the hallway. You decide it's wiser to go for a pee first.

Your stomach is hard with the effort of holding it in and it takes some deep breathing before it relents. Meanwhile, the banging on the door gets louder.

You flush and walk downstairs.

'Who is it?' you shout.

'It's a neighbour and I want to know whose that white car is parked outside our house.'

'I don't know,' you tell him.

'Is it yours?'

'No, it isn't mine. I don't drive. Will you please go away. You gave me the fright of my life.'

'Okay, cool.' His footsteps fade.

You are left alone again in the empty house in the small hours, trying to get to and remain asleep for the rest of the night. You would like to sleep now and wake up about June to find the trouble between you and Ray is over and your boss isn't on to you about some things that have happened at work recently.

You go back upstairs. Your bedroom is large and white with insomnia. It shines on everything you've done wrong and everything that's gone wrong.

There's to be no sleeping here.

You turn and walk downstairs. In the kitchen, you switch on the kettle and then you jump because you think there's someone in the back garden looking in at you.

You back towards the kitchen door and realise it's a street lamp through the hedge.

The house is cold. You put the heating on despite the fact you can't afford it, and a coat on over your jumper.

Ray might be in bed by now. You wonder if he's sleeping. Ray can no more be reached than someone on Pluto. He will be surrounded by his aura of white-cold fury, which no one can penetrate. It will fuel him to finish the accounts and deliver the food to work, and still have time to go to the all-night supermarket. He will wheel round the trolley, looking at no one, putting in staple food: bread, milk, corned beef, coleslaw, cheese.

Last summer, you had these things together on picnics, but with green salad instead of corned beef. They seemed a little less basic in the sun, with the dark green deck chairs he'd got from the supermarket, for when neither of you fancied the ground.

Ray gets into bed on auto-pilot and his anger burns white acid into his room. If you rang him, his voice would be clipped and taut and would hurl you off the phone.

So you stay on your own in the house, because basically you are on your own, as much as Ray is with his family dispersed and indifferent to him. Then you think, as much as Dave was in his final days when he kept losing consciousness, even though there were nurses and doctors coming in and out, even though your brother was sitting beside him.

You remember the day Dave died, when you were going to meet Ray in the big building where he'd been to a meeting. You went through a wooden door and it slammed shut behind you. Through a large glass door, you could see a conservatory with white walls. Light was shining through a window.

There were people walking around, so you knocked. But they just walked past you, some very near. Outside, rain was banging on the wooden door. You tried to open it, but couldn't. The place smelled of dampened wood and the draught made you shiver. You continued knocking intermittently for twenty minutes. Then you tried the outer door again. Tugging at the latch, you managed to get it open. The rain had stopped. A voice called 'you're here then, are you?'

You turned to see Ray standing behind you, a grin radiating from his face.

That night, you visited your mother, who told you Dave had died between ten and ten thirty, the time you had been stuck behind the glass door.

Ray's grin has gone and he will not be beaming at you for some time, if ever. Dave has gone. The world will not come back tonight except in the shape of enemies and terrifying thoughts.

Three a.m. This is when your chickens come home to roost.

You're off work at the moment and you realise you might not have a job when you get back.

Of course, you've been reading up about rights and employment tribunals, but you're not sure how to argue this one. You're not sure who's right or who's wrong or to what degree. But you know these things always happen in February.

The word has that sound to it: sharp, harsh, like someone spitting quickly.

This has been building up for a while, though. And now you can see your boss's face and hear her words when you lie down, spat out like acid, like February.

All right, at this time the first snowdrops are supposed to come out, a sign of hope that spring is on the way. Some people only hate January. But snowdrops get frozen by frost before March is out. This month trails on, leaving its mark until May.

You search for incidents to match the words in the letters: 'disrepute' 'conduct having a negative effect on others' 'gross misconduct'. But when you try to think, the words clash like symbols out of sync and you feel a breath of panic rise in your chest, approaching a scream.

You thought you were doing all right. But if you were no good at this after all, what will you be good at?

The future looms, a huge, white void.

February changes things forever. White is the colour of innocence. February shows you you will never be that again. Ray's unspoken accusations swirl in your head.

Ray would have had you in a white wedding dress: innocence, purity, fidelity; 'to have and to hold, in sickness and in health, til death us do part.

You have never fancied marriage. Maybe deep down you know feelings can change like the seasons, so there's no point in making such a commitment. Ray's the one from a broken family and you are not. He clings to these uncertain certainties.

You were never sure you wanted to be had or be held, not on a permanent basis. Now you know what it's like to feel alone, the way Ray's always felt. This alone time is no time. You can not picture the frost-white of morning breaking it.

In the summer, when everything was green and flush-pink, you betrayed Ray. Ray, shut in his dark-brown secrecy had opened up and let you in. He had told you things he'd never told other people. You had held them in during winter and spring. Then in summer, you had spilled them out to Anna, like a sunflower shedding seeds.

One night, in the pub, you told her about his family dispersing and the problems with his breath and the woman he split up with fifteen years ago, who he can't bear to speak to. Ray's insecurities slopped out onto the pub table as you sipped Guinness. Then your own about how you liked it when his voice was very quiet, but the way he picked at his nails made you wince. That you didn't feel right enough about him to take it further, but you couldn't seem to finish it, and you weren't sure why. That you fantasised about having sex with one of his friends.

You told her how he really felt about his job.

Now it's February and Ray has found out. Anna let it slip to Gill, who told her partner, Andrew, who works with Ray.

Ray sat alone in the armchair last Tuesday, staring straight ahead. He said 'I've been talking to Andrew.'

You asked what they'd been talking about.

Ray put his cup down on the coffee table. 'You fucking cow,' he said.

Then he left. The door echoed.

Keeping things to yourself is like lying under a shroud of snow. You want it to melt, and to share things, not just be a couple ensconsed in smothering secrecy.

You don't want to be alone either, not for too long.

The man next door has snowdrops in his garden. He tends them well. He says 'hello' when you meet occasionally and is normally O.K. with you. Except when there is a car outside. Then he participates in the car wars like the rest of the neighbours. His wrinkled face hardens. He starts shouting.

A man was attacked because his car was parked in the wrong place. Two weeks in hospital. He returned wrapped in bandages, an improbable snowman.

You sit at the kitchen table, drinking another cup of tea, even though you don't want it, and a picture of Dave and your brother comes into your head. They are sitting at your mother's kitchen table, both aged seven, cutting out paper snowflakes. You do some yourself and then it's time to go out to Girl Guides. You are eleven and have just graduated from Brownies. 'Always do your best,' 'think of others,' that kind of thing. You thought you had. You always seem to be trying to. But it doesn't work out right. Your boss thinks you're unemployable. Ray thinks you're an inconsiderate cow.

The kitchen table is white with paper snowflakes, as you leave for Guides, aged eleven, full of ideas about doing your best, about becoming a doctor, or a teacher, or a mathematician.

Dave didn't get to adulthood. When he reached fifteen his white blood cells began to propagate and attack the red ones. An early sign was when he came on a family trip to Scarborough. Dave, large built, muscular at fifteen, fell asleep in the car. When he woke, he said he ached all over. Your mind flashed back to the record of him having a chest X-ray you'd seen while working over the summer as a hospital cleaner.

Then, he didn't come to the house for ages. There were reports of chemotherapy, anaemia. They were trying to find a bone marrow match. He turned up one day completely bald.

Dave died in mid-February, one and a half years after his leukaemia was diagnosed. The church was full. The flowers on his coffin were red and yellow and blue and green, significant for the absence of white.

Outside, the air is death-white.

'In sickness and in health.' Ray injured his back again a month ago, had hardly moved. His doctor said stress hadn't helped. You heard about this from Anna.

You wondered if you should go to him. You weren't sure he'd want that. You had things to do. Finally, you left a card and some sweets with his landlord.

Now you are sick, sick-note sick, sick of work, of winter, of February. Ray will not come near you.

''Til death us do part?' Life is parting you. Might as well forget the wedding dress.

You manage to comb over some memories: of the man with the big face who comes in to the library. The way he plants this face opposite yours. How you feel this pressure in the back of your neck when you see him, which you've identified as hatred. How your fist clenches round the stamp when you jab the date on the Westerns he gets out, after he has hovered by the section for half an hour.

There's the kid, who comes in with its mother, who screeches and the screeches feel like a knife through your head.

There's your supervisor, Emily, with the cold grey eyes, which seem to be constantly watching you. Her voice is taut and jarring. Your ears feel like they're stretching to absorb the sound.

You don't see Audrey, the boss, much. When you do, you notice the maroon skirt suit she often wears, the curly hair, piled on the top of her head, the smell of Eau de Cologne. She has rarely said anything critical to you, but then she has rarely said anything.

There have been the shortened break times, the new targets, things you're supposed to say to 'customers' in a certain way, which you can't quite get the hang of. You're not sure if they've come from Emily or Audrey, or someone higher.

Maybe there have been off-hand words, not much you can think of. You know the days have come to feel like a pressure vacuum of white heat.

Anna said she's heard Ray is having trouble at work at well.

You close your eyes and behind them Ray's face blanches with fury, his eyes red with anger-pain. He is jabbing a finger at you. It mingles with your boss's face, now pounding into yours, her expression telling you to go.

You go to your room and take out one of the hospital white pills the doctor has given you. You use them sparingly because she hasn't given you many. 'You need to be able to sort things out for yourself. It's not that bad, you know,' she beamed. You glared at her dark blue mini-skirt, crease-free, her dark orange jumper, presumably designed to cheer patients up.

You wait for the world to go dreamy and it seems like you're waiting a long time. The house is heated up and could lull you into sleep. Spring will be here soon and flowers will grow in white and blue and yellow. This time will pass.

You close your eyes and pictures come in front of them of snowdrops and paper snowflakes and pretty ice crystals.

Your body jerks. Someone is banging on the door.

Next Stop Hope

Introduction
Ian Daley

Next Stop Hope is a series of commissioned pieces, and is a timely re-gathering of the writers who regularly graced the pages of route issues one through to thirteen. Up until this point, the route series has been issued in newspaper form. The premise has always been a simple one, to create a platform for new writers, drawn together from different parts of the social spectrum with a selection policy that often trod further into the margins of acceptability than comparative publications. Then, place that work together in one publication and reflect on what emerges.

Route issues one to thirteen were published from February 2000 to January 2002, chronicling an unexpurgated state-of-mind that spanned the millennium to September 11th and its immediate aftermath. The flavour of those issues was characterised by the contributions of the writers gathered here. One year on, each were commissioned to submit new work, no strings attached, by a set-time towards the end of 2002. What follows, in the main, is what was sent in.

Next Stop Hope is a borrowed title, and one that was declared independent of any prior consultation with its content. It follows that the title's relevance is best measured in juxtaposition to the body of work that has become it. A piece of writing is only as good as its reading. The writing is done and the onus is now upon you. Read well.

The Sculpture of Gorian Drey and the Ensuing Chronicles of Vomit

Val Cale

For Oscar Wilde's foreskin
Rot In Peace

This is a story that starts with the creative cultivation of a small sticky snot, arrives reluctantly at the dining table of my deranged parents, crosses the Atlantic in a winged tin can, buses itself to Tijuana and culminates in an extraordinary session of debauchery unlike any I've had before. It involves a road trip I took from New York to the wastelands of Mexico with a wacky Scottish artist called Gorian and a blow-up doll with an 'inviting anus' who we met along the way. The theme of the piece, as you've probably worked out, is, *chucking your ring up* and anything else that happened which doesn't directly pertain to puking has been omitted.

The world can be a sick place, but this tale isn't about the sickness of the world, this is simply about a few things that could make you throw up. It's a competitive interactive piece that requires the reader to have two things for optimum effect, a photograph of George W. Bush and a full stomach. Pin the photo on the wall close to your person and if what you are about to read makes you heave, heave on George, let the vomit dry and mail me the final product. If you haven't eaten and don't feel sick, find a dog turd, toast it for a few minutes, garnish it with offal or lime-scale from your toilet bowl rim, roll it into a ball and suck on it. If that doesn't make you puke...you're already up to your inverted asshole in serious shit. The best entry will receive all the other entries and a monthly supply of multiracial orifice debris from exotic and benignly diseased areas around the globe. If you're so sick that you don't chuck up, feel free to shit on his face or squirt anything you like on his forehead and there'll be a runner-up prize for the best choco-coated or fluid-stained Bush.

230

We all know people who do strange things; people who have odd outlandish obsessions, people who collect toenail clippings and bum fluff balls and store them in jars, people who are downright spooky and absorbed in the very pith of their throbbing madness...people with *peculiarities*. I've met a lot of crazed individuals on my travels over the years but I've never met anyone quite like the guy I am about to tell you about here. My Glaswegian friend Gorian Drey Campbell studied fine art and sculpture at the Crawford College of Art in Cork City, Ireland. To get straight to the point, he was an acid-eating, mushroom-champing, whiskey-guzzling, red-bearded artistic genius. A wild Scottish bastard with scraggy locks of fiery hair, a well-defined beer gut and glass-green eyes studded with the tiniest slivers of hazel. He lived to create and took the concept of his art further than any other artist I have ever seen or heard of. He eventually took it to prison, or rather that is where it eventually took him, and that is where it left him, although in his esteemed madness he never fully understood why...

Gorian had a small studio next to a unisex toilet on the second floor of the college overlooking the pea-green river Lee and one day while he was sitting on the crapper in the cubicle pondering the delicate workings of his final year assignment, noticed that somebody had begun to write their initials on the toilet wall in...of all things...*snot*. It looked really good too, all the colours of influenza and thrush mixed with all the consistencies from dribbling diarrhoea to a hot flush. Snot of all shapes and sizes, bloody and caked, visceral and oily, sticky and stale. Snot from good days and bad, sad days and glad, sick days, healthy days, hungover days, sober days, stoned days and days when you had nothing better to do than sit on the holy bowl and revolve your index finger around your snout. You could tell the health of the nasal miner from the pickings on any given day. There was green snot, red snot, black, brown, yellow and all sorts of mustard-coloured snot. A grimy kaleidoscopic collection of gunky nose droppings pasted to a wall, depicting half-constructed letters, all in the name of *art*.

Gorian was so impressed with what he saw that he started a Snot-Art installation in his own bathroom that evening and invited his dwindling friends to contribute with their own mucus, nail clippings, pubic hairs, toe jam, skin flakes, dingleberries, bum fluff, nail dirt, boil jam, scabies scum, cyst juice, throat phlegm, genital smatterings or anything else that naturally left their bodies. Soon he had the makings of a surreal landscape constructed from discarded body products on the wall of his bog...and very few friends but me.

For four months he splattered his crazed creation with gizzum and snot and anything else he could release until his girlfriend Suzy told him that she'd leave him if he didn't dispose of it and get his act together. In an attempt to save his relationship he painstakingly salvaged what he could from the wall, put it in a plastic container and deposited the lot behind a bag of dried cranberries at the back of the fridge. This wasn't the greatest idea Gorian ever had though because Suzy unwittingly sprinkled some of the mess on her cereal one morning, threw up and left. The last trace of her was a pile of puke, a toppled bowl of muesli on the sofa, a note saying *You're a sick bastard Gorian, you need help!* and the remnants of a Tupperware of salvaged Snot Art humming beneath a trio of mesmerised flies on the kitchen floor of his filthy unfurnished flat.

The break-up of the relationship devastated Gorian. Suzy had been one of the few remaining links he'd had with 'reality' and after her departure he sank sadly to the lowest point of his life. The great artist was now reduced to a man focused on little else but picking his nose. His time at college was coming to an end and he had an important assignment to produce a sculpture for his final college exhibition. The piece was to be a 'multi-media...self-portrait...experimental work of sculpture...depicting the relationship between the artist and the materials used by the artist to convey an image of himself.' Gorian had an artistic brainwave and soon his snot-collecting hobby found new faith and converted to a serious compulsion. He decided to keep it up until he had made a life-size bust of himself from body gunk, and, to make up for the time and snot he had lost due to his ex-girlfriend's erratic behaviour, started to use just about every other body juice he could get his hands on; ear wax, anal excavations, fingernail dirt, peeling scalp, dried skin, hair follicles, piss, shit, blood, sebum and especially...... scabs.

Gorian Drey Campbell developed a fascination and what could only be called a freaky fetish for scabs. He'd wait for them until they were about to fall off and prematurely pick them from his body like a dedicated philatelist peeling a rare collector's stamp from an ancient envelope. He got so carried away that he soon had a miniature bust of himself constructed solely from his own snot and congealed juices. His passion for scabs was unholy, uncompromising and wholly unhealthy. He'd wait for the congealing blood to become infected and turn strange shades of yellowish gangrene green like the pus dogs often accumulate in their eyes and are unable to lick out. He had an infatuation for the beauty and esoteric qualities of his scabs. He wanted them to complete the face of the sculpture, to show the pain of the true artist in his work, to create art from the most developed artistic creation God had devised. To create an image of himself from *himself* and he became so engrossed in his obsession that the mad cunt actually began to mutilate his body to get the necessary materials to stick to his creation. He started to slice himself in places that no one would see and watch the development of his scabs until they turned the colour he desired. Then he'd peel them off carefully, one by one and stick them to his sculpture with semen, snot or any other sticky substance his body would release. The work would reflect the artist in the truest sense imaginable, there would be no paints, no glues, no clays or artificial materials, only the purest components available to man. Gorian was convinced that his work would be a masterpiece, the greatest sculpture since God had created Eve from a spare rib.

As the piece slowly developed he invented strange tools for getting pus, wax, shit and anything else he could find out of his orifices. Clothes hangers were twisted and inserted in private cavities and matchsticks were repeatedly jabbed in his ears, hemorrhoids were milked, cysts serrated, pimples pulverised and blackheads amputated from filthy pores. He left himself susceptible to catching colds so that he'd have more snot to dribble on his art and grew his finger and toenails long thinking they could be used as teeth in the final production. He found colours on his body that were unique and could not be copied. If each human were ultimately different, then so were their scabs...no two were totally alike. In his mind Gorian Campbell was creating the purest form of art. In his meandering blob of grey matter he had reached the stature of genius. He had devised an idea for the most innovative sculpture ever fashioned. The irony of the snotty situation was that the idea had come to him while he was taking a shit on the porcelain bog.

Gorian indulged his creation with every spare second he had and the original singular snot soon snowballed into the beginnings of a creative biological work of art. Unlike other sculptures, this one would not only deal with the surface of the piece but the composition *inside*. The surface of the brain would be made solely of semen and snot, the cerebrum of ear wax, eye pus and phlegm, the cerebellum of ass, toe jam and bum fluff. He wanted to define the different parts of his think-box, the lateral and the linear, the conscious, subconscious and the half-awake. The sculpture would not just be about the physical representation of the outer visage but the make-up of the interior would ultimately dictate the very essence of the final artistic expression. He became so engrossed in his creation that time passed him by unwittingly and one day in a moment of panic he realised that at his current rate of progress it would take him an eternity to complete his masterpiece. In a moment of inspiration he decided to recruit outside help. After all, snot was just *snot,* every last squidgy titbit didn't have to be *his*. He started hanging around hospitals looking for mucus on walls and floors, rummaging through the trash for minute traces of human shedding, going around to public toilets and collecting greenballs from walls. Even once in desperate whiskey delirium, picking up a whore riddled with STDs and genital warts and trying to pick them off and slyly rummage through her cavities while she slept. His daily collections never really amounted to much, a few grams of toilet-wall snot, some Unidentifiable Fragments Of Shit, maybe smatterings of dry phlegm from a window-pane or whatever he could find in the trash. He always found something though, especially snot. It seemed that no matter where you went, people were always picking their snouts, flicking their excavations indiscriminately into the air or depositing them on doors or tables or seats or walls.

No matter where you went, if you knew where to look and you looked carefully, you could find a particle of human snot. It was the one thing nobody had ever invented a vessel for its collection and disposal. It seemed that humans had unknowingly given themselves free rein to deposit their mucus wherever they wanted, gradually, unconsciously marking their territory with little sticky green nose balls like animals staking their territory with scratches and piss. The collection grew slowly until Gorian had another moment of wild inspiration and started to leave messages in bathrooms all over the city. He'd draw a rectangular box on a cubicle door, put an arrow underneath and write,

In the name of Unholy Art
Please excavate your nose
and leave your snot here...
Go on, Pick us a Winner!

After all there were six billion people in the world and if each person deposited a mere milligram of mucus daily it would amount to over four million kilos of snot each week. He left his message all over the city, in every bar and restaurant, every night-club, betting office, café and college dorm. Soon the mysterious collector had a reputation around town. Everybody had seen the wacky toilet advertisement but nobody really knew why anyone would be collecting 'snot'. It came in all shapes and sizes and started to turn up everywhere, little boxes of fresh green balls stuck to toilet doors in the unlikeliest of places. Vicars would go to the dentist and end up leaving a bogey on a door. Midwifes would go for a tinkle and wind up doing the same. There was snot from students and bankers, bakers and wankers, businessmen, slaves, kids, old ladies, senators, butchers, cowards and maybe even Indian braves. Soon he had enough mucus to build a green army, but he needed more than just snot. He needed different fluids, dissident sticky substances. He began collecting his knob cheese in a small jar, eating strange stodgy foods to invite constipation and the turds that he eventually squeezed out of his neglected ass would be so viscous that they'd stick straight to his radical work of art. He stopped brushing his teeth and collected the minute amounts of plaque that grew between his yellowing stumps. He stopped washing and let his body fester and stink until he could collect daily offerings of rancid, foul-stinking shit from his navel, toe cracks and butt cave. He even started farting into a balloon and dousing his creation with ass gas! Gorian worked on his sculpture night and day, arranging the array of human disgust, moulding it in his hands until he had a bust of himself almost ready for the final show. The bust of Gorian Drey made *from* Gorian Drey and a little help from anonymous friends who had discarded parts of their bodies on toilet walls around the city.

Finally it was ready...the most disgusting sculpture ever crafted. Months of snot, puke, dribble, drool and fuck knows what, congealed and coagulated together in a clotted curdled mass. A festering orgy of revolting filth solidified together in a gross example of human turpitude. It was bad enough to look at, unbearable to smell, unimaginable to even think about. But that wasn't enough for the mad Scot, NO! That wasn't enough, mere ART was never enough alone! It must make a statement, it must tear down barriers, it must exist as an entity alone, confront *all* the human senses and in the case of Gorian's ART, terrorise every fucker in sight. Gorian would have his cake and eat it too and that is precisely what he did. He sprinkled the completed masterpiece in essence of mint and vanilla and painted it with a fine coat of melted dark chocolate. On the night of the final exhibition, amongst the endless canvas' and carvings, the etchings, collages, murals and multimedia extravaganzas, there stood, on a pus-pink podium, the bust of Gorian Drey......on a tray......in the midst of a pile of paper plates and plastic forks. And it was with a strange and sadistically sick pleasure that the artist watched his portrait being curiously sampled by hungry onlookers. At last they could really *taste* the art of Gorian Campbell......scabby bastard that he was.

* * *

We had planned to fly to New York together after the final exhibition but Gorian drank a bottle of Scotch and had an idea that he should circumcise himself with a Stanley knife one night and that put me off. I told him I'd meet him there, half-afraid of being on the same plane with a man in the throes of developing a habit of self-mutilation.

Shortly before I left, my father was hospitalised and due to have a relatively simple yet extremely uncomfortable operation. He's always had a bad nose and I was beginning to think I had more in common with him than I like to admit because at the time my own nozzle felt like a blood-clotted rectum that had been sadistically stuffed with something Gorian might have concocted to represent the last hour of the Apocalypse. It could have been related to the array of powdered Colombian substances I'd been sniffing that week but whatever the reason, I was having difficulty breathing and sounded more like an animal grunting than a human indulging in the art of speech. My dear old dad isn't the most clearly spoken of characters either but at least he has an excuse for his ceaseless snorting. His nose is riddled with dozens of whelk-like growths which look like droopy cat's testicles that have been methodically peeled and pumped full of something which may have seeped from Gorian's ass. They're disgusting things, often oval in shape, full of pink and purple pus and they stink like raw sewage when burst. They grow in wombs or rectums too and in some extreme cases, if left to ripen, can travel through body passages like ballooning eyeless penises and protrude from vaginas, assholes and nose holes like translucent radioactive grapes threaded with fine sinewy veins. I've seen some strange shit over the years visiting my old man around the nose wards of Ireland. If you hold the things up to the light they look like embryonic cataracts encased in a bloody congealed mess, miniature deformed ostrich foetuses enclosed in a horrid translucent epidermal lining. There's nothing pretty about these growths, they have no redeeming traits, in fact, next to the photo you've hopefully already puked on, they're quite possibly the ugliest things on the planet. I'm not sure how they're removed but I've heard that in olden days they were strangled with string, snipped and the entire ball of festering jungle juice was amputated like a bulbous black grape being picked from a heavy vine. They're known to the medical world as *polyps* and have to be removed from my father's nasal passage by a nasal surgeon, two or three times a year. The poor guy has had so many operations by now that the bone at the bridge of this snout is eroded and looks sunken and ready to cave in at any moment.

He was conscious when I arrived at the South Infirmary but the ensuing conversation was like talking to a man who had a randy rodent stuffed up each nostril and a golf umbrella being jammed down his throat by an invisible iguana. *'Hello son'* sounded exactly like *'Hangha Sha'* and the communication process was all a bit too much for yours truly, stoned off my face on purple skunk. Soon my father could just as easily have been speaking a rarely-used dialect of Korean. The conversation turned into a very bad comedic selection of charades and before long I realised that there was no point sticking around listening to a man harbouring obese hamsters in his head. I made some daft excuse and told him I'd call down to his house the next day after he was discharged. He'd had the growths removed that morning and on my way out I jokingly asked him to bring them home in a jar so I could have a look. He grunted and I thought nothing more about it until I arrived at his house, stoned out of my box again, a couple of drizzly Irish days later.

The old fucker can be a bit analytical at the best of times and he's always boring people to death rambling on about the different industrial processes he overlooks at the chemical plant where he works. He's a simple man with simple pleasures but when he takes an interest in something he really goes the whole hog and finds out pretty much everything there is to know. If he unexpectedly took an interest in theology or philosophy I'm sure he'd probably work out the meaning of life in a few weeks. It turned out that he had taken a macabre interest in the biological makeup of his nostril growths and fuck me! he *had* gone, as I had jokingly suggested and brought the extraneous flesh growths home and put them in a plastic container in the freezer for safe keeping until my arrival. Not only that but his doctor had given him other samples of polyps which had been removed in the hospital that week. He had a few ounces of the things in the freezer and was about to indulge me in what could have turned into a sordid show when my mother arrived home cold and wet and signified her arrival and disgust at the world by viciously slamming the front door and nearly relieving of us of the front window. She was pissed off and cranky and screamed something at the old fella about the state of the weather and the cheek of the neighbours so rather than face the wrath of Kali incarnate we sneaked off to the living room to watch a nature documentary on the Discovery channel about the sex life of North American polecats. (My dad joking that had we been feline it would have been the equivalent of watching a hardcore porno flic.)

We sat down to dinner later, me with my vegan Chinese rice noodles and the other two with plates of Irish stew my mother had concocted while myself and the old fella were flicking between a poll tax debate and a polecat orgy on the box. I was too afraid to try and make small talk because Kali was in foul humour but halfway through the meal the old man opened his mouth and, probably for the sake of something to say, said 'These meatballs are great love!' as he slurped up a spoonful of meat to his mouth. His attempt at deleting the awkward silence from the air certainly worked, for she looked at him like he was an idiot and said 'Meatballs! What fecking Meatballs? There's not a thing left in the house, I had to put every last bloody morsel we had in the freezer into that stew, it'll last a few days but we'll have to go shopping tomorrow or there'll be nothing but leftovers for Sunday dinner.' The old fella went a strange shade of ghoulish green, excused himself and went to throw up in the bog. I spluttered, laughed and tried to keep a straight face as I watched my mother chewing her husband's internal nose boils and then smacking her lips. We didn't have the courage to tell her what had happened but there were leftovers for two more days and apparently my brother raved about them. After dinner they drove me to the airport and seven hours later I landed in John F. Kennedy airport and that's when the madness intensified tremendously.

* * *

The first American I spoke to in the U.S was a grossly overweight immigration cop with an odd-looking beefy tomato in place of a nose, who slowly grilled me at customs like I was the chief kebab at a barbecue. When he was finished another one accosted me at the baggage carousel and asked me if I were the guitarist in a death metal band that his wife loved. I had a lump of dope in my pocket the whole time of course and this was a distraction but the most distracting thing about the whole episode was the green immigration card I was handed to fill in on the plane. It was so retarded that I really felt like turning around right there and then and saying 'F*uck this*! I can't be bothered with this country, put me back on the next flight and get stuffed.' This was *really* sick. Sick and stupid. And if there's one thing that does my head in, it's blatant 'stupidity'. In fact the thing that I'm most afraid of on this planet right now is *stupidity*. You don't have to be a genius to realise that it's very much in vogue these days. Take George Bush, the leader of the *free* world. The idiot is a moron, no, he's *not* a moron, the imbecile has a degree in Moronism, actually NO! he has a Masters in Mutated Moronic Monomania and a Doctorate in Delusional Dumbness. Take one look at the retarded face of Sir George Wankalot Bush and you will realise what the 'W' stands for. Even *Wankalot* is a compliment to this blockhead. I'd rather have a discussion with the wrinkled underbelly of my mother's sagging tits than talk to that murdering fucking moron.

Really, I couldn't believe the shit I had in my hands, I couldn't believe that human beings had gone to the trouble of chopping down life-giving trees, mashing them to pulp, turning the pulp into thousands of little rectangular cards, dyeing them green, perforating them with lines of holes, and then printing them with the most senseless shit you're ever likely to see. I'd recommend going to the States just for the experience of reading the customs literature. Actually you don't have to bother because it's all right here on this very page, courtesy of yours truly and if Sir Wankalot is able to fill in the blanks without the aid of a translator I'll eat my snots.

The I-94W non-immigrant arrival form asks the following questions. You'll soon deduce for yourself that it's a load of finger-fucking, arse-banditing bollix, conceived by braindead moronic twats who are locked up in office blocks all their lives for the specific purpose of making anyone with half a brain throw up. Fools who don't have the slightest concept of what it feels like to be alive. Fools who are in government offices all over the world and for some reason keep our society going with their silly bits of paper and their countless forms and their bureaucratic piles of nonsensical shit. Fools who drafted the remarkable, highly intellectual paper the glorious American government asks you to fill in upon arrival in the richest, most politically influential country on earth. A bullying country that indiscriminately bombs the fuck out of anyone anywhere anyhow, and not only get away with it but actually entertains massive international help with the carnage. As Sir Wankalot said, 'You're either with us or against us!' or in other words, 'You either help us murder who we want or we murder you!'

Anyway here it is, the I-94 form...answers an' all, and I think it's sick.

Do you have a communicable disease, physical or mental disorder, or are you a drug abuser or addict?

Yes I do, in fact I *am* a disease, Mr. D. Isease. Physically and mentally disordered, dysfunctional and downright demented. Laden down with herpes, halitosis, haemorrhoids, Hepatitis A though C, HIV, hungry hordes of head lice and a hangover from Hell. I'm coming to the United States to bang every known and unknown narcotic available to man straight into my groin with an industrial nail-gun and smoke all your shit. I hope you don't mind.

Have you ever been arrested or convicted for an offence or crime involving moral turpitude or a violation related to a controlled substance; or been arrested or convicted for two or more offences for which the aggregate sentence to confinement was five years or more, or been a controlled substance trafficker, or are you seeking entry to engage in immoral activities?

Yes, I once had a chicken farm in Ohio where I often watched Gertrude the God-fearing hen as she was repeatedly fertilized by the rooster Turpitude. I was also briefly engaged to an immoral thought related to the aggregation of a dyslexic sentence and entertained the

241

idea of spicing up my sex life with a frozen turkey while confined in traffic with a substance five years ago.(I wonder how many people actually know what *turpitude* means?)

Have you ever been or are you now involved in espionage or sabotage or in terrorist activities or genocide, or between 1933 and 1945 were you involved in any way in persecutions associated with Nazi Germany or its allies?

Shit, you got me there! Damn it to fuck! I am a Serbian spy on a top secret genocide mission, and even though I'm only seventeen years old, you're right. I was involved in Nazi persecutions from 1939 to 1945, my job, handing out sachets of new and improved 'two in one' shampoo and conditioner at the washrooms of Auschwitz. I was later promoted to cleaning up after Goebbels' orgies in Berlin. (They conveniently don't ask you if you were involved in the nuclear invasion of Japan in 1945, the annihilation of Vietnam in the sixties or the obliteration of Afghanistan in 2001.)

Are you seeking to work in the US or have you ever been excluded and deported or previously removed from the United States, or procured or attempted to procure a visa or entry into the US by fraud or misrepresentation?

Yeah, I've spent six grand getting a fake passport from Iranian goat herders, and now I am going to tell you *all* about it. Not only that, but I've been deported eighteen times and often enter the country by means of a secret tunnel cleverly disguised as the entrance to your ass.

Have you ever detained, retained or withheld custody of a child from a US citizen granted custody of the child?

No, but I've made soup from their toes and sucked on their eyeballs while someone else retained and detained them with a cattle prodder.

Have you ever been denied a U.S. visa or entry into the U. S. or had a U.S. visa cancelled?

Only that time I was caught with the two-foot rubber dildo and the cage of pheasants in various stages of suspended rigor mortis.

Have you ever asserted immunity from prosecution?

Oh for Fuck sake. Alright! Alright! Alright! You've got me there! I really thought that I'd get away with it. The truth is my name is Count Boris Von Shitass, I'm a Nazi spy working for Osama Bin Liner, Sadass Hummein and Sa Tan. I'm responsible for innumerable acts of genocide, fratricide, infanticide, pesticide, shiticide, fuckicide, pissicide, fruit'n'veg'icide and generous portions of happy-hour international anthraxidic carnage. I've been addicted to crack for eleven years and been refused a visa to the States thirty-two times. I drink a litre of lukewarm domestic bleach for breakfast each morning and eat my own faeces with a fresh semen sauce at lunch. I'm here to engage in seriously dodgy sexual activities with domesticated barnyard animals and postal workers.

   I couldn't for the life of me understand why a document of such sheer stupidity would be handed out in such quantities and with such nonchalance. I couldn't believe that they would expect anyone to answer any of these questions. How stupid does the government think we are? And if the government is stupid enough to think that we *are* that stupid...how stupid are we for electing the government? God only knows.

* * *

I was in the good old US of A contemplating the contemptible nature of man and in dire need of a beer. Gorian showed up the following Friday wearing a new ring around his finger, 'an ancient symbol of cyclical purity' he joked. In reality it was no more than the dried-up foreskin from his newly circumcised knob, varnished and strengthened with copper wire. A week after that I stumbled across a cheap second-hand laptop in a junk shop in New Orleans and on a whim, decided to add a new member to the collection of shit I had in my pack. It worked fine for a while but as soon as we hitched our way to Arizona the thing packed up and no matter how many times I tried to turn it on, just would *not* boot up. I couldn't figure it out so one day decided to find a computer store and see if anyone could shed some light on the situation, it was really starting to get on my nerves. Flagstaff is the nearest decent-sized town to the Grand Canyon and it can get pretty hot in the summer. By the time I found a computer shop I was soaked in sweat and as soon as I stumbled through the door an enormous savage-looking dog came out of nowhere, snarled and accosted me. He was so ugly that if I hadn't just taken a dump I'm pretty sure the mutant would have literally frightened the shit out of me there and then.

There are three breeds of dog I can't stand, Pit Bull terriers, Bulldogs and Rottweilers. This one looked like his mother was a delirious Pit Bull on smack, his father a professional Bulldog and he'd been battered at birth by a Rottweiller wielding a bludgeon. He looked like a cross between a very deformed tree sloth and an enormous rabid rodent and the flash of luminous pink from his groin suggested that he may have had a seriously dangerous weapon growing stiff between his hind legs. For the most part I like dogs, but this bastard was one canine I didn't want to have anything to do with. I froze in fear as he started sniffing my knees and shins and I wasn't sure whether to pet him or not and I was thinking 'for fuck sake......what's a brutish hairy quadruped like this doing in a computer store?' I didn't realise then that a lot of retail outlets in the States have ugly animals engaged in service to protect them from burglars and such like. This ugly bastard could have protected it from an army of upright assholes on wheels.

I was dressed in shorts and sandals and I could feel his hairy pink tongue slobbering against my skin and his sickly dog breath warming my legs. By the time he started snorting around at my feet we had a few onlookers and I was statuesque in the middle of the shop floor waiting for the bloodthirsty bastard to finish his business and get the fuck off me. By then I was amazed that someone hadn't come to my rescue but I was stoned out of my gourd and that didn't help my rational thoughts one bit. He was sniffing my toes, maniacally, like a starving pig looking for buried truffles when suddenly my feet started to feel unnaturally warm as if they had miraculously increased ten or twenty degrees in temperature. It was then that I looked down and saw the foul orange liquid seeping out around my feet. They were covered in a huge pile of pickled slime and I realised the bastard was after *puking* all over them. Jesus! Human spew is smelly and gory enough but Fuck Me! dog puke is just rancid. Man! There I was, standing in a store, up to my naked ankles in dog vomit, afraid to move, waiting for someone to come and ask me if I was ok as a slavering mutant burped loudly and indiscriminately barfed a second time all over my paws. I could feel the puke between my toes, feel the solids settling between my little piggies and the rest slithering between the carpet and my soles. Fuck knows what that beast had been eating that day, I wouldn't have been surprised if his owner just let him hunt for his own food. He probably hunted homeless humans in airless alleys. He was probably a canine serial killer on the prowl. Luckily a sales assistant noticed that something was wrong, screamed at the dog and started apologising frantically. He then disappeared into a back room and reappeared with a bucket of soapy water and a big wad of paper towels. I went outside, washed the puke off my feet and started laughing. The guy repeated his apologies a billion times and assured me that this had never happened before and reinforced my theory that I have the smelliest feet in the world. By then he must have felt compelled to attend to my needs and did so by asking if there was anything he could do for me. I showed him my computer, told him I hadn't been able to turn it on for days and asked him if he could have a look. He said 'sure' in a southern accent, opened up he case and plopped it up on a table. He turned it to face him, plugged it in, hit the 'on' switch and twitched with confusion as the fucking thing beeped and booted up faster than it had ever done before. That was an embarrassing moment, I had just been puked upon by a dog and now I felt like a complete fool, so I thanked him and fucked off to find Gorian and drag him out for beer. The only explanation I could come up with was that I must have been some bad-assed fool in a previous life and I was paying for it now. The computer has worked just fine ever since.

We were on a road rolling down the west coast of California; its origin San Francisco, its destination Fresno, as they say in bus-speak. There were seats on that bus next to windows, forty-five seats in forty-five different spaces playing forty-five tunes to the sound of numerous different wheels revolving over a manmade trail surfaced by a sticky black substance invented by a Scot called Macadam. Outside the window windmills stood on hills, twirling slowly in a soft desert breeze. Jack rabbits with huge floppy ears poked heads from burrows and waited for Sancho Panza and his groovy acidhead zonk of a mule-riding master to pass by on their journey to the promised land of zany hallucinations. Cacti stood alone like spiky green erections and tiny twisters waltzed with each other in the dusty distance.

There was a sky too of course, a dusk sky, streaked in haphazard oranges, randy reds and oleaginous baby blues, hanging like a vomited tarpaulin above a cacti-flecked desert. Strange colours to mix unless you blend them together in the Californian stratosphere. Strange colours to contemplate as one unless you're on the road to Tijuana nursing a tequila hangover and a lunatic with the tip of his knob wrapped around his little finger. Beneath the Quixotic horizon mountains lay like snoozing elephants and cumulonimbus clouds clustered together like flocks of swallows gathering to head south for the winter. Rain dribbled down from the heavens like saliva from the mouths of people who are too old to care and too fucked in the head to notice. Jet black tyre threads lay splattered on the road like dead geckos curled up on the tarmac as we passed through a forest of electric transformer pylons and broken umbrella graveyards. Forward through the drizzling dusk and the barren beige fields coated in the stubble of cacti...alone with each other...two crazy fucks heading for the Mexican desert.

We were seventy-seven miles from Fresno, doing ninety in the fast lane, heading south, moving a mile every forty seconds through the hazy landscape. Forty-five seats in a metal box on wheels, forty-six if you included the jolly black giant behind the steering wheel of the Greyhound, infinite numbers if you're off your head, none if you're asleep, any amount if you are insane. Who knows how many seats were on that bus? The oranges faded to pale grapefruit and the neon pink 'Wal Mart' and yellow 'Subway' signs flickered along Badger Flat Rd competing with the McDonalds signs which said 'billions and billions sold' and I had to wonder, 'billions of what?…Souls?' Pacheco Boulevard passed by on the right along with a sign for Mercy Springs Road. The bus driver appeared to know where he was going and that was good because the guy sitting on seat forty-five listening to Electric Ladyland on his cheap Japanese Discman had no idea. I know that for a fact simply because I *was* that guy. Soon we were heading for the Mexican border, following the ancient footsteps and needle tracks of renegades and writers once on the run from stars and stripes. The natural light was almost gone and trees and telegraph poles displayed different characteristics in the new-born blackness. Animated silhouettes became more magical. The darkness had a way of bringing certain things to life. Seat sixteen moved forward at the same speed as seats seventeen, eighteen and nineteen. Everything was moving harmoniously and in good faith toward the most frequently crossed border in the world. Forward, past Santa Fé in our Tijuana Taxi. There were four of us I guess. Hendrix in my ears making his Stratocaster axe sound like it was tripping on acid and ether. Gorian's head out the window puffing my blow. Hunter S. Thompson sitting next to me between the Penguin covers of his 'Fear and Loathing' thing, and me, the occupant of seat forty-five wondering exactly where the fuck I was going and what the fuck I was going to do when I got there.

By morning we were in Mexico, drinking real Mexican beer in Hussong's cantina in Ensenada, two hours south of Tijuana in Baja, California. Within an hour we had decided it would probably be a good idea to drink a lot, buy a couple of cowboy hats and grow moustaches. There was a Mariachi trio buzzing about playing flamenco guitars and singing about lost love, an enormous deer head nailed to the wall and men all around drinking tequila like hungry blue whales might filter Arctic plankton. The cowboys were drinking their worm water faster than I could down my beer. Behind the bar dusty shelves were stacked with liquor from every corner of the ball. The sign on the mirror said *If you drink to forget, pay before you drink* and its Spanish translation underneath said 'No credito sin exepcion.' The T-shirt on the guy in the corner said 'Everyday I add another name to the list of people who piss me off'. And I thought *No assholeos sin exepcion*. We were in Mexico at last but there was no way I was starting on the worm water yet. I'd be eaten alive by the stuff.

My liquid breakfast was served by a moustached man called Pepé. Life became a movie and it seemed that maybe the images so often portrayed on TV were closer to reality than I wanted to admit. It was one of those bars that must have seated writers on the run. William Burroughs, Ken Kesey and other Merry Pranksters could easily have sat there gurgling tequila. I could hear their ghosts throwing up and jacking up in the john and wondered if they could speak Spanish or whether, like me, they just pretended that they could. 'Un autro cervesa por favor amigo?' that much I learned fast, although nothing moved fast in that place but the levels on the tequila and hot sauce bottles and the music tripping through the smoky air.

The guys in the bar whispered 'loco' and that was just fine. They could call us what they wanted as long as they didn't shoot us dead with their six- shooters. We drank all day and eventually ended up in a dodgy cantina where we started on the tequila with the locals. Mexican beer is pretty good and they don't fuck around with Bud and Coors and Bud light and shit like that. We were the only gringos who'd probably been in there for quite some time and the décor behind the bar was a fascinating eclectic mix of strange shit. There was a framed photo of a naked blonde woman with an enormous plastic cock coming out of her cunt in the corner by the TV. There was a black and white football game on the screen, next to that, a sign saying *No hay servicio para damas en la barra!* a set of deer antlers to the left and a portrait of the Virgin Mary with the words 'Bendicenos Madre Mia' beneath. Above all this, looking down over the lot from the ceiling was a godlike photo of the masked Lone Ranger on his horse Silver, a tattered yellowing map of Mexico and a window with eight concrete blocks for glass. The whole scene could have summed up the various stages of the evolution of Mexican man, from the dark ages of religion to the stone age of cowboys, the bronze age of beer, the iron age of football to the age of enlightenment when every Mexican finally realised the ultimate truth......Jesus isn't the Son of God, the Lone Ranger is.

* * *

We were back on the bus the following day and water towers stood aloof like alien craft in the distance as I scraped at the wax in my ear with a paper mate pen and pondered the existence of extraterrestrials and the purpose of ear wax and snot and all the other bits of shite that emanate from the various orifices of our bodies. Gorian had somehow managed to shoplift a blow-up doll we had seen in a sex shop in Ensenada and he was blowing it up in the back of the bus and sticking her head out the window to freak out the passing Mexican motorists. Her mouth was huge and circular, in permanent blow-job position and she looked ridiculous but attracted a lot of attention. The blurb on the box she came in advertised her as a high class doll with an 'inviting anus' 'soft supple skin' and vibrating vaginal and anal love holes which required four AA batteries per orifice. Not only that but she had...TITS YOU COULD FILL UP WITH ANY LIQUID YOU LIKED! Fuck me! You could drink beer from her plastic jugs while you banged away at her *inviting* anus and stuck your fingers in her ear-holes for that extra aural stimulation.

How a synthetic woman made from petrochemicals could have an 'inviting' anus is beyond my primitive levels of comprehension. If there's one thing that an anus could *not* be surely it's *inviting*. A hole in the back of your butt that squirts out shit in all stages of viscosity is *not* an invitation, it's the arsehole of the human earth! I was getting worried about Gorian by then. He had his fingers up the doll's ass and was flying her out the window to the delight of some motorists and the horror of others. I wondered if he'd eventually start fucking her. There are people out there who fuck these things and they can cost up to a thousand dollars a doll. I bet Sir Wankalot has a closet full of them. I bet he puts Saddam Hussein and Osama Bin Liner's masks over their heads and buttfucks them nightly singing the *Star Strangled Spanker*. As far as I'm concerned people can do as they will when it comes to their own sexuality, whatever gets them off is fine by me once it doesn't involve inflicting too much pain on anyone else. But people who fuck plastic dolls and fill up their tits with cider have got to be weird. I'd always assumed that blow-up dolls were primarily abused by sad lonely fuckers alone in dingy rooms reeking of semen and sin. But watching Gorian in action I had to wonder how far these people would really go. If you're willing to spend $500 or more on a doll made of petrochemical compounds and you're going to have sex with this doll on a regular basis then surely you'd buy her clothes, lingerie, uniforms, make-up, wigs, lipstick, jewellery and maybe even flowers and chocolates to spice up the evening. Perhaps you'd even have dinner with her and wipe her arse after. You'd want to be a very, very sad individual to purchase one of these items but they can be bought in any city in the world and this implies that there must be a market for them. Admittedly it would be handy if real live people did actually have tits or genitals that squirted cider (or whatever beverage tickles your fancy). It would be nice to have a beer while you're making out, but a *plastic* woman with beer taps for tits...that just wouldn't do it for me. Then again if you could buy a model with a built-in water bong and get high while you screwed plastic. That just might swing it.

I wonder if dolls are used by single people who can't get laid or are they used by happily shacked-up couples? Imagine a seventy-year-old couple wrinkling away on top of a plastic doll, she drinking cider from her nipples and he pumping away at her 'inviting anus'. It'd be like an undulating sea of wrinkles wobbling in the wind. There must be a lot of people who own these dolls and keep them secret from their partners. It could be a lesbian day-care worker or a garbage collector or a bisexual celibate of the cloth. It could be your mother, your father, your friend or your boss. Maybe there are secret clubs where groups of men and women with strap on dildos meet on Tuesday nights and have a go at it. I wouldn't fancy fucking a doll full of someone else's semen though. It might be warm and comforting but I really don't think that psychologically I'd be able to come to terms with it. Dripping sperm goes cold quickly and that's probably the one thing I don't really like about it. Cum and mucus are strange substances, you could probably make a great glue with them......then again, people probably already have.

Onward trundled the forty-six rickety seats. The sun dripped down like runny honey over a toasted desert as Suzy's head passed a sign for a 'hard shoulder' and I wondered why they didn't warn you about the soft ones. Sometimes only the *hard* things on this planet seemed to matter. On TV they're allowed to show limp cocks...that's ok...they can show a *soft* penis in a shower scene or something like that...that's fine, BUT a *hard* cock. NO! that's not allowed, that will be banned, restricted and probably denounced as hardcore porn. Hard cocks are simply *not* allowed to be seen on regular TV at any time of the night or day. It's almost like we are denying the reason for our existence, denying the thing most men wake up with every day of their lives. Unfortunately the only real difference between a hard cock and a soft one...is blood. It takes very little for a man to get sexually excited and when he does blood rushes into his bollocks and makes it hard. It would seem then that only a certain type of *blood* is banned on TV!

It's estimated that by the time the average 'westerner' is sixteen years old they will have witnessed over 300,000 murders on TV. That's a lot of blood, but *cock* blood, NO! Alright you probably think that I'm taking the piss now and you're probably right but let's just think about hard-ons for another minute. Every single person who has ever lived or died owes her or his life to a hard-on, even test tube babies aren't exempt. Hard-ons are the basis for humanity, without them we'd have absolutely fuck all. Yet what do we go and do? *Ban* the fucking things.

* * *

I knew Gorian was a sick puppy and he must have thought I was an ailing bastard too but what happened after that got completely out of hand. You could say that it plummeted into the Death Valley of depravity. If you ever see the cacti silhouetted against the skyline in the Baja wasteland, you'll have some idea why we wanted to find peyote and trip through unexplored clouds on a mystical Mexican flying poncho. In this magical place we wanted to get high and dance with the spirits of ancient desert shamans in the dunes.

We got off the bus in a small deserted tumbleweed town, checked into a hotel and went out for beer. By the end of the night we were razed to the optimum limit on tequila and in the mood for some madness so we decided to try and score some hallucinogenic cactus. I gave a demented-looking moustached cowboy with silver teeth a hundred pesos, he grinned a far-out grin and put a brown paper bag in my hand. I didn't know how Gorian would trip but trusted him anyway, I had a pitiful weakness for trusting lunatics. We were looking for peyote, but neither of us even knew what it looked like. The bag looked like dried mango slivers but we had no idea. Moustache man laughed and said 'You think you loco now? You think you loco? Ha! You no know loco......this make you *very* loco.' After drinking a Bloody Mary Gorian had concocted without vodka or tomato juice I had to admit that he was right.

I don't know what that stuff was, I don't know if it was peyote, some kind of wacky fungus or something else but it reduced us to very sad cases indeed. Sad gibbering wrecks of human beings, three-year-olds in adult bodies on mad hallucinogenic drugs. Whatever we were on was incredibly strong and made me feel very, very small. My brain felt gargantuan but my body felt very, very minute. I was sitting in front of a small bottle of Corona and I felt that this little golden vessel was twice my size. I felt like an ant drowning in the mud at Woodstock, an amoeba in a dolphinarium, a goldfish caught in a current with a school of blue whales. Gorian was obviously having a similar experience because he kept missing his beer bottle every time he reached for it. What happened next though was his fault, of that I am sure.

We were back in the hotel, loaded, completely full, undergoing total madness. Gorian said he'd make some Bloody Marys but instead puked in an empty glass while I was in the toilet and filled it straight to the top with an orange reddish soupy vomit. When I returned he laughed and said…'I made you a drink,' I asked him what it was and he said that if I drank it he'd tell me and then he'd be my slave for the rest of the night. I momentarily thought we were sitting on a golden beach drinking cocktails, grabbed it and drank it down in two seconds flat. I held it for another brief second, puked it straight back into the glass, wiped my chin, lit a joint, looked at the clock and said 'It's now 1.27 a.m., I own you for the rest of the night.' I then passed him the twice regurgitated glass and said 'Finish it slave.' He tried heroically but sprayed vomit all over his bed in the attempt and the stench of foulness set in as he said, in his ultimate lunacy, 'Sorry master.'

The hallucinogens were so vivid it was like being in a magical land with its own dimensions and laws. Whatever sick arrangement we had just contrived was now carved in stone and there was no way either of us could change the statutes of the trip. From then on it was master and servant. Our new world had rules and we were compelled to comply with them. Gorian knew it too. I had a slave until the mango slivers wore off. The plot grew thicker than drying balls snot. A myriad of ridiculous requests ran through my mind...'Sit on the TV and stick the controls up your arse!...Ring room service and ask for a gladiator...Shave your body and head......Stand in the corner and oink like a pig...Make stick men out of your shit you bastard, drink, throw up, drink, throw up, drink, throw up, repeat it like a mantra, repeat it like your last breath!

I was the master, he was the slave. I was tripping out of my jolly green gourd and I was going to make Gorian Drey wish he'd never dared me to drink his puke. I had risen to the challenge and now he was going to pay dearly for his actions. I didn't know what to do but Campbell was going to drink my puke if it was the last thing I did that night. The bastard had gone too far this time.

The tale ends here in many ways, yet its repercussions continued long into Gorian's life and I expect he has calmed down a little since. I had swallowed his puke and you can't fuck with someone like that and expect to get away with it. Gorian thought he was the world's maddest bastard but I showed him a thing or two that night he would never forget. On the table in front of me sat half a bottle of tequila, a camera, a dozen dead beers, a sheet of Mexican stamps, an envelope, a pen, an address book, a half eaten ear of corn and the deflated torso of Suzy. I stared at the assortment of things wondering how I would satisfy my revenge and then it all floated into place like a meteor shower exploding into electric clarity on Mars. Everything I needed for ultimate revenge was right there at my disposal and to top it all off, the trippy shit we had eaten was making me nauseous. Suzy's saucer-shaped nipples twisted off anti-clockwise and that's how you filled her tits up with liquid. I doubt if the manufacturer had ever intended his love creation to have artificial mammary glands filled with vomit but I was tripping and I was mad and that's what I filled them with. By the time I had screwed the nipples back on she was fully inflated and her tits were topped up with puke. Gorian's final order before we passed into the purgatory of delirious dreams was to drop an envelope in the mailbox in the lobby of the hotel. It's contents were short and sweet…

Dear Mother and Father,

I met this wonderful woman in Mexico and we are really crazy about each other. Please develop the enclosed roll of film as soon as you can and introduce yourself to the new love of my life.

Love and best wishes,

Your Son, Gorian.

I never saw the photos myself and I doubt if Gorian did either but if they came out ok they would have shown more than one picture of Gorian Drey, tripping out of his box, with his erect one-eyed member inserted in the 'inviting' anus, vagina and mouth of plastic Suzy. They would also have shown the Scot suckling Irish vomit from brown plastic nipples as he inserted a half-eaten cob of corn into a vibrating vagina.

* * *

You can spit that dog turd out now if you still haven't puked. But for the sake of human decency, don't waste it, launch it at the face of George Wankalot Bush, mail it to the White House and voice your disgust before the dumb-assed moron starts the war to end the world.

Makeovers From Hell

M Y Alam

It's not entirely unusual, two souls passing through at the same time. Though two birds with one stone works wonders in terms of workload, multiple harvests are by far the most efficient means going. Crashing aeroplanes and sinking boats are all well and good but it is la crème de la crème of reaping scenarios that he lives for. Nothing quite notches up the numbers like an odd war or two.

A combination of bad luck, bad kids, bad weather and bad breath killed them. To this day members of the public still remember reading and hearing their untimely ends. The tributes didn't exactly pour in, but the point was made by colleagues and friends. Two of their own number had been killed. Life was finite after all and that was the greatest tragedy. In response, fellow presenters, soap opera 'stars' and the occasional sports personality who was trying to break into media did the done thing: one after the other, they lined up to look solemn and speak to camera about these now dead heroines of modern times as if they were a pair of Princess Diana clones. Celebrities, as an idea and as individuals are bad enough but once they die, they become bigger and so much better than they could ever have possibly been. It's just the way of things.

Pippa and Jemma worked in television-land as presenters in the general area professionally termed 'Daytime Lifestyle Programming'. During their short careers as fashion and design advisors to the average and intellectually stunted they had managed to crawl up the three-rung ladder of celebrity and had reached the dizzying heights of… C. Considering the B list is where the old, wrinkly and never-that-good-in-the-first-place-and-now-one-step-away-from-senile-dementia celebrities continue to reside, this was not such a grand achievement but it had been something of a remarkably rapid rise, even in the modest though egomaniacal world of Daytime Lifestyle Programming. Now that they were no longer living their sudden but tragically post mortem leap into the A list was guaranteed.

On his way to some of the more exclusive fashion houses in Knightsbridge with a cargo of designer clothing, Keith 'Fizzy' Fletcher, was busy chatting up Hailey 'Flora' Stone when the car in front, a 1998 Renault Clio, braked a little too rapidly for Keith's liking. Keith muttered something under his breath and for the next two miles, rode the Clio's bumper. Hailey, impressed by this show of manly stupidness, snuggled up close to Keith and started massaging his leg, before moving on to rub his hairy but flabby chest. Keith smiled to himself. This was the kind of run he'd do for free.

Keith had backed off substantially by the time Hailey's hand had wandered towards his groin as riding the Clio's bumper and looking forward to riding Hailey at the next service car park required far too much concentration. The distance between his articulated lorry and the Clio shrank back to nothing once Hailey started talking to him. She wasn't just talking; she was very purposefully arousing him. Keith freshened his breath with a spray and at that precise moment, disaster got ready to strike. The driver of the Clio, a vacuum cleaner salesman by the name of Gavin 'Flash' Scott who loved nothing more than tormenting lorry drivers by braking hard when they were least expecting it, found himself for once being forced to genuinely brake hard as a breeze block fell from the bridge he was passing under. Gavin swerved around the lump of building concrete, swore at the little bastards who were no doubt still stood laughing on the bridge and then finally broke into a cold, sticky sweat once he realised the weekends of go-karting were not a waste of time and money but had in fact saved his life. Keith, still distracted by Hailey's roaming hand and dulcet, sensual tones, tried to follow suit but he fell at the first hurdle as his eighteen wheeled monster was nowhere near as friendly or as responsive as Gavin's four-wheeled Papa-and-Nicole-Mobile.

Cheryl – the name Keith had given his rig in honour of Cheryl Baker from *Bucks Fizz* and later *Children's TV* – jack-knifed immediately and skidded for two hundred and some yards before finally coming to a sharp stop thanks to Pippa's two-week old Porsche Boxster which happened to be sitting on the hard shoulder, minding its own business, waiting for 'a man' to come and change the punctured tyre that had been running flat for the last six miles.

Next to Pippa was Jemma who promptly shat her pants as soon as she caught sight of the oncoming hunk of metal in her door mirror.

'Something the matter?' asked Pippa as she looked in her rear view mirror.

'Jesus…' managed Jemma.

'I know,' complained Pippa. 'It might be a truck but isn't black just an awful colour? I mean, come on! When will people learn? It needs to be much more slender to get away with black.'

Keith and Hailey survived virtually unscathed. They ended up falling in love and then marrying. A month later, they were falling out of love, a turning point in their relationship which they symbolised by both having affairs with each other's former partners, each other's siblings, before catching each other in bed with the siblings of each other's former partners. All was not lost. In fact, quite the opposite as this led to a much needed source of income for all concerned. A researcher got in touch with Hailey and asked her if she would be happy to go on *Trisha* in order to tell the world about herself, her partners and what embarrassments to the human race she and they really were. Soon after this first showing out on *Trisha*, Hailey and Keith divorced only to remarry a month later simply to repeat the whole process for the sake of giving the nice people at *Trisha* a little twist to their story and something for the producers of *Cheryl* – an up and coming, competing Real-life talk show hosted by the ever popular *Cheryl Baker* of *Bucks Fizz* and later *Children's TV*. With a total three divorces, and three ruined rigs (Kelly after *Kelly Marie*, Sheena after *Sheena Easton* and now Cheryl who needs no introduction) Keith was fed up with lorry driving as a living and felt it was time to move on. For Hailey, being much younger than Keith, this was it. She always had this thing – an affinity, they called it – with television: watching it, changing the channels on it, moving the aerial around for better reception and even recording the best bits of *Top of the Pops* off it seemed to come to her as if it was second nature. Uncanny. This was what her whole life had been getting ready for. It was all too much like a dream she'd had as a child, she told Trisha the third time she was invited as a guest:

'It's all too much like a dream I had as a child, Trisha.' she said while Trisha nodded falsely.

Back to Cheryl, not *the Cheryl Baker* of *Bucks Fizz* and *Children's TV* but Keith's rig. Although the Boxster is one of the safest cars in its class, and with performance, comfort and above all prestige scoring way above average, its presence, style and refinement was no match for Cheryl's mass which ended up doing the world something of a favour by killing Pippa and Jemma in a somewhat grotesque but sadly instant manner.

Death hears their bells toll and arrives to do his duty. Keeping their opinions to themselves, for now, Pippa and Jemma smile politely at what they see as possibly their next but greatest challenge. Death doesn't get it but more importantly, feels a little annoyed by their ignorance. Talking about him as if he's not there is simply rude and, what's more, makes him feel a little uncomfortable.

'Your time has come,' he informs them in a low… deathly tone.

They carry on as if he has no voice. He clears his throat.

'Yes?' asks Pippa. 'We weren't listening.'

'Your *time* has *come*,' repeats Death and turns his back on them, expecting them – all but willing them to follow him. That's how it is; that's the system that's worked for aeons but these two, they seem oblivious to such ways.

'I think you're the one whose time has come…' says Jemma, expecting Death to fill in the blank.

'I'm Pippa,' smiles Pippa. 'And this is Jemma.'

'And who might you be?'

'Erm… Death.'

'Right. Well, Mister Death… any first names? Sounds so formal, calling you Mister,' comments Pippa.

'Like a headmaster.'

'Erm… no, just Death.'

'Oh! Do you mean like Eminem?'

'Em-in-em?' ponders Death.

'Eminem is so happening right now. That Trailer Trash look is so original.'

Death finally realises what's going on. He's about to get a makeover from a couple of posh, arrogant and altogether vulgar tarts who think they know what they're talking about but the odd thing is, the idea appeals to him. He's been feeling a little… a little uninspired, perhaps even depressed, of late. Maybe this is it – maybe this is just what he needs to get back on track.

'Sorry,' says Pippa. 'Did you say Death?'

Death nods.

'Death as in… as in The Grim Reaper?'

Death nods again, this time slowly – as grim as it gets.

'Well,' beams Pippa, clapping her hands like a kid looking forward to a Big Mac and Shake, 'this *is* a challenge!'

'Care to give us a twirl, Death? Nice and slow if you would.'

Death, for once in what seems like an eternity, feels hopeful. He duly obliges and gives them a twirl, nice and slow, just like they've asked.

'Hmm…'

Jemma ponders also.

'I think reinventing such a strong image could be a lot of work. You know, when people think Death, there's a certain image that immediately pops into their minds.'

'Well, I thought precisely the opposite was the problem here: people don't notice Death any more. Death's just too…'

For a moment, Death is surprised and just a little upset that even these two halfwits can comprehend this slow and painful demise that started way back during the Enlightenment. Bloody smart arse seventeenth century Europeans, getting all high and mighty without once considering the implications. Descartes, Newton and even the likes of Da Vinci and Galileo didn't look so smart when Death came a calling.

'W-e-l-l… boring, really.'

'Boring?' says Death, hiding his offence the best he can.

'I think I see what you mean,' says Pippa, Death's meagre protest failing to even register. 'Yes… what he's wearing… dull, old fashioned – I think we need to get rid of that before we do anything.'

Death might as well not be there. He decides this is not something to get annoyed about. Instead, he'll take this all with a good pinch of salt. A small price to pay for a happier future.

'Surely somebody must have said something. Surely a friend could have given you some advice.'

'Well, this is something else we need to think about: Death has no friends.'

'I don't want to sound mean but I'm not all that surprised, frankly. I'm pretty sure I'd lose all my friends if I started parading around in the same old thing, day after day, week after week…'

The patronising tone and ignorant demeanour still surprises Death but he will, for the time being, choose to live with it. It's not as if this is for ever.

'So. How do you think we should begin?'

'Well, for starters, I think Death should be seriously considering shedding – and shredding – his current wardrobe. Might look the part for your average fifteenth Century Southern European Catholic-'

Pippa motions at Death's get up and says:

'But *all* of it has to go.'

'The question is,' ponders Jemma. 'What instead?'

'Sex. We need something that says sex.'

'What about a sporty look? Shorts and t-shirt or a singlet, even. That beach bum volleyball look is big right now.'

Jemma mulls over the idea for a moment and then, as if divine inspiration has interceded, she sits bold upright, her lips spreading into a broad smile.

'I think I have it,' she says, slowly nodding to herself as her mind paints Death in his all new look.

Death's not keen but he can't get a word in edgeways; hardly surprising considering they love the sound of their own voices. Once they get into their stride, all external noise is filtered out automatically.

During the course of this makeover, they insist on talking to camera even though it's not there. Far from annoying Death, this is a constant source of amusement. The clichés, the sound-bites and the wisdom of materialist narcissism is incessant: *Out with the old and in with the new… Style is about look, not always about the buck… Sexy beast… Comfort has nothing to do with style… Style has nothing to do with taste… Taste needs to be learnt… Clothes tell the world more than you can ever say… Minging… Let's just work with what we've got… When all else fails, accessorise… My grandma's got better taste and she's been dead ten years… Let's just jazz it up, in a Pippa and Jemma stylee…*

After spending the best part of a day working with the Gurus, Death is finally done. Pippa calls his look 'Death Chic'. Death, however, is still not too impressed. Yet another chunk of TV speak is offered in response:

'You have to give it a bit of time to get used to it.'

'And it's about what other people think; about how they see you that matters.'

'Stop being so selfish.'

'You have to give it a chance.'

'Why don't you see what people say?'

'Yes – let's see how people react.'

The rain comes but it's cold. Soon enough rain turns to sleet then snow which drops quickly through the dark night air. Tommy Boyd is on Talk Radio and as usual, he's talking shit about asylum seekers, teenage mothers and gun crime. Ever since Dullah saw him on *Magpie*, Tommy's been like this: full of shit, sanctimonious with it but Dullah's never been able to stop himself from listening to idiots. Like tonight: do a job delivering a bit of blow and be rewarded handsomely for the trouble. The people Dullah has worked with are a mixed bunch. Some he likes – considers friends, others he simply knows whereas there are a few he would sooner see dead. Most are precious about their word. They have honour and Dullah likes to think he's the same: the honourable will cross the road to walk with the honourable whereas those with nothing are destined to stay despised, miserable and alone.

This job pays well but it is a lot of trouble. Dullah is rolling on two treadless tyres and two that are on their way to baldness. The heater that might as well be a refrigerator and the headlights have the temperament of a dozen spoilt brats. Thankfully, the road is clear – not a car in sight with it still being Christmas.

'The things you give up for the love of money,' he sighs before reminding himself that Christmas is not and never has been for him.

Still, it could be worse, as arrogant fucks like Tommy Boyd might say. Nothing coming, nothing going except for Dullah. A respectable but reasonably safe forty miles an hour on a stretch of motorway that might as well be a skating rink.

He's been driving upwards of twenty years and he's never experienced anything like it. He knows the rules of vehicular physics he knows the moves to deal with them. Stay in low gear at all costs, go with the skid as soon as it happens and tap the brake pedal quickly and repetitively until control is established. Not for nothing that Dullah's got a reputation for an above competent pair of driving hands and feet. But the car's got a life of its own and nothing – not Dullah, not his twenty years of driving and not even the physics of Newton, Einstein or even that gimpy little Hawkins guy can put a stop to it. Still, he has to try, has to put up some semblance of a fight. Dullah wrestles with the wheel for a while but like the car, it spins around like a kid's toy. From the outside it looks like a poetic, graceful kind of choreography, like ballet only a much more anarchic series of spins, flips and bounces. The funny thing is Dullah doesn't seem to feel too effected by what's going on. The pounded roof pushing his head into his shoulders, the crushed doors cracking his ribs one after the other and the wrecked steering column squashing his legs beyond any kind of meaningful repair seem to matter nor hurt not one bit.

From his now stationary but upside down perspective, Dullah sees two lights coming at him. They get bigger and then their size, for a moment, stabilises but just as quickly, starts to get bigger once again. Dullah tries to shield his eyes but his hands are firmly trapped between the steering wheel and his legs. For some reason, he thinks now is a good time to try and wiggle his toes. He tries and they don't. The coach, carrying happy Boxing Day footballers on their way back from a humiliated Old Trafford, turns to its side, flips over and lands on Dullah's car.

It's dark. Dullah wonders what happened, how he got out of that. Maybe he got lucky. Sounds sort of reasonable.

'Try to relax,' says a voice.

'Where,' croaks Dullah, then, after clearing his throat, tries again: 'Where am I?'

'It's okay,' says the voice. 'Nothing to worry about.'

'What happened? Where am I?'

'You were delivering some drugs from a man called Tony to a man called Vinny. You were driving a car with illegal tyres, no MOT, no Road Tax and no insurance. The motorway was icy, your car skidded and collided with the Aston Villa Football Club team coach.'

'Shit. Was anyone hurt? Was anyone....'

'Killed?'

'Yes. Did anyone die?'

'Just one person. Just you.'

It doesn't take long for a being such as Death to convince Dullah that this is the truth. Death shows him all the proofs necessary and Dullah sees them without once opening his eyes. For some reason, Dullah tells himself that if he was of the Catholic persuasion, now would be a good time to let the Hail Marys roll:

Hail Mary

Full of grace

The Lord is with thee

Blessed art thou amongst women...

Dullah smiles to himself. He never knew he knew the whole thing. All that Catholic Confessional stuff sounded great, so dramatic yet meaningless in the movies: *Bless me father for I have sinned...* but Dullah had never bothered to learn the whole *Hail Mary* thing but here he is, saying it in his head even though he thinks the whole thing is a scam. For a few moments, Dullah tries to recall where he might have heard it or learned it but there's nothing doing so instead of completing the lines of penance as accorded by the Catholic Church, Dullah decides to recite the words penned and recorded by a player of a slightly different nature, a slayer of countless rap features. As the Notorious B I G might have said when it was his time:

Hail Mary

full of grace

smack the bitch

in the face;

take her Gucci bag

off her back

jab her if she act

funny with the money

Oh you got me

mistaken honey…

I don't wanna rape ya

I just want the paper…

Dullah finds himself feeling comfortable. It's not that Death seems harmless or anything but Dullah does get the sense that he's a straight shooting, honest kind of soul even though his preceding reputation might be otherwise. The even stranger thing for Dullah is the complete absence of fear. Death, so it seems, isn't such a bad thing. Polite, calm and remarkably understanding.

'Don't worry, everything will be just fine.'

As long as Dullah does one thing. Death doesn't ask for a lot but he'll know if he's not getting it. In exchange, Dullah will live once again and with him he'll be given the usual near death memory that comes with all near death experiences: a dearly loved but now departed relative telling him to stay away/come into the white light.

'What?' asks Dullah. 'What can I give you?'

'Your opinion. Your honest opinion.'

'On what?'

'Open your eyes.'

Dullah remains silent. Not stunned but amazed. Lost for words.

'Well?'

'Erm…'

'Yes? You've nothing to fear. Please, be honest.'

'It's just that… it's just that you're not what I expected.'

'I see. In a good way or in a bad way?'

The last living, popular incarnation of Death that Dullah recalls was undertaken by a certain Mister Bradley Pitt. Pitt's Death was smooth, suave and an altogether younger, cleaner and in some ways much hipper sort of personification. That figure would have been fine even though it was a human incarnation and even though Death as Pitt was just too nice and bent the rules far too easily for Dullah's liking. This Death, however, looks ridiculous.

'I think,' begins Dullah.

'Yes?'

Dullah sighs.

'You have nothing to fear,' says Death once again.

Dullah nods.

'Can I ask you if you chose those clothes?'

'No you can not. All I want is your opinion. Your judgement.'

So Dullah tells him. Dullah tells Death that he looks like a malnourished Austin Powers, only with better teeth and probably better comedic value. He also tells Death that there was nothing wrong with the old, dark and fearsome stereotypical look he had before he got all bloody 1970s retro. That, at least, had a sense of personality, a sense of identity and what's more it worked. That look – hooded cloak, the shining armour and the scythe worked like a mother fucker because it was enough to shit the life out of anyone which was a pretty useful effect in case he came across any not-quite-dead people. This look, however, is a mistake. A bad joke. If Death thinks this shit looks good, then he's in serious, serious trouble.

Although Dullah's opinion is blasted out in less than a minute, Death considers the judgement for what seems like an age. For Dullah this is a bad sign. So Death, like the Devil, is a liar, then? Nothing to fear? That's what he said but Dullah is scared. Maybe he should have lied and told him he looked slicker than Slick Rick.

'I am a joke,' says Death. 'You're right.'

Death sounds like one of those old men who's grown tired of being constantly ignored. Sounds like one of those old codgers who fought in some war or other that's now been forgotten by all the people he helped save. Death is bitter but not only that, there's a trace of weakness in his voice. It's almost as if he's ashamed of himself.

'That's not what I meant,' says Dullah. 'It's the clothes, that's all.'

Death sighs. Of late, Death's gone pretty cold. He's been feeling like this ever since the 1950s when advertising started doing the job of religion. Religion used to be great. Religion was more powerful than any drug going and as long as he had all those dealers in his pockets – priests of one description or another – Death had a job worth doing; had a certain spring in his stride, a bit of a pep in his step. Nothing, except eternity, lasts forever. Instead of fear and control, advertising turned the tides by instilling optimism, power and liberty into one population after the next: when the Chinese finally embraced this new ideology, Death knew Socialism, and more importantly, his own existence, was close to being finished.

Dullah doesn't know where all this leads but he does think that perhaps Death, like everyone else, is subject to certain pressures. Suddenly, it makes sense. Death is to be pitied because he is useless, no longer necessary nor appreciated. Consumers have no problem being owned, controlled and killed by the things of consumption but the all powerful, all devouring and increasingly incessant consumer, simply can not and will not even try to relate to the one concept that, to all intents and purposes, consumes them without having the good grace to give them anything in exchange, other than liberation. Death is no longer a real, spiritual or even remotely intellectual concern for anyone. To all intents and purposes, Death, like substance itself, is dead.

'I'm sorry,' says Dullah, 'but you did ask.'

'And you did tell me.'

'Now what?'

'I might be Death but I walk with honour. You have nothing to fear.'

Dullah comes out of a coma after fifty-four days. Police, doctors and even religious leaders described his survival as nothing short of a miracle: the car and its contents were destroyed by the blaze that consumed it moments after impact. Dullah's burns were mostly superficial; his lungs no longer suffering from the effects of smoke inhalation and any bones that were broken were well on their way to being repaired. The first thing he said when he came to was:

'Death's not dead.'

For Jemma and Pippa, Dullah's judgement means a swift jump to the front of the queue into hell. They were going to hell before Death interceded but Death gets a certain pleasure informing them that, for once, they are proven as wrong. For them hell is not a problem. Jemma and Pippa return to the land of the living but with conditions: they are to spend the rest of eternity with a wardrobe made up of all the clothes they have previously consigned as tasteless, drab and 'so not happening'. For them, hell is being all the people they so readily and eagerly belittled. Death may be Death but he has honour and even a sense of poetic justice not to mention humour on his side which more than can be ever said for the likes of Pippa and Jemma.

Fifteen Minutes Just Got Longer
Daithidh MacEochaidh

Given the success of instant fame shows, rumours are rife that a new talent show is soon to hit the small screen with all the celebrity impact of the proverbial **** hitting the fan. (The fan in question as yet remains un-named.) A group of acne & angst ridden writers are forcefully removed from the rest of society, made to perform a couple of *Ready, Steady, Book* manoeuvres, thereafter set loose in the media jungle, protected only by close circuit hidden cameras as they are voted at by the public, made to perform the usual demeaning stunts, copious crying, heart on sleeve juggling and selling the dirt on other contestants.

The first day's elimination round is a light entertaining assault course of alcoholism AKA Malcolm Lowry styl-e, being put on a wall and having one's genitals examined in the manner of Virginia Woolf, ending with being injected with Franz Kafka's particular strain of tuberculosis. At any point, a contestant can be released from this trial by ordeal by shouting the magic words, 'Get me out of here, I'm not Ernest Hemingway!'

Complaints of taste regarding the second day's tripe and tribulations have been received prior to shooting. The so called *Byron Day* whereby, contestants are lamed, made to drink wine from a skull, before committing incest, has surprisingly being objected to on the grounds of taste and decency. A spokesperson from the media company in question nailed this complaint with all the laconic excess of Dash Hammett, 'Since when as taste mattered?...' You can't fight the moral high ground where viewing figures are concerned —very seemingly.

It is day three that might prove the most troubling to the wantabe writers, having to perform an abstract of *Finnegans Wake* in the style of their favourite impressionist. For this event, they've had to wheel out Mike Yarwood to do the judging as Monet was unavailable due to gardening commitments with the *Ground Farce* team. The urbane spokesperson remained un-phased, explaining that he had a whole team of stand-in stunt stutterers, guaranteed to pull a few purse-strings with the all important teen market.

It has been suggested that rather than bringing on new writers, rather than introducing the public and the wantabees to the literary cannon, that all this show amounts to is a crass mimicry of other programmes, selling out culture for rating figures. This charge brought short shrift from the producers, 'Look at Chris Tarrant, look at Spit-the-Dog' — then come back and talk to me about selling out' —— no argument there then.

As to the more incisive complaint that such shows are all part and parcel of a general dumbing down, the response was expansive. The company in question (a questionable company) in cooperation with the BBC''s costume department franchise Ltd.. have agreed to a mere six episodic version of Proust's *la recherche du temps perdu*. 'Don't talk to me about dumbing down, we even got the hot lesbian scene written into the contract, provided that 'Darcy' can watch!' In reply to the question, what scene? The spokesperson, tipping the winkle, freely admitted that he'd never seen the original film, and thereafter muttering something incomprehensible about the polyphony of inter-sexuality.

There were other rumours but because of contraceptional reasons and the fear that other producers might steal the baby, these will have to remain under wrap. Who knows, with luck, they may stay there. However, there was one highly improbable bit of plagiaristic gossip which suggested that 'Big Brother' had been lifted from a book, a real work of literature ...Oh well, enough of the telly, me and my rather dated buddy, Eric Arthur Blair, are settling down to listen to the third programme on the wireless; it's really quite pleasant here, cup of char, comfy seat, a bit of culture for a change —this place is not called Room 101 for nothing ...

As economically forecasted before being broadcasted, the show was a crass hit. A pregnant, fresh-faced youngster who talked with a limp was given the book deal — not that a book was written, just reassembled, after all as one cultural theorist proudly denounced, 'The artist as modernist super-hero is dead — all is quotation — all is pastiche — all ironic reference ...' There was more, but the quote in full was bigger than the book that wasn't written. Which, incidently, went straight to number one in the Amazon charts by clever bulk-buying strategies, just as the data was sampled ... not that the sampling was original, just someone else's tunes, now on CD. Which, incidently, went straight to number one in the charts by clever bulk-buying strategies ... Sorry, I feel that you've heard the last sentence before, but don't quote me on that. Instead, remember what dear old Ezra wrote in the good old 'in for a penny, in for a pound' days —— MAKE IT NEW!

Beautiful Ruins
Adrian Wilson

Late Autumn 2002 I travel to Istanbul, where business hospitality is a kind of luxury twenty-four-hour surveillance – a little like being in the 'Big Brother' house, only the conversation is significantly more strained and you can simply order food from room service rather than having to perform like a nineteenth century circus seal.

We visit working factories on roads turned wild by the earthquakes and subsequent storms – ravines of tarmac and churned earth – and inside them survey endless lines of women standing at sewing machines, all in black.

In a club overlooking the Bosphorous, its shores lined with hazy palaces and mosques, we listen to a fat man in a cummerbund sing mournful traditional songs for a radio station launch – agitated semi-tone shifts with brash orchestration – about which my hosts seem somehow embarrassed. Inevitably, I am forced at some point to squirm with a belly dancer by a swimming pool, on the top floor of a five-star hotel. Her dark eyes dart much quicker than my hips. Then I take the ferry across the Sea of Marmara to Bursa, a teeming industrial city to the south. On the trip, strangers douse my hands with lemon cologne and children survey me slyly.

* * *

They've built a new exhibition centre in Bursa, and on the way to it one morning, we pass a building block in the middle of nowhere which I am strangely drawn to.

You see plenty of ruins in Turkey, but not anything being knocked down.

Ruins – even ancient ones – usually just have new bits tacked onto them. So after a couple of days, I feel compelled to go and have a look. Managing to give my well-meaning hosts the slip, I trudge across mounds and gullies which seem deliberately placed to stop me getting to it, though it's only a quarter of a mile at the farthest.

It reminds me of a 1950s Butlin's holiday camp. There's a tiled communal toilet and washroom with a huge tree sprouting out of it. It couldn't possibly be a holiday camp, I decide, and is too luxurious to be some kind of open prison. I guess it might be some kind of workers' residence built by an idealistic manufacturing plant owner – Bursa's own Titus Salt perhaps – though there's no such business in sight. All the apartment blocks have been smashed in at the same end, as if there's some unknown plan, and mounds of stones, tiles and metal placed in front of them.

I stumble around for ten minutes, taking pictures, then I notice a group of men sitting silently behind a clump of trees and alarm bells ring. This is the kind of silly curiosity that gets you in trouble. Here I am, in the middle of nowhere really, carrying a significant amount of US dollars, a camera, a laptop, passport and credit cards. They may be the demolition team having a long lunchbreak or alternatively just vagrants. The fact that the Turks are almost insanely honest doesn't totally reassure me and I decide the best thing is to make my exit as swiftly and silently as possible.

* * *

When I was editing the 'Tubthumping' collection of short stories for Route a couple of years ago, some old bloke sent me a series of photos of the Bradford factory in which he worked for forty years. There were both exterior and interior shots of the place in its heyday, then more of it lying semi-derelict and graffiti-daubed in the 1980s, and finally shots of it being demolished in the 1990s. The photos – a kind of sequential metaphor – were accompanied by a heart-achingly sad reminiscence in long-hand. This detailed the often pointless rituals, the hierarchial wranglings, the skills required to operate extinct machinery and the patience – or resigned helplessness – needed to see through days, months and years of monotonous repetition. Any characters mentioned were shadowy and half-formed and the deference was all towards the building itself.

It will be nigh-on impossible for anyone looking back and trying to find the point of their existence through a life of work to capture the same sad sense of loss through photographs of early twenty-first century abandoned call centres, offices and warehouses. What would you photograph? Coils of abandoned cable across a stretch of beige carpet? Tiers of numbered shelving?

There are still abandoned mills and factories all over West Yorkshire, of course, and with the exception of Salt's Mill and a few others, it's proved impossible to really turn them into anything else. So they rot at the epicentre of back-to-backs which used to hole-up their labour. Their contents have been plundered, and brass plaques, machine parts and tools, clocking-in machines and hand-written ledgers are finding their way into themed pubs and restaurants scattered around the globe.

I'm not alone in finding all this intriguing.

'I photograph modern ruins because I find it disturbing to find familiar objects and technology to be abandoned,' says photographer Phillip Buehler. 'I'm reminded that nothing is permanent, that everything is always in a state of transition. And we see ourselves in our own transitions, sometimes too focused on where we're going to notice and appreciate where we are.'

His Modern Ruins site (www.modern-ruins.com) is devoted to America's grass-filled cracks in the pavement – from the World's Fair grounds in Queens to overgrown abandoned freight rail lines of the East Coast. Particularly haunting are images of the old Alcoa factory in New Jersey near the Hudson River. Contaminated by toxic chemicals known as PCBs, it remains unused despite a prime location on the waterfront. Cleaned out only a few years ago in an attempt to put in condominiums, nature is now ravaging the old building with little respect for the industrial age. Inside, chemical stalactites drip from support columns.

A similar US site is that of artist Lowell Boileau's 'The Fabulous Ruins of Detroit' (http://detroityes.com).

'In the summer of 1971, I returned to Detroit after two and a half years in Africa, the Middle East and Europe where I had visited numerous ancient ruins,' he explains. 'Detroit was restive, as the social revolutions of the late 60s played out their effects, and in transformation, as its population began vacating the city to the surrounding suburbs. Still, Detroit seemed little changed from its model developed in the teens of the twentieth century when it became the pre-eminent industrial city in the world.

'Unseen to the eye, during that hazy summer, immense economic, social and political forces, that had been set in motion years prior, were to render large sections of the city and its industrial structures into ruination. Could one be instantly transported from that time forward twenty years it would appear as if large areas of the city had been carpet bombed leaving behind huge hulking ruins – ruins larger and more extensive than those I found in my travels to Zimbabwe, El Tajin, Ephesus, Athens, or Rome.'

Biggest of all Detroit's fabulous ruins remains Henry Ford's Model T Automobile Plant in the Detroit enclave of Highland Park, which is still in partial use as a warehouse.

Home of the moving assembly line and designed by industrial architectural giant Albert Kahn, the world beat a path to its door, fuelling the second industrial revolution and catapulting Detroit to wealth and fame.

Built in 1909, it once produced one thousand 'Tin Lizzies' a day. It ceased production in the 1970s, and has suffered greatly from neglect ever since.

Dutch pilot Henk van Rensbergen also has something to say on this subject (home2.planetinternet.be/henk/).

'I can't go to any place in the world without looking for that open window, that hole in the fence or that unlocked door. In the beginning the biggest thrill was to venture inside the building, always on my own, explore and discover...'

'Today, the pyramids of the industrial revolution just uselessly stand in the way, they're a scar in the landscape,' he adds. 'The deafening noises have been replaced by silence, but if you listen carefully they will tell you their story.

'Abandoned hospitals where you can still smell the anxiety of the ill, where you can hear the coughing of the TB-infected and where once doctors and nurses walked through the shiny corridors.

'A one hundred years-old hotel, standing proudly at the waterfront, arrogantly overlooking the beach and fiercely withstanding all the storms of the past century, a decayed symbol of wealth for the rich.

'Why are abandoned places so attractive?'

* * *

Raiztlin da Wizard, aka Master of Chemistry Violator and the Twisted Machinist, aka Meisseli, are two young men who make trips to abandoned sawmills, factories and power plants all over Finland (http://people.jyu.fi/~raiztlin/www/eu_gallery.html).

'We are definitely not interested nor involved in vandalism, satan worshipping or similar activities sometimes connected to such locations,' they say. 'We're not graffiti writers either. Our only interest is to search, explore and photograph these places. It's not uncommon that young boys are charmed by boiler rooms, basements and ghost houses. So were we back in 1980s. However, our interest didn't fade awywhere, actually it has grown.'

Inevitably, there is a magazine devoted to this new modern pastime – Infiltration – 'the zine about going places you're not supposed to go, devoted to the art of urban exploration' (www.infiltration.org).

Infiltration features editorials, exploring advice and information, articles on recent expeditions, and interviews, all illustrated with maps, pictures and diagrams. The current issue of Infiltration (September 2002, #19), subtitled 'Houses of the Holy', takes a thorough look over, under, around and through the secret spaces of churches.

* * *

One of US photographer Phillip Buehler's other landmarks is that of Ellis Island, which he has photographed at intervals from being a student in the 70s.

During its peak years – 1892 to 1924 – Ellis Island received thousands of immigrants a day. Each was scrutinised for disease or disability as the long line of hopeful new arrivals made their way up the steep stairs to the great, echoing Registry Room. Over 100 million Americans can trace their ancestry in the United States to a man, woman, or child whose name passed from a steamship manifest sheet to an inspector's record book in the great Registry Room at Ellis Island.

With restrictions on immigration in the 1920s, Ellis Island's population dwindled, and the station finally closed its doors in 1954. Its grand brick and limestone buildings gradually deteriorated in the fierce weather of New York Harbour. Concern about this vital part of America's immigrant history led to the inclusion of Ellis Island as part of Statue of Liberty National Monument in 1965. Private citizens mounted a campaign to preserve the island, and one of the most ambitious restoration projects in US history returned Ellis Island's main building to its former grandeur in September 1990.

* * *

Which brings us conveniently back to Turkey. The country has just learned that it will not be invited to join the EU in 2004, though twelve other countries, mainly from East Europe, will. The EU has cited Turkey's human rights record as the prime reason for its exclusion. Turkey has retorted that there are moves to keep the EU 'a Christian club.'

The US, which is not exactly adverse to its own Christian clubs, has backed Turkey to the hilt. The EU is where Turkey belongs, despite the fact that its sixty million population are predominantly Muslim – a faith towards which the US does not appear to be currently so well-disposed.

But Turkey of course, would probably be prepared to allow even more US planes to point at Iraq from its land, if push comes to shove, and there is also the little matter of the $3 billion pipe being built across Turkey in a bid to avoid future US reliance on Saddam's crude oil.

The US is probably quite right, a Europe with Turkey inside it is probably quite capable of sorting out any little cultural and religious differences this might throw up. But woe betide any Muslim trying to chance his arm by trotting uninvited up the steep stairs to Ellis Island these days.

* * *

The day after my walk to the Bursa ruin, I mentioned it to Ahmet, my host, who found it very amusing.

The city's state-owned brothel, he explained, had to be moved to the other side of town, because it was too near the new exhibition centre, and foreign visitors might not understand.

Four Poems
Mark Gwynne Jones

Addressed in Braille

Point taken
and chewed
through mandibles
of logic.

Teeth cracked,
gums bled.

I sucked the eyeballs
from your head
and viewed the world
from your perspective.

Decided that
I didn't like it.

So here they are
in a brown paper bag.
Bloodied, bruised
and addressed in Braille:

Yours, I believe!

Brassed Off Billy Monty

The's plenty mek a song n'dance
play the trumpet in the' pants
sing inside an old string vest
wi' rain poundin' cobbled streets
or fillin' up *that* tin bath
to drown the kids or wash the cat
but none can spek o' pain and graft
like our Billy
brassed off Billy
brassed off Billy Monty

And them that ses they've 'ad it tough
sleepin' out
sleepin' rough
sleepin' out's a holiday
when sharin' bed wi' family.

It's the nicotine stained nostalgia show
the only north you'll ever know
hanging in a photograph

That's our Billy in the cot
puffin' on his mother's fags.
A dog with mange, uncle Fred
and twenty siblings shared his bed
but deprivation does him good
put some coal dust in his blood
that smoulders in the neighbourhood
of brassed off Billy Monty.

Cos when the town's thro'
and shuttered up
jilted like a £5 slut
and Katy's pregnant before she's twelve

and heroin's the only help
and you're falling out with your finger nails
as the family turns in on itself
and even your mates are no longer pally
it's time to join the Royal Ballet;
it's time to pray for that second chance
and take to the stage in your underpants:
Come on Billy show us all!
and blow your trumpet at the Albert Hall
where the people cheer and bay for more
…more …more
of our Billy
brassed off Billy
brassed off Billy Monty

Mr Walker was a Hitchhiker

A thud and a crash and the blood did splash
and I couldn't get it off with my windscreen wipers.
It was just another one of those bloody hitchhikers.
A no hoper. The dope smoker, slimy viper,
costing me a fortune in windscreen wiper fluid.

It happened in Wales, a place in Clwyd.

Well, he would have had a blade in his pocket
or a knife behind his back.
A gun inside his sandwich-box
and a head full of smack!

Furthermore,
I just hate people climbing into my car
when they're soaking wet.
He should have got a job
and bought himself a better way of life.

So sayeth the man in the Mercedes Benz
who never ever stops not even for his friends.

Well I suppose that's one way of picking people up,
on the bonnet!

And I'm staring at box cars box cars
with people boxed inside.
The look of loneliness is one per car
but no-one gives a ride.

We're paranoid and paralysed
Look at all them freaks!
Parallel yet polarised
our lives no longer speak.

And the road was like a river of steel.
Humming with the power of the passing car.
And on the banks of the river
all I could feel
were unknown lives flashing far
out - on
                off.
Gasping between
the watchman's cough,
breathing only the fumes of the passing car.
The planet was turning away from our star
and evening fell.

Nigh-time.
        Suburbia.
Lights flicker, flash
in a thousand rooms.
In a thousand rooms
people, alone,
            living alone
are watching the same
program,
program their minds.

But the road never sleeps.
And out there on the streets, from the
chrysalis of night,
juggernauts have woken as dinosaurs.
And I
            a waster
The Socialist Wanker
deranged by the dark
have become
                    a psychopathic killer
loose on the road…

Oh for a Draught of...

Season of mists and magical fungus,
Brother and guide to the Abraham Heights;
Pull from the earth its psychic juices
In fruiting bodies that push for the light.
Ah season of mists and magic mushrooms
And strangers worrying the bleating sheep,
And farmers advising *Mind it Boyo!*
Between the brook and burning leaf.
Where the drowsy wasp and dead can speak
Of cracks in the world at the end of time
Where the gates are tied with bailer twine.

It was there they walked with heads hung low
In search of heaven between the grass.
Both 'shrooms and steeples point to the stars!
Some they ate and some they bagged.
Ah season of mists and magic mushrooms,
The skies were full of bleating sheep
And farmers advising *Come By! Come By!*
To a puzzled dog that sits beneath.
Where the babbling tongue of the water speaks
In the voice of Phil Drabble.

Where is reason now?
Yes, where is that slippery fish?
Thrashing on a plate, perhaps
                    Gasping for its breath.
Mouthing words we cannot hear
Like a tickled trout.
Round and round the microwave,
        shall we let it out?

Ah season of mists and magic mushrooms,
Flocks of sheep are now calling my name:

*Maaaark…Maaaark…*a heavenly chorus
Between what's real and what's insane.
Where public, police and priest complain
Of cracks in the world at the end of time,
Where the gates are tied with bailer twine.

No Stranger To Sequins

Chloe Poems

Family life was like the moaning and groaning
of a tone-deaf orchestra
Warming up to performance,
Family life was the drowning and stoning of an innocent woman
Condemned to death for ignorance.
Family life was the worst bits of everything
before it could be anything beautiful
Anything beautiful was spread thin
Like margarine before dole day
Beautiful
Was the fairest skin scorched by sunrays.
Beauty was silence before it could talk
Beauty was knee-capped before it could walk
Was second-hand before it was worn
Sentenced before it was born.

I was born to believe I could never achieve
Beauty.

When I was young
I'd watch old men
And wonder why age happened and how
How did lines appear and why
Why did they suit flat caps
Perhaps I'd never know
I was never gonna be that
No way I'm ending up fat
Old man, you're a lonely place to me.

My old man disappeared

Followed the van and cleared off with my mother's money
and beaten heart
Before I was three
Before I started the school I never attended
Before I was ever apprehended
Before a girl ever condescended to kiss me.
He dillied, he dallied
Fucked off and married his whiskey
"A bottle a day keeps the family away"
A proverb he wore to his grave.
Was he ever happy to play with the child
Whose life he helped pave with uncertainty
And did he wear a flat cap
Like the chap who first gave me money?
Ten pence a wank, that's what he paid me
"Baldy nuts" is what he called me
Now I had more sweets than the boy next door
Which confused him and his ma 'cos we were poor
I wasn't one for keeping score
But I'd smile all the same
It was his dad who paid my way
Helped rot my teeth, gave me my name.
I liked that feeling
Made me unique
Liked how I felt when I was paid
Excited, strong
A child, a man
Somehow belonged to both worlds
And it never crossed my mind
I was still kissing girls.

Old men are easy
They've worn out their dignity
Keep it under wraps
And selected flat caps.

Old men are liars
Families haven't a clue
The age and sex of granddads latest screw.
Old men are arrogant
Old men are scared
Old men have wisdom
Like babies have beards
Old man, you're a lonely place to me.

There's an art in being rent
And you don't have to be bent
To paint the pornography of old men's desire
Their colours are simple
Jaded
Faded colours of fire
And I'm the canvas of sexual aspiration
But how can they aspire
When it can take just one stroke
To earn an old man's fiver.

'There must be room for love.'
I read it on a toilet door
It stood out like plain clothes police in clubs
Graffiti made poetry
By the filth surrounding it.
The thought of playing soldiers ran wild in my head
Because, as a child, it was the only thing I ever loved.
There wasn't room for my army to tread in this cubicle
I felt as alien as it.
There must be room for love
Did he mean the toilet was too small
Was he crying out for help?
Love on a toilet wall
Is a contradiction in itself.
Then I realised
I needed help

Like a bomb needs a target
A trader needs a market
Like a Catholic needs a saviour
And a warehouse needs a raver
Like a hand needs a glove
The old man sucking my cock ran off
As I screamed
"There must be room for love".
I sat down
Ramshackled as my trackies
Round my ankles
Shivering
Not with cold but with shock
This emotion was like a sniper's bullet
Aimed not to kill
But to stop me in my tracks,
I just sat, faced the facts
I've had no choice, never
I could only ever have been me
And the other boys who wear street corners like coats
Their voices are choked
And harmony is as strange to us as its always been
Unseen, like the Queen's knickers
Or actresses shagging vicars.
What you've never seen
You can only dream of.
It was then it dawned on me
I've only ever dreamed of love.

My love was never a man or a woman
Never a cottage
Soft focused
By a Vaseline-covered lens
It was something I couldn't touch
Couldn't fully comprehend
How can you visualise love

When you've never even had it
From family and friends.
I knew it was there somewhere
But not what it was for
Some people find it in books
I found it on a toilet door.
There must be room for love
I had to agree
Tidy up
Find space amongst my emotional debris
Mind was overcrowded
With people who couldn't think
Buildings had no windows
Eyeless towers
Cars without wheels
Dishes corrupted every kitchen sink
And broken crockery industry touched the sky.
It would take something great
To bulldoze this.

When we met it eventually did.

I'd only ever been to Wales
Taken on trips by middle-class Social Workers
Shamed into concern.
They took me to its countryside
Expecting me to change
But trees are just pretty coloured clutter.
When I muttered
Dared to utter I was bored
They condemned me for my truth
As if this messy foliage
Could be some kind of answer
To my equally messy youth.
They asked me to trust them
But how can you trust people who are paid to care

I mean, who'd dare trust a rent-boy.

The beach was vast, deserted
Hell bent on pebbles
Perfect opposite
To my necessary wreckage.
I stood and dared the November wind
To chill me
Force me away
As my arrogance won over the elements
I almost heard the wind say
'Welcome to the first day of the rest of your ...'
Didn't finish its sentence
But I knew what it meant
I felt it had been sent like a singing telegram
Of congratulation.
The air and my skin were moist
As his harmonic voice
Reinforced the strength of my first proper choice.
I thought of the boys on the streets
Almost wished them here
But they can't belong to my fantasy
This is my heaven, these are my eyes
This is my lumpy, sandy paradise
My own private hidey-hole
Grey, bare as old men's heads.

The pebbles felt like cobbles beneath my feet
As I hobbled along the shore
It again reminded me of the streets
Maybe that's why I felt I'd been here before
Didn't think I could feel so pure.

I buckled,
Foot was pulled from under me
Almost as a reminder, my hand hit oil

For a moment
I felt like the flipside of the beach
Empty, soiled
I recoiled
As another truth fell -
The decision to pollute it
Was made by old men as well.
But it was still here
Still belonged
As much a part of everything as anything was
And no matter who, no matter what
The beach is all it's got
A born survivor
It doesn't need an old man's fiver.

I love this place
Feel at home…love…home
Words meaningless until now
Almost forget my reason for being here.
I look for the hut
And it's there, a shy wooden creature
Sitting in the not too distant future
Soon to be an instant feature
In the continuing adventures of my life.
I smile at this cliffhanger
Because it won't take a week
To find out what happens next.

Heart stops as if punctured by an arrow
Wind suddenly makes me cold
Doubt is inseparable from paranoia
As deceit descends into this view,
What if he's not there?
His promise could be false
Just another old man
Who's allowed my romance a fictitious chance

To waltz like the greatest dancer
I could be playing out his fantasy
Without him even being here
He might be just another toothless wanker
Sitting in his chair
Drooling over young boys on his video.
Aggression makes a comeback
Like a battered boxer
Defending his pride
Can't hide my emotions any longer
Anger gets stronger
Foot catapults from the floor
I kick down the door.
Not angry any more
As the shack becomes a palace.

I step inside
A single stride takes me from the beach
Into fairyland.
Words aren't spoken, although breath taken
We just stand still and breathe.
Heady scented smoke fills my nose
We bathe in the glow of waxen flame
And I remember when I was told
All that glitters isn't gold

He's standing there
She looks beautiful
His arms open to greet me
She smiles hello
He takes my hand, she draws me and he kisses me,
The strength in his fingers and lips
Is enough to render me helpless
Tough, tender, somehow selfless
As she shares with me his honesty.
There is no confusion

This union is its own
Everything is real
Total, supreme
Like the best meal you've ever tasted
The best time you've ever wasted
The way rain feels when you're naked.
This is just the start
The beautiful woman in the rickety shack
Wants to make love to me,
Says things that excite me
Touches where skin tingles
Tongue lingers over nipples
Waiting to be bitten
Teeth greet flesh
Stain lipstick red all over my body.
I arch, stretching to his giving shapes
I hold him
Her sequins are jagged harsh
Stab at me
Digging furiously, leaving marks
A feminine legacy of masculine delicacy
And I'm ready
He's ready
She holds me tenderly
As he enters me
It's warm, welcome
As I was a short time ago.
I feel love
And it's …

I realise, believe
For the first time in my life
I've achieved
Beauty.

Five Poems
Michelle Scally Clarke

Somewhere

Somewhere over the reignbow
Is the forgotten you leave behind
There you'll find me dancing
Swinging on my lullaby's

I was born in a thousand heavens
Watched while you teef my stars
You sat me down in a desert
I created oasis out of Jupiter and Mars
You tried to stop my heart bass
See me skipping with my skipping rope
Whilst we belly laugh through hunger
Strange fruit still rot and choke

Somewhere over the reignbow
Is the forgotten you leave behind
There you'll find us dancing
Swinging on our lullaby's

Witness of your blood
Bored by your greed carnage and anger
Does my smile disturb your plan
Or the space you take from roun' us
As we breathe with our children

I gave you my son
Watch you charge for his moon
But we laughin' now
We feel we cry
Distant but distinct
In the milkyway night
I gave you a fresh bud
Watched your silent screamed face
For you dared to see me blossom
For it hurt to see my grace

Somewhere over the reignbow
Is the forgotten you leave behind
There you'll find we dancing
Swinging on our lullaby's
Ghetto style

She Is

Did you run away as a little girl?
Can you see her when you look into her walls?
She's on your hands
She's your flaws
She's your rise
She's your fall

Worse than a period pain
Or panther claw
She rips out your heart
Then she'll come back for more
Enters your body
Leaves from your pores
She is warm fat raindrops
On volcanic fall
She is light
The softness you held
As a child
She is your wombliss
Your womb man blitz
Then you dis
Then you dis
Then you dis dis dis
She is
The smell of your pillow
When you wake up in morn
She gets into your body
And comes out of your pores
When you fear
When you rape
When you call her a whore
She's your mother
She's your very first smile

Did you run away as a little girl
Can you see it when you look into her walls?
She's on your hands
She's your flaws
She's your rise
She's your fall
She is your mother

It Wasn't Just a One Night Stand

It wasn't just a one night stand
Was it?
Though you'd be pressed to understand
My need to be held by a man
I didn't just give myself away on a plate
Did I?
You had so much
You filled your face
Are your eyes too big for After Eights
Can't you make more room
Fit me in
Or I didn't open a can of worms
Did I?
To all my fears
Still have to learn
To walk not run
Be still stay strong…..

It wasn't just a one night stand
Was it?

Will

Will the blackbirds and sun shine for me?
When I close my final eye
Will you read my poetry as you tell them of my smile?
Just remember the light in me
The play mate and the life
My love for forget me not blue skies
My love for Hayfield night
Will you read my words eloquently?
As in life you treat my soul
Do not forget my children's tears
For I am in their bones
Lay me in the earth
Beneath a willow tree
An' laugh as you explain
I was sometimes melancholy

Wake

Blessings rain bittersweet grief
Photographs pass a tear moving picture
Tears fall in heart attack
You're not coming back
        Friend

Slow to recover feel old before time
Sharp as the weather cuts still your smile
Bills still come in
     After you dead
     You always said
        Friend

Backbone
Anthony Cropper

There was hail here yesterday evening. I sat at the kitchen table, not thinking about much, and it started, all of a sudden. I listened for a while without turning to look. Listened to the cracking of ice pellets on the window, on the roof and the flags. Then, I looked and saw the huge grey-white hailstones, thousands of them passing by in a flash, blocking the view to the garden.

It lifted me in some way, to be sitting here watching and listening like that. At that moment, it woke me from something more than any other weather could have. I thought if that was snow, or a shower, or a thunderstorm, then it wouldn't have had such an impact. But that ice, bouncing around off the roof and battering the window made me stop whatever it was I was thinking about.

Things didn't seem so bad during that storm. I went to bed not long after and thought long and hard about that moment. I thought about that thin white layer that had been deposited on the rotten window sill, on the uneven flags, on the long straggly grass, on the branches of the sycamore tree, on the uneven garden fence.

Now, Sal's over by the sink. She even manages to make water from the tap sound angry. I can't think what I've done to get her in this mood. I asked her before, I said, are you ok? But she just said she must be tired or maybe she has a cold coming on. I just don't feel that happy, she said.

It's funny how she can manage to get round the house and keep her back to me. We've not looked at each for hours. She's got slightly rounded, hunched shoulders. She tells me she's got a long back, and that it makes it difficult for her to sit up straight or stand straight. She had some guy feel down her backbone one night, years ago. We were at a friend's house and this man with a beard said he was a masseur, a therapist. He said he can fix people when they've got twisted muscles, trapped nerves and things. He said to Sal about her back. He said there's probably a joint out of place in her spine.

She liked that sort of attention and asked him to have a look. She'd been drinking. She was smiling, and had thin purple marks on her lips from the wine.

The man with the beard sat to her side, started at her neck, and worked his hand down her backbone. We were all round, watching, waiting for him to speak. The music was quiet and these friends of ours had the lights down low. You could see people leaning forward in their seats. The fingers on his other hand twitched slightly, like he had the shakes or was old or ill. He had his eyes closed, too. It was dark, but you could see he had them closed, and it was like he was talking, his lips moving slightly apart.

After about five minutes he stopped and said, here. There's a slight kink, just here.

Sal smiled, took a sip of her drink and nodded at her friend, Cath.

Then the man with the beard said he could fix it. Give it a few months, he said, and he could gradually get that part of her backbone into place. He said it'd help her with her breathing. You must get a sniffy nose, he said.

Sal looked at Cath again. That's exactly right, she said. I was told it's hay fever or an allergy to alcohol.

No, he said and smiled. It's not alcohol. It's this, here, and he reached out and placed his fingers in between her shoulder blades again. It makes you stoop, he said, and that puts pressure on your lungs, which stops you breathing properly. All that causes an irritation in your sinuses. It's all interconnected, he said. The body always responds in some way to a problem. It's just a matter of getting to recognise it, he said.

I told Sal she should go. On the way back in the car I said, go. You've been having trouble with your back and your breathing since I've known you. Give it a try, I said.

She shifted slightly, pulled at her skirt, then said, I don't trust him. His hand felt funny on me. He pressed his fingers into me in a funny way.

She was almost asleep in her seat, tired after drinking, but you could see she wanted the conversation, she kept slowly angling round to it, asking what I thought of the guy with the beard, whether I believed that sort of stuff, what I thought of his shirt or shoes, whether I thought he was some kind of pervert.

Then don't go, I said. Take more of those tablets for your breathing, blame it on the weather, blame it on booze.

It was late, maybe three in the morning. The streets were wet after the rain. The car hissed through patches of water.

But I am allergic to drinking, she said. Just wine, red wine. You know what I'm like in the morning, I'm all bunged up. It's not just coincidence.

You should go, I said. You never know.

The next I knew she was asleep, her head lolling over towards me. I thought about slowing down and pushing her back up into her seat, so she was straight, so she wouldn't get an ache in her neck. We had an hour or so to go and I thought if she stays like this she'll be stiff in the morning. I can't understand why, but I left her like that, her head stretching the muscles on her neck. I turned the radio on and listened to night-time music, all the while keeping my hands tight on the wheel, looking at the wet black road in front of me.

Now, Sal's chopping onions. She said she'd make shepherd's pie tonight. I'm amazed. I can't remember the last time she cooked. She's still got her back to me, we haven't spoken in half an hour or more.

She sneezes, wipes her nose on a piece of kitchen roll, takes a drink of wine and breaks the silence.

This'll be done in twenty minutes, she says. Remind me to take it out, will you?

I look over at the steamed up window, at the streaks that catch the reflected light. I watch her as she moves the couple of feet to the sink and begins to wipe the chopping board with a cloth. She's wearing a tight white top, black jogging trousers and the slippers I'd bought her for Christmas a few years back. You can smell the onions and the potatoes in the air. It's warmed the kitchen, made the air heavy, sickly.

She places the chopping board on the side next to the sink, switches on the kettle and takes two mugs from the rack that's over near the fridge.

I'll make some tea, she says. You want some tea?

Yes, okay, I say, but the words feel awkward in my mouth. It's like this kitchen is filled with too many things. There's the food cooking away in the oven, the kettle pouring steam out into the air, the pan of potatoes bubbling away on the stove. There's all this silence that's been building between us. There's all these years of sitting round this table, talking and laughing, falling out and singing and fighting and splitting the finest of hairs.

I watch Sal for a while. I watch her from behind and think about that man with the beard laying his hand on her, saying he could sort everything out. Give it two months, he said, and all your problems will be gone.

She sneezes then wipes her nose on the same piece of kitchen roll. I watch her shoulders, watch them move as she pours water from the kettle. I think about that joint in her backbone, about the problems it's caused, about whether I should go over to see if I can ease the pain.

Dust
Susan Everett

Eighty percent of dust is made up of human skin. She knew that for a fact. Though the proclaimer of such useless information had long since been forgotten, the statement still remained.

Mary wiped the top of the china figurine so lightly the cloth hardly touched its pale face. She wondered if that fact was really true, and if it were, would dust differ in colour in different countries?

'Right, love. I'm off to measure Mr Soames. Be back tea time.'

She didn't bother to answer as his guilt-free words filtered soft into the room, just visualised his solid-set back as he strode out through the doorway to the drive. She liked to imagine his self-inflicted muscle span swelling up all on its own and wedging him between the beams.

Sometimes she wondered why she felt so bitter.

Then she remembered everything.

Be back tea time, would he? Expecting steak, as usual. With sauté potatoes on the side. As usual. Somehow Reggie's aspirations of grandeur and his bid to escape the family's mining ancestry meant that frying whole potatoes instead of sliced up chips made him feel more upper-class. In a way she pitied him.

Sad, isn't it? That everything you once admired in a person, everything that attracted you to them in the first place, then mutates into everything you most hate. Like that old repeated story, charming when it was new to her, of how the pit caved in and Reggie saw the light. He dug his thirty-year-old form through blackness with air so dark you could hear it painting on your lungs. As oxygen seeped silently away Reg understood his true vocation. His light at the end of

314

the tunnel. His future.

Death... he loved it. That first encounter with a couple of dead humans was the single most exhilarating experience of his life to date. Those crushed corpses were as beautiful to him as his second sexual experience with Eva Brightman on that illicit trip to Blackpool which proved more illuminating than he'd expected.

He'd been an undertaker now for twenty-five years. That's how she met him. Harking back ten Christmas's ago, she remembered how understanding he had been, how comforting. Listening to her sobs and inadequate ramblings as if he was actually interested and not just there to put a body in the ground.

Her father was dead, you see. It wasn't what you could call an impossible surprise. He'd been ill for years but neglected to notice, preferring instead to put assortments of symptoms down to hereditary arthritis and slow rising damp.

A policeman broke the news. Your father's dead, he said, in a way that made her smile and be glad she had a visitor. She never had many of those, male visitors. Apart from the local priest but he didn't count as she put him down as neutered.

The post mortem showed her father was riddled through with cancer, so many organs it was like a shopping list. Mary was glad he hadn't had to know. It was quick, they said. He wouldn't have felt a thing. And all she felt was numb. Only when she identified his cooling body did she understand the full impact of what had happened, and realise she'd never need to buy a pound box of Quality Street and a Father's Day card again.

There was one thing that really bothered her though. Why had he taken up hang-gliding in the first place? And was his equipment rented or self owned? What possessed a sixty-three year old man to propel himself off Malham Cove at the mercy of the winds, supported by mere fabric and metal she'd never understand. Picturing it now, she saw his beaming, pink blushed face, battling the elements as they tossed him through the air. Shadowing rocks and crannies. Staring down at frozen grass and scatterings of rabbits. He'd probably loved it, but the thud of landing would have played hell with his arthritis.

If only he hadn't landed near those cows, if he'd only picked another field. All those Yorkshire Dales and he picks an acre of intrigued cattle. You couldn't blame them. Any normal animal would be a little bit bemused when some alien creature drops unannounced from the sky and shouts 'Mushy peas and Tetleys all around' in high-pitched decibels. An eyewitness said there was no way Dad could have averted their stampede, not once they started racing. Perhaps if he hadn't kept hold of the glider they wouldn't have dragged him quite so far.

At least some good came out of all this tragedy. Her Dad achieved his lifelong ambition of being remembered by having a lengthy obituary in the Yorkshire Post and a column in 'Tour Guide's Companion To Strange Country Spots'. And she met her future husband, Reggie Mood the undertaker.

Their courtship was unexpected, especially by her. When Reg bit into her sausage pie a spark flashed through his eyes. Then as he masticated apple crumble the vibrations in the air made it seem quite feasible that sex was on the cards.

She'd never used food as foreplay before. She'd never used much of anything. Reg sat drooling on the sofa as she recited her way through books of sumptuous recipes. When they reached Lemon Pavlova he touched her breast for the first time. By the end of Orange and Carrot soup she was a changed woman.

Sex and food seemed a good enough basis for a relationship. At first shocked by Reggie's pleas for erotic escapades in the back of the hearse and assorted coffins, Mary succumbed with much enjoyment. The presence of death made her feel that much more alive.

They were a perfect partnership, successful too. Death was a constant growth industry, not hit by recession. He did the bodies and she did the baking. 'Moody, Dead and Fed', the undertakers with crudities as well as corpses. Hors d'oeuvres as well as hearses. They moved from bigger hearse to bigger house, collecting china people every time they sunk a corpse. He talked to those pot people more than he ever did to her.

She casually dropped his figurine to the floor. Smash. Fragments of white china spread across the carpet.

Reg was having an affair. She knew that for a fact. Ironic, wasn't it? He'd been comforting the widows for at least eight years of their marriage. Eighty percent. When he came back from those outings it was more than just his own skin that would flake off into dust.

She often wondered if he'd been like this before. Before she met him. Before copulation and crispy crust pastry became official. And she wondered when the exact moment was when he decided to go out looking for another cake shop.

She could forgive anything but this. Almost anything. But this time he'd gone too far. Too often. Too damn close to home. Him and her own niece, for God's sake. Taking his tricks around the parish was one thing, but in her own family? And the girl was even ringing him. Here. At their house. Mary knew who it was because she knew her voice so well, due to years of feeding baby food and birthday cakes. On the occasional times that the phone wasn't put down when Mary answered, the girl covered up by lightly asking after Auntie. How are you, Auntie Mary, she would chirp. Are you keeping yourself well? Not quite so well as you, the woman thought. I know what sort of shape *you're* in, my dear. I've even seen the photographs. And I'm dying to ask who took them as you and my perky husband were obviously far too entwined to work the flash.

Mary bared her soul to Mrs Ryan, who never interrupted or yawned with boredom or aimlessly pored over the Independent crossword as if it was some life-enhancing experience to crack the puzzle. Dependable, Mrs Ryan. Even more so now she was dead.

Teasing the woman's curly hair with a soft brush, Mary made her look her best and reapplied more lipstick. She hated how their mouths went blue. Mary told the silent woman all about her trip to Liverpool the previous year, when she went to see an old school friend who actually bored her senseless. In order to escape dreadful nostalgic ramblings Mary had taken a trip to the docks and fallen in love. His name was Kevin. They sat in a cafe and talked about deceit and daffodils and diamanté jewellery. They had nothing much in common, which was a start. He had given her his address and said if she ever needed a break just get in touch. The memory made her shiver, more with regret than cold. She should have rung him up.

Mary put a yellow sticky note on the coffin to remind herself to re-powder the woman's face before the relatives came. She shut the lid in case any more children came round bob-a-jobbing and ran out of the building screaming, dropping their hard-earned coins on the driveway and running home to parents with tales of bodies and assorted human accessories in the garage down the road. Only to be given clouts round the ear-holes and sent off up to bed.

The wind attacked her fresh permed hair as she carried waiting trays over to the hearse. Reg wouldn't like this. He'd drone on about health regulations and respect and ethics but that wouldn't get the pasties, porkpies and sandwiches to the function and anyway the other funeral wasn't until three so this hearse was standing spare. At least it started without self-induced spark plug electrocution, which was more than could be said for her own car.

Reg wasn't happy. He wasn't very pleased. The funeral was fine, he said, but you should show respect for dead, and still keep all the people fed. She told him to sod off and carried on serving entrees.

There was quite a crowd of mourners there today. As Mary wandered with the melon boats she wondered if Reg had had the widow yet. If he had given her some comfort. Some soft, warm fumblings and whispered words of understanding loss. Of needing to reach the heights of ecstasy to escape the depths of gloom. The full service, including VAT.

She watched as Reggie took the widow's black cloaked arm and led her to a corner. As Mary saw the strawberry flush run up the woman's face she knew it wouldn't be too long before one of Reggie's little visits.

He pretended nothing happened, just bounced right back to his quiet wife and said how nice her tarts were. Then bit into a piece of speckled quiche as he began to chat.

Mary didn't listen. She watched his mouth move but didn't register the words. There was a piece of spinach on his teeth. She focused on it until it got too irritating, then looked around the room at all the sad personas, and back at Reggie's round, excited face. And that fleck of green. There was spinach on his teeth and it was getting on her nerves.

The widow was ensconced in black, shadowing a chair, pondering if she should sit down or stand up and look less relaxed and more unhappy. Reggie smiled across and received a little queenly wave.

There was still spinach on his teeth.

Getting on her nerves.

Mary put the tray down on some vanilla slices and squashed them completely flat.

She took her apron off and deposited it on a rosebush as she left. No one seemed to notice as she made her escape in the waiting hearse and headed for the M62, just her and a corpse for company.

Mas Se Perdio En Cuba

Pedro González

The nine-hour flight had done nothing to help the hangovers that John and Bea were still nursing from the farewell party at a friend's pub the night before. The drinking had continued until the early hours, leaving just enough time to pack parcels with medicines and rush to Manchester airport. The captain announced 'In ten minutes we will be arriving at Jose Marti airport, Havana, we hope you enjoy your stay.' John's suffering was lifted by the prospect of finally arriving in his adored socialist paradise. He tried to catch a glimpse through the window, but all he could see was the dark. Bea squeezed his hand.

Manolo was sitting patiently outside Jose Marti's airport waiting to collect the two tourists. A dental assistant in the Cayo Hueso clinic, he had been sent by his boss to look after the visitors. Smoking cigarettes was his distraction; he lit one after the other. He had fought the habit before the accident, but he did not fight it any more. One day, three years previously, he forgot to check the supply of anaesthetic when injecting the child of his neighbour, Ramon. The 'special period' during the nineties, as it was called by the government, was at its peak and the scarcity of many medical instruments and drugs was an everyday problem. The doctors were using alternative drugs that, in some cases, brought fatal consequences to the patients. The son of Ramon was to be yet another hidden fatality in the tragic statistics of the Cuban national health. The fall of the Soviet Union had devastated Cuban life through isolation. During the eighties Cuba was proud of the high standard of health care it provided, but things had

322

changed. The accident was covered up by his boss, Dr Felix Agudo, an old man with a high sense of justice and pride, only overtaken by his blind faith in the revolution and the government. He knew that Manolo, although young, was an experienced nurse who usually approached his work with great diligence. This mishap was a fatal mistake, but in the eyes of Dr Felix Agudo, not sufficient to end the career of such a promising young nurse. Ramon sued Manolo for negligence and the loss of his son. The case was dismissed when Felix intervened on Manolo's behalf.

Manolo had never seen medicine as his ultimate goal in life. He was hooked on music and his dream was to sing with his own orchestra. His lively attitude and exaggerated way of telling stories made him the most popular nurse in the clinic. But the strong dose administered on Pedrito took not only the little child's life but also Manolo's ambitions and joy. From that point on Manolo became a solitary man with a tendency to weep and he developed a hopeless soul. His dreams of becoming a singer and leading his own orchestra were over. Music and dance, which had been his reason for living, now didn't mean a thing. He was forced to move home twice to avoid being hassled by the family of Pedrito. Ramón had tried to kill him once, waiting in the gloom of the night outside the clinic. He pounced on him with a knife, the resulting brawl took Manolo to the hospital for two weeks, seriously injured in the leg and left him with a permanent limp. Ramon was held up the following day and taken to Cuba's worst prison, where overcrowding, violence and rape finally drove him to finish his own life.

Bea was the first one to walk into the arrivals lounge where a crowd of people were gathered to see their families, friends and to collect tourists. She saw their names written on a piece of paper that somebody with a sad smile was holding above his head.

The rainy season of September was just starting and John and Bea were greeted by a torrential downpour, forcing everyone to stop and wait. John joked in Spanish of thinking he was still in England. Manolo explained to him that this was the rainy season and they'd better have brought raincoats with them as the weather was going to be very unsteady. They waited under the roof of the airport until there was a break in the rain. John took the opportunity to ask questions about the situation in Cuba. Manolo sadly smiled, he knew what the European socialists wanted to hear. 'Things are getting worse but Cubans are happy to resist and keep the revolution going ahead.'

Just as John expected.

The dark Cuban roads were naked to Bea. None of the commercial billboards that she was so familiar with were present, in their place were propaganda messages about the revolution, its heroes and the defiance to the US embargo. She watched John as he looked through his side window pleased to be seeing Cuba exactly how he imagined. Bea was concerned that this adventure in Cuba was not going to be so much fun for her. John's passion for Cuba was incurable and maybe, she thought, this trip would put his feet on the ground and hopefully he could lay to rest his socialist craze. She didn't expect to like Cuba and her first impressions did nothing to dispel this. Her preference was to travel to Turkey, even Spain, rather than Cuba. Her savings for the whole year were going to be spent on John's whims. It was nothing against Cuba but she didn't understand why holidays had to become a declaration of principles. Didn't John enjoy summer package holidays in resorts? Of course he did but after losing his good job in that bloody accounting company, in a case of unfair dismissal, he had joined the Socialist Party in protest. Paul Rowland, John's best friend since childhood, was a distinguished member of the party. It was to him he turned when he lost his job and Paul offered his full support, recommending a very good labour lawyer who managed to claim good compensation from John's ex-company. Now his life was devoted to fight the system but how strong were his beliefs? He was afraid of demonstrations, he'd never read a book of politics in his life and he would never confess his socialist ideas to his beloved father, a Conservative councillor in Carlisle.

Dr Felix Agudo was standing outside his fenced house in one of the suburbs of Havana speaking to a boy when they arrived. He greeted his guests with a serious and polite smile. John, in good Spanish, after spending a year living in Spain teaching English, carried out the introductions. 'My friend Paul Rowland in England told me to send you regards and gave me this parcel of medicines for you.'

'Thank you so much, you can't imagine how valuable these medicines are for us. I've known Paul for a long time and know if you are his friend you should be another good person and socialist.' John felt a bit embarrassed, he had never being called that before and he didn't know how to react to this compliment. His membership in the Socialist Party had been for a scarce eight months.

Bea tried to distract the attention by apologising in broken Spanish for not being able to speak any language other than English. Felix told her that his English was good enough to communicate but, lamenting, that he was not very proficient as he hadn't practiced for a long time. Manolo was unloading the car. 'You are in good hands with Manolo, he is a good man. Life here is hard and some may try to take advantage of visitors, but Manolo, you can trust. You can pay him your travel fare now, ten dollars will cover it.'

The contrast between the street outside and Ramon's house was prominent. The badly asphalted roads and rundown houses ended at the big fence, behind which Felix had a beautiful clean house with perfectly painted walls. John and Bea's tiredness forced them to kindly reject Felix's invitation to dinner and they retired to their room which had a ventilator hung from the ceiling and a big old bed. There was also a TV set. He switched the TV on and a presenter stood in front of a blackboard and wrote down the main themes of her lecture on the industrial revolution. She was talking about Manchester's industrialisation and the origins of modern capitalism. Young students were at their desks listening and taking notes.

'What kind of a boring programme is this?' asked Bea. John was defensive. 'Cuba is an educated country and TV is educative, not like the rubbish that we have to put up with in England.' 'TV programmes are to entertain not to lecture people.' John didn't reply, he was knackered and didn't have the energy to argue now.

John was getting annoyed with Manolo's silence and short answers. John wanted to know everything, his travel book was too boring to read. Manolo guided them around Old Havana, deliberately impeding the hustlers from disturbing them. The heat was so strong that Bea was growing uncomfortable. She suggested they stop and have a drink. They had their first mojitos at the Museo del Arte. A trio were playing traditional Cuban songs for tourists in the patio. Bea recognised *Guantanamera* and began to sing along quietly. She loved singing. She wished she could speak Spanish as she was a quick learner for lyrics and melodies. The cocktail was having an effect. John felt glad to be in Cuba. The music, the beautiful ladies with their shaking hips and sexy walking and the calmness of the place were a perfect scenario for a promising holiday.

For the first time Bea could see a glint of a lively expression in Manolo's face when the trio announced a new song. She asked John to ask him if he liked music. 'Not much,' was all Manolo said.

Once they finished their drinks they asked Manolo to come to collect them in two hours as they felt like a stroll around Havana. Havana's streets were unpaved and the colonial houses, once surely beautiful, were in a poor state. Walking around the Prado Street several times they were stopped by people speaking in broken but comprehensible English complimenting them with kind remarks on the greatness of English football and pop music and then offered them cohibas, Cuban coffee or CDs burned off Cuban music for a few dollars. They carried on walking, ignoring the hustlers. Hustlers were very persistent but not dangerous, anyway, the permanent presence of police all around Havana made them feel safe. They wished they could walk without being noticed as tourists but their pale complexion, with their shorts and sandals formed their physical passports. As they walked to the Malecon long promenade road of Havana, prostitutes tried to stop them and propositioned John, without being concerned of the presence of Bea on his side. The traffic was a good example of Havana's contrasts, the old elegant Chevrolets circulating side by side with the Ladas, the ugly soviet functional cars, and the *Camellos*, the monstrous bus carried by a lorry, overcrowded with passengers. John said to Bea that they should travel in one of these buses instead of having Manolo driving them around, he wasn't happy to stay in Cuba as another spoilt tourist. 'No way,' answered Bea.

At the Floridita they met another British couple. They were from Newcastle and were passionate on salsa dancing and, hence, decided to come to Cuba to follow a course with a master dancer. They suggested John and Bea join. 'That is an impossible mission. I've two left feet,' said John. However, Bea liked the idea and John reluctantly accepted to have a go at the dance lessons given at the Palacio de la Salsa the next day. The Geordies were staying at the Hotel Sevilla in the centre of Old Havana. They all agreed to meet next day at noon in the lobby of the hotel.

Manolo made them a gesture of greeting as he saw them. John really wanted to know Manolo. Although he was sparing with words and very serious, his sad and benign expression made him likeable. After having so many cocktails they felt more chatty and wanted Manolo to join them in their tipsy mood. So they proposed to have some more mojitos in whatever bar he wanted to take them. Manolo accepted with a shy smile and took them to the other side of the Malecon. There in a little tower bar with loud salsa music and spontaneous dancers they sat down outside and ordered their drinks. Manolo asked for a glass of *añejo*, the seven years rum, with no ice. Once he got served he drank it in one gulp. John insisted he get him another but Manolo declined. He knew that if he carried on drinking he wouldn't stop until fainting on the ground. He didn't enjoy drinking with people as he tended to find his sadness. Bea's tipsy mood took her to dance and after trying hopelessly with John she gave a look at the skinny black guy that was walking with a beautiful young mulata. As he saw her looking at him, he started to dance with his partner in Bea and John's direction. Then they swapped partners. Bea loved the way she was led by this talented dancer. She felt as though she was a good dancer too. How easy is dancing salsa with a real dancer, she thought. She was aroused by the closeness of their dancing. She couldn't stop giggling as the skinny guy paid her compliments, how beautiful she looked and what a good dancer she was. John stopped dancing when the mulata was taken by another dancer so he sat down with Manolo and enquired on his well being. He said that he shouldn't bother with him and that his only concern was to provide his guests with a good time in Havana. 'Have you ever been abroad?' asked John. 'Long time ago,' he replied, 'that was as a volunteer nurse to Angola and Zimbabwe, but I've never been to England, although I would love to.' John promised to invite him to visit them. He answered with a smile. He knew that he would never be able to leave the island.

Bea came over and introduced her new friend. Raul was his name. He was still holding her, his arm to her hip. John was never a jealous man and liked the guy from the beginning. He liked people with big smiles and an easygoing attitude. In England, he thought, everything was so stiff and forced. As they were all sat down around the table, John asked for more drinks. Manolo looked at Raul with distrust. Manolo told him that he thought that they met before. 'Maybe at Cayo Hueso barrio?' Raul said that maybe, but Cayo Hueso wasn't his barrio. Bea's tipsy mood was getting hotter and she wanted to carry on dancing with Raul. She got up and dragged Raul to the centre where all the dancers were. Soon John and Manolo lost sight of them. Manolo tilted his head to John's side and in a grave voice told John to call his girlfriend and go immediately. He didn't understand why but the seriousness of Manolo made him feel doubtless about the dodgy situation she may have got involved in. He hurried up to look for Bea, followed by Manolo. She and Raul weren't among the dancers. He was sweating nervously. Manolo put a friendly arm on his shoulder to calm him down. 'They are over there,' said Manolo. They were leaning on the bar with two drinks and were very close to each other. Now it was Bea who was embracing Raul by the hips. Manolo walked to Bea and told her in perfect English that it was time to go now. Bea surprised at Manolo speaking in English for the first time and in her slightly drunk state, realised that she had to obey. Raul hastened to give her a telephone number where she could contact him.

Once inside Manolo's car, driving around the Vedado area, she angrily asked what happened. 'That black was a pimp that could get you in a big trouble. You should be aware that here things are not the same as in England.' Still confused by Manolo's good command of English and upset by the way they had to go, she asked him angrily why he had taken so long to talk to them in English. He confessed that he learnt English in Zimbabwe as he'd had an English girlfriend there, and he thought tourists prefer to speak freely without the inconvenience of having somebody who could understand what they are saying. He told her not to be angry with him as he knew Raul, who is a notorious troublemaker in the barrio he worked. 'These people know how to flirt and flatter tourists only for them later to realise that they had been robbed of all their dollars.' 'How do you know him?' asked John. 'I was one of them for some time. We never met but I heard a lot about him and when I was introduced to him I recognised his name and the collar he wore. That used to belong to an ex-girlfriend of mine. I was told that some time after she left me she started to hang around with him. Lately, she died of Aids and probably he took her jewellry. She was a precious mulata with a lust for gold and good life. She had been doing prostitution for him for five years.'

In the Palacio de la Salsa Bea and John struggled to get the right steps. The salsa teacher, a handsome Cuban with brown skin and green eyes, was a lively and flattering man that captivated his female pupils. Italians, Spanish, Germans, Americans, Canadian and British were the nationalities of this mixed group of salsa learners. Some were already good dancers. Somebody loudly asked the teacher: 'Miguel. When are you going to have the party?' 'On Saturday night, I will bring a band of hot Cuban music. So reserve your tickets now before is too late. They run out quickly,' he replied. Bea assured her new friends that they would be there.

Manolo was waiting for them outside the Palacio de la Música. John wasn't in a good mood. Once when they were in the car, John complained to Bea that his trip to Cuba was to contact political organisations and meet leaders for the solidarity group in England to work with and not to dance salsa. John didn't enjoy the salsa lessons. He never liked dancing, it made him feel clumsy and useless, hence, feeling vulnerable. He liked to be in control of things and making a fool of himself trying to learn the aerobatics of salsa wasn't his goal. He was proposed by the committee of the Cuban Solidarity Against Embargo, a group of left-wing and some apolitical goodwill people, to establish some contacts in the industrial sector to channel their help and donations. In order to do that he had to speak to some high ranks in the government of Castro. Felix Agudo was his passport and main introducer to the Cuban bureaucracy. Without him, he wouldn't have much chance to get through the rigid communist hierarchy, thus, his travel would have been fruitless. His first meeting was that afternoon in a few hours, and he was very nervous. The salsa lesson didn't help him to feel better.

The office of the High Comissioner on Transport and Roads Industry was a very modest little room which was deprived of even the little personal touch of an occupier. The customary picture of the revolution heroes, Che Guevara and Camilo Cienfuegos were above the civil servant's desk on the back wall and served as the main decor. Also some posters on the sidewalls with propaganda slogans such as *Resistiremos* and *Patria o Muerte* were giving the solemn and serious touch to the otherwise aseptic room. The talk finished shortly, the bureaucrat thanked him for his visit on behalf of the Cuban government and promised to send him a document with details of the priorities that Cuban urban transport requires. He was given two complimentary tickets to the Tropicana as special guests of Cuba.

John was happy to have finished his meeting and thought his mission accomplished, he could now rest and think of more pleasant enjoyment, of how to spend his days in Cuba. He really disliked politicians and he felt out of place discussing with them. The only reason to have been nominated to represent the solidarity volunteers group was his command of financial matters. The group had a small financial power but although scarce in resources didn't want to waste their funds in useless efforts. There were five more days to spend and he thought that he wouldn't like to be around official offices and it would be a good idea to move from Havana to Varadero to enjoy a bit of sun and beach.

Bea was taken aback by this sudden change of plan. 'What made you change your mind so quick? Ain't you socialist anymore?' He replied with a solemnity, not convincing enough, that even good socialists like enjoying their holidays in the same way as the rotten capitalists. Bea smiled cynically and gave him her hand. She knew that something had happened inside that office. John's face was expressionless, he maybe realised the futility of his little organisation, she thought. She started to play mind games with him suggesting they go to the Cuban countryside and live in a farm with the locals to savour a more genuine Cuban life. Now John was the one more interested in spending a typical tourist holiday just as she was getting increasingly curious about Cuba. She had never practised salsa before as she saw it as one of those things that mature women got into after a bad relationship in order to get a new partner, if possible a sexy Latin partner. Bea was a radiant young girl that enjoys clubs and going out. Her music was dance music, specially garage and soul, and never felt any interest in Latin forms of music. But now all of sudden, she was enjoying this music and liking the way Cubans were. She became Cubanised by the effect people had on her. Even with her little Spanish vocabulary. She enjoyed the calmness, the friendliness and, of course, the sexiness of Cubans. Their way of walking was so cool and sexy. A place of extreme, manhood and womanhood living together and marking their own roles with one needing the other to exist. Compared to England, where macho culture was just a bunch of lads in short sleeves and shaved heads drinking heavily and pulling girls or fighting, and that bloody girl power thing was girls wearing exhibitionist clothes, even in the most chilling winter, to go out and behave as aggressively as men. And all that was just a weekend thing, not like Cubans who express their sexuality and flirting games almost every moment.

Late in the evening Manolo went to pick them up at Felix's house, dressing very smart with black trousers and a long sleeve white shirt. John and Bea were advised not to wear casual clothes as the Tropicana entrance policy was very strict. They decided to invite Manolo as they enjoyed his company. Moreover, he was the only Cuban they met that could speak good English. He was still quiet but gradually more extrovert and communicative with his new friends. The table reserved by the high official for them was quite close to the main stage. The advantage being they could enjoy the show at a very close distance but the drawback was that dancers could bring you on stage to dance with them at any moment. John was terrified of being taken by the dancers and even the several cocktails he had didn't help his blush when two beautiful mulatas hugged him from each arm and took him to the main platform where he had to dance with the chubby vocalist. The band playing were a combo of five beautiful girls that were making a lot of noise. Their musicianship was outstanding. The prettiest played the congas with one of them slightly inclined to her lap as she rounded the instrument with her naked legs. Bea enjoyed every minute of the show and was more than eager to join the Conga dance where the audience and dancers joined in a long line and went over every corner of the roofless Tropicana. She felt two big hands holding her back and a familiar voice calling her name. She looked at her back surprised to see the skinny black guy from the Malecon bar. She remembered the warning of Manolo and stopped dancing, Raul followed her and asked her if she wasn't happy to see him. She told him to please leave her alone. Manolo came up quick to assist her. Raul stared at Manolo and threateningly spoke to him and left. Bea thanked him so much for intervening. 'Not at all,' said Manolo and took her to sit down. John had seen what happened and was about to intervene when again Manolo stopped him. He said: 'I know how to treat these people. Leave it to me'.

On the drive back home John asked Manolo what Raul had told him. 'Nothing serious, just the usual threat,' replied Manolo. 'Can't he be very dangerous?' asked John. 'That is how life can be here.'

'I thought that Cuba was a safe country.'

'And it is, especially for tourists. Nobody will intimidate you in the streets as in other places in the Caribbean. But Cuban barrios are not a safe place where pimps and secret societies have their own networks and can always get away with revenge and crime.'

'In that case why didn't you let me intervene?'

'Because they also can get you. Not tonight, but they will look for you and I can assure you they will eventually find you. Don't worry about me. I have survived in this jungle for too many years to be bothered now.'

Bea, moved by Manolo's courage, touched Manolo's shoulder from the back of the car and kissed him on the cheek. He let escape a sign of emotion in his expression and told her: *'Muchas gracias Señorita'.*

While John was laying down in a hammock beside the swimming pool, Bea ambled along the shore, lost in her thoughts. Her skin was getting a nice suntan after being scorched in their first day in Varadero. Tomorrow they were leaving Cuba and she was worried about how her relationship with John was going downhill. The week in Havana made them more aware of their differences than their similarities. John was getting more alienated from his purpose and now he was getting pissed every day and made advances to some beautiful Cuban girls before her eyes. Their worlds were tearing apart but that wasn't her main concern. She was noticing changes in herself too. She was discovering new things in her feelings that alarmed her. She couldn't stop thinking of Raul. It wasn't just his attractive appearance and exultant manhood that attracted her. The sense of danger was turning her on. She wasn't afraid to recognise it even though it saddened her. She needed emotions and these were scarce in her life with John. He wasn't enough of a man for her. Once he was. That lively young man she met at her friend's party who couldn't stop telling jokes for a moment and his self-assurance made her give him her telephone number. After that, dating was the normal step and three months later she moved in to his. She felt comfortable living with him as they continued to have their own lives even though living together. But now the passion and love was long ago gone and it was time to move beyond. John was never going to change and neither was she.

When Bea entered the bar of the hotel, she saw John leaning against the wall talking to a sexy young girl. She went up to them and asked John if she was her new friend. John, a bit drunk, told her to look for another man. They all could have a good time together. 'Well thanks for your advice. I know what to do now. You can have your mulata and now I will go to look for my man. Don't wait for us, as maybe I am not coming back. Hasta la vista baby!' She went to their double-room and took that scrap of paper with a telephone number.

The taxi driver asked Bea if she was meeting friends in Havana. 'Si un amigo', said Bea, feeling happy to understand and be able to converse a little bit in Spanish. She met Raul in the Café Paris of Calle Obispo in Old Havana. She was happy and excited to be with him. He was suave and knew how to flatter women. Although aware that he was a womaniser, she enjoyed his company and compliments. He suggested to go to see a salsa band after having a dinner in a good paladar, the private run little restaurant of a good friend.

The paladar was in the other side of Havana, separated by the sea, in the Barrio de la Regla. There, a big black woman, the landlady, with a compulsive noisy laughter-made them welcome. It made her feel that she was waiting for them. They passed to a cosy room with a table in the middle and two chairs. The room was adorned by African imagery and a strong but nice smell of herbs. The candlelights were the only light. He recommended her to have a special dish called Ropa Vieja, a selection of pork meats accompanied with rice, beans and vegetables. He sat down close to her and took her hands. She was losing herself in his hands. The big woman brought a bottle of Añejo and an ice bucket. He filled two glasses and toasted the start of a new friendship. She never had tried straight rum before and she liked it. It made her feel happy and lively. There was some drumming sound coming from somewhere outside. She asked what it was. 'They are preparing for a ceremony for the Santos,' replied Raul. Then he explained that the African gods were twinned with Christian saints since the times of slavery and this mixed religion, which had survived Spanish inquisition and the anti-religion communist ethics, had many followers in Cuba. Bea asked him if the Santerias was a kind of voodoo. He laughed and said that in the Santeria's ceremony, they don't kill chickens. He confessed to her that he belongs to a Santeria family called the *Abakwa*. After that, they kissed.

At the Salsoteca in the Miramar playa, Bea saw the illuminated sign announcing the orchestra of Adalberto Alvarez y su Son. She asked Raul if they were popular. 'Of course, Adalberto is the Phil Collins of Cuban music,' said Raul.

'I hope he is better' said Bea smiling.

Inside the club, Raul shook hands with many people. He seemed to be very popular. She remembered the warnings of Manolo. Two beautiful mulatas in night dresses shouted at Raul, something that Bea couldn't understand but their laughing and way of looking at her made her feel uncomfortable. The band was announced by an elegant presenter and soon everybody started to dance to the rhythmic music. She also felt the urge to dance and took Raul's left hand as her other hand rounded his hip.

In the lavatory a woman bumped into her and asked her the time. She looked at her left wrist when the woman cut a scratch off her blouse with a pair of little scissors and told her to run away and leave her man now otherwise she would regret it when she put a terrible curse on her. She was taken aback by the vicious temper of her attacker and decided to leave but not before telling Raul what had happened. Raul told her not to be afraid and he went to look for the woman. She followed him through the dancing crowd. Bea saw Raul talking to the woman and he took her out. She tried to reach them. Once outside Raul shouted at the woman and hit her several times. The woman got her scissors and tried to attack Raul. He twisted her arm, got the scissors and stabbed her in the stomach. She was bleeding, laying on the ground. Bea couldn't believe what she saw and called a taxi that was passing at that moment. Raul saw her leaving in the taxi and ran after her.

Gasping for breath she asked the driver to go to the Monaco district. She went to see Felix and told him the story. He called a police inspector friend of his and explained the story. Later that night, Bea was asked to identify Raul. As she was afraid of him, she went with Manolo. When they left the police station Manolo took Bea back to Varadero. All the way he kept serious and quiet. He even didn't ask how it occurred. She apologised to him for being so foolish and for not following his advice. His face was expressionless again.

John and Bea hand in hand entered the Jose Marti's airport, their eyes covered in black glasses. Manolo was pushing the trolley with their bags. They didn't speak to each other. Silence was their farewell from Cuba. In the queue to pass customs, John passed first. Bea left some tourist to pass her and went to Manolo. She hugged him and crying, she asked for forgiveness. Manolo let a tear go, ashamed to cover it with his hand, he told her not to worry.

John had his first interview, after losing his job, for a consultation Company which were appointing a financial adviser for its office in Birmingham. Bea moved to her best friend's house and started to see an ex-boyfriend.

One day after a long shift Manolo was on the way home when he was stopped by a young guy on a bicycle. He asked him for light. When he was putting his hand in his pocket the kid hastened to cut a piece off his shirt. He left pedalling fast. He only turned round to call him: '*Chivato*, friend of the tourists. You will die like a rat.'

The same day Bea's telephone rang. John wanted to see her. Bea agreed to meet in the old pub where they used to meet. John was already there when she arrived. They sat down in the same corner as they used to do. He informed her that he got the job in Birmingham and was moving next day. She told him that she was happy for him and that she had been promoted in her company. 'Do you think of Cuba?' he asked.

'I wish I couldn't. But, yeah, I still think about it. And you?'

'I think Cuba will haunt me all my life. You know there is a Spanish phrase that says: *Más se perdió en Cuba*. Literally, *More was lost in Cuba*, but its actual meaning is, *It is not the end of the world*. For me Cuba will always be the end of my little world. You know that day when I had the meeting with that bureaucrat I realised how false was my dream. I hated that man and hated myself. My concern on people's well-being was as false as his. I despised hypocrisy but I was the most dishonest as I just wanted revenge. I wanted to fuck the system and the whole world if I got the chance.'

Bea put her arm on his neck and kissing him, she cried on his shoulder. They left the pub together without saying anything. Once outside they looked at each other and went their own ways. Not a simple *call me* was said. They knew they would never meet again.

What Money Can Buy
M S Green

The man who was chained to the tree surely knew survival was beyond him now. There was something of the martyr in those deep alert eyes - seeing all around, yet making no attempt to communicate, be understood. Grim reconciliation: this was the only way. The nightmare that had haunted for years revealing itself to have been a premonition.

A ballooning swelling disfigured the flesh of the man's right cheek. His bloodied nose was pushed and flattened towards that sore, stark decoration of violence as if an invisible hand was incessantly exerting pressure. Pain. Though partially concealed by the chains the man's clothing was evidently in some disarray. White shirt ripped, blotched scarlet; black trousers torn at the thigh, both knees. The stains of grass and earth.

It had been a struggle to bring him here.

There were three other men. They crowded the small clearing in the woods that the chained man could not help but face. Captors and captive. The three captors were uniformly dressed - military green bomber jackets, faded jeans, outdoor boots. A black balaclava was roughly stuffed into one of the men's rear jeans' pocket.

The first captor, rugged, unshaven, looked up high: a summer blue jigsaw piece of sky framed by dense greenery, the high branches of the trees on the edge of the clearing. The sun that could not be seen from here would be setting in a short while. Perhaps that is why he then checked his watch, looked to his allies with an expression that was undeniably affirmative.

Finally he focussed on the captive: 'trees and trees and trees for miles and miles and miles. No one will hear you if you shout so, now the gag's off, at your leisure, kick up all the fuss that you want.' Lighting a cigarette the blond, crew-cropped second captor continued to nervously pace two yards forward, turn, pace another few yards, turn and on. Walking the spot. 'Yes, shout for all your worth but if the sound of your voice gets under my skin... well, I wouldn't like to be in your shoes.' Despite the victim's vulnerability the threat lacked daggers of menace; the man puff-puffing tobacco had not the same villainous aplomb of his comrade. The man chained to the tree gave no sign that he had heard any words. 'I wouldn't like to be in his shoes, anyway.' Now the third spoke. All six-and-a-half hulking feet of him. The man mountain with the greying beard, thinning crown: he was maybe a decade the senior of the others. His huge frame leaned on the spade with which they had done their digging, somewhere amongst the trees, close by. The man chained to the tree could not recall hearing the giant speak before. The giant narrowed his eyes, while the first captor grinned with pleasure. 'Drop-dead gorgeous.' Full of mockery of that beaten figure shackled by industrial links, padlocks. Chains that twisted round midriff, pinned arms and legs to bark as they wrapped and trapped around the thick tree-trunk.

'The fashion world doesn't know what it's missing.' A taunting guffaw. The nervous smoker sniggered sycophantically when the joker turned to see if the joke had been appreciated. Not everyone could be likewise persuaded. 'What's his game?'

'Game?'

With raised brows they watched the giant scratch at beard, mystified by the victim's reticent hold on dignity despite the brutality suffered, the poison black cloud over him. 'Why doesn't he plead for mercy?'

'Knows it would be no use. Knows why he's here.' The grin might have vanished but the scorn remained. 'To die a death and make my world.'

'He's too chicken scared to talk.' The second captor's quick cautious glance towards the first was a glance that sought approval. It received only a smug nod. Some private notion had perhaps been confirmed. 'Chicken scared,' the second reiterated striding the few yards to halt right there, on top of the prisoner. A bully-boy smirk, a lengthy drag on the half-gone cigarette - blue-grey smoke rings blown in the pummelled face. 'Are you chicken?' Sneering, flicking the cigarette butt away. A clenched fist held inches from the mess of the broken nose. Unblinking, meeting his tormentor eye to eye, the captive's tongue refused even a whisper.

'He's chicken.' The fist unfolded, a mouthful of spit splattered the ground.

'Well then, we all know why we're here and, it's getting late, we'd better get it over with.'

The eye contact suggested that the giant had no real further part to play, was merely a spectator.

'Who'll do it?' The second rocked on his heels.

'You know who'll do it. We drew straws didn't we?'

'Yes, we drew straws,' words uttered with much reluctance. Drawing straws had not been the right way to come to such a sombre, significant decision.

'Wait!' The word was emphasised by the slamming of the spade into the earth. 'We'll see what he has to say for himself.' The huge man spoke with authority, as if he too had come to a decision. The first looked on with displeasure.

'You're not getting cold feet, too, are you?'

'No. But I'd like to hear what he has to say. Speak.'

From face to face to face. Sullen malice; fear and uncertainty; unspoken questions, beginnings of pity. The captive did not speak as had been decreed however.

'See... Let's get it over.'

'There's something that isn't right.'

'Isn't right? There's nothing wrong with justice.'

'That's what this is called, is it? Justice? Such a high and mighty word.'

'Damn you!' Judge, jury spun round, showed his back in anger. 'Damn you!' Stomping over to a tree he kicked out, chipped the bark with his wrath. 'We go through it all, down to the finest detail, everything goes to plan... then, on some cowardly whim you change your mind right when it matters most!'

'Maybe we need to do things right. A last request?' He who had drawn the short straw - he who was to be executioner - had grown in confidence now he knew at least one of his fellow conspirators also had qualms. Maybe, just maybe, he wouldn't have to be the one who did the killing after all. If only there was enough time. His fingernails tap-tapped the cigarette packet.

'Just get it done.'

He dared ignore the order, strode before the captive again. This time a cigarette was pulled from the near empty packet, gently placed between puffy red lips. 'Smoke?' He was about to reach in his pocket for a light when the cigarette fell to the floor.

'Get it over with,' the first commanded impatiently.

'I'm trying to...'

'I know what you're fucking trying to do. Get it over with.'

'Why doesn't he say anything?'

'Does it matter?'

'He fought hard enough to stop being dragged into the van.'

'That's right. My ribs still ache.'

'That was a mistake. We should have used the gun to get him in the van. No one was around. And should someone have passed we could have drawn attention to ourselves by giving the fool a chance to fight back. But he was placid enough when we put the gun to his back and led him up here, through the woods. He was placid enough while we were digging his grave.' A cruel smile flickered over the speaker's mouth.

'The sod gave me a nasty bang to the jaw, too.'

'What the hell! You went about things like a wimp. But you've got the pistol now. You swore you'd use it with a drink down your gullet. You swore there'd be no problems.'

A gruesome truth. And nothing but. Complexion drained to a ghostly pale as if staring down a barrel himself. Jacket unzipped, hand reached inside. The small black handgun. That equivocal, doleful expression seemed to say that he would give anything for someone else to be holding it. The safety catch was flicked.

'Are you sure this is the right man?' The big man wanted to know, his voice clear, resolute. He wanted no mistake. He had to be certain.

Not for one moment had he imagined the victim to be capable of that brave fight that had earlier been put up. And then this wordless obstinacy in the face of death. This was not how the man they had been told to execute had been portrayed to them.

'Of course I'm sure he's the right man.'

'What's your name?' Doubt was gnawing away. The captive glanced disregardfully away. At the outset it had been a great stubborn sense of injustice that had rendered him mute. It had been the same sense of injustice that prevented him breaking down, falling to emotional pieces. No matter what, the belief that this should not happen to anyone would not allow him to give them further opportunity to gloat. He'd swallowed and swallowed the lumps that formed in his throat. He had not even begged for the sake of his young daughter and wife. Now, watching his captors debate and wrangle, hope had been reborn. Maybe all was not lost. Maybe he could getaway yet. It was about timing. Timing the roll of the dice. So don't give them anything yet. Let them talk. Let them talk each other out of it.

'We know his name. He's the right one.'

'Have you got the photograph?'

'The photograph? No. I've burnt anything that could be used as evidence. Once we're out of the district they'll be nothing to say we've ever been here.'

'But you're the only one who saw the photograph.'

'Do you think I'm stupid enough to snatch and shoot the wrong man? One thing you both should remember - I'm in this for the money. I haven't personal feelings about this.'

They deliberated. 'No, I don't believe you would get the wrong man, but...'

'Maybe we should let him go.'

'Let him go! Let him go!' Enough was enough was enough. Right arm violently swished through the air, the hysteria of a fanatic stoning an heretic. 'And let him go running straight to the law! Don't forget he's had a good look at all of us! Get it over! The job done, we get our money and that's it. We don't have to get involved in anything like this again.'

'If you hadn't talked me into it I wouldn't be here in the first place.'

'And if he is the wrong one...'

'Listen to yourselves! Listen!'

'Don't do it. Don't let him talk you into murder.'

At the hushed rasping urgency of the voice all froze. Long seconds passed.

'He's the one. Don't forget what he once did.' Having recovered, the first captor, unmoved, held his ground. 'And I want the money. You know I could have done this on my own. I could have asked someone else to join me, someone with more courage. But I thought you were my friends, the very people who could be trusted. I gave you a chance. However much you might want to blow that chance he's not going to get away. He gets away over my dead body! Give me the gun!'

'Don't do it. Don't let him talk you into murder.'

'Pass the gun! I'll do it! I've had more training in situations like this. I'll have to do it. Fucking cannon fodder regiments!' Features contorted, embittered with ugly intent. And away from that rising reckless craziness the second captor stepped back. 'I'll do it! If I have to, I'll fucking do it! Pass the gun!' The first shadowed, hand outstretched, fiercely demanding. Hand it over? A point-blank refusal. Tracking further away. Didn't use the gun to ward the first off, the gun aimed down - this, a blind retreat. And the stalker stalked. He had noticed the boulder jutting from the earth, knew that his prey would unsuspectingly stumble. An abrupt lunge, hand grabbing at hand that had finger on trigger. Another hand gripped and crushed throat. By some miracle the finger on the trigger did not squeeze, it slipped harmlessly from danger. The struggle for power began. Like a fight between actors, a fight choreographed. Wary delicate trickery, thrusts of grunting brute force. The loaded weapon struck fear into both combatants, neither wanting the confrontation yet neither wanting to back down, lose. They had to have the gun. The gun controlled the future. They grunted and pushed, tripped, made fists to slug. Fingers tried clawing eyes. 'If you don't watch it the weapon will fire!' Alarmed, the bearded third held head in hands. Which side should he take? Should he step in, use his colossal body and brawn to end the

343

lunacy? Would the gun accidentally be fired? And dreading the consequences if it was. The warning had some effect. Though the first wrestled on, snarling, undaunted, his fast tiring opponent was influenced to relent. Allowed the gun to be wrenched from his grasp. He had not been determined and strong enough to win.

They crouched over, panting, catching their breath.

'You should have said you didn't have the heart right at the beginning. Now we've come so far we can't turn back. You'll do better to think about the money and the money alone.'

'I don't want to be responsible. I didn't...'

'Nobody ever does. But don't you realise that someone would have taken the job? Someone who dared not to care. Someone who knew the value of money. Making a mortal enemy of a rich man was not a clever thing to do.' A finger condemned the man chained to the tree. 'For his sins he has to pay. Maybe the best legal team money can buy wouldn't stand a chance, couldn't nail him - for what he did. How could it? But there are always other means. Money buys those other means. Us. Together. We can nail him. We've been careful. They'll be nothing to connect us to the death. Trust me, I've made sure of that.'

'What if the paymaster refuses to pay?'

'He'll pay.'

'They'll be no way we can make him.'

'He'll pay!'

The giant man frowned, reflectively stroked his whiskers. 'It has to be done.' Now the gun had changed hands he knew that there was no turning back, that it was over, no room for discussion. 'It's true, if we let him live he'll be able to identify us all. The law will be alerted that there's a price on his head, they'll know who put it there. Then they'll be a price on our heads for screwing everything up. This is a secluded spot, maybe the body will never be discovered. Whatever, we have to see it through now.'

Both the second captor and the captive closed their eyes.

Marching to the tree where the captive was held the man who had won the gun looked to be without conscience. A tigerish stare revealed no emotion only the nerve that had never once wavered. Without ceremony the gun was pressed against the living dead's temple. 'Our time on earth is full of good-byes.' A sadistic tone of enjoyment. The others grimaced, looked away.

Their ears could not be averted to the crack, the sudden vicious blast that echoed through the woods, sent unseen animals scrambling, birds flapping, caw-cawing. The same blast that sent shudders up and down their spines. Not wanting to but needing to know they turned to see if it had really happened. Immediately they turned away. Another shot rang out. A few wet, bludgeoning thuds. The face would be beyond recognition.

They heard a clanking of chains, a solitary dull, heavier thud. Something being dragged along, twigs snapping. The giant stared at his boots, sighed, took a deep breath. Get it over. He left the second captor standing dazed, gazing into emptiness. In no time the sound of the spade working. Filling the shallow grave that each had taken turns to dig.

Shaking fingers fumbled to light a smoke while the corpse was dealt with. How many cigarettes he went through, how long the deed took, he did not know. Shortly, eventually, they rejoined him. They were three again. 'Pity about the mess on the tree. The muck I've thrown on it conceals it reasonably enough though.' The heavy load of chains was thrust into idle hands. 'Make yourself useful, carry these.' The recipient of the chains could not avoid shrinking back, disturbed by the thick, fresh blood on the arms of the killer's jacket. 'Don't worry, I'll not wear it to a dance.' A casual glance over shoulder. 'It's done.' The killer motioned with the gun: 'we might be unlucky, that might have been heard by the old gamekeeper. I know he likes to visit a pub in one of the villages four or five miles away at this hour, likes a whiskey or three before last orders, but to be on the safe side we should make a move. It would be typical if tonight of all the nights he decided to stay sober.'

A reply was not forthcoming.

And they left wordlessly, in single file. Down a mossy rocky slope, to the dry mud path, into the darkening depths of the woods. The rattle of chains, the tramp of boots, diminished. In no time the trio were lost from view altogether amongst the twilight and trees.

Five Poems
Jo Pearson

Tune In, Turn On, Bale Out

The sky is crying
Noah won Olympic gold for t'third time
in the rowing
Jesus he wor right
nitrates, carbon dioxide
my chest feels tight.

Strappelli emigrated
followed the scrying screen of Nostradamus
the guy in the film built his boat
on top of a multi-storey building.

Can't hold the rain back with a giant tarpaulin
be same for the next fortnight
a greeting wee boy
did crap in the swimming
fitted the new council bath
leaked from downstairs' ceiling

no tax rise gridlock
wettest September since 1811
when I wor a lass
sea didn't come in
tv said to watch out for sewage.

I am sailing
off on the foam of a fig leaf
with a rough twig sail
two giant piano fingers lofted
and the wings of a starling.

Hell, I don't want to live there either

Kramer vs Kramer
our house all week
in each tweaked floorboard
and suppressed heart beat.

Against the pillow
one eyelash
blinks the bairn awake.

Autumn already
pokes its bony finger
whips a clipped breath
across the street

I take to heart
Damart
and a chink in the warm air heater's
warm air heat.

Sink my teeth
into another Cadbury's toothache
15 Potty Lane
the devil, the old ball and chain

better I know
my number's up
mark the cards
throw the game.

3 Colours Red

So now we live
in one of those red houses
by the iron bridge
me son demolished
the big red building bricks

and sits there in his red shoes
two holes for big toes
Naked Lunch all week
flies humming out the woodwork.

Fireworks spatter
like winter weather against the window
light the whole sky bonfire red
the kind of spitting rain that stings.

Destined for the shit bins
six months on Teletubbies
snatch Po's red scooter
and do a flit.

I don't want to hear
next door's Coronation Street
soap wars between the walls
have to switch on Neighbours
for that warm red community shit.

There is no eldorado
he makes me cry
just like me dad did
mother's ruined rag of tissue
and bottle of red sleeping pills.

The history I tried so hard to shake
laps me red faced
wallpaper pattern dancing
in front of eyes rimmed red.

Losing Edna

An old 5 pence piece
slow motion down the grate
along with the house keys.

Embedded fella's knees
and varicose veins like road maps
- ordinance survey.

3 letters received
2 cardigans me son wears
after 17 years.

Her face probably
still a tongue sandwich
between 2 slices of bread lips.

Those glasses always
fit for a bunch of gladioli
while she fills his snap tin.

The Earwig and the Rose
after Tom Waits

That's the way the milk pours
that's the way the tablet scores

that's the way the paper cuts
that's the way the cigarette butts

that's the way the knuckles rap
that's the way the roads map

that's the way the beauty spots
that's the way the ink blots

that's the way the vice tightens
that's the way the dawn lightens

that's the way the fence leans
that's the way the ceiling beams.

I met my love on the old tip road
down by Tang Hall where the flowers grow
in the summer hot as coal
an earwig and a rose

Four Poems
Bob Beagrie

Cu chulaind's Lullaby

On double time, Cash in hand

Snort, burlesque bull-bouncer
low on Exchange Square,
scanning herds in wattage orange

the valley's folded Christmas zeal
pours Nativity scenes from garage mouths

all the streets, gritted roads
brittle avenues n' frosted groves
fight n' race for grottodom
to be the first He'll visit

ah promise yeh

without a doubt, the doormen tap-dance
sly with segs, slide 'n' shuffle, soak up stares
like buffalo mounds in freezing fog

hulking shadows, black on grey
around megaliths, worn tumuli
knee-high bollards n' thin black ice

blart n' bother clinging tight
copping slurred snogs n' covert gropes
underneath the Green Man's bleep

early doors

the queues are safe in the crack
of a 22 carat tooth, ironed out
by a bleached blonde stare

six pupils swimming in each eye
six irises like jade tigers dancing the jitter
of Red Bull, tuned-in to the overflow
of mood n' booze n' powdered highs

says yeh then nah, in green, in red
nods 'em in then holds 'em back

no fuss

this hound will smile polite
to' suss the yabber
even take a pinch of raw-faced cheek

he cooks his paws
in white vinegar n' herbs, trained 'em
to kill with a simple tap

his bark has become rose quartz
spends the days carving edges
marking points in shifting maps

last orders

waits like a nail bomb for some tanked
-up bloke who's out to prove
a bitter point n' knows a few good moves

the hound is wired n' licensed to warp
the night back into shape, diffuse
the situation with a raised full glove

n' lead with his nut in a cold tamed rage
to gore with receded horns n' guard
the rites of Yuletide's turn

in dark dawn

after a parmo, a sleet squall drives
Cu chulaind home, inch by inch
he scrubs the night scents from his pours

before sneaking-in
between warm sheets to spoon
his body about her sleep.

Snake Eye

'Narcissism appears realistically to represent the best way
of coping with the tensions and anxieties of ultramodern life.'
      Christopher Lasch. *The Culture of Narcissism.*

Warning: one of every twenty images may be harmful to your health.

One causes two nights of fever dreams in the humidity
Of August, legs tying themselves in the sheets.
Two sandwiched days of shuffling like I'm forty years
Older than my years. Retinas burning winces
From deep aches and surface spasms. It came on
Like a cobra-bite, started with a cold shiver
Till it felt as if someone had stabbed my left eye.
I took a few days off to crawl inside my shell.
Batten down the hatches to wait out the worst of it.
Spend some quality time with my old ghosts,
And new ones, with their deadline deliriums,
Their forked impossibilities flick-sniffing me out.

The second night the pain grew blunt, but spread
behind my cheek and jaw. The snakes were back.
Slithering thru the creaks of the hot house, thru the pipes,
And the marrow of it. Spitting phone calls not made
E's not returned, letters unwritten, reports, arrangements
Expectations not met. All I wanted was to strip off my face
Burn my name, shed the constrictions of my skin.
Wondering what's going on. What on earth have I seen?

Was it that wasp-sting in the eye from a few months back?
Maybe, it didn't just sting, but laid some eggs as well
And they've hatched to start devouring my brain!
Or maybe my best mate, who I cut short last week
Has since crafted a doll around a hair I left, inadvertently
On his carpet and is slowly working his needles.
Or else it's Wisdom arriving in my mouth - that seems

A little far fetched, but on Nights of the Snake, you rule
Nothing out. I'm prone to these crashes once in a while.

It was bright again by the time sleep came. But today
I was more my usual shape, though less prone to movement.
Filled-up by the sunshine on the water, the water-light's
Shimmer on the underside of the bridge. Well gifted,
As we drifted on the river, ate ice cream by the cathedral.
Paid our respects to Hilda and Cuthbert, felt unusually
Comfortable with Slow. The Nights of the Snake have slid
Into my back-brain drawer, leaving a twinge in my kidneys
One nostril that refuses to work. But that's nowt –
Why! Tomorrow I'll be fit enough to turn cartwheels
Down the hillside, heading straight for white water
Staring wild and stopping short before the rocks.

Never Enough

Too much cholesterol in too many
bites of cake too many bargains in
too many window displays, too many
shoes to wear in one week & far too much sex
on today's t.v. too many carrier bags crammed
under the stairs too many scratch cards & coupons
stuffed into her purse not enough notes folded flat
to the lining lying back to back & not enough
change to make a decent rattle.

Too many years of too many fags
sitting on her chest in too many queues
for a reduced perm & set that's had enough
of coping with too much
rain
Too much
sea wind
being kept under-wraps
by a history of headscarves & a season of hats.

Too long at the sink thinking
there's not enough days till the Christmas crush
& not enough days to save for next year's holidays
in Blackpool, The Lakes or the Costa del Sol
too many pinched days spent nibbling the corners
of never enough endless days to be basked away
on lie-lows like a babe in the shallows
& sipping too much sangria

Not enough days & not enough days
not enough hands & not enough eyes
not enough sweet nothings poured into her ears
& not enough ears to hear the too many
tales of old wives on too much tamazipan

& not enough laughs while these not enough
days stretch into too many yesterdays & not enough
tomorrows already filled too the brim with too many
spiders lurking in too many baths with too many
legs & far too much hair

& that bus driver's smile's missing too many
teeth from too many fights after too many
drinks or too many bites of his wife's fruit cake,
muttering to himself under his too much moustache
that he's spent too long squatting a double yellow line
behind too many arseholes driving too many cars
under too many middle-managers making too many cuts
& too many changes to the old bus routes.

There's not enough seats or there's too many people,
too many sneezes & too many germs not enough
flu-jabs to deal with the threat of the expected epidemic
in the Christmas crush, there's not enough days,
& there's not enough days & she's beginning to feel
that it's one of those days when she's lived one
too many of these not enough days.

On a Trip to Leeds

(Verwundeter Mann – Arno Breker 1940)

I strolled around a wounded man, king of tree-lined streams,
who'd formed a cage of his own form. Head hung low,
loose arms on knees. Stilled veins traced the backs of hands,
the bulge of lats and abs, relaxed, with lead-lined heart.
The giant man, who's seen the age yet never aged,
the mad spark in the artist's eye, who knows the furnace
of this perfect form of knowingness, overseen the ideal,
the crematoria; and never let a wrinkle rise, no doubt lines,
crows feet, or fearing crease along the brow, save that
which he was given within his cage of classic form. I saw
the limp prick harder than stone, the gaze toward his navel.
Kept my distance from this doomed god who could take a swipe,
tear off my head, stamp me under perfect foot, before settling
down upon his rock to brood on 'Why, and how and when?'

Graffiti Dipped Wonder

Ricky Venel Stone and Mawnie Sidran Moon

This is a collaborative poem written over the internet at www.urbanpoetic.com. Urban Poetic 'seeks to be a collaborative online community that embraces the fly tracks of poets the world around all seeking to elevate the word movement'. Ricky Venel Stone's words are in normal text, Mawnie Sidran's are in italics.

She breakbeat sampled my heart
took me near and far
put me on the stars
dressed me in stripes and bars
followed my lines
motorwaying my future path in half
...without maths
gave me static and feedback

feeding me love
to his willingness I succumb
breakbeat samples of lust...
spinnin on wax
bboy found bgirl at last...
searching has stopped
and love was found
hiphop junkies addicted to the sound
of that urban flow beat
poetically producing heat

She blew me up!
...and I died
consecutively dying
her freedom still fights
her black skin bites the nice heat
...I take ice when I sip her sweet skin satin
she grafitt-ed my skin pattern opportunity
broadened my horizons and my community
ruthlessly she deepens me
I'm lost in her oceans

I'm hoping to em-sea her sound
swim and drown
be as profound as her statement
she gives me her streets
accepting no payment

With pilot markers I streak
colors of his skin
hangin from heavens
I mark easily with my pen
illustrations
of his heart
sprayed with krylon
I mark
the outline in dark
his name is my art
profound is the statement
I seem to produce
as I color the depth
of my favorite muse

Many times in many lifetimes
she blew up like a fuse
I can't hold the love
pennies for my thoughts
...love my temptress
left hand on the mic
right hand grabs her waist tight
fitting like gloves
I'm in love!
bgirl found bboy at last...
and its not corrupt
...I amplify the high
while her lips fight much love
I gasp much love above the night
till and from moontide

with or without light
we poets write insight
breakbeat tight
streaming movements of fingertips
I touch her skin and scribe
tattooing eyelids
and dreams
singin 'ol pirates'

By Jah we stay blessed
love to watch as he creates this mess
with one lick of my lips
he starts the cypha again
and were stung by love
like mattress springs we stay sprung
tight on this method
crystal like dreams
by any means
I stay tucked
up under his wing
bboy egyptian king
the answer to my hiphop dreams
he amplifies my thighs
deep into every night
till and from moontide
with or without light
keepin our breakbeats tight
his melody escaped touch
sharin headphones listenin to Buckshot
I stay locked
inside his clutch
he's on top
and i'm on the unda
drenched beneath my graffiti dipped wonder

My lips bent on french vanilla
I tend to melt with her militancy
...our lines besieged
she's west I'm her east
graffiti hearts beat yin and yang
she sprays in phat nozzles who I am
she has released my scratch
bought my love beat back
sharpened with attack
like orchestral violins and harps
mark these words she writes me sooooo high
I need to be careful of the space
there's no air
I will die
...and the soft killin offence
is not arrestable
I dipped in wonders of
bgirl american dreams
my soul spirit bleeds
cuz I swear we're original like Adam and Eve
butterlip wings scent
nutmeg and cinnamon
she's my poison my ointment
and my vitamin
...plus in the dark
when my eyes rove over her-art
she's my filament!

He fills me
sends me...
deepens me thoroughly
throughout each and everyday
in each and every way
I'm in love
his radiance outshines the sun
producing earth movements from above

half way around the moon
and past heaven
I fly
deep into his eyes
and envelop history
discovering past lives
and times
of man and wife
poetry scribes
his words write me sooooo high
I died
a million times
at the dipped wonder of my dreams
ancient love
you solomon
I sheeb...
and like lessons
I study the magnificence that's kept
in the discovery of what's next
I read I scribe I search and I find
that the peace I was searching for
I found in your eyes
and I'm stung
with kisses that taste like cinnamon
and so I see
you mark easily with your pen
as I drip your name in bubble letters sprayed from within
...plus in the dark
when my eyes rove over his-art
I start to scribe wonder
images dedicated to my graffiti dipped wonder

Biographies

M Y Alam's debut novel, *Annie Potts is Dead*, was published in 1998 by route. His second novel *Kilo* followed in 2002. His work draws on hip-hop and American gangster movies as well as life in inner city Britain. M Y Alam has numerous published articles and short stories to his name and he occasionally writes for *The Big Issue in the North*. He currently works as a lecturer at Bradford University, in the Department of Applied Social Studies.

Bob Beagrie has worked as a freelance artist, writer and creative writing tutor for many years. His poems have been published in two pamphlets, *Gothic Horror* and *Masque* by Mudfog Press, as well as appearing in various anthologies and magazines. In 2002 he won the Biscuit Poetry Prize and his first full-length collection *Huginn & Muninn* has just been published by Biscuit.

James Bones has just finished a degree in cybernetics at Bradford University. He currently has a head full of murder stories and a bank account full of debt. To anyone who wants to offer him a job or advance on a novel: mum's the word.

Peter Bromley lives and works in the North East of England having moved around most parts of Britain to follow his chosen job, which is conservation. Currently he is the Regional Director for English Heritage. Married with three children and several stick insects, he has had work published in *The Echo Room* and *New Voices:North East*. *Sky Light* is his first piece of published prose.

Val Cale was born ass-first in a hospital in Cork city, Ireland in 1971 but is now proud to have no fixed abode and fewer possessions than you could shake a pint of Guinness at. Val's been travelling the world for the last eleven years. He's lived in Japan, Taiwan, India and the Middle East amongst a myriad of other strange lands. He's recently completed an overland trip from the foot of South America up to the Arctic Circle. He subscribes neither to organised religion nor politics but is a true believer in chaotic madness and a connoisseur of illicit hors d'oeuvres. His novel *The Blackstuff* was published in 2001.

Lolita Chakrabarti trained as an actress at RADA and has been working on stage, television and radio for the last twelve years. She began writing seven years ago. Her stories have been broadcast by the BBC and are read up and down the country via the Interact network. She is currently working on a play and her first novel.

Anthony Cropper was born in Fleetwood, Lancashire. His first novel, *Weatherman*, was published by Route (October 2001). Since then he has appeared at a number of literature festivals, including performances at Crossing the Border Festival in Amsterdam and the Vaasa Literature Festival in Finland. He has had a number of short fictions published, and some of his work has recently been translated into Swedish. Anthony collaborated with four other writers in order to generate text for the Orpheo Five concerts and he was recently commissioned to write the text for *Wanderlust,* which was performed at Scarborough Festival of Light. He is currently completing his second novel.

James Dean Garside is a quiet man with scary handwriting, he studied English in North Wales, got a Creative Writing MA in Bath, then returned to Yorkshire to repent for his sins. He's had poetry and short stories published in anthologies, community publications, and literary magazines. Intends to write a novel if he can stay out of bed long enough.

Susan Everett worked as an illustrator before concentrating on her writing. After winning the Carl Foreman Screenwriting Award (in association with BAFTA) in 1993, she went to film school in America where she wrote scripts and directed a short film, *White Rabbits*. Her first novel *Crazy Horse* was published by route in 2000. She wrote a two hour TV thriller for the *A Mind to Kill* series, broadcast in 2001. The same year she directed another short film, *Moose*, which was followed by a commission from the Film Council/Yorkshire Media Production Agency to make her latest short film, *Puss Puss* in 2002. Susan splits her time between writing and making films, as well as teaching scriptwriting in Leeds.

Rachel Feldberg's current work includes a Radio Four drama commission, a short story commission from *Time of the Signs* and re-drafting her first novel with the support of a Yorkshire Arts award. *Jigsaw* is one of a quartet of stories, written as part of a UK Year of the Artist Award, which were inspired by journeys with local taxi drivers to the four points of the compass.

Daniel Fox was born in Sheffield, 1979. He's just graduated from Hull University and will be studying some more in Manchester in the Autumn. Presently, he's working part-time as a 'legal representative' for a company in East Yorkshire 'the plucky underdog taking on the suits, etc, etc. I'd like to write a book. Make it into a film, script it and direct it myself, and have final say over the sound track. I want Melvyn Bragg to interview me at the gates of my old school on a crisp morning for a South Bank Show profile. You might think my tongue is in my cheek. It isn't.'

Pedro González is a DJ of a cultural bent, playing such events as film festival openings as well as being the resident DJ for route's live poetry events. Currently he plays *Mestizo Sound* every Sunday night at Big Hands in Manchester. As much as he likes to play music, he also likes to talk and share his passion; he writes articles for route and for the magazine *Vida Hispánica* and also gives occasional talks on music at cultural centres and events. *Mas Se Perdio En Cuba* is his first piece of fiction.

MS Green is an ex-journeyman musician who has been drunk at - and played - the seedy venues of many major UK cities. During the mid-nineties he co-formed and promptly helped bankrupt a small independent record label. He penned a fast-selling Manchester -based music fanzine around the same time. Several of his stories appeared in *Warehouse*, and he is currently working on his first novel.

Mark Gwynne Jones is a performance-poet with a growing reputation. His highly regard film-poem collaborations appear on the website www.psychicbread.com His first collection *Pickety Pockety Poems*, was published in 1997 by Last Gasp Records and his next collection, *Psychicbread*, will be published by route in June 2003.

Roddy Hamilton lives and works in Aberdeen. His stories have been published in various literary magazines in Scotland and broadcast on Radio Four as part of a season of new Scottish writers. Currently working on a novel, he is also interested in digital fiction and video film-making.

Philip J. Hancock, AKA Marvellous Phil, is the author of SOHO... A collection of link poems describing twenty-four hours in W1. He is currently working on a new collection of poems.

Bernie Hare was born in End Park, Leeds. He's worked as a social worker, car mechanic, van driver, foster carer and removal man. He's interested in most of the arts and sciences, drugs, music, comparative religion, philosophy, and horse racing. 'Last year, I started up as a freelance writer and editor and now I'm almost starving to death.' He is currently working on a novel, *Urban Grimshaw and the Shed Crew*.

Lee Harrison is twenty-five, lives in Hull – a top ten City of the Stigby. 'For my current day job, I order books for the Hull College library, but would like to write for a living.' He's done a degree in Religious Studies but can't remember why; something to do with *Indiana Jones and the Temple of Doom*, he thinks. 'In my spare time I lie face down on the floor listening to three CDs at once as I plan ways to win the hearts of THE LADIES using enemas, organ donation and my amazing Elvis leg technique.' Additionally, 'I believe there is a tune for every occasion and have incidental music playing in my head at all times.'

A S Hopkins Hart has a number of published stories to her name. In the early days of jazz criticism, the ultimate accolade was to say the performer 'lived the blues' A S Hopkins Hart is like that about surrealism. She lives in Otley.

Helena Hoar grew up in Derbyshire. Studied in Southampton and Leicester; also at Rutgers in New Jersey. Worked as a teacher in Cheshire. Worked as other things in Warwickshire. Now teaches small children in West Midlands. Can't help writing.

Daithidh MacEochaidh is a published novelist, short-fiction writer and poet. His work ranges from the blisteringly experimental to 'in your face' neo-realism. His sad, disturbing yet poetic novella *Travels with Chinaski* is to be published by *Wrecking Ball Press* in 2003. Meanwhile he has set up a web initiative to promote shorter fiction: www.skrev-press.com. He currently lives in Wales.

Oliver Mallet lives in Leeds and is 'very busy wasting my life. When not working for the civil service or sitting around doing nothing I am trying to complete my first novel.'

Denis Mattinson was born in a Yorkshire pit village. He left the pits to serve in the army, spending three years in Malaya. Since then, he's been a gamekeeper, a curator of birds and subsequently, an entrepreneur.

Andrew Oldham is a nominee for the London International Award, his writing has reached over one million listeners, none of which know him or give a crap. His work has gone on to irritate leaders of the Methodist Church, family value groups and his PC; they believe his work is now the only single thing responsible for destroying the fabric of society, which has resulted in the writer receiving hate mail and sex videos. The writer now sleeps like a baby. In his spare time he has been nominated for the Jerwood-Arvon, received a Peggy Ramsay award for stage writing, written for BBC Drama, Independent TV/Film and patented his smug bastard look.

Dai Parsons was born in Ystradgynlais, South Wales. Now living in York, Dai is training to be a psychiatric nurse. Dai 'wanted to be a Fire Engine when I grew up. But despite painting myself red, hooting a lot, and having the propensity to piss anywhere, I still find it much easier to pass myself off as a writer. Spent most of my life in an autistic daze, clambering into pillar boxes, locking the door, posting the key back through the slit, and then trying to find my way out by battling like a rare one with anyone else I found in there.'

Jason Parry has recently moved to London, having lived in Leeds for the last eight years. He is a researcher by trade, which means he gets to look at the internet a lot. Having completed an MA in screenwriting at the Northern Film School, he is getting a good response to his screenplays; waiting for a friendly producer to start writing him cheques, as he is fed up with the apprentice work of being asked to do rewrites and trial scripts for free. He has had short stories published on a number of websites and magazines.

Jo Pearson hails from Ossett in West Yorkshire. A musician and simple mum, Jo currently lives in York. Her collection of poetry *Talking to the Virgin Mary* features in the route title *Half a Pint of Tristram Shandy*

Chloe Poems has toured nationally over the last eight years. Frequent hits at the Edinburgh Festival, these shows toured up and down the country, from Aberdeen (where Chloe was Cover Girl for Miss Alternative Aberdeen) to Portsmouth.Chloe recently completed a tour of England with dissident Spanish novelist Juan Goytisolo and is featured in the new BBC TV poetry series *Live Poets Society*. Chloe's first anthology *Universal Rentboy*, was published in 2000 by The Bad Press and her second *Adult Entertainment* by route in 2002.

Jo Powell is a former journalist and lawyer now finishing an MA in Creative Writing. She has previously published stories and also won a crime story competition in *Writers' News*.

Michelle Scally Clarke's book/CD *I Am* was published by route in 2001. Michelle regularly performs around the country, solo or with her band, she is also an inspirational workshop leader. She lives in Leeds with her two children.

Jane Scargill grew up in West Yorkshire, has lived in Coventry, the North East and France. Currently lives in Lancaster where she completed an MA in Creative Writing and is now training to be an NVQ Assessor. She writes short fiction, poetry and is working on a novel.

Mawnie Sidran Moon - 'Urbanpoetic for me was a place where I could write and read some of the most familiar and self related poetry, I have ever experienced. It gave me the freedom to write and express myself in ways that other poets understood. I found early on, from the very first pieces I read from Ricky, that he had a style similar to mine. I was easily moved and instantly inspired to become part of his writing.'

Ricky Venel Stone - 'Hidden behind the online aliases - Mine: *Che Energies*, Mawnies: *Wisdombody* - poets inspired from a variety of word movements, come together from all over the globe to discuss, to read, write and collaborate freely, sharing commonalities of experience and of course, Hiphop. Writing with Mawnie inspires me. It's a beautiful exchange of slang, diaspora and life.'

Adrian Wilson is a writer, journalist and musician. His novels *The Righteous Brother* and *Very Acme* are published by route, and he edited the acclaimed 1998 collection of short stories *Tubthumping* for the same publishing house. Adrian is the editor for a trade magazine for which he gets to travel in luxury around the world, about which he grumbles considerably. But then, he is from Wakefield.

The Route Series

An important aspect of route is to keep work fresh, of its time and highly visible. The route series is a valuable tool to achieve that aim. A combination of commisions and submissions, mixing short fiction with poetry and articles from an assortment of writers. The first thirteen issues were newspapers.

For online content and to purchase
back issues please visit

www.route-online.com

Warehouse - *MS Green, Alan Green, Clayton Devanny, Simon Nodder, Jono Bell* - *Ed Ian Daley* - ISBN 1-901927 10 5
Warehouse is a unique type of social realism, written by young warehouse operatives from the bottom end of the labour market in the middle of the post-industrial heartland, it steps to the beat of modern day working-class life. A soundtrack to the stories is included on a complimentary CD, warehouse blues supplied by *The Chapter* and urban funk grooves from *Budists*

One Northern Soul - *J R Endeacott* - ISBN 1-901927 17 2
If that goal in Paris had been allowed then everything that followed could have been different. For young Stephen Bottomley something died that night. *One Northern Soul* follows the fortunes of this Leeds United fan as he comes of age in the dark days of the early eighties.

Kilo - *M Y Alam* - ISBN 1-901927 09 1
Khalil Khan had a certain past and an equally certain future awaited until gangsters decided to turn his world upside down. They shattered his safe family life with baseball bats but that's just the beginning. They turned good, innocent and honest Khalil into someone else: Kilo, a much more unforgiving and determined piece of work. Kilo cuts his way through the underworld of Bradford street crime, but the closer he gets to the top of that game, the stronger the pull of his original values become.

The Blackstuff - *Val Cale* - ISBN 1-901927 14 8
The Blackstuff is a true story of a road-trip that sees Val Cale in trouble in Japan, impaled in Nepal, ripped off at a vaginal freak show in Bangkok, nearly saturated by a masturbating Himalayan bear in the most southerly town of India and culminates in a mad tramp across the world looking for the ultimate blowjob and the meaning of life.

Weatherman - *Anthony Cropper* - ISBN 1-901927 16 4

Alfie de Losinge's machine was designed to control the weather. Instead, amongst the tiny atoms of cloud formations, he receives fragmentary images of events that slowly unfold to reveal a tender, and ultimately tragic, love story that skilfully draws a picture of life inextricably linked to the environment, the elements, and the ever changing weather.

Very Acme - *Adrian Wilson* - ISBN: 1 901927 12 1 £6.95

New Nomad, nappy expert, small town man and ultimately a hologram – these are the life roles of Adrian Wilson, hero and author of this book, which when he began writing it, was to become the world's first novel about two and a half streets. All this changes when a new job sends him all around the world. *Very Acme* is about small town life in the global age and trying to keep a sense of identity in a world of multi-corporations and information overload.

Like A Dog To Its Vomit -*Daithidh MacEochaidh*- ISBN:1901927 07 5

In this complex, stylish and downright dirty novel, Daithidh MacEochaidh belts through the underclass underachieving postponed-modern sacrilege and the more pungent bodily orifices. *Like a Dog to Its Vomit* is a must read for anyone who has ever poked their weary toe into the world of critical theory, many of the postmodern textual games and strategies are on offer, used, abused, open to derision, and yet strangely sanctioned in the end.

Crazy Horse - *Susan Everett* - ISBN 1 901927 06 7

Jenny Barker, like many young women, has a few problems. She is trying to get on with her life, but it isn't easy. Her beloved horse has been stolen while the vicious *Savager* is on the loose cutting up animals in fields. She's neither doing well in college nor in love and fears she may die a virgin. *Crazy Horse* is a wacky ride.

Adult Entertainment

Chloe Poems

ISBN 1 901927 18 0 £6.95

One of the most prodigiously gifted and accessible poets alive today, Chloe Poems has been described as 'an extraordinary mixture of Shirley Temple and pornography.' This collection of political and social commentary, first presented in Midsummer 2002, contains twenty-three poems of uncompromising honesty and explicit republicanism, and comes complete with a fourteen track CD of Chloe live in performance.

Half a Pint of Tristram Shandy

Jo Pearson, Daithidh MacEochaidh, Peter Knaggs

ISBN 1 901927 15 6 £6.95

A three-in-one poetry collection from the best in young poets. Between the leaves of this book lies the mad boundless energy of the globe cracking-up under our very noses; it is a world which is harnessed in images of jazz, sex, drugs, aliens, abuse; in effective colloquial language and manic syntax; but the themes are always treated with gravity, unsettling candour and humour.

I Am

Michelle Scally-Clarke

ISBN 1 901927 08 3 £10 Including free CD

At thirty years old, Michelle is the same age as the mother who gave her up into care as a baby. In the quest to find her birth parents, her roots and her own identity, this book traces the journey from care, to adoption, to motherhood, to performer. Using the fragments of her own memory, her poetry and extracts from her adoption files, Michelle rebuilds the picture of 'self' that allows her to transcend adversity and move forward to become the woman she was born to be.

You can hear the beat and song of Michelle Scally-Clarke on the CD that accompanies this book and, on the inside pages, read the story that is the source of that song.

Moveable Type
Rommi Smith
ISBN 1 901927 11 3 £10 Including free CD
It is the theme of discovery that is at the heart of *Moveable Type*. Rommi Smith takes the reader on a journey through identity, language and memory, via England and America, with sharp observation, wit and wry comment en route. The insights and revelations invite us not only to look beneath the surface of the places we live in, but also ourselves. *Moveable Type* and its accompanying CD offer the reader the opportunity to listen or read, read and listen. Either way, you are witnessing a sound that is uniquely Rommi Smith.

Route Subscription

Route's subscription scheme is the easiest way for readers to keep in touch with new work from the best of new writers. Subscribers receive a minimum of four books per year, which could take the form of a novel, an anthology of short stories, a novella, a poetry collection or an issue in the route series. Any additional publications and future issues of the route paper will also be mailed direct to subscribers, as well as information on route events and digital projects.

Route constantly strives to promote the best in under represented voices, outside of the mainstream, and will give support to develop promising new talent. By subscribing to route, you too will be supporting these artists.

The fee is modest.

UK £15
Europe £20 (35• approx)
Rest of World £25(US$40 approx)

Subscribe online now at www.route-online.com

To receive a postal subscription form email your details to books@route-online.com or send your details to:
route, school lane, glasshoughton, wf10 4qh, uk

Next Stop Hope is a title on the route subscription scheme.